Matt stared at her. This was a new twist. "Are you asking me if I'm passionate?"

Although the thought amused him, he just didn't see Kendra putting that sort of question to him. It didn't jibe with her personality—at least, not the way he perceived it.

Was he wrong? And if so, about what, exactly? Less than twenty-four hours in the woman's company and she was becoming one huge, intriguing enigma. A puzzle he found himself wanting to solve.

"No," she contradicted, a flash of embarrassment over the misunderstanding sending heat up her neck to her cheeks—as did the unbidden thought of his being passionate. "What I'm asking you is if your fellow co-workers know the first thing about what makes Matt Abilene tick," she asked. "Or do they know only what you want them to know?"

Dear Reader,

Welcome back to the Cavanaughs. We continue to explore this latest branch that has recently come to light. This time, we peek into the life of Kendra Cavelli aka Cavanaugh, who, when her fiancé dies, distances herself from personal relationships, avoiding them like the plague.

For his part, her new partner, Matt Abilene, liked relationships just fine. The more, the merrier—and the lighter, the better. He'd learned to keep any sort of commitment out of the picture by watching the way his mother, desperate for someone to love, had been taken advantage of over and over again. He wanted to keep her safe and swore to himself that he would never follow in her footsteps.

But love, Kendra and Matt come to learn, is a very hard thing to shut the door on when it comes knocking. Come watch it unfold with me.

As ever, I thank you for reading and from the bottom of my heart, I wish you someone to love who loves you back.

All the best,

Marie Ferrarella

CAVANAUGH RULES

BY
MARIE FERRARELLA

First published in Great Britain 2012
by Mills & Boon, an imprint of Harlequin (UK) Limited,
Eton House, 18-24 Paradise Road, Richmond, Surrey TW9 1SR

© Marie Rydzynski-Ferrarella 2012

ISBN: 978 0 263 89567 4
ebook ISBN: 978 1 408 97747 7

46-1012

Harlequin (UK) policy is to use papers that are natural, renewable and recyclable products and made from wood grown in sustainable forests. The logging and manufacturing processes conform to the legal environmental regulations of the country of origin.

Printed and bound in Spain
by Blackprint CPI, Barcelona

Marie Ferrarella, a *USA TODAY* bestselling and RITA® Award-winning author, has written more than two hundred books for Mills & Boon®, some under the name Marie Nicole. Her romances are beloved by fans worldwide. Visit her website, www.marieferrarella.com.

To Nik
Hearts really do heal,
If you let them

Chapter 1

Detective Kendra Cavelli remembered reading somewhere that life was a series of leavings. At the time, she'd thought this was a very pessimistic point of view. But, she realized now, she'd been a lot younger and full of hope then.

Granted, no one would consider her old by any standards, except for maybe when measured against the life cycle of an everyday fruit fly. But the truth of it was, these days she felt a great deal older than what the age indicated on her birth certificate.

And who knew? Maybe the year that was written down wasn't as accurate as she'd once thought. Certainly the last name had turned out not to be.

She'd spent more than twenty-six years thinking she was a Cavelli, only to be told that she wasn't, that she and her brothers and sisters were actually Cavanaughs because her father was really a Cavanaugh. Thanks to a distraught maternity nurse who had been enveloped in grief the day her father and the *real* Cavelli baby were born, the two infants had accidentally been switched before either was a day old.

Former police chief Andrew Cavanaugh had done some research into the matter once it had come to light. It seemed that a nurse on the maternity floor, a Jane Allen, had just been told that her fiancé, Private First Class Wade Johnson, had been killed in some unnamed battle halfway around the world. Grief-stricken, Jane had gone through the paces of her job, utterly dazed and confused.

And because of that, Kendra's father and his subsequent offspring had lost their identities. Her father was taken home by the Cavellis while the real Sean Cavelli had been claimed by Seamus Cavanaugh and his wife.

And now, several months into what she and her siblings referred to as the "great revelation," she was still having trouble centering herself. She felt trapped between the past she'd *thought* was hers and the completely new present that loomed before her.

Maybe she'd have less trouble adapting, Kendra thought now as she cut across the hall of the second floor of One Police Plaza, if this name thing had not been tangled up with the loss of her own fiancé and now, on top of that, the sudden exit of her partner.

The first had all but destroyed her when he had deliberately blown himself away to the next world, and the second had just recently—and voluntarily—retired. The upshot was that both had left her to deal with things as best she could on her own.

She doubted that either one of them had given her

so much as a thought when making their final decision. God knew that Jason hadn't because if he had, he'd still be alive today. And they'd be married.

Instead, here she was, feeling incredibly isolated and alone. Alone even though her immediate family, counting her father, Sean, and her brothers and sisters, came to a grand total of seven people—plus her. At this point, Kendra didn't know if she was even allowed to count the family members she was no longer actually related to.

As for the "family" she was suddenly *supposed* to be part of, she hadn't gotten around to doing a successful head count there. All she knew was that, when gathered together, they could probably fill up half a stadium. God knew they filled a great deal of the Aurora Police Department, of which she was a proud part.

At least that hadn't changed.

At least, she now amended silently, she *assumed* that wouldn't change, even though she'd just been summoned by the chief of detectives, Brian Cavanaugh, who, along with the former chief of police, was one of her two "newfound" uncles.

Walking into the chief of detectives' outer office, she stopped at the desk positioned just in front of the door to the man's inner sanctum.

The entrance was guarded by a very capable-looking young woman in her late thirties. As Kendra crossed to her desk, the woman raised her eyes to Kendra's and quietly waited for her to say something.

"Detective Kendra Cavel—Cavan—" Kendra stumbled, not having decided which name she was going to use now that she was aware of the whole story. It wasn't as easy a decision as some might have thought.

Thomas and Bridget had already both opted to go with *Cavanaugh,* as had her father, but she wasn't sure if she wanted to abandon the name she'd used for more than a quarter of a century.

The decision to do so was particularly difficult for her in light of the fact that she already felt as if *she* had been abandoned. If she abandoned her name and the people she'd once regarded as family, what did that say about her?

Tabling her unsettling thoughts for a moment, Kendra said, "I'm here to see Chief Cavanaugh."

Lt. Reta Richards, the chief's administrative assistant for over ten years, smiled at her and nodded knowingly, as if she understood and sympathized with the dilemma Kendra was facing these days.

"The chief is on the phone right now," the lieutenant told her. "But he said to tell you that he'll see you as soon as he's through. Please have a seat." She indicated the chairs to the right against the opposite wall. "It shouldn't be long."

With a preoccupied nod, Kendra crossed to the chairs and took a seat.

That was when she noticed that she wasn't the only one waiting to see the chief of detectives. Occupying one of the other chairs was a tall, dark-haired, strikingly handsome man who despite his athletic build seemed to fill the room with his presence.

Making eye contact with her, the room's other occupant flashed her an easy smile. The kind of smile that said he was comfortable in his own skin and welcomed visitors regularly.

Kendra was well acquainted with the type. Not a serious thought in his head, except for having fun. Her engagement to Jason had rescued her from men like that.

Or so she'd thought at the time.

Instead, her engagement to the late firefighter had introduced her to a world of devastating grief and heartache.

She nodded absently at the man, acknowledging his silent greeting, and then took her seat. She was not about to start a conversation with him; she fixed her eyes on the inner door.

Kendra was torn between hoping the chief's door would open immediately, separating her from the possibility of having to make small talk with a man she didn't know who most likely just wanted a receptive audience, and hoping that Brian Cavanaugh would take his time getting to her because she had no idea what to expect.

The problem was, she had trouble waiting. Her father had commented affectionately, more than once, that she was not one of his more patient children.

It was hard not to shift restlessly in her seat. The man to her right occupied his chair as if he didn't have a care in the world. And when he smiled at her, all it seemed to do was increase her restlessness, although she couldn't explain why.

As it turned out, Kendra didn't have all that long to wait. Less than five minutes later, Reta saw the light go out on the phone's multiline keyboard and looked up. "The chief will see you now."

Since there were two of them and the lieutenant hadn't specified which of them she was speaking to, Kendra heard herself asking, "Which one?"

"Why, both of you," Reta replied pleasantly.

The man to her right was already on his feet. God but he was tall, Kendra thought as she rose from her chair. He had to be almost a foot taller than she was and she stood close to five-seven in her stacked heels.

For some reason she couldn't pinpoint, she felt a strange ripple of foreboding in her stomach.

She had a bad feeling about this.

Kendra walked in first, whether because she was just a little faster, or because of some latent gallantry on the man's part, she wasn't quite certain. Not that it mattered all that much, she supposed. What mattered was why she'd been sent for in the first place.

Old-school all the way, Brian Cavanaugh rose from his chair and leaned forward over his desk. He shook Kendra's hand warmly, as if they had known each other all her life instead of just a little while.

Oh, she'd known *of* him, and the chief had been the one to give her her gold shield at the ceremony when she'd been made a detective just shortly after she'd become engaged. But she hadn't actually known *him* until the "great mixup" had come to light. After that, there had been a slew of miscellaneous invitations—both for actual occasions and for no reason at all—to attend family gatherings, usually at retired police chief Andrew Cavanaugh's house, but not always.

Not everyone attended each gathering, but she'd seen the chief at these unofficial parties often enough. He'd worn the very same smile then as he was wearing now. Did that mean that she should relax?

Or was he just trying to soften the blow that was about to come?

She'd been born suspicious and while that was help-

ful in her line of investigative work, it did wreak havoc
on her personal life.

"How's everything going, Kendra?" the chief asked
her as he silently indicated the chair to the left of his
desk.

By *everything,* she assumed he meant work. Her
partner had retired two weeks ago and she was alter-
nating between missing the man's grumpy countenance
and being summarily angry at him for his abrupt retirement. Never mind that Det. Joe Walsh was approaching
almost seventy and had well earned this retirement. The
widower had led her to believe that he was planning to
work forever. She'd allowed herself to get comfortable
with the idea that she could count on seeing Joe's hang-
dog frown facing her each morning across their desks.

"I'm managing," she answered in a pleasant voice
that neither confirmed nor denied her statement. Until
she knew what was going on, her guard was going to
remain up.

"And you, Detective Abilene?" Brian asked, looking
at the tall, rangy man who'd stretched his long legs out
before him the moment he'd sat down.

From this angle, the man seemed to be all leg, Kendra caught herself thinking.

"The same," the detective replied, nodding toward
Kendra as if that meant he was echoing her assessment.

Brian smiled then and Kendra's uneasiness grew.

Part of the reason she disliked departures so in-
tensely was because they were wrapped up in change.
She'd never cared for change. It was a very real fact of
life, but that didn't make it any easier for her.

Lately there'd been so many changes, she couldn't keep track of them all.

Brian laughed softly, causing both of the other two people in the room to look at him curiously.

"I'm getting ahead of myself," Brian said to them. "Introductions are in order. Detective Matthew Abilene, meet Detective Kendra—"

He paused then, realizing that he hadn't been apprised of her official decision yet. Each of the Cavellis, like the four stepchildren who had come with his marriage to his former partner, Lila, and the triplets from his late brother Mike's hidden family, had been given the option of changing their surnames and officially becoming Cavanaughs if they so chose.

So far, the family name was batting a thousand, but he was not about to jump the gun with the few who were still undecided.

"Have you made a decision about your last name yet?" he asked her.

Because the chief was being thoughtful rather than pushy, she offered the man a grateful smile. "I'm still working on it, sir."

He nodded understandingly. "I understand. It's a big step to take," he agreed. "Let me know what you decide." His intent was to let her know that while he was interested in the final outcome, he refused to apply any undue pressure on either side of the argument. "Anyway," he continued briskly, "it's come to my attention that the two of you have both recently lost your partners for one reason or another. Yours took his long overdue retirement," he said to Kendra, then turned to Matt. "And yours—"

"—picked up and left the state when his girlfriend decided she wanted to live somewhere where it's always raining," Matt commented. Glancing toward Kendra, he added, "They moved to Seattle."

Her eyes narrowed as she looked at the handsome face. Was he talking down to her? The man might be good-looking enough to have his own fan club, but she took offense. "I figured that part out on my own," she told him coolly.

"Sharp," Matt murmured. Whether he was just making an offhanded comment or being sarcastic, she wasn't sure. But she leaned toward the latter—in which case he needed to be taken down a few pegs even if she never saw the man again.

"Yes, she is," Brian replied in no uncertain terms. "Which is why I've decided to partner the two of you up."

Kendra frowned. She'd had a vague, uneasy feeling that this was coming but somehow, hearing it caused a jolt. She didn't want this. She knew she couldn't just pick a new partner, but this man was as far from her first choice as humanly possible. Any man *this* handsome would be trouble. She could feel it in her bones.

"Are you in Homicide?" she heard herself stiffly asking the other detective.

Because if he was, he and the partner who'd been dragged to Seattle had to have been next to invisible. She didn't recall seeing either one of them around and, annoying though he promised to be, Abilene was *not* the kind of man who blended into the woodwork. Once upon a time, before she'd been so terribly disillusioned, she might have even felt a flutter—or three—

in Abilene's presence. But those days were long gone. Still, she would have taken note of him—had he been there to take note of.

"Major Case Squad," the other detective corrected her.

Major Case? That didn't make sense. Why was the chief pairing her up with a detective from another division? Kendra turned to look at the man she was supposed to regard as her uncle.

"Then how—"

Brian anticipated the rest of her question and spared them both by answering, "I've decided to switch Detective Abilene to Homicide."

"You're taking me off Major Case?" Matt asked, surprised. Why? What had brought this on? His record was clean, exemplary even. He would have been aware of any complaints from his captain.

"Just for the time being," Brian told him mildly.

It was his way of helping his people adjust to new circumstances. He allowed them to believe that a change was temporary while they did their best to fit in. After the initial period of adjustment, he'd discovered that most times getting the same people to transfer back out—and leave their new partner—in order to go back to their old division required the assistance of a crowbar.

He was counting on that here.

"There's not that much to do, even with Seth gone," Brian pointed out to Matt. "Until it picks up, we could use a mind like yours over in Homicide." And then he instinctively turned toward Kendra and added, "And that in no way was meant to be a negative reflection on the caliber of your work. It's just that with Joe retired, you need a new partner."

Kendra knew that. And she knew that the chief was only trying to be helpful, even though she didn't want any help. But the only time detectives went solo was when their partners were either in court, testifying, out sick or on vacation. Otherwise, if detectives left or asked to be transferred out, the resulting gaps were filled as quickly as possible.

This was just a little faster than she'd expected. Or liked. Even if change hadn't made her feel uneasy, Abilene, with his perfect smile, did.

Joe's chair was still warm, she thought ruefully. She hadn't thought she would have to get used to someone new for at least another week. Maybe longer.

So much for longer.

She was well aware of procedure, but that didn't mean that she liked it. And she had the uneasy feeling that she'd just been partnered with a hotshot who got by on his looks. Granted, she was going by a gut feeling, but her gut had always been fairly accurate.

Kendra made up her mind to ask around about Abilene. Or maybe she would have Tom do it for her. Her older brother had a way of finding things out that didn't rub people the wrong way, while she, well, she hadn't quite managed to successfully develop that talent yet. At least not when she found herself heavily invested in something. Such as now.

She slanted a glance at the man sitting beside her. He seemed to be fine with the arrangement. Or at least he wasn't protesting it. But then, there were many ways to protest something, not all of them vocal. Abilene's expression gave her no clue as to what he was thinking even as, for one unguarded moment, it seemed to ripple directly into the pit of her stomach.

Definitely needed to have Tom ask around, she decided firmly.

Right now, she needed to know one thing. Taking a breath, Kendra asked the man sitting across from her, "Is this permanent, sir?"

Uncle or not, she knew that her family connection didn't figure into this right now and she didn't want him to think she was questioning his judgment. On the other hand, she really needed to know what she was facing here. Forewarned was forearmed.

Brian smiled and looked at the two people sitting before him, one at rigid attention, the other in a seemingly relaxed mode. He had a positive feeling about this. Although probably not immediately evident to either one of them, pairing these two was a good thing.

"We'll see," he answered. Turning his attention to Abilene, he gave the man an opportunity to voice any protest, although he had a feeling that there would be none forthcoming. It wasn't that Abilene was a dutiful "good soldier," but he rolled with the punches and took whatever came his way. But by no means was he a pushover. This would be a healthy blending of styles.

"So, unless you have any objections, Detective Abilene, you'll be moving your things over to Homicide, effective immediately."

Matt nodded. His expression remained the same, even while his eyes swept over the woman to his left, as if taking measure of her. If there was a verdict one way or another, he kept it to himself. There was neither eagerness nor covert annoyance in his voice. "I'll get right on it, sir," he promised.

Let the adventure begin, Brian thought.

Like a mechanic with an ear for the machines he worked with, Brian liked hearing the sound of a well-tuned engine. He had a feeling that was what he had here. Kendra would just have to get over the initial period of adjustment. But it would be worth it.

"Well, unless there's anything else," Brian said, a note of finality in his voice, "you're dismissed." And then, as the two rose to their feet, he added with a smile, "Make me proud."

"Yes, sir," Kendra replied, forcing a smile she didn't feel to her lips.

"Do my best, sir." Matt fired off the casual promise as he turned to leave. He caught the dark look that his new partner shot him.

The woman was very attractive, but she didn't know it. He'd never had a female partner before. This was going to be interesting. *Very* interesting.

Kendra strode out of the inner, then outer office ahead of him, putting distance between them quickly. She didn't bother to pretend to want to talk—because she didn't. She was busy dealing with this latest curve that Fate had tossed her.

Matt merely stretched his legs and shortened that distance to nothing in a matter of a few steps.

He caught up to her way before the elevator, but she kept on walking, not acknowledging his presence. It was as if she'd been encapsulated in a world all her own.

If only, she thought.

"So what do I call you?" Abilene asked as he reached

over her head and pressed the Up button on the wall before she could.

Forced to acknowledge him, she had a feeling her best bet was to put him in his place right from the very beginning. If she was wrong about him, there would be time enough to soften her approach.

Kendra looked up at him—she was going to need to get higher heels, she decided, then almost instantly rescinded that thought. A little distance between them might be a good thing. Being too close to him might blunt the edge she would need. There was no getting away from the fact that he *was* bone-meltingly good-looking and close proximity might cause her to forget.

"Good at my job," she answered.

Matt considered her reply for a second and then nodded. "Okay, but that's a little long. How about I just call you 'Good'?"

The elevator arrived and she turned her back on him as she entered, silently cursing Joe for having left her to undertake a life revolving around fly-fishing.

Chapter 2

When Abilene got off behind her, Kendra turned around to look at her new—and hopefully very temporary—partner. Why was he following her?

"Shouldn't you be going up to your floor to get your things?" she asked him.

Just for a moment, he'd allowed himself to watch her walk, appreciatively taking in the way her hips swayed ever so slightly. Her question pulled him back to reality. He nodded toward the squad room just behind her. "I thought I'd see where my desk is first."

"And what?" she asked. "If it doesn't meet with your standards, you'll stay where you are?"

Abilene grinned, amused. "Is that a hopeful note in your voice I hear?" He studied her for a moment, looking beyond her high cheekbones and her fascinating eyes. "You don't do change very well, do you?"

The last thing she wanted to put up with was being

analyzed. Kendra's eyes blazed as she tossed her head. "What I do or don't do is none of your business," she informed him.

The way he saw it, that wasn't quite true. "Some of it will be. And I want to see where my desk is so I don't have to wander around aimlessly when I come down with an armload of my stuff." He looked at her with eyes that seemed earnest. "Does that meet with your approval?"

Rather than answer him, she merely sighed and beckoned him to follow her through the door. Crossing the floor, she stopped at what seemed to be the center of the room.

"This is yours," she told him, gesturing toward the cleared expanse of desk that butted up against hers.

A greater contrast between the two areas would have been difficult to find. One desk was the picture of virgin territory without so much as a scrap of paper on it, while the other desk bore silent testimony to a very cluttered style. There was a computer off to one side, its keyboard stretched out before it rather than neatly tucked out of sight. The rest of the desk was buried beneath files and a snowstorm of scattered, interweaving papers. Not so much as a square inch of desktop was visible.

Matt made no verbal comment, but the way his mouth curved seemed to say it all. At least, she read a great deal into it.

Kendra took umbrage at what she perceived as criticism from her new, God-help-her, partner. Periodically, she went through everything on her desk and cleared spaces, trying her best to organize the raft of papers into some sort of a system, but inevitably, the stacks would bleed into one another again, merging and creating a chaotic pile.

"I've got a system," she retorted defensively in response to the amusement in Abilene's liquid-green eyes.

"I'm sure you do." To the untrained ear, Abilene's mild tone sounded completely agreeable. Why, then, did it make her want to scratch his eyes out or at least challenge him to a weapons proficiency contest on the gun range?

Absently, Matt opened the center drawer of his new desk, then checked, one by one, a few of the other drawers. Like the surface of the desk, they were all pristinely clean.

He shut the last drawer. "Your old partner did a thorough job cleaning things out. He didn't leave anything behind."

"Not even any hope," Kendra murmured under her breath. The amused sound coming from her new partner told her that her voice hadn't been quite as low as she'd thought.

Great, Pretty Boy has hearing like a bat.

Stepping back, Abilene pushed his chair into his desk. "I'll go get my stuff now."

"I can hardly wait," Kendra deadpanned, pasting a pained smile on her lips.

Matt paused for a moment, his eyes slowly sliding down the length of this sharp-tongued woman. Thanks to his chaotic upbringing, he was basically nomadic in his lifestyle and his relationships. It gave him the ability to take whatever came down the road because, good or bad, he knew it was only temporary and would eventually change.

"You know," he told her, "I'm really not such a bad guy to work with. Not as good as some, but better than most. You might want to put the pitchfork down, Good, and reserve judgment for a while."

The fact that Abilene wasn't heaping endless laurels on himself surprised her. Someone like him, who exuded sensuality with his every movement, ordinarily had the inside track on vanity, possessing an ego that made passage through narrow doorways an ongoing challenge.

She supposed she could be wrong about Abilene, but she didn't care to debate it with herself right now, one way or the other. She wasn't feeling all that magnanimous or friendly.

"The jury's still out on that one," Kendra informed him.

Matt supposed that was the best he would get for now. And maybe that was good because he could see himself being attracted to her, but that might complicate matters. And all he was interested in for now was a truce while he got his bearings. Later might prove to be another story, he mused, but right now, he just wanted to settle in.

He flashed an easy smile. "Sounds fair enough," he replied.

Turning on his heel, he was about to leave. All his things could be packed up and transported in one trip. Unlike his new partner, once he closed a case, he didn't hang on to the papers that went with it. Instead, he placed everything onto a flash drive and preserved the information that way. It took up a great deal less space. And it made for a neater desk. He worked better that way.

Matt got exactly three steps toward the squad room door when he heard his name being called.

"Hey, Abilene!"

When he turned around again, Matt found himself looking down at an older man with thick silver hair and a far thicker waistline. Rather than hiding the latter behind the all-forgiving folds of a jacket, the older man had left his jacket in his office and was wearing just his shirt. The sleeves of his slightly rumpled shirt were rolled up and his tie appeared to have been hastily loosened, as if leaving it in its initial position would have eventually wound up choking him.

"Abilene?" the older man repeated, this time turning the last name into a question.

From the looks of the man, this had to be his new boss, Matt thought. He doubled back in long, loping strides.

"Yes, sir," he responded easily, extending his hand to the other man, who stood only slightly shorter than he did. However, his slumped shoulders gave the impression that he was shorter than he was.

After a beat, the older man took Abilene's offered hand. The handshake was surprisingly hearty. "I'm Lt. Holmes," Isaac Holmes told his newest detective. "You're just in time."

Abilene cocked his head, the very gesture a query. "For?"

"You and Cavelli—you're still Cavelli, right?" Holmes asked Kendra, sparing her a quick glance, then turning away before she had a chance to answer. "Just caught a case," he concluded.

Matt jerked his thumb in the general direction of the hall—and the elevator. "I was just about to bring down my stuff," Matt told him.

"Your stuff can wait. It's not going anywhere. But you are." Tearing off the top page from his pad where he'd written down the incoming information, the lieutenant pressed the paper into Kendra's hand. "Super found a dead body. Not the one he expected to." Glancing over toward Abilene, he added, "Welcome to Homicide."

Kendra glanced at the paper Holmes had handed her, then tucked it into her pocket. "The Super *expected* to find a body?" she questioned.

"Not expected-expected," Holmes clarified. "Guy who lives there hasn't been seen for three days, so his boss sent someone to his apartment. When he didn't get an answer, the kid got the super."

"And they found a dead body in the apartment who wasn't the guy who lived there," Kendra guessed.

Holmes nodded. "I want you to find out whose body's in the apartment and see if you can get a handle on where the guy who pays the rent is. Apparently, he's still missing."

"You got it, boss," Abilene promised as he fell into step beside Kendra.

"Jump right in, don't you?" Kendra commented as she increased her pace. But even so, Abilene more than kept up. Man had legs that belonged on an ostrich, she thought darkly.

"Isn't that what I'm supposed to do?" he asked innocently as they went into the hall. If this wasn't going to be an all-out territorial war, he needed to do what he could to put her mind at ease. He was definitely not out to become king of the hill—at least, not this hill. "Look, I'm not trying to snag your territory, if that's what you're worried about. From what I hear, there's more than enough work to go around for everyone. This isn't a competition."

He was analyzing her again. Kendra gave him a cold look as she yanked open the door to the stairwell. She *hated* being analyzed. "Nobody said it was."

Abilene stopped short. Was she taking the stairs? "Hey, aren't we supposed to be taking the elevator down?" he asked.

"Go ahead," Kendra tossed over her shoulder. "Nobody's stopping you."

Like a door to a tomb, the stairwell door all but thundered as it closed behind her.

Peace at last.

Kendra's heels met the metal steps, emitting a quick, rhythmic staccato sound as she hurried down to the first floor. She was only halfway down the first flight with three more to go when she heard the stairwell door above her opening again. She didn't have to look to know that Abilene was now behind her—and catching up fast.

Couldn't she get at least a couple of minutes away from this man? She wanted to be able to clear her head and having him around was not at all conducive to that.

He had no idea how the woman's mind worked. Was she intent on trying to ditch him, or make him fail in front of the boss? Was she just playing some sort of a game where only she knew the rules? He wasn't about to take a chance on being left behind on the first assignment that he—that *they*—had just caught.

He was a firm believer that you never got to redo a first impression—and he knew that they were the ones that tended to last.

Shadowing his new partner's every step, Matt was half a beat behind her as they came to the bottom of the last staircase. She'd just reached the door when he stretched his hand over her head and pushed it open as she turned the doorknob.

Kendra bit back an annoyed retort. She felt as if she was almost encompassed by the man's long arms. He seemed to take up all the space around her, she thought grudgingly. *And* all the air. There was no other reason why, just for a second, she'd felt so hot and so light-headed.

"I can push open my own door, Abilene," she informed him crisply. Out of the stairwell, she took the opportunity to pull fresh air into her lungs. The feeling of heat began to recede.

"Nobody said you couldn't, Good," Abilene replied mildly. "Just doing what I can to help. It's a heavy door."

It *was* a heavy door, but she wasn't about to say anything to that effect. She didn't need some hotshot thinking he was her knight in dented armor.

Muttering a couple of choice words under her breath, Kendra all but marched into the parking lot. She went straight for her old Crown Victoria. Number 23, the one she used to share with Joe, before the man had been seduced by the idea of retirement.

"I've got the address, I'm driving," she crisply informed Abilene.

Wide shoulders rose slightly, then lowered again in what seemed like the most careless of fashions, as if the matter of who drove was the last thing on her partner's mind.

"Fine with me," he told her. "I like riding shotgun anyway." Opening the passenger door, he folded his long, lanky frame into the seat, then pulled out the seat belt and secured it. "Never cared much for driving in traffic."

Kendra frowned as she started up the vehicle. So far, Abilene seemed to be going out of his way to come across as agreeable. But she wasn't about to be lulled into a false sense of security. Joe had tripped her up several times before they'd found their work rhythm. Since he was her first partner after she'd been awarded her gold shield, she had nothing to compare the older man to and assumed that all male partners were going to challenge her straight out of the box until she proved herself capable.

After being on the job for over two years in the Homicide Division, she found it more than a little annoying to be sent back to square one. But that was the price she had to pay for being a woman—and for being related to the brass. Because her father was head of the CSI lab, she was acquainted with accusations of nepotism. But now that she was connected to the Cavanaughs, she had a feeling that she would never know a peaceful moment again.

She spared Abilene a glance as they took off. *Nope,* she thought. *Never again.*

* * *

The five-story apartment building where Lt. Holmes had sent them was located in the more well-off—although by no means rich—section of Aurora. Leaving the unmarked Crown Victoria parked in a space intended for deliveries, Kendra made sure that the police light was visible before she and Abilene went up the four flights in the elevator to the scene of the crime.

"What, no stairs?" Abilene asked, amused when she opted for the elevator.

"I thought I'd let you save your energy in case there's a need for some heavy lifting," Kendra told him without missing a beat.

"Thoughtful," he quipped as they got off.

The forced smile came and went in a blink of an eye. "I try."

"Yeah, me, too," he said, looking at her significantly.

Something in her gut undulated for half a heartbeat. She banked it down and walked faster.

The apartment in question wasn't hard to find. The immediate area directly before the crime scene was crowded with curious people. Apparently people from the building's other apartments, as well as an influx of others drawn by word of mouth, were gathered about the hallway in clusters like bees circling a hive.

The yellow tape strung across a doorway must have attracted them, Kendra couldn't help thinking.

The superintendent, when they finally located him, appeared rather young, inexperienced, and seemed completely distraught. Every few minutes he kept nervously repeating that this was his "first dead body" and that viewing it wasn't nearly as "cool" as he'd thought it would be. He seemed genuinely disappointed about that.

Kendra called the slight man a few choice names in her head, but for now kept them to herself. She glanced in Abilene's direction and guessed by his expression that perhaps a few of the same names for the super had occurred to him as well.

Maybe they weren't that different after all, she mused.

Getting down to business, Kendra went directly toward the body. Lying facedown in the middle of the living room, the victim was completely covered with a king-size blanket that appeared to have been taken from the lone bedroom. No limbs were peeking out at either end, but a pool of angry dark red blood haloed the blanket, bearing silent testimony to the fact that someone had indeed died in this apartment. No one ever lost that much blood and survived.

Squatting down beside the victim, Kendra raised a corner of the blanket and got her first view of the dead woman. Her reaction was always the same. Her heart would feel as if it was constricting in her chest as sympathy flooded through her.

The victim, a woman most likely in her twenties, was lying facedown on what had been a beige rug. The back of her head had been struck hard and was apparently the source of all the blood on the floor. Kendra's first guess was that the blow to the head appeared to be the cause of death.

Dropping the blanket back over the dead woman, Kendra rose carefully to her feet, ignoring Abilene's extended hand, offering her aid.

"Our killer knew the victim," she commented, more to herself than to Abilene. She wasn't quite ready to talk to him just yet, at least not in the role of her partner. She regarded him more as a casual observer. Baby steps, she counseled herself. "And apparently he felt remorseful enough to cover her up so he wouldn't have to look at her after he'd ended her life."

"Or she," Abilene interjected.

Caught off guard, Kendra stopped and looked at him quizzically. "What?"

"Or she," Abilene repeated. "The killer could have been a woman. Doesn't take much to pick up that statue and swing it hard enough to do some major damage at the point of contact."

Abilene nodded toward what appeared to be a rather cheap bust of Shakespeare lying on the floor not that far from the prone body.

Kendra stared down at the faux bronze bust. Shakespeare, no less.

You just never knew, did you?

Her first thought would have been that someone who'd gone out and bought something like that would have been mild-mannered and cultured. So much for being a profiler.

"No, it doesn't," she agreed.

Moving over to the bust, she squatted down for a better look at it. It was the murder weapon, all right. There was a thin red line of blood at one corner. The killer had obviously come up behind the victim and hit her when she hadn't been looking.

A lovers' quarrel? Or calculated, premeditated murder?

Too bad the bust couldn't talk.

More than four hundred years after the fact and the bard was apparently still killing people off, Kendra thought cynically. Except now they didn't get up for a final bow once the curtain fell.

With a suppressed sigh, Kendra rose to her feet again.

And then, just as she turned back to look at the prone figure lying on the floor beneath the ginger-colored blanket, one of the crime scene investigators who had arrived earlier came over to bag the ancient-looking bust.

"That comment about the killer knowing the victim," Abilene began.

For one tension-free second, she'd actually forgotten about him. Too bad that second couldn't have lasted a bit longer.

Abilene's remark, hanging in midair like that, had her looking at him sharply, anticipating some sort of a confrontation regarding her thought process.

Was he going to challenge something else she'd said? Already?

Kendra eyed the man she knew her sisters would have thought was a living, breathing hunk, trying to see past his chiseled exterior. She waited for the verbal duel to begin.

"Watch a lot of procedural television, do you?" he asked.

"I don't have to." Although she did, she silently admitted. The shows intrigued her. But he didn't have to know that. She debated saying anything further, then decided to go ahead. "My father's the head of the Crime Scene Lab."

"Boy, you sure have every angle covered, don't you, Good?" he laughed.

Kendra bristled. "I really wish you wouldn't call me that."

Now that was definitely amusement in his eyes. "Would you rather I called you Bad?" It was clearly a teasing remark and perhaps under other circumstances—before life had trampled all over her heart—she might have picked up the banter, even enjoyed it. But she was what she was and there was no going back.

Still, it didn't stop her from noticing that the man had the kind of smile a woman could get lost in—even a sensible woman.

But not her, of course.

Still, she wished the chief hadn't picked him to be her partner. Going it alone—even with an increased workload—would have been better for her in the long run.

"What I'd rather was that my old partner was still around."

He surprised her by leaning in and whispering, "Lemonade, Good. When life throws lemons at you, you make lemonade."

Her eyes held his for a long moment. Until she found herself sinking into them. She backpedaled quickly. "I don't like lemonade."

He laughed, shaking his head. "Why doesn't that surprise me?" he murmured before turning back to the murder scene.

Chapter 3

"Hey, Abilene, what do you—"

Kendra stopped abruptly. She'd assumed that the detective was behind her, but when she turned around, she only saw the crime scene investigators in the room.

"Great," she muttered. "Now he's wandering off." Biting off a few ripe words, she went to look for him.

She found her new partner in the bedroom. Abilene stood before the narrow mirrored closet. The sliding door was in the open position and he was staring into it.

Glancing over his shoulder, Kendra saw nothing that would have captured his attention so intently. Was she missing something, or was he one of those people who stared off into space as he pieced things together in his mind?

"So, what do you think?" she finally asked him.

If she'd surprised him by coming up behind him,

Abilene gave no indication. Turning from the closet, he looked at her as he lobbed her question back to her.

"You're the expert."

Did that mean he was unwilling to state an opinion, or that he was giving her her due? So far she really had no idea how to read this man and that bothered her. More than that, it annoyed her.

Hell, everything about this man annoyed her, not the least of which was that he seemed to be getting under her skin and this was only day one of their temporary partnership. What was she going to be like a month into this ordeal? She didn't want to think about it.

Kendra was aware that learning to pick up signals from this man would take time, but she'd gotten more impatient in this difficult past year and it made her less willing to wait. Jason's accident and subsequent suicide had made her want to seize things immediately, solve crimes yesterday. It was hard regaining her stride when all she wanted to do was run, not walk and certainly not stroll.

Abilene was still looking at her. Waiting for her opinion—or at least pretending to. Either way, she gave it to him.

She glanced back toward the living room, then said, "Looks to me as if Ryan Burnett and his girlfriend got into a fight—cause unknown at the moment—and in a fit of temper, he hit her with that bust. When he realized what he'd done—and that she was dead—he apparently got scared and took off."

"Stopping to pack?" Abilene asked.

He indicated the cluster of bare hangers in the closet. Off to one side of the tasteful, small bedroom was a black lacquered bureau. Several of its drawers were hanging open. From the disarray left behind, it was obvious that some items had been hastily grabbed from there, too.

She shrugged, amending her theory to fit the scene. "Maybe Ryan decided to take off permanently. Man's going to need more than a toothbrush if he's starting a new life somewhere else."

"That shows clear thinking," Abilene protested. "It doesn't jibe with a supposed crime of impulse," he pointed out.

Kendra saw no contradiction. "The man's an accountant. He's supposed to be a clear thinker. It's the nature of the beast." She glanced at the bed. It had no comforter or blanket over its crisp, coordinated navy blue sheets. That confirmed her initial theory that the blanket in the other room, now spread over the murder victim, had come from here.

That brought her back to the theory that Ryan hadn't meant to kill the woman. Things had gotten out of hand for some reason. But what had triggered the argument? And why now, at this particular point? The answers to that might explain everything.

Seeing one of the two officers who had called in the homicide, she crossed to the man and asked, "Do we have an ID on the victim yet?"

The officer nodded and offered her the wallet he'd gotten from the dead woman's purse.

"Her name's Summer Miller," he told her. He handed over the wallet, exposing the driver's license for her benefit.

Kendra looked down at the small picture on the license. She'd seen a larger, framed photograph of Summer in the bedroom on the bureau. She was standing in front of a smiling young man. His arms were wrapped protectively around her. The two appeared very happy, as if they didn't have a care in the world between them.

They did now, Kendra thought grimly. She assumed that the man in the photograph was the missing accountant, Ryan Burnett.

"Well, at least we have a name for his girlfriend," she said quietly, closing the wallet for now.

Spying a pile of plastic sealable bags used for evidence, she picked one up and slipped the wallet inside. She closed the seal before tucking the wallet into her pocket. She wanted to hand-carry this piece to her father personally. There were questions she wanted to ask.

And then she turned toward Abilene. "You up for some canvassing of the neighbors on the floor, see if anyone heard or saw anything that might prove to be useful?"

"Lead the way," he said, gesturing toward the doorway. "But—"

Kendra crossed the threshold, then looked at him over her shoulder. "But?" she echoed.

"Shouldn't we inform her next of kin first before we start canvassing and flashing her picture around?" he asked.

"Since we're here, we'll canvas the floor first." Kendra didn't like wasting time and she sincerely doubted that word of the young woman's murder—as well as her name—would get out in the next hour. "She'll still be the victim of a homicide—and dead—in an hour," she assured Abilene. "Plenty of time to break her family's heart in an hour instead of now," Kendra added with a resigned sigh.

That was the worst part of the job as far as she as concerned. Informing the family of a death, then watching the light go out of a parent's or a spouse's eyes. They should have a special group of trained professionals who only did that—and rendered grief counseling while they were at it.

"I suppose you're right," Abilene murmured in a deep voice under his breath.

She knew he didn't mean it, but she took it as a token victory. In response, she paused to flash a quick, satisfied smile in his direction.

That he smiled back pleased her more than she was happy about.

They wound up canvassing the apartments on the crime scene floor. All the people who had been milling around the hallway had mysteriously disappeared when they came out, going back to their lives and choosing not to communicate with the police.

It turned out that only a few people—three, to be exact—were in their apartments to answer their doorbells when Kendra and Abilene came around.

The first was a young woman with a brand-new baby. The baby looked to be less than a month old. The new mother had all but physically dragged them into her apartment when they rang her bell. It was obvious that she was desperate for adult companionship, even companionship that involved being questioned about a murder.

It was clear that while she loved her infant son, the

woman was more than ready to return to work—or at least to be in the company of human beings who knew how to do more than spit up, cry, wet and sleep.

Moving like a woman who was sleepwalking, she admitted to not having heard anything out of the ordinary that day: no sudden shouts, no raised, angry voices, no loud crashing sounds.

They thanked her and left as soon as they could extricate themselves.

Two doors down, a night watchman finally opened the door after Abilene had given up ringing the doorbell and resorted to knocking—hard. Rumpled and bleary-eyed, the man appeared none too happy to be woken up. He was no more helpful than the new mother had been, shaking his head in response to the same questions.

"No, man, I didn't hear anything. I took a sleeping pill," he explained, then whined, "Only way I can get some sleep. It's just not natural to have to try to sleep during the day," he grumbled.

"Maybe you should try getting another job," Kendra suggested tactfully.

Her words brought an instant, almost malevolent look into the man's dark eyes. "Don't you think I would if I could?" he snapped at her. "I was a damn aerospace engineer before all those useless companies started to bail and move out of the state. This damn night watchman job was the only thing I could find after looking for five months." He glared at her accusingly. "Now I probably won't be able to get back to sleep because of you."

She was about to say something placating and apologetic to the belligerent watchman when she noticed Abilene shifting beside her. The next thing she knew, he was placing himself between her and the man in the doorway.

"Take it easy, man," Abilene advised, his voice mild. "Might help you fall back to sleep if you calm down a little."

By his subdued expression, it was obvious that the night watchman had become aware of the rather pronounced differences in height between him and the detective. Rather than say something sarcastic or cynical, the man nodded and backed up into the security of his apartment. The next moment, he'd shut the door.

For a second, Kendra was stunned. Turning, she was all set to tell Abilene that she didn't need him to run interference for her or play the big, bad guardian, but then she decided to let the matter drop. Maybe Abilene, in his own clumsy, heavy-handed way, was trying to be helpful. Even, perhaps, protective.

The last thought shimmied through her, creating a shiver she managed to tamp down. Maybe she was just working too hard. But she couldn't stop now.

Two doors away from the crime scene they found their third person to interview. Unlike the other two tenants, he was neither half-asleep, nor bleary-eyed and belligerent. Tyler Blake, a "currently" out-of-work actor according to his own description, was both friendly and more than willing to answer questions without seeming desperate for company.

And, also unlike the other two tenants they'd interviewed, Blake admitted to having heard something earlier that day.

"It sounded like two people arguing, but I just thought that someone had their TV turned up loud," he admitted ruefully. "I didn't pay attention and then it was quiet again. Sorry," he apologized, flashing a contrite smile at Kendra.

"Nothing to apologize for, Mr. Blake. You couldn't have known what was going on," she told him. Another question occurred to her and she asked, "Were you by any chance friendly with Mr. Burnett?"

The out-of-work actor shrugged. "Just small talk at the elevator and the mailbox. You know, 'Just another great day in Paradise,' that kind of thing. We never talked about anything personal, anything that mattered," he clarified.

"Did you know his girlfriend?" Abilene asked out of the blue. Up until now, he'd been rather quiet, letting her take the lead and choosing to listen rather than to question.

Tyler looked surprised at the question. "You mean to talk to, or by sight?"

"You tell us," Abilene replied, leaving it up to the actor to fill in the blanks.

"Well, I saw them leaving his apartment a couple of times, but I never had any conversations with her, if that's what you mean." A self-deprecating laugh escaped his lips. "Fact is, I'm not sure if I could pick her out of a lineup if I had to."

"Well, lucky for you that won't come up," Abilene told him. "Burnett's girlfriend was found dead in his apartment this morning."

Tyler's eyes widened in absolute shock. Perfectly round and black like small marbles, they gave the impression that they would fall out of his head at any minute.

"He killed her?" he asked in disbelief, his voice trembling.

"Right now, that seems to be the working theory," Abilene told the actor. "Unless you know something different." He paused, giving the actor a moment for the information to sink in. "Any thoughts on that?" he prodded.

Tyler *really* looked surprised then. "Me? No. No," he assured Abilene while trying to suppress a shiver of his own. "Just all sounds kind of creepy, that's all. When I did see them together, they looked happy—I guess," he tagged on with a shrug.

"You guess," Abilene repeated slowly, watching Tyler's eyes.

Tyler drew himself up to be a little taller, a little straighter. Abilene still towered over him. "Well, yeah. I didn't stare at them or anything. I've got my own life," he said. "And my own girlfriend," he added with pride. "She's my fiancée, actually," he clarified. "And she doesn't like me staring at other women," he added with a grin.

"I hear you," Abilene said with a conspiratorial laugh. "They can get really jealous on you for just being yourself. Nothing wrong with a guy just looking."

"If you think of anything else," Kendra said, interrupting what looked as if it had the makings of a guy fest and taking a card out of her pocket, "call this number." She tapped the phone number beneath her name. "Ask for Detective Cavelli."

"So, is that the name you're going with, Good? Cavelli?" Abilene asked as they walked away from the actor's apartment.

Why did his questions immediately get her back up?
It was, after all, a legitimate question. But coming from
Abilene, it got under her skin.

Just as he did.

She supposed she was being unfair—but that still
didn't change her reaction.

"It's the name on the card," she told him. They
stopped at the crime scene one last time. The crime
scene investigators were apparently wrapping things
up, she thought. That was their cue to leave. "I didn't
want to confuse him. So far, this actor's our most lucid
witness."

"Or at least he's playing the part of one," Abilene
commented as they walked over to the centrally located elevator. His comment had her looking at him
quizzically and he shrugged. "Hey, he's an out-of-work
actor—they need audiences like most people need air."

"Speaking from experience?" she asked.

"In a way," Abilene admitted. "I dated an actress
once." And then he laughed. He'd dated several of
them, actually. At different times. Beautiful women
with beautiful faces, all clamoring to be used—finding a personal hell on the other side. "Hard not to in
this state."

"Dated an actress," Kendra repeated. Probably a
whole bunch of them, possibly at the same time. He
had the charm to pull it off, she decided. If you liked
that sort of thing, she couldn't help adding. "How nice
for her," she commented dryly.

"Nice for both of us," he said, then added with a
smile, "Short and sweet."

Something in his voice caught Kendra's attention—

and, though she wouldn't have admitted it in so many words, it also aroused her curiosity, among other things she chose not to explore.

"Is that a requirement with you? 'Short and sweet'?" she repeated when he just looked at her.

His mouth curved devilishly. "As a matter of fact, yes, it is."

She'd been right about him, she thought as she got in behind the wheel of the Crown Victoria. Abilene was a player, trading on his exceedingly good looks and satisfying his appetite whenever the spirit moved him. She bet it moved him a lot.

"Where to now?" he asked as he buckled his seat belt.

"Back to the precinct to see what kind of information we can find about the late Summer Miller." She turned on the ignition. "By the way, what was that back there? With the actor," she specified.

"It's called being a detective and gathering information. Also questioning a witness. Why?" he asked her. "Wasn't I supposed to do any talking? Am I just supposed to be your strong, silent backup?"

She sincerely doubted the man *knew* the meaning of the word *silent*. For now, until she got used to him, she just wanted him to stay out of the way, not suddenly step up and take the lead. She had no problem sharing that position if the person she was sharing it with had respect for her. But Abilene wasn't giving off any of those vibrations. At least none on a frequency she was receiving.

"I only thought, this being your first case, you'd just observe," she told him.

"This is my first *homicide,* not my first case," he corrected. He wasn't some wet-behind-the-ears rookie to stand in awe of her. If that was what she wanted, she should have gone with one of the department's newly minted detectives, not him. "The actor just brought up some questions for me. Sorry, was I supposed to clear them with you first before asking him?"

It wasn't exactly a belligerent question, at least not in tone. But she could feel him challenging her nonetheless. Rules and boundaries needed to be established, here and now. Or maybe she was just reading too much into it. These days, she wasn't sure of anything anymore.

Maybe she just needed to unwind. Find a way to relax a little. She wondered what her sisters were doing after work tonight. Bridget was usually all caught up in her fiancé these days, but that still left Kari.

Maybe she'd give Kari a call—after she called Thomas to ask him to look into her new partner's background. She'd feel a lot better if she knew the kind of person she would be working with. Hotshots and red-hot investigators tended to come across the same way sometimes. It would be good to have a second opinion on what, exactly, she had on her hands here.

"Well, was I?" Abilene pressed.

Kendra blinked, then realized that she'd lost the thread of the conversation. She needed to ask for clarification—and that annoyed her.

"Were you what?" she asked, sparing him a quick glance as she eased the car to a stop at a red light.

Abilene suppressed an impatient sigh. "Was I supposed to clear it with you first before I asked the actor any questions?" This time, there was an edge to his tone.

That would be nice.

She knew the detective was being sarcastic. She supposed, in his place, she would have felt the same way.

Okay, so she was being testy. But that was because she didn't like change and she didn't like the fact that he had a way of looking at her that made her stomach muscles cramp up.

Kendra did her best to temper her own voice. "Of course not. I was just surprised to hear you asking questions, that's all."

Matt decided to give her the benefit of the doubt. Shrugging, he stood down and relaxed again. Maybe the woman wasn't a class-A pain in the butt. She just came across like one. But maybe she had a reason to—one that he intended to find out, provided there *was* a reason.

"Look," he said amicably, "there's going to be a period of adjustment. I get that. If we're going to make this work, then we need to get things out in the open."

She was on her guard again. "What things?" she asked.

"Things that bother us about the other person."

She could feel his eyes on her. It made her feel like squirming. So much for a truce. She would still hang on to the hope that this collaboration of theirs *was* only temporary.

Kendra made a right turn at the next corner. "I've got a better idea."

"Okay, I'm game."

Pushing down on the gas, she flew through the next

light just as it was turning red. She wanted to spend as little time in close quarters with this man as possible. For some reason, he seemed to deplete her oxygen supply. "Why don't we just see if we can find out who killed Summer Miller and just where Ryan Burnett ultimately ran off to."

He laughed shortly. Yeah, that was definitely another option. "You mean just work the case."

Kendra continued to look straight ahead as she drove. "I mean just work the case."

Abilene tempered the sarcastic retort that rose to his lips. "It might surprise you to know, but that was what I was doing when you asked me what I was doing," he told her.

Kendra blew out a breath. Maybe the key to surviving this union was to exchange as few words as possible—and to keep to well-ventilated areas. "Point taken. Okay, Abilene, as you were."

He grinned. "Wouldn't have it any other way."

Kendra wondered just how long she had to wait before she could officially request a change of partners without having the chief think that she was being unreasonable.

Chapter 4

Utilizing a couple of prominent social networks, a little more than an hour into her internet search, Kendra discovered that Summer Miller had no immediate family in the state.

The only listed relative turned out to be a distant cousin, someone named Sandra Hill, who lived in Springfield, Illinois.

But even that proved to be a dead end. When she tracked down the cousin's phone number and tried it, she was informed by an automated voice that the number she had dialed was "no longer in service."

Dropping the handset back into the cradle, Kendra sighed and shook her head.

Abilene looked up from the list of newly accumulated phone numbers related to the case. "Something wrong?"

"Just hit a dead end, that's all." Her frown deepened

as she stared at the last site she'd pulled up. "Hopefully not the first of many," she commented. In response to the questioning rise of Abilene's eyebrow—the extraneous thought that her partner had incredibly well-shaped eyebrows for a man floated through her head out of nowhere—Kendra filled him in. "The victim's cousin's phone is currently disconnected and I can't seem to find anyone else to call."

Although relieved not to have to notify a grieving family member of the young woman's untimely death, she felt sad to think that no one was there to make funeral arrangements for Summer Miller.

"Maybe there's a roommate or a best friend who can supply us with the names we need," Abilene suggested. "We can go check out where she lived. You still have her license, right?"

She'd almost forgotten about slipping that into her pocket. Her intent had been to drop the wallet off with her father at the crime lab—it would give her an opportunity to ask him some questions about the body—but then she'd gotten sidetracked. "Right."

"All right, then. Let's go," he said, already on his feet. "We've got the address, let's see if there's a roommate or a talkative neighbor."

Before she could rubber-stamp his suggestion, Abilene's cell phone rang. He paused, digging it out of his shirt pocket. Glancing at the caller ID, it was his turn to frown. Without thinking, he dropped back into his chair and turned it almost 180 degrees, deliberately cutting himself off from his partner.

When he spoke, his voice dropped down a couple of decibels.

Either action would have aroused Kendra's curiosity. That he did both increased her curiosity a hundredfold. Ever since she could remember, she'd always had this almost overwhelming desire to know—*every*thing—to get to the bottom of any matter.

This was no different.

As she pretended to write out her notes and some of the points she wanted to touch on later, Kendra listened intently, taking in what Abilene was saying to whomever was on the other end of his call. Lucky for her, Kendra had excellent hearing because her partner's voice was so low, it almost could have qualified for mental telepathy.

"No, I can't right now." He sighed, like a man searching for the right words and the strength not to raise his voice and yell in utter frustration. "You knew that this was going to be just temporary. Yes, you did," he insisted. "You're smart enough for that. No," he said in a firmer voice. Then, in the next moment, as Kendra continued to eavesdrop, she heard her partner relent. "All right, all right, don't cry," he told the person on the other end—obviously a woman. She could tell from his tone that he was a man who really hated tears. "Okay, I'll see you after work," he agreed. "We'll go out." Abilene paused, listening. As did Kendra, trying to piece together what was going on without being obvious about it. "It's the best I can do."

With that, he terminated the call. Dropping the cell phone back into his pocket, Abilene blew out a frustrated breath. As he glanced toward his partner's desk, it took him less than a second to come to the conclusion that she'd been listening in on his half of the conversation. Given her nature, it didn't surprise him.

His eyes met hers and he waited. He wasn't about to say anything unless she was.

He didn't have long to wait.

"Former girlfriend you dumped?" she asked, nodding toward the pocket with the cell phone in it. Getting up, she pushed in her chair.

"No," was all he said. They went into the hall together.

The single word vibrated with finality and an entire collection of No Trespassing signs.

So be it, she felt in a moment of empathy. If the tables had been turned, she wouldn't have wanted to be quizzed, either. She thought back to a little more than eighteen months ago. There'd been some really intense, poorly muffled conversations with Jason in the days before his suicide that she wouldn't have wanted to repeat, either.

"Sorry," she apologized, hitting the Down button for the elevator. "None of my business."

He hadn't thought that she was capable of an apology—at least, not one to him. Not when it came to something like this.

Because she had backed off, Matt found himself loosening up just a little.

"That was my mother," he told her.

Kendra looked up at him sharply. That wouldn't even have been her tenth guess.

"Your mother?" Kendra replayed the short conversation in her head, viewing it in a completely different light. She was still convinced that the other woman had been crying. Compassion flooded through her, not to mention a new, warm feeling as she regarded the man who'd been sitting across from her.

"You need to see her, I can cover for you," she offered.

Matt shook his head. Running to his mother's side wasn't going to help anything—or change anything. "Thanks, but no. This isn't anything new, even though she never seems to see it coming." The elevator car arrived and they got in. He paused for a second, debating whether or not to say anything else, then shrugged. It wasn't all that much of a big deal, he told himself. "My mother's got a habit of getting mixed up with the wrong kind of men."

Kendra thought of her desk and the brand-new notes she'd just written that now rested like so many new snowflakes on top of her other, older notes. Who knew—maybe that was ultimately Summer Miller's story as well. "A lot of that going on lately."

"Yeah, except that at her age, you would have thought my mother would have developed a little common sense and learned not to be charmed and taken in by some con artist's smooth line."

Rarely did the heart listen to reason. If it did, Kendra would have known enough to back away, to insulate her heart right after Jason's accident. That way his suicide wouldn't have almost destroyed her when it had happened.

"The heart wants what the heart wants," Kendra replied simply. The elevator doors opened and she led the way out. "Besides, it's a misnomer."

He caught up to her in less than one stride. "What is?"

"That bit about common sense." God, this man *really* had a long stride. She would never be able to beat him in a race. The realization annoyed her even though the need to outrun him would most likely never come up. "Sense isn't common. At least not when the heart is involved."

"You speaking from experience?" he asked her, moderately intrigued.

She was, but she wasn't about to go there. Not with someone she didn't know. It was hard enough to talk with her family about Jason and how she'd failed him—not that she actually did. For the most part, she avoided the subject altogether, even when one of her siblings—or her father—prodded her to go out socially again. She hadn't been out on anything even vaguely resembling a date since Jason had put that gun to his chin and put himself out of his misery—and greatly intensified hers.

"No," she replied with studied casualness. "Just a general observation."

She'd paused, Matt noted. Paused just long enough to make him think that his question had a positive answer, one that she was unwilling to talk about. Why? Had a relationship of hers gone sour?

Whoever it was probably never stood a chance against that tongue of hers, he surmised. It would take a hell of a man to go toe-to-toe with her and survive, Matt reasoned.

He tucked away the thought for future review. Right now, they had a job to do. No one had to tell him that he had to make a good first impression. That meant not just solving the case, but solving it as quickly as possible.

Coming up to the Crown Victoria, he opened the passenger door automatically. She seemed to enjoy driving and he enjoyed not having to bicker with her. As far as he was concerned, it was a win-win situation. He'd been the one to suggest going to Miller's apartment, but he recalled that this had all started when Ryan Burnett had been reported missing. Maybe they should go back to that salient point and begin the investigation from there.

"You want to check out the victim's place of residence, or where our missing accountant-slash-suspect worked?" he asked her.

"Let's go there first," she agreed. "Get a little more insight into what this guy is capable of." About to get into the car, she paused and looked at him over the roof of the car. "You sure you don't want to go see your mother? My offer to cover for you still stands."

He shook his head, although he appreciated the offer. Appreciated, too, the way her features seemed to have softened just now. He felt something distant stir inside him.

"I'm sure," Matt said as he got in.

There was a pattern to his mother's behavior. A well-worn pattern. For the next couple of hours, his mother would cry, long and hard. Cry as if her world was literally coming to an end and she didn't know how to go on. But, eventually, when her entire body would be drained of any and all moisture, she'd sink into a peaceful, albeit reluctant, acceptance of the events and begin the arduous task of trying to rebuild her life.

But first she would consume a half gallon of rum raisin ice cream.

It never ceased to amaze him, how his mother could remain as thin as she did. Most people who consumed that quantity of ice cream—especially with the regularity that she did—would eventually begin to tip the scales to an ever-increasing number.

But his five-foot-three mother had always been a size six. He supposed it was nature's way of compensating for allowing her to drag her heart through the prickly briar patch time and again.

"Your mother been divorced long?" Kendra asked casually as she pulled out of the parking space. She guided the car carefully to avoid hitting anything.

He glanced at her, then decided not to ask the obvious: what made her think his mother was divorced? Divorced or widowed, the upshot was the same. His mother had no permanent man in her life—other than him. There were times when the weight of that felt almost overwhelming.

"Yeah," he answered absently. *More like forever.*

She prodded him a little more. "How long is *long?*"

"I don't remember ever meeting my father," Abilene said after a beat that had gone on way too long.

His answer made her understand why he had almost not said anything. "I'm sorry," she said with genuine feeling.

Her father had *always* been there for her. However, in her case it was her mother who was missing from her life. And had been ever since she was a little girl, when her mother had lost her battle against cancer. She and her siblings had grown up with their father doing double duty as both mother and father to them. He'd more than held his own in both capacities and she loved him dearly for it. But she knew what it meant to miss a parent deep in the confines of her heart.

"No need to be," Abilene told her offhandedly. "All in all, it wasn't a bad life. A little nomadic, maybe," he allowed, "but not bad."

She spared him a glance as she continued down the main drag, away from One Police Plaza. "Nomadic?"

He couldn't think of a more descriptive word for a lifestyle that involved picking up in the dead of night and vacating the premises—quickly. "I figure that would be the best term to use for sneaking out in the middle of the night—ahead of the landlord—when my mother couldn't pay the rent."

She could feel her heart going out to the boy he had been. A life of being one step ahead of the creditor was no life for a child. Had he been afraid? Ashamed? It took her a moment to reconcile the man who projected such a laid-back exterior with the person she now believed was buried inside.

That was the moment, she later realized, that he stopped being this annoying man she was forced to put up with and started becoming her partner.

"Did that happen often?" Kendra asked, not bothering to mask her sympathy.

His shrug was dismissive. "Often enough, or at least it felt like it when I was a kid. Back then, I thought it was a big adventure," he confessed. "Until I was old enough to realize that you're not supposed to run off without paying. Sometimes," he recalled, "when she found a decent-paying job—or a guy who initially spent money on her before he took her for everything she had—my mother would send money back to the landlord she'd skipped out on. She'd send it in an unmarked envelope so he couldn't trace it back to her."

His mother had always had good intentions—just not such good luck when it came to choosing men.

"She really didn't like not paying," Matt explained. It was impossible to miss the fondness in his voice when he spoke of her—even if she had made him sigh before. "More than that, I think she was afraid I'd turn out to be a thief if she didn't make me understand that you had to take responsibility for your life—or at least your bills," he said with a quiet laugh.

Taking it all in, Kendra nodded now. "Sounds like a decent woman who just wanted to be loved," she said.

Abilene shrugged again and stared out the window. He'd said too much. Since when was that a failing with him? It wasn't like him to talk this much. He was going to have to police himself a little more around this woman—no pun intended, he added with a bemused smile.

"Yeah, maybe that's it," he agreed dismissively. And then he looked at her. His partner had subtly pulled all this out of him. Why? Was she going to use it against him somehow? She seemed and sounded sympathetic right now, but he didn't trust her yet. That was going to take a little time. *If* it happened at all. "What does this have to do with the case?" he asked, the edge back in his voice.

"Nothing," she told him honestly. "I'm just trying to get a handle on the guy I'm working with."

"You could get that out of my file."

She didn't bother telling him that she didn't have enough clout to have his file pulled—yet. The chief, of course, had access to it and probably so did her father, but she didn't try to pull strings like that. If she did, then she would deserve all the unflattering terms that were tossed her way by people who didn't know any better, who didn't know *her* better. Shortcuts were for emergencies, not to satisfy your curiosity or for some self-serving purpose.

But for now, she said none of this. If, for some reason, they remained partners after this case was over, he'd find out what she was like on his own.

The thought didn't bother her nearly as much as it would have initially.

"Won't tell me as much as you would. I'm not interested in You the Professional. I want to know what kind of *man* I'm trusting my back to. I already figured you were a decent enough detective or the chief wouldn't have transferred you down to Homicide."

"Why? Is that where the elite go?" he asked. The amusement in his voice hid the slight chip that had emerged on his shoulder.

"That's where the best are needed," she informed him. "I'm told that the chief tends to view this not as a job, but as a mission to protect his city. He wants to keep the people who live here safe. That's done by keeping killers off the streets and putting them behind bars. And *that's* done by putting the best detectives on the job."

He laughed shortly as she made a sharp right. "Now you're beginning to sound like a city council poster trying to get people to move here."

That was the *last* thing she would have wanted, to have more people move to Aurora.

"God forbid. Aurora's got enough people here already. Any more and it's going to get way too crowded for the people who initially moved here to get away from the big cities."

Her father would tell her stories about the city when the main thoroughfare had only two lanes, one in each direction, and there were only three traffic lights between the two freeways that buffered Aurora. That was when the developments could be counted on one hand and there were almost as many cows and horses as people living here.

Those days were far in the past, but somehow, Aurora had managed to maintain its small town *feel* even if it was far more "city" than "town" these days.

Silence descended over the vehicle and continued to travel with them for a couple of miles until Kendra decided to tender an invitation to Abilene or, actually, to his mother.

Even as the idea formed in her brain, she had a hard time believing that she would say this. But people in pain had a way of getting to her and from what she'd overheard earlier—and what he'd just told her now—Abilene's mother was in pain. Decent people shouldn't have to be in pain if there was any way around it.

"Look, I'm still just getting used to this whole deal about actually being a Cavanaugh and not who I thought I was—"

"A last name doesn't change who you are," he pointed out. "Although," he added with a touch of whimsy, "saying that you're a Cavanaugh might make things a hell of a lot easier for you."

"Or harder," she countered. "A lot of people think that just because I'm related to a Cavanaugh, I'm getting a free ride, that I don't have to work as hard as the next guy—I work twice as hard as the next guy."

"Unless the next guy happens to be me," Abilene said, his mouth curving.

Damn but he had a sexy-looking mouth, even when what came out of it annoyed her. "I work twice as hard as the next guy," she repeated with feeling. "No matter *who* the next guy is."

"The lady doth protest too much." The way he said it, it was more of a question than a statement.

It still wasn't received well. "The 'lady' is busy working her tail off to prove she can do the job each and every time," she said with feeling.

He seemed willing to take her at her word. With a casual shrug, he said, "Okay, we got that out of the way. Now, where were you going with all this before we got sidetracked?" he asked with a grin.

Right, the invitation. For a second, she felt awkward about extending it. After all, he might get the wrong idea—that she was interested in him. Which she wasn't. This wasn't for Abilene, she reminded herself. This was for his mother.

"That the former chief of police, Andrew Cavanaugh, likes to have people over for breakfast—or any meal. He sets a really good table and, personally, I have no idea how the man does it, but there always seems to be food ready. A battalion could come by and I think that he would have enough to feed them until their sides ached." She'd been present a couple of times when the man had juggled fifty guests and never broke a sweat. She found that incredible. "What I'm getting at is maybe you and your mother might want to drop by some morning, like on a Saturday," she suggested. "More specifically," she continued, suddenly remembering that her father had said something about there being a party of some sort at the former chief's house this weekend, "*this* Saturday."

"As your guest?" he asked.

She was about to say no, afraid he'd read into that, but then she relented. After all, it might make things easier all around if that was the initial invitation.

"Yeah. Sure. Why not? As my guests," she agreed. "It might just do your mother some good," she added so that there wouldn't be any misunderstanding about why she was suggesting this in the first place. If he thought she was interested in him, their budding working relationship would get shot to hell. "There's a lot of warmth and love coming from that group." She could testify to that firsthand. "Gives a person a feeling of well-being."

Abilene liked to keep his private life just that, private. But he needed help here. So he rolled her offer over in his mind. He loved his mother dearly and while he wouldn't have traded her in for anything in the world, what he *would* have changed about her was her emotional neediness.

She'd always been there for him and had done the best she could to raise him so that he wanted for little. If he had one wish in the world, it would be to see her finally happy—and secure.

Maybe she'd learn how by associating with people like the Cavanaughs.

"Sounds good to me," he finally told his partner. "Count us in."

She nodded. Now all she had to do was ask her father if she'd overstepped her bounds. She made a mental note to talk to him tonight.

The list of people she wanted to touch base with once she was off duty was growing.

Chapter 5

"No, I've never had any trouble with Ryan Burnett." The man they were talking to looked surprised to even be asked such a question. "If I had, I would have fired the guy, not sent someone to look for him when he didn't turn up at work or call in. Why?" he asked suspiciously, looking from one detective to the other. "What's going on?"

Lou Maxwell was the senior accountant and founder of the company that boasted a number of celebrity clients as well as doing the accounting for a large number of small corporations in the area, all of which he'd parlayed into a thriving business. The man had a booming voice, which was in complete contrast to his rather small, thin frame. Expensive clothes hung on his body like suits on a hanger, waiting to be pressed into service by an actual live person.

If Maxwell was aware of the shadow he cast—or didn't cast—he gave no indication of it.

When neither of the two detectives who had come into his spartan office to question him about his missing accountant answered his question, he went on to ask another.

"Kennedy said he saw a dead body on the floor," he said, referring to the junior accountant he'd sent in search of his missing employee, "but that it wasn't Burnett's. Whose was it and where the hell is Burnett?" Maxwell demanded.

Kendra shook her head. "We really can't discuss an ongoing investigation, Mr. Maxwell."

"You people wouldn't *have* an 'ongoing investigation' if I hadn't sent Kennedy to find out what was going on. Now I'm down two men instead of just one because Kennedy is still throwing up in the men's room and you won't tell me anything." He glared at the detectives when they still wouldn't tell him anything. "Look, someone on one of the news channels or one of the millions of blogs on the internet is going to find a way to ferret out the information and splash it all over the airwaves, so you might as well tell me now. I have a right to know."

Maxwell had a point. She could see by the look that Abilene gave her that the other detective thought so, too. She was surprised that Abilene was leaving it up to her rather than just stepping in and taking over. Maybe he did respect protocol—in his own way. He was turning out not to be such a bad guy after all. Then she cautioned herself to continue reserving judgment. After all, she didn't exactly have a sterling track record when it came to being right about men.

Determined to control the amount of information that came out, she kept it short and precise.

"We found a woman in Mr. Burnett's apartment. We didn't find him. Would you know where he would be inclined to go if he couldn't stay at his apartment?"

Maxwell shook his head. "Not a clue," he confessed. "Nice guy, but he kind of kept to himself. That's why I liked him," Maxwell underscored. "Worked hard from the minute he came in until the minute he left. No goofing off, no internet surfing on my time." He paused for a moment, thinking. "About a couple of weeks ago, I heard him mention he was going to get engaged."

"Who did he mention it to?" Abilene asked before Kendra could. It was a natural assumption that the woman was the same one found on Burnett's floor, but there was always an outside chance that it wasn't.

"Kennedy. That's why I sent him," Maxwell added. "Thought maybe they were friends." The small, deep-set brown eyes narrowed further, appearing to grow even smaller. "You telling me that you think Burnett killed the girl?"

"I'm not telling you anything," Kendra reminded the man tactfully. "Right now, we're just asking as many questions as we can think of, trying to see what we can find out. See what flies," she added, borrowing some of the accountant's short, clipped terms.

Maxwell snorted. "Well, if he did kill her, then I'm a rotten judge of character." It was evident by his demeanor that he didn't believe he was.

Kendra, however, wasn't as sure as he was. "Let's

hope you're not, Mr. Maxwell. Do you mind if we talk to your people? See if perhaps they might have anything to add?" They could do it with or without his permission, but with was always easier.

"Do I mind?" Maxwell echoed. "Yeah, I mind. If they're talking, they're not working. But go ahead," he concluded, waving them on to the outer office where the accountants who worked for him were all seated. "Get this over with. The sooner you do, the sooner you're gone and they get back to doing what I'm paying them for."

"Don't think anyone's going to be nominating him for Boss of the Year any time soon," Abilene commented under his breath as he and Kendra closed the door to Maxwell's office.

"Could be worse," Kendra deadpanned. When Abilene raised an eyebrow, she said, "He could have told us to come back and talk to the other accountants after hours."

Abilene took a chance that she was being serious and said, "Maybe he knew he'd be overridden and didn't want the hassle. Guys like that only pick fights they figure they'll win."

Guys like that in this case meant guys in control. Was Abilene referring to himself as well? She took it as another possible small piece of insight into the man assigned to work with her.

"I'll keep that in mind."

Abilene heard something in her tone and deduced the rest. Partnering with her would be a constant, ongoing battle of wits. He found himself kind of liking that. It would keep him on his toes.

"Not all guys," he interjected.

Okay, he's exempting himself, she thought, amused. She looked at Abilene for a long moment—and just for a second, caught herself thinking things that had no part in the investigation.

Doing an abrupt mental about-face, she murmured, "Good to know."

They both turned their attention to the accountants, taking them aside one by one into one of the small private offices meant for client-accountant interviews, and asked their questions.

The accountants were all of the same opinion. Talking to them just reinforced the initial impression of a hardworking, affable young man who was willing to pitch in when necessary but for the most part, kept to himself. No one had a bad word to say about him.

What Kennedy, the accountant who'd gone to Ryan's apartment, had seen had already made the rounds at the firm and to a person, they were convinced that Burnett couldn't have killed the girl. What they did believe was that the missing young man was perhaps in trouble or even imminent danger.

"Maybe somebody broke into his apartment and kidnapped him," said Gina, the accounting firm's one administrative assistant, a very young-looking blonde who seemed to favor braids as a hairstyle, her blue eyes wide and earnest.

Kendra decided to make the young woman work to put over her theory. "Then how do you explain the dead woman on his floor?"

Gina didn't even hesitate or need time to think. She'd

obviously figured out the kinks in her theory while waiting her turn to be questioned.

"She walked in on it and the kidnapper was forced to kill her because he couldn't take them both prisoners." Having advanced her theory, Gina seemed exceedingly pleased with herself. The next moment, she was looking to Abilene, rather than to the woman questioning her. She definitely looked interested in *his* reaction.

He didn't disappoint her. Instead, he nodded. "We'll take it under advisement," he told her in a quiet, thoughtful voice.

In response, the young woman lit up like a Christmas tree.

Her reaction was not lost on Kendra. *And another one bites the dust.*

Since this was the last interview, Abilene followed Kendra's lead and started to rise. He felt the administrative assistant place her hand on top of his, meaning to momentarily detain him.

"You'll let me know if that was what happened?" she asked hopefully. "That poor Ryan was kidnapped?"

"You'll be one of the first to know," Abilene assured her with solemnity.

"Laying the groundwork for a future conquest?" Kendra asked in a quiet, unfathomable voice as they left the outer office.

"Letting her think she said something important and useful," Abilene corrected. "And who knows? That woman's theory makes about as much sense as anything else right now."

Kendra relented. She supposed she had to agree at this point.

"One thing does seem to be clear right about now," he continued.

She would have been lying if she had said that she hadn't braced herself before gamely asking, "And what's that?"

"The guy who worked shoulder to shoulder with those other accountants in that office wasn't the kind of guy to kill his girlfriend in cold blood."

No, not according to the way they had perceived him. But there was also another explanation for what had happened in the small apartment. "How about in the heat of an argument?"

They stepped into the elevator. Abilene shook his head. "Didn't sound like a very passionate guy to me, either."

"How about you?" she asked without any preamble. She pressed for the first floor.

Abilene stared at her. This was a new twist. "Are you asking me if I'm passionate?"

Although the thought amused him, he just didn't see Kendra putting that sort of question to him. It didn't jibe with what he knew of her personality.

Was he wrong? And if so, about what, exactly? Less than twenty-four hours in the woman's company and she was becoming one huge, intriguing enigma. A puzzle he found himself wanting to solve.

"No," she contradicted, a flash of embarrassment over the misunderstanding sending color up her neck to her cheeks—as did the unbidden thought of his being passionate. "What I'm asking you is if your fellow co-workers know the first thing about what makes Matt Abilene tick," she asked. "Or do they know only what you want them to know?" Which was the more logical conclusion.

After a moment, Abilene nodded his head. They reached the first floor and he waited for her to step out first, then darted out just before the doors closed on him.

She didn't tell Abilene he looked rather adorable just then, even though the thought flashed through her mind.

"I see where you're going with this," he told Kendra.

She laughed, waving away his words. "I wasn't trying to make it a mystery—unlike who killed Summer and where our missing accountant is at the moment."

"Right now, I'd say the key is in their relationship," he speculated.

She seemed a little uncertain, even as she said, "Right now, I tend to agree."

Right now. Abilene smiled knowingly. "Don't commit fully, do you?"

She couldn't make up her mind whether she liked his smile—or found it distractingly annoying, not to mention unsettling.

"Not easily," she admitted when he was obviously waiting for her to say something.

He nodded. "Me, neither."

Tell me something I don't *know.* But out loud, she said, "I already figured that part out," all while sporting a pleasant, completely unreadable smile.

Abilene followed her out to the street. "Where to now?"

It was getting late. Shadows had begun to form, tagging one another on the ground. "I think you put in enough time on a first day," she told him.

He hadn't expected that. She reminded him of someone who pushed, who worked into the small hours and expected no less from those who worked with her. "I'm not a novice," he reminded her.

"No," she agreed, "but you do have a mother who's waiting to see you. And we're not about to solve this thing in a few extra hours tonight. Go, see your mother, Abilene," she urged. "Make her feel better." She thought of how much, after all these years, she still missed her own. "You only get one mother."

He snapped his fingers. "And here I was, getting ready to swing by the Mother Store to see if I could trade mine in for another model."

Sarcasm was a weapon—and a defense mechanism. Which was he using? "You always crack wise like that?" she asked.

"Not always," he admitted, his voice even, giving nothing away. And then he looked at her significantly. "Only when I'm inspired."

They'd come up to the car and she pressed the lock release. A small *click* had all four locks opening and standing at attention.

"C'mon." She opened the driver's-side door. "I'll drop you off at the precinct."

"Okay. I owe you a drink."

That stopped her for a moment. She glanced at him over the hood of the car. "How do you figure that?"

He dropped down into his seat, then waited for her to do the same before continuing. "Isn't the new guy supposed to buy drinks at the end of his first day?"

Buckling up, she shut the door. Kendra shook her

head just before turning on the ignition. "I was the last 'new guy' in our squad and they bought *me* drinks."

His laugh seemed to fill the interior of the vehicle and rippled along her skin.

"That works, too," he answered with an agreeable nod.

Kendra had a feeling that he would hold her to that drink.

They parted in the parking lot, with Abilene going his way and Kendra, supposedly, going hers. She watched his car pulling out of the lot in the distance. Only then did she get out of her vehicle and go back upstairs.

Tom was waiting for her. By request.

Taking the elevator to the Missing Persons squad room, she got out, entered the room and crossed to Tom's desk. Wearily, she dropped down into the chair positioned next to it.

"What do you know about him?" she asked. "My new partner," she added for clarification. And then, because it occurred to Kendra that she wasn't being at all clear, she backtracked and said what she should have mentioned in the first place: her new partner's name. "What do you know about Matt Abilene?"

The wide, muscular shoulders rose and fell in a minor, offhanded movement. "Off the top of my head— nothing," Tom admitted. "But I can ask around if you'd like." He looked carefully at Kendra, as if trying to discern if everything was all right. "I heard that the chief gave you a new one," he confirmed. "Is he giving you a hard time?"

She didn't want to answer that one way or another. To say yes would get her brother's protective side up and Abilene wasn't actually being condescending or disrespectful toward her, which meant that she couldn't say that he was giving her a hard time. It was more that he was irritating her—mostly in ways she couldn't talk about or explain, even to herself. Besides, knowing the way Tom thought, he just might interpret her words in a completely different and unwelcome way.

So, for now, she remained evasive. "I just like to know the kind of person I'm working with, that's all," she said in the most innocent voice she could muster.

"Wouldn't you figure that out after a few days of interacting with him?" Tom asked, putting the logical assumption out there.

For that, at least, she had an answer. "You know I'm the impatient type."

Tom grinned. "Which is why this new partner of yours gets more of my sympathy than you do," her brother told her.

Kendra eyed him impatiently. "So you're not going to help?"

"I didn't say that."

No, she had to admit that he hadn't. And that relieved her. For a second. "You just like to yank my chain."

Tom didn't bother suppressing the laugh. "Something like that."

Nothing new there, she thought. And then she remembered something else. Something she had jumped the gun on. Was this going to create problems now, she wondered uncertainly.

Kendra took a breath, then said, "Mind if I ask you a question?"

"Go ahead."

She pressed her lips together, then pushed ahead. "Think that the chief would mind my bringing two guests with me to his Saturday brunch thing this week?"

"Which chief?" he asked for form's sake, although only one of them really cooked. Brian just put up the tables. "We've got two of them in the family now," he reminded her, tongue in cheek. "It might be clearer if you refer to them as Uncle Andrew and Uncle Brian."

She couldn't bring herself to do that just yet. They were people she respected and in Brian's case, was honored to work with. But they weren't her uncles. Maybe in time they would be, but not yet. Not now.

"Doesn't feel right, yet," she told her brother. "And you know I'm talking about the brunches the former chief has in his house—Andrew, all right?" she tagged on, exasperated as she used the man's name.

Tom ignored her irritated tone. There was a more interesting question here than why her temper kept spiking. "What guests?"

She would rather not have said anything until later, but since he asked, she had to tell him. There was no easy way around it. "Abilene and his mother."

"So you're getting along with him, then," Tom assumed.

She wasn't about to launch into any long explanations right now. "One thing doesn't have anything to do with the other," Kendra countered.

Tom crossed his arms and leaned back in his chair. "All right. Educate me."

She sighed. "Abilene got a call at the office from his mother today. She was upset. From what I could gather, her boyfriend walked out on her. Abilene said it wasn't the first such occurrence. That it's a pattern." She recited the facts as she recalled them. "She sounds like a good woman who's made a lot of bad choices because she's afraid of winding up alone. Apparently, there's no other family. I just thought…"

Kendra let her voice trail off. Tom was the smart one here, she let him fill in the blanks.

"—that being subjected to the Cavanaugh family might help her feel less alone?" he guessed.

"Something like that," she acknowledged. "But I don't want to do something that'll make the chief think that I'm taking advantage of the so-called family connection."

Tom shook his head. "It's not a 'so-called' family connection," he corrected her. "It *is* a family connection. *Our* family connection. Like it or not, Kenny, Dad's a Cavanaugh. And so are we."

"Yeah, I know. But—" She paused for a moment, searching for words that didn't seem to want to materialize. "What do we do about…you know…the *other* family?"

"We don't 'do' anything about them. The way I see it, Kenny, we just got more family, we didn't trade one bunch in for another. You can't close your eyes to over twenty years of life and pretend it never happened. We thought they were our aunts and uncles, *they* thought they were our aunts and uncles. No reason for anything to change."

He was missing the huge elephant in the room—and

she knew he was too smart not to see it. So why was he taking this stand?

"Except that they're *not* our aunts and uncles," she insisted.

"Just a technicality, Kenny. Finding out about the hospital mix-up doesn't suddenly erase them, or make all those memories of Christmases past disappear. It sure doesn't erase them from our lives. They wouldn't want it and *we* wouldn't want it." He leaned forward in his chair, his voice gaining enthusiasm. "Life just got better, Kenny. And you don't have to choose between one camp or the other. This is one of those times when you can have it all and it's really okay."

He smiled at her as he rose. When she did as well, Tom gave her a quick, hard hug. "Give yourself permission to be happy again, Kenny. The rest of us are worried about you." And then he glanced at his watch. "Now, if you'll excuse me, I have a very sexy lady waiting to light up my life and I don't want to keep her waiting any longer."

That would be the detective who'd transferred from New Mexico after working with her brother on her niece's kidnapping case. Kaitlyn Two Feathers. Their family would become larger by one very soon. Kendra was happy for Tom, even as she felt an unexpected pang in her heart for what she no longer had. And maybe never did. Jason's suicide, despite all her efforts to help him, was evidence of that.

"Say hi to Kait for me. Tell her to treat my big brother well."

He grinned. "Will do."

She stood there, watching her brother leave and then,

quietly, she doubled back to the Homicide squad room. She made her way through the nearly deserted room until she reached her desk.

Taking a deep breath, Kendra sat down and started to go over all her notes on the current case from the beginning.

Again.

Chapter 6

Sabrina Abilene's impressively unlined, heart-shaped face lit up when she saw her son walking toward her booth.

She'd been sitting there for the last half hour and was thinking about leaving. She knew that Matthew's career didn't always remain between the lines. Sometimes he was forced to work around the clock. And while she worried about him a great deal because of his chosen career, she was also incredibly proud of him.

"You came," she cried once Matt was within earshot. Surprise and pleasure were evident in equal parts in her voice. "I didn't think that you were going to."

Matt slid into the seat opposite his mother. This was where they came whenever they wanted to celebrate an occasion. Or just to get away and talk.

It was the latter he was faced with now.

Somewhere along the line, their roles had gotten reversed and he'd become the parent while she was the child, at least when it came to matters of the heart.

"When have I not come?" he asked. Then, before she could reply, he said quietly, "You're getting me confused with all those other men in your life, Mom. The ones who keep disappointing you and running out on you."

"No, I'm not," she protested with a sad smile. "I just expect you to get fed up with holding my hand whenever I wind up having this happen to me," she told him honestly. Her eyes smiled as she looked at him. "I'd never confuse you with anyone else." Sabrina looked down at the one glass of wine she allowed herself to have whenever she came here. There were no answers in the light pink liquid. "Why do they keep running out on me, Matthew? What's wrong with me?" she asked in a very small, defeated voice.

Matt didn't bother with the menu. He knew what the restaurant had to offer by heart. The people who ran Haven knew when not to mess with a good thing and had left it unchanged for the past few years.

When the waiter approached their table, Matt ordered the lemon chicken. His mother echoed, "Make that two." Once the waiter retreated, only then did Matt answer his mother's question.

He hated seeing her like this. And hated what he had to tell her, even though they both already knew this. "You have lousy taste in men," he told her honestly. "And a good heart," he added to temper the harsher remark. "No matter how many times this happens to you, no matter how many men take everything you have to give and then disappear, you just can't seem to make yourself believe that not everyone is like you, that some- one could actually be cruel on purpose."

His mother laughed shortly. "I guess that makes me a sucker."

"No," he told her carefully, "just a good-hearted per- son who really needs to be a little more cautious about opening up."

She began to speak, then waited until the waiter who'd returned with the basket of lemon chicken pieces that was to be their dinner left again.

"It's just that I get so lonely sometimes," she con- fessed quietly. Bright blue eyes looked up at him. "I miss your father."

"I don't think he'd be too happy about what you're going through, either, Mom," Matt pointed out patiently. "Listen, I have an idea. Why don't you do some volun- teer work at the local hospital?" he suggested. "They could use the help and it'll make you feel as if you're doing something useful for people. That's a plus. You also might run into a better class of people than you do at your present job. Definitely another plus."

But Sabrina shook her head. "I can't do that and work," she protested. "My job takes up a great deal of my time."

The place where she worked—a bar named Sparky's—was not the place where he wanted his mother. It was the last in a long line of less than A-list places where she'd worked.

"Waiting tables at that...club—" he finally settled on the word rather than calling it a bar "—also puts you right out there with a whole unsavory class of people. Men just looking for women to take advantage of."

She pressed her lips together. "Meaning me."

"Listen." He leaned in closer. "You can quit that job. I have some money put away—"

"No, no, no, that's out of the question." She was his mother, Matthew wasn't supposed to have to take care of her. "I won't have you spending your hard-earned money on me—"

"My money, Mom," he told her. "I get to spend it the way I want to." He smiled at her, remembering the good times—and there had been good times. She'd tried very hard to give him a decent upbringing and he'd never doubted that she loved him. The rest of it was hard to take. "Can't think of a better way than helping you out."

"I can," Sabrina told him firmly. She placed her hand over his and patted it. "Your taking time out of your busy day to see me is all I want from you. That's already more than a lot of sons would do," she insisted. And then she forced a smile to her lips, putting up a brave front for him and trying at the same time to convince herself that from now on, it was going to be different. "I'll try to do better," she promised.

He nodded and pretended as if he believed her, but this was nothing new. His mother had made the same promise before, time and again, and she'd meant it.

But each and every time she'd wind up losing her soft heart to the first charismatic con man who crossed her path.

It was as if there was some kind of electronic bulletin board with her picture on it. The note beneath it urged anyone with larcenous tendencies to come find her because she was the perfect mark.

His mother had good intentions, but this pattern of

hers wouldn't change unless he found a way to do something about it.

What he needed, Matt told himself, was to find a way for his mother to mingle with a better element of people, he thought. That was when he suddenly remembered the invitation his partner had tendered. He had his doubts if the cocky detective actually meant it once she had the time to think it over, but whether or not she meant it, he decided he needed to take her up on it.

Or rather, his mother needed him to take her up on it.

"By the way," Matt said casually as he selected another piece of chicken from the basket—he favored drumsticks—"we've been invited to the former police chief's house on Saturday."

Sabrina's light green eyes widened in surprise. "Why? Is something wrong?"

"If something was wrong," Matt answered, doing his best not to laugh at his mother's dazed expression, "we'd be going to the precinct, not his house. Turns out that my new partner's one of his nieces and the former chief of police has a real penchant for having a lot of people over to his house for brunch and other get-togethers. Word has it that the man's one hell of a cook." A deep fondness filled his eyes as he grinned at his mother. "He probably can't hold a candle to you, but we might as well give the guy a chance. So what d'you say? Will you go with me?"

When Sabrina didn't answer right away, he prodded her a little. "Could be a lot of fun, being around a house full of honest people for a change—and me, of course," he winked.

As if he had a dishonest bone in his body, Sabrina

thought with a gentle laugh. She was and always had been very, very proud of him. Matthew was the very best part of her.

Sabrina leaned over the table and their basket of communal chicken and kissed his cheek. "You always could make everything all better just by talking to me, Matthew."

"Maybe I should tape-record my voice, leave you with that to listen to when I'm not around."

The smile on her lips was also reflected in her eyes. When she looked like that, his mother was downright beautiful. But, beautiful or not, she didn't deserve to be taken advantage of the way she was. And she certainly didn't deserve to have it happen to her over and over again. Maybe some time with the Cavanaughs would help her break that pattern, let her see the way decent people treated one another. Who knew—it might even help to build up her confidence.

"It's worth a try," she laughed, referring to the tape.

"Yeah, maybe it is, at that." Matt was only half kidding.

"'Morning, Good," Abilene said cheerfully as he slid into his chair and took his place behind his desk. "By the way, my mother says thank you for the invitation. She'll be very happy to attend the chief's brunch this Saturday."

About to get started with the files he'd left on his desk last night, Abilene took a sip of his coffee. That was when he took a good look at his partner for the first time.

He wasn't much on noticing a woman's clothes, but

he was fairly certain that he'd seen his partner wearing this same outfit yesterday. In his experience, most women didn't wear the same thing two days in a row unless they hadn't been home the night before.

He eyed her over the rim of his container. "Did you go home last night?"

Kendra looked up ruefully. It wasn't something she was happy about acknowledging. Sleep last night had come when she'd least expected it and she'd wound up with her head on the desk, getting about four hours, perhaps less. It hadn't been restful. Her neck was killing her this morning and she was pretty sure that beneath her sandy bangs was the imprint of a staple.

None of that put her in a good mood, or even a tolerable one. The edges of her temper were already pretty frayed. And it was still early.

"Let's get one thing straight. You're my temporary partner, not my guardian angel," she told him.

"Temporary, huh?" he repeated. "Is that what you think?" If it was, that explained a lot, he reasoned.

She shrugged, not about to discuss it when she felt so overwhelmingly underarmed. Her mind fuzzy, she was still having trouble focusing.

"Everything's temporary one way or another. Who knows?" She threw the ball into his court. "Things might not work out and you might be the one asking for another partner."

She was a Cavanaugh. He wouldn't jeopardize his career like that. You didn't get very far by complaining about the chief's niece.

"Or you might." And that, he knew by the way she'd

said the word *temporary,* was a far more likely scenario in this case.

"There's that, too," Kendra agreed with a dismissive sigh he couldn't quite interpret. "What was that you said about your mother?" she asked, looking for a way to change the subject.

"I said she wanted me to thank you for the invitation to the chief's house." Had the woman been here all night? he wondered. Working on the case? She certainly didn't look as if she'd found anything for her trouble. He doubted she'd be quite this surly if she had.

Why was it so hard for her to think clearly? Kendra wondered, annoyed with herself and the fog that had set in on her brain. She used to be able to get by on four hours' sleep—just not four hours grabbed on top of a desk, she reminded herself.

What had Abilene just said about his mother? Oh, right. That the other woman had extended her thanks. She stitched together the rest of the conversation, then, just to be clear, asked, "Then she's coming?"

"Took a little persuading—my mother really doesn't like to feel as if she's imposing—" he explained, to forestall any further misunderstanding.

"Trust me, from what I know about Andrew Cavanaugh's get-togethers, she's not," Kendra assured him.

"But she is coming," he said, finishing his sentence despite the fact that they seemed to be talking over one another here. He paused for a second, then asked, "You were serious, right?"

"Absolutely."

Right now, given her present state of nonclarity, she wondered what had possessed her to invite Abilene, but then she recalled that he'd told her about his mother's penchant for getting taken by the men she let into her life. She supposed, in a way, Abilene's mother and she had something in common. The men in their lives had ultimately disappointed them.

Except that in her case, it wasn't so cut-and-dried. She was disappointed because, on some existential plane, she had failed Jason. If she hadn't, she would have been able to make him come around and renew his hold on life. Instead, he'd gone ahead and romanced a gun, using it to end his life, rather than fighting his way back from the depths of the black hole he'd slipped into.

"So how do you want to work this?" he was asking as she distanced herself from Jason and the memory of that awful day, of finding him like that, lifeless and bleeding.

She took a breath, then focused her attention back on the case. "Well, right now I'm having a lot of photos of Burnett printed up so that we can show it around in all the train and bus stations and at all the airline terminals at the local airport. This way, if he's leaving town any other way than by car, we've got him."

"Great." He nodded, but that wasn't really what he was asking. "But I meant on Saturday. At your uncle's house." She really wasn't here, was she, he thought, looking into her eyes again. He couldn't help wondering what was going on in her mind.

Kendra blinked. It took her a second to refocus her thoughts, shifting them away from the case and reluctantly onto her personal life. She almost corrected him about Andrew being her uncle—except that, when she came right down to it, she really couldn't. He *was* her uncle. Not in name only, but in actuality.

It was just going to take a lot of getting used to.

"Oh, that. Well, I could meet you at your place, or you could—"

She was about to say that he and his mother could meet her at her place, but then that meant she'd have to give him her address and she wasn't in a place emotionally where she was willing to give out that kind of information to him just yet. She preferred doling out personal information slowly. When she knew Abilene better—*and* he was her partner of record for a while—*then* she'd let him know where she lived.

Maybe.

"Why don't I swing by your place, pick you and your mother up and we'll go from there?" she suggested pleasantly.

"All right." He wasn't about to ask her why she'd doubled back so abruptly. He had a feeling he knew. The woman was very guarded and she didn't immediately "work well and play well with others," as they used to say on grade-school report cards from decades gone by. "Give me an approximate time so I can pick up my mother first and have her back in time for when you do your 'swinging by,' Good."

She could feel her temper shortening drastically. She wished he wouldn't call her that, but obviously the more she asked, the more he seemed to "forget." The only way to deal with this was to ride it out.

For some reason, while Abilene wasn't being exactly sarcastic outright, it was pretty damn close, she realized. Why? Kendra silently demanded. Was he reacting to something she'd said, or—?

She was overthinking again. Her brothers and sisters always said that was her biggest fault. Thinking things to death. She hadn't always been like that. But having a fiancé kill himself on what was to have been their wedding day sent ripples through a person's life. Big ripples.

There were times, in the very beginning, when she'd secretly marveled that she was simply putting one foot in front of the other and not just huddled somewhere in a fetal position.

After that horrible accident, which had claimed the lives of four of his fellow firefighters, when Jason lay there in the hospital bed, so much of his body scarred by the fire, she'd come to see him every day. She and her family had been his cheering section and she had sworn to him that it didn't matter to her if he had one leg or two, didn't matter if he met her at the altar in a wheelchair or on crutches, just as long as he was there.

She loved *him,* she'd insisted, not just some part of him, or, in this case, a missing part of him.

It had gotten to the point where she thought he believed her, but obviously she'd failed somehow, failed to convince him, failed to save him. He hadn't believed her when she'd told him that she loved him, that she would be there for him and that she wanted to help him regain his enthusiasm for life.

If he'd believed her, wouldn't he still be here?

The thought vibrated in her brain. Tears gathered in her eyes.

"Hey, you okay?"

Abruptly, Kendra came back to her surroundings.

She noted the concern in Abilene's voice. She also realized that in her momentary lapse, his butt had somehow gotten planted on her desk. Obviously, he'd come around when she hadn't answered him and had sat on her desk to look down into her eyes.

Not only that, but he had one of her hands in both of his and she *knew* he wasn't just trying to shake it.

Something warm and unbidden rose up in response within her. Startled, she was quick to shut it down and pulled her hand away.

"I'm fine," Kendra retorted.

Ordinarily, he would have retreated and said "the hell with it." But something in her expression caught his attention. And captured his concern. Something was out of sync.

"Yeah," he agreed. "For a woman who's a million miles away."

Damn but having him as a partner had a definite downside. During the past couple of years, she could count on Joe dozing at his desk half the time. He certainly didn't play Twenty Questions and probe her like this.

"I was just thinking," she tossed off carelessly.

He laughed shortly. "I kind of figured that."

"Good for you." Rising abruptly, Kendra pushed her chair in. The armrests banged jarringly against the desk. "Let's see if the people where Summer Miller worked know if her boyfriend was hot-tempered enough to kill her."

Sounded like as good a place to start this morning as any. Abilene gestured toward the doorway. "Lead the way."

Her eyes narrowed. Did he think she was waiting for his permission?

"Thanks," she said frostily. "I will." Lengthening her stride, she walked out of the office quickly.

"Hey, Good," he called after her, increasing his own stride. It didn't take much to catch up to her. He saw her shoulders tense in response to the name he called her, but pretended not to. "Did I say something to set you off?" he asked.

You mean today? Or just in general? "Yes."

"What?" he asked, curious.

"Everything," she fired back at him, stabbing at the Down button on the wall between the two closed elevator doors.

"In other words, you don't want me to talk?"

She came very close to saying yes, but she knew damn well that she was being unfair to him. Just because she had issues didn't mean that she should take it out on him. Or chew him out.

It wasn't his fault she wasn't woman enough to save Jason.

"Sorry," she apologized with a heartfelt sigh. "I get crabby when I don't get enough sleep. I didn't mean to make you feel I was chewing you out."

"You want to go home and catch a couple of hours?" he offered. "I can handle questioning Summer's employer and coworkers," he told her, then added, "The lieutenant doesn't need to know," in case she thought he was planning on telling their boss.

"I can handle my own problems," she informed him.

Talk about being touchy, he thought. "Didn't say you

couldn't. Just thought you might handle things better with a couple of hours' sleep under your belt."

She had to admit the offer was exceedingly tempting. Every fiber in her body suddenly begged her for the opportunity to just curl up on a soft surface and shut her eyes. But there was no way she had any intention of shirking her duties.

"Thanks, but no. I'll manage," she insisted.

"If you say so," he answered glibly.

"Yes, I do."

Kendra's tone was firm even if her resolve wasn't quite there yet.

Chapter 7

When questioned about Summer Miller, the heavy-set man with the curly, faded yellow-white hair sadly shook his head.

"No, I had to let her go. PartyTyme! is owned by this family-run corporation and they have very strict rules," he told them solemnly. He paused for a moment to reengage in his ongoing battle with his ever-sinking trousers, pulling them up to just beneath his expanded waistline. Temporarily, they hung on his hips before once again beginning a slow descent. "There's zero tolerance for drugs. Summer failed the last random test we had and bam, she was out the door."

"Summer had a drug habit?" Kendra asked. According to the M.E., the first tox screen had been negative. Maybe further testing was in order.

Harvey Abernathy raised his seriously sloping

shoulders in a hapless shrug that seemed over before it started.

"I never saw any evidence of it in her work, but, yeah, I guess she had to," he concluded. "Otherwise, she would have passed the test. But there are no second chances here. So I had to let her go, even though I didn't want to. She was a good worker."

"When was this?" Abilene asked.

"A week ago last Monday. My guess was that she had to have been partying all weekend for it to still be in her system like that. But I don't really know," he quickly added, his small eyes darting from one face to the other. "I don't do things like that myself." His voice was breathless and almost wistful as he told them this.

"Was she close to or friendly with anyone here?" Kendra asked. She glanced over her shoulder at the cubicles scattered about the floor. There was a person within each enclosure, manning a phone. Planning parties, she imagined.

"You could try talking to Suzanne Del Vecchio," he said, pointing to a cubicle on the left. A thin brunette was seated at the desk there. Unlike the others, she wasn't on the phone. She was typing something on the keyboard. "I saw them going out to lunch a few times." Abernathy shook his head again. "Too bad Summer had a drug problem," he said with real feeling. "She really *was* a good worker when the chips were down and we had a deadline to meet."

Kendra forced a smile to her lips. "Thank you for your help, Mr. Abernathy." She closed her notepad and tucked it back into her pocket. "We'll just go have a few words with Suzanne and maybe a couple of your other employees, if it's all right with you."

The sloping shoulders rose a little and collapsed again. "Have at it," he told them, gesturing vaguely toward Suzanne's cubicle and beyond. He watched them as they left his cluttered, claustrophobic office.

"Drug problem?" Abilene questioned somewhat skeptically the moment they left the supervisor's office. The idea seemed rather clichéd, but then, clichés existed for a reason.

"The M.E. didn't find any needle marks on her," Kendra offered.

"Lots of ways to take drugs," he reminded her.

She glanced at him. What was this, Rookie 101? "Thank you, I did not know that," she said, enunciating each word.

Rather than retreat because he was obviously rubbing her the wrong way—again—Abilene grinned and inclined his head.

"Glad to help." He saw his partner's lips move, but whatever she was saying, it was too low for him to hear. He had a feeling that it was probably better that way—for both of them.

"Yeah, we hung out together sometimes," Suzanne Del Vecchio told the two detectives who'd entered her cubicle and asked about Summer Miller. "Whenever her boyfriend was working overtime," she qualified. "Otherwise, she was always with him. They were going to get married, at least that was what she kept telling me."

"You didn't believe her?" Abilene questioned.

The brunette shrugged. "I figure men tell you a lot of things they don't mean just to get their way."

Amen to that, Kendra thought. "You never met him?" she asked the other woman.

"Once or twice," Suzanne allowed. "He seemed nice enough, I guess. Why? You think that he's the one who killed her?" she asked eagerly. When neither of the two detectives answered her, she told them, "The story's all over the office. Personally, he didn't look like a killer. But then, you never can tell."

Kendra was tempted to ask the woman what she thought a killer was supposed to look like, but that was only being testy, so she kept the question to herself. Instead, she focused on the new piece of information they'd just discovered.

"Your supervisor said she was fired for having a drug problem. What do you know about that?"

Suzanne blew out an impatient breath and snorted contemptuously. "Summer didn't have a drug problem. *He* has the drug problem," she accused, her brown eyes momentarily darting in the direction of Abernathy's glass-enclosed office. "Always watching people like some card-carrying Nazi."

"Your company has a strict no-drug policy," Abilene pointed out.

"Well, maybe it shouldn't," Suzanne said defiantly. "Besides, Summer didn't have a drug problem, she *did* drugs."

"The difference being?" Kendra asked.

A slight look of condescension entered Suzanne's brown eyes. "The difference being was that Summer did drugs socially. Like once in a while. She wasn't an *addict*," Suzanne said with feeling. "She could take them or leave them. Her boyfriend was strait-laced so she made sure she never had any on her around him."

"And when she was doing these drugs 'socially,'" Abilene began, using Suzanne's terminology. "Where did she get them?"

Suzanne frowned and looked at the corner of her desk. "I don't know," she said, annoyed at being asked the question.

"You're lying," Abilene told her, his voice mild. When the girl glanced up at him sharply, a denial ready to burst from her lips, Abilene went on talking. "CSI 101: you just said that without making eye contact. If you were telling the truth, you wouldn't have stared at your desk. Now why don't we save everybody a whole lot of time, and you tell me who Summer's drug contact was."

When Suzanne's look turned defiant with an underlying element of fear, Kendra set her mind at ease the best she could. "We're not out to make a drug bust, Suzanne. All we want to do is find out who killed Summer. This dealer who provided her with happy pills might be able to point us in the right direction. Don't you want whoever did this to Summer to pay?"

Torn, the brunette began to waver. "Well, yeah, sure. Oh, okay," she finally relented, exasperated. Opening her purse, she pulled a card out of her wallet and handed it to Abilene, then belatedly said, "I was just holding that card for her."

Abilene exchanged looks with his partner. *The hell she was,* he thought, even though he nodded solemnly at her statement. "Lucky for us you were." He indicated the card. "Mind if we take this?"

Relieved not to be arrested, Suzanne merely waved the card away. "No, keep it for as long as you want. Keep it forever. I don't have any need for it now that Summer's gone." The last word echoed of sadness as the reality of the situation finally began to penetrate.

Abilene glanced at the card before tucking it into his shirt pocket. He frowned. "This is the address of a pet store."

"Yeah. It's his day job," Suzanne told them. "That's his name on the bottom."

"'John Smith,'" Abilene read out loud. There was no missing the sarcasm in his voice.

"Original," Kendra commented dryly.

"Probably all he could come up with while on his designer drugs," Abilene speculated. He looked at the young woman who'd given them the card. "We'll be in touch if we have any more questions." He could have sworn the brunette cringed a little.

The pet store on "John Smith's" card was located at the end of a strip mall in one of the older sections of the city. The entire block had seen better days and most of the businesses that had been here then had gone off in search of those days, leaving behind empty windows and emptier stores. The pet store had once been next door to a video rental store. The only thing left to testify to this was an old poster for *The Lord of the Rings* that had been abandoned in the window and was now burned by the sun and curling away from the glass. The glue on the tape used to keep the poster in its place had long since dried up.

The pet shop itself, while still operational, was a rather sad-looking place. There were no energetic little puppies or kittens or rabbits to snare the attention of people passing by. For the most part, there were no people passing by and that was just as well. Rather than pets looking for a good home, shredded newspaper remained as the makeshift bathroom for whatever small animals had once been in the window.

Looking through the dirty glass, Kendra scanned the interior. "Looks like it's closed."

"No, I see some movement," Abilene contradicted. "There, in the back. Next to that rear door."

As he said it, the tall, somewhat scruffy-looking thin man who had caught his attention bolted through the same door.

"Guess he's not interested in making new friends," Kendra quipped as they quickly rounded the building to the back of the store and the alleyway that ran the length of the strip mall.

"Maybe he's just shy," Abilene responded dryly.

When they reached the alley behind the pet store, there was less than a beat before someone started shooting at them.

The moment he heard the sound of the first gunshot, Abilene yanked Kendra's arm and pulled her to the ground, throwing himself on top of her to shield her from the bullets. Discarded large cartons that had once contained giant supplies of pet food provided partial shelter.

Despite the dire situation, Abilene was not unaware

of the feel of her body beneath his. Nor was he oblivious to the very strong reaction he was having to her.

Forcing his mind back to the immediate problem, Abilene scanned the area to see where the gunfire had originated. His body still pressed completely over hers, he pulled out his own weapon and returned rapid fire.

"I'll cover you," he told her. "You get back into the building."

"The hell I will. But you can get off me," she ordered. She couldn't breathe with his weight on her and more than that, she didn't like the reaction she was having to his body aligned with hers this way. Every inch of her body was aware of his. Big-time.

The sudden guttural scream told them that despite all odds and very poor visibility, Abilene had somehow managed to hit the fleeing suspect who was firing wildly at them.

"You shot me!" The bewildered, belligerent accusation echoed in the empty alley. "I'm bleeding!" the dealer cried in panic. "Help me! I'm dying!"

"That's one hell of a drama queen," Abilene commented.

"You're still on top of me," Kendra pointed out through clenched teeth.

"So I am." Abilene drew back slowly. On his feet, he offered her a hand, which she ignored.

"If that's a chuckle," she warned as she scrambled to her feet, "you're a dead man."

"Just clearing my throat," her partner told her innocently.

Kendra gave him a dirty look, then turned her attention to the man who was still screaming that he was dying.

"We can get you to a doctor," she called out, raising her voice above the panicked dealer's cries. "But you have to throw out your gun."

"John Smith" was all but sobbing now. "Okay, okay, okay, here it is." He tossed it out then came out himself from behind the Dumpster he'd used for cover. "Now get me some help before I bleed to death!"

On her feet, she was about to take the lead and was utterly surprised when Abilene caught her arm again. But this time, rather than pull her down to the ground, he merely switched places with her, going first.

She knew what he was doing—putting himself in harm's way instead of her, just in case the man had another weapon hidden somewhere. While a part of her appreciated the fact that he was trying to protect her, that was *not* the way a partnership like theirs was supposed to work.

What was with this man, anyway? Were his testosterone levels off the chart?

"What?" she demanded, trying to pull him back—it was like trying to move a mountain, something else to annoy her about him. "Are you suddenly bulletproof?"

"Didn't you know that?" he deadpanned. "It's right there in my résumé. Page two: Bullets just bounce off me without leaving a dent."

"Must have missed that part." Her own weapon drawn, they approached Summer's alleged recreational drug supplier, watching for any sudden moves. But the part-time pet store employee had morphed from preening drug supplier to a frightened stuck pig. All he wanted was to have the bullet removed from his arm and the bleeding stanched.

"Can you stop the bleeding?" she asked Abilene. Her plan was to extract information from the man in exchange for taking him to the hospital—but she wanted the information first, because she knew if it was the other way around, the drug dealer would renege and give them nothing.

"You mean like putting my finger in the hole?" Abilene asked innocently. "Yeah, I can do that."

Even as he said it, Abilene placed his thumb over where the bullet had entered the dealer's shoulder. The man let loose with a blood-curdling scream.

"I need to get to a hospital," he cried. "You gotta get me to a hospital." The man was practically begging now.

"As soon as you tell me why you killed Summer Miller," Abilene told him.

The man stared at him, bewildered. "Who?" he cried, shaking his head at the same time to actively deny any wrongdoing.

"Summer Miller." Kendra dug into her back pocket and pulled out the photograph of the dead woman that the M.E. had given her. Summer was lying on the autopsy table, waiting to be taken apart bit by bit. "You supplied her with drugs."

Squinting, the man finally nodded, obviously recognizing the dead woman. "Yeah, I supplied her, but I didn't kill her." His head jerked up as he demanded wildly, "Why would I kill her? That's bad for business." Hysteria punctuated his words. "I'm bleeding to death here. You don't get me to that hospital, I'm gonna die!"

"If you didn't kill her, then maybe you can tell us

where you were three days ago, say all day?" Abilene asked him.

The dealer shook his head, the ends of his dirty hair swinging about like stretched-out commas. "I don't know," he wailed.

It wasn't easy, since at bottom she was a caregiver, but Kendra remained firm. "Not good enough," she told him with a shake of her head. She looked at her partner and asked, "You have a Band-Aid on you, Abilene? I'm fresh out."

"Sorry, never carry any," he told her, playing along for the dealer's benefit.

The latter was becoming genuinely panicked. "Wait, wait, I do know. I remember. I was in San Francisco," the man cried. Relief flooded his expression because he remembered. "At this big party."

"San Francisco," Kendra echoed somewhat skeptically. "And you can prove this?"

He looked at her wild-eyed, sweating profusely and seemingly light-headed.

Kendra knew they only had a couple of minutes left, if that much, before they lost their advantage and had to take the man to the nearest E.R. He was losing blood and at this rate, he would pass out on them.

"I got money from the ATM down the block from the party. I had to make change for this big ape who only had hundred-dollar bills on him. He was showing off for this skanky-looking girl he was with." The man was babbling now. "They've got cameras, right? The ATMs, they've got cameras? You can see it's me on the camera. I wasn't anywhere near that dead girl."

Abilene was as calm as the other man was agitated.

"They're supposed to. You'd better hope that yours was working."

The next moment, he was forced to catch the dealer as the man's eyes rolled up in his head and, passing out, he pitched forward.

Holding him upright, Abilene looked at Kendra. "Get enough?" he asked.

"Provided he was telling the truth and the camera was working, yes, we've got enough to either clear him or put him closer to the scene," she answered. And then her eyes narrowed as she saw a bright streak of red across the back of Abilene's shirt. It was dripping down his sleeve. "What's that?" she asked, even though, as far as she was concerned, it was a rhetorical question. When Abilene turned his head and looked at her quizzically, she pointed to the back of his arm.

Craning his neck, Abilene glanced at it and then shrugged off her question and the streak. "The guy's blood."

The hell it was. "I don't think so," she said flatly. "Not at this angle." Inspecting his upper arm quickly as Abilene held onto the drug dealer to keep the unconscious man from sinking to the pavement, Kendra bit off half a curse. "Dammit, you're hit. He shot you, probably while you were playing at being a bulletproof shield and draping yourself over me."

Abilene grinned broadly at her, despite the stinging sensation that was beginning to penetrate his consciousness. "Was it good for you, too, Good?" he cracked.

"Abilene—" There was a warning note in her voice that told him to back off. She didn't consider this a laughing matter. And she definitely didn't want to revisit that one flash of heat she'd felt when his body had pressed into hers.

Again he shrugged in response, but this time there were consequences to the action. She saw the wince he tried to cover up.

"All in a day's work, Good," Abilene told her cavalierly.

"Yeah, if you're working as a superhero," she countered, her temper fraying. He could have been killed, playing the hero. And it would have been her fault, she thought with a twinge of guilt. She couldn't have been able to handle that, having Abilene die because of her. "You didn't have to throw yourself over me like that," she insisted angrily. "I have a gun and I know how to use it."

Rather than argue with her—something Matt was quickly learning just led to nothing but one dead end after another—he caught her off guard by quietly saying, "You're welcome."

The two simple words stopped her cold in her tracks even though she continued to glare accusingly at him. She knew damn well that she would probably have been the one with the bullet in her if he hadn't played the hero.

And who knew? That bullet could have gotten lodged in a fatal place. In effect, he could very well have saved her life, even if she was having trouble admitting that fact.

"Yeah," Kendra finally acknowledged with more than a little reluctance, all but spitting the word out as if it had turned bitter on her tongue. "Thanks."

He laughed. "Sugar and spice" was definitely not a

description that could easily have been applied to her. She was more like hot sauce and wasabi.

"Don't worry, Good. I'm not about to say that your life's mine now or anything like that just because I saved you." Moving quickly despite his wound, he cuffed the unconscious dealer's hands behind his back. "I just didn't want to disappoint my mother and tell her that the invitation was canceled." With that, he hefted the skinny man up over his good shoulder, ready to transport him into a vehicle.

"Get in the car," she ordered, pointing to their unmarked vehicle. "I'm driving."

The second he did, after depositing the unconscious drug dealer in the back, Kendra took off.

Abilene braced his one good arm against the dashboard, thinking that perhaps the invitation would have to be canceled after all. Dead people didn't attend brunches.

Chapter 8

"**W**ho taught you how to drive?" Abilene asked less than ten minutes later as they peeled into the hospital's E.R. parking lot.

The entire trip whizzed by in a blur with his partner going way over the speed limit and flying through yellow lights less than a beat away from turning red. He'd white-knuckled it all the way, wondering if they would make it to the hospital in one piece or if her driving would land them in the morgue instead.

"My brother, Tom." Kendra brought the car to a jarring stop. "Why?"

Abilene silently released the breath he'd been holding for the last nine and a half minutes. "By any chance does your brother have anger issues?"

Kendra shot him a warning look. "No, but I do."

Jumping out of the car, she rounded the hood before Abilene could get his door open and was at his side as he slowly rose from his seat. She saw that he needed to hold on to the side of the vehicle to do it. The whole side of his sleeve was now crimson.

This was not good, she thought, concerned and disturbed by what she saw. "Dammit, Abilene, you could have been seriously hurt!"

He forced a smile to his lips. "Ah, Good, I didn't know you cared."

"I don't, wise guy," she bit off. "I just hate filling out reports in triplicate—and God only knows who they'd give me as a partner this time around, seeing as how they're already scraping the bottom of the barrel." She looked at him accusingly.

"Stop, you're making me blush," Abilene protested, pretending to hide his face.

"You wish," she retorted. In contrast to his shirt-sleeve, he looked exceedingly pale. "My God, Abilene, right now it looks like all your blood is draining out of your body."

"My body's just fine," he assured her, then made her an offer, smiling weakly. "Care to check it out for yourself?"

"I'll pass, thanks." She hoped her flippant retort would hide her concern. "Stay here, I'll get someone to bring a gurney for our friendly neighborhood dealer," she told him, nodding at the unconscious suspect in the back seat.

"You know where to find us," Abilene called after her as she hurried away. Still holding on to the side of the vehicle, he lowered himself back into the passenger seat.

Kendra returned quickly, leading an orderly and a

nurse back to the parked car. Between them they were pushing a gurney.

"Stayed right where you told me to," he declared, trying to sound cheerful and carefree. Watching Kendra approach, Matt pulled himself back up to his feet again. It took more energy this time.

"Good, looks like you're finally learning how to listen, Abilene," she quipped, doing her best to hide how worried she was. She came around to his side as she got out of the orderly's way. "Now if only—Abilene?" she said uncertainly as she saw the towering man swaying ever so slightly.

When he turned his head to look at her, Matt felt his knees start to buckle. He did his best to stiffen them and remain standing.

Seeing him begin to sink, Kendra reacted instinctively. She pushed her shoulder under his arm and turned herself into a human crutch. Holding on to his arm, which she'd leveraged around her neck, she braced her partner against herself and struggled to keep Matt upright. Her free arm immediately tightened around his waist as she felt his weight begin to shift.

"A little help here," she called out to the orderly. The other man had his hands full transferring the unconscious drug dealer to the gurney.

But it was Abilene who answered her. "You're doing just fine," he drawled. There was the hint of an amused smile in his voice.

She looked up at her partner suspiciously, wondering if he was doing this on purpose, but something in her gut told her that he wasn't. He was just reacting to losing so much blood.

"I need another gurney for my partner," she called over to the nurse, who was already helping the orderly guide their prisoner back through the hospital's electronic doors. "Now!" she ordered.

"I love it when you throw your weight around," Abilene muttered, his words tumbling into one another.

"Shut up, Abilene," she warned.

"Right away," the nurse was saying, responding to the request for another gurney. "We just need to get this one inside the hospital."

"I don't need a gurney," Abilene protested with what he thought was feeling, but he was just short of slurring his words. "You're doing just fine propping me up like this, Good."

She slanted a look at him. "Don't tempt me to drop you." Dammit, didn't he realize how serious this could get?

Just then, Abilene gazed down into her face, his eyes on hers. Something inside her warmed and sent out pulses through her whole body. She couldn't begin to describe the feeling it generated—or maybe she could, but thought it best not to.

"You wouldn't do that," he told her in response to her threat.

He wasn't baiting her, daring her or even teasing her. He was telling her what he knew to be true. That even though their partnership was still in its infancy, he absolutely *knew* beyond a shadow of a doubt that she had his back and that he could count on her not to let him down no matter what.

Kendra chose not to respond, not because she felt he was putting undue pressure on her with his assumption but because she struggled with the implications of his statement. It took the partnership out of the realm of the temporary, which she considered nice and safe, and tossed it into the dependable and permanent, which, given her track record with permanent, scared her.

She preferred looking to the future in terms of day by day, not with any sort of a permanent plan. It was far safer that way.

"Just shut up and try to keep upright until they come back with a gurney for you," Kendra instructed him testily.

"Yes, ma'am," he murmured.

She could feel him growing more lax, could feel his limbs growing heavier. She wasn't sure how much longer she was going to be able to sustain him in his present vertical position.

"C'mon, Abilene, stop playing around," she ordered, doing her best to sound really annoyed.

She knew he wasn't playing around, that he was doing what he could not to collapse against her completely. But berating him might get Abilene to rally faster than merely tossing encouraging words at him. The man responded to a challenge, she thought.

The nurse, followed by two orderlies and an E.R. doctor, returned just in the nick of time. The moment they did, Kendra felt Abilene go completely limp. Another second and they would have both been on the ground with her finally succumbing to Abilene's lax body and sinking under his weight.

"We'll take it from here," the physician told her as he and an orderly each took one side of Abilene to ease him onto the gurney.

"But we were doing so well," Abilene protested dryly.

"Shut up, Abilene," she ordered.

She heard him suck in a lungful of air before being able to make any sort of a response. "Yes, ma'am."

Stopping before an empty trauma room, the doctor turned to her as the orderly and a nurse pushed the gurney and her wounded partner into the room.

"Do you have a number where we can reach you?" he asked her.

"Lean out of the room and shout," she told him. "I'm not going anywhere."

"He's not in any immediate danger," the doctor assured her, apparently thinking that might be why she wanted to stay.

"I'm not going anywhere," she repeated.

"Don't argue with her," Abilene advised the E.R. doctor weakly just before the door closed. "You'll never win."

"Jerk," she muttered under her breath as she stood outside the room, hating the fact that she was left out in the corridor to pace and wonder and worry—almost against her will—until someone came out to talk with her.

Because she didn't want to dwell on what was happening behind closed doors, Kendra took the opportunity to make a few calls. She called her lieutenant and filled him in on everything that had happened, including the fact that they had a drug dealer in custody at the local hospital. *And* that Abilene was being stitched up.

"Does the dealer look good for the murder?" the lieutenant asked.

"Well, he *says* he was in San Francisco at the time and took some cash from an ATM at approximately the time of the murder. I need to get a look at the footage from the ATM camera to confirm his alibi."

"I'll turn you over to Wong," the lieutenant told her. "He can check it out for you. Let me know how Abilene's doing," Lt. Holmes tacked on just before he terminated the phone call.

"Most likely I'll find him flirting with a nurse once they've got him all stitched back together," she prophesied.

But she was talking to dead air. With a sigh, she closed her cell and put it away.

She went back to waiting.

Impatiently.

But when it was over, she didn't find Abilene flirting with the nurse in attendance, even though she was rather cute. Kendra couldn't help wondering if they'd stitched up his libido as well.

The E.R. physician had paused to give her a quick update on Abilene's condition when he was finished with the minor surgery. Abilene's wound had turned out to be just a flesh wound. The reason he had lost more than the usual amount of blood was because he'd been popping aspirin to help ease the pain of an old knee injury. The aspirin, in turn, had rendered clotting generally elusive, thus contributing to the inordinate amount of blood flow and his weakened state.

Given the go-ahead, when Kendra walked in on her partner, Abilene was already sitting up on the gurney, struggling to put his shirt back on over the rather bulky bandage.

"Doctor said it was 'much ado about nothing,'" she told him dryly as she walked into the small recovery area where they had placed her partner after his surgery.

His back to the entrance, Abilene twisted around slightly to look at her. "Here, give me a hand with this, will you?" he requested. "My arm's a little sore from being used as a pin cushion."

"Your arm shouldn't be 'a little sore,'" she informed him, picking up his casual shirt and easing one of the sleeves over his arm and shoulder. "It should be in a sling."

His expression told her what he thought of that suggestion. "The bullet just nicked me." He said it as if it was an everyday occurrence.

"Tell that to all the blood you lost." And then her agitation and exasperation got the better of her. "Don't you know better than to pop aspirins like they were candy?"

He paused to smile at her. "That's what I have you for. To be my nagging Jimmy Cricket."

"Jiminy," she corrected. "I think you might mean Jiminy."

He'd never been up on all those kids' movies. Beyond the fact that Snow White knew seven dwarfs, the extent of his knowledge was rather limited.

"Whatever." He waved away the correction. Leaning forward, he felt Kendra slide on the other sleeve. *Houston, we have liftoff.* "I could have just slapped a couple of butterfly Band-Aids from my medicine cabinet on it and been okay."

"The doctor told me that you had to be given a pint

of plasma as well. Got that in your medicine cabinet, too?" she queried innocently as she flagged down a nurse who, it turned out, had Abilene's discharge papers ready for him to sign.

The man signed the papers in just under the speed of light. He was more than ready to go. The plasma must have given him a boost of energy because he was feeling more like his old self. And that old self was definitely reacting to the volatile little firecracker giving him all this lip. The woman aroused him.

"You always like to have the last word, don't you, Good?" he asked mildly as they stepped out into the E.R. parking lot.

She made him stay where he was—the car was only a short distance away and she brought it back to the entrance to pick him up.

"When I'm right—which I usually am," she said, picking up the thread of the conversation again as if there had been no long pause between sentences, "then, yes, I like having the last word."

Abilene deliberately eschewed her offer of help—it was a matter of male pride—and lowered himself into the passenger seat as smoothly as he could.

"I'm honored to be driving around with a saint," he told her evenly.

Having rounded the hood and gotten in on the driver's side, she glared at him as she buckled her seat belt again. The car hummed to life. "Now, I didn't say I was that, did I?"

Their eyes met for a very long, electricity-filled second and he murmured, "Oh, God, I hope not." Because saints didn't do the kind of things that just being around this woman seemed to keep conjuring up in his mind.

Kendra slowly released a breath, wishing she could steady her pulse as easily. Why she felt suddenly enveloped in a blast of heat she had no idea, especially since not a single other factor around her had changed even minutely.

Talk, idiot, before he thinks you've been struck dumb. "Do you want me to take you home?"

The smile on his lips unfolded slowly. Sexily. "Is that a proposition, Good?"

She didn't bother trying to get him to stop calling her that. Apparently, it was a useless exercise.

"No," Kendra replied as evenly as she could, "that's a question related to your so-called flesh wound. After losing all that blood, I thought you might want to go home and rest instead of going back to the precinct and all that paperwork."

Well, maybe he wasn't chomping at the bit to get to the paperwork, but the rest of it sounded pretty good to him. This case had become almost personal for him. Maybe because it was his first in Homicide, but he was determined to solve it, to close it. And that meant being there, not going home and lying down. He needed to prove himself to her, to show that he had something to contribute to this partnership, other than just being a human shield.

"Nope. I'm definitely good to go," he told her solemnly. His eyes never left hers as his mouth curved teasingly. "And I'm pretty much ready to work, too," he added.

Why did she feel as if he was propositioning her?

And why in heaven's name did she want to take him up on it? What was wrong with her? Was it just a matter of her not having been with a man for over eighteen months? The last time had been just before Jason had been so badly burned. After he'd killed himself, her heart had just slipped into solitary confinement and she'd withdrawn from everyone but her family.

These days, she still didn't mix work with her personal life beyond grabbing an occasional drink at the local hangout with some of the people she worked with.

So why the change now?

Maybe because your last partner looked like an aged lawn gnome and this one could raise the body temperature of a dead woman.

Snapping out of it, she slid the key into the ignition.

"Okay, Wong is checking out 'John Smith's' story about using that ATM in San Francisco at the time of Summer's murder. Let's get back to the office and you can write up your notes."

"Notes?" he echoed.

Had he taken notes? And where was his notepad, anyway? His brain still felt a little fuzzy and unfocused. The only thing that seemed to be coming in loud and clear was his reaction to Kendra. Ever since his body had pressed hers to the ground, he'd detected a low-grade hum running through it.

Celebrating.

"Yes, notes. You're right-handed, right?" Kendra glanced at his hand resting on his knee.

"Right, but I think it's experiencing sympathy pains for my left arm," he told her solemnly. To "prove" it he held up his hand and pretended to try to flex his fingers. Under his watchful eye, they moved stiffly, like sticks bowing one by one. "See?"

"I see, all right. I see a fraud. Now, you can't have it both ways. You can't go back to work and then milk everyone for sympathy and not do anything," she pointed out.

Because it amused him, he played the game a few minutes longer. "Wow, they didn't tell me you were this hard-hearted."

She doubted if anyone even had any sort of opinion about her. "You just didn't ask the right questions," she countered flippantly.

"Apparently not," he agreed. His voice was lofty again and seemed to be regaining some of its former volume, along with a little wry humor.

"Seriously," she told him, her expression reflecting how she felt about his almost getting killed protecting her. It was what partners were supposed to do, watch one another's backs, but had he been killed, she would have had a great deal of trouble coming to terms with that. "I don't want you doing that kind of thing again, all right?"

"Okay," he responded glibly. "Next time I see someone pointing a gun at you, I'll just let them go ahead and do what comes naturally." He looked at her pointedly. "Happy?"

"Happy" would have come with another partner. One who didn't constantly keep stirring her up this way, Kendra thought.

"You know what I mean," she bit off.

"Sadly, most of the time, no," he confessed with a sigh. Shifting in his seat, he looked forward. His body started to ache something fierce. Whatever effects the local anesthetic had had on him began to vanish, leaving behind a light residue of pain and exhaustion.

"It's been a long day, Good, and it's not nearly over yet. Tell you what, just let me close my eyes for a minute and you just drive us to the precinct." Matt glanced at her to see if she had any objections. "Is that okay with you?"

She didn't answer. Instead, she pointed out what he'd neglected to do. "You forgot to buckle up."

"It's a little awkward, reaching for the seat belt from this angle," he confessed.

"You're a detective. You're supposed to set a good example."

"For who? You march to your own drummer anyway. As far as I see, you're the only other person in this car, Good."

With a sigh, she leaned over him and grabbed hold of his seat belt, then pulled it across his body and slid the metal tongue into the groove. Though she tried to avoid it, that involved getting very close to him and all but brushing against his torso. Granted, it was not nearly as close as he had gotten earlier, pressed against hers, but it was still something that didn't exactly go unnoticed by either one of them.

"Thanks," he murmured when she was finished.

"You're welcome," she answered, doing her best to sound casual even as a warm blush crept up her cheeks. Backing out of the spot, she put the car in gear and drove.

And pretended she didn't hear him laughing softly to himself.

Chapter 9

At first, Matt thought it was his imagination. But it only took the short ride from Sabrina Abilene's apartment to his own to convince him that something was off with his mother. He needed to find out what before his partner showed up to take them to the former chief's house.

"Everything all right, Mom?" he asked as he studied her.

Over the years, he'd become pretty much of an expert when it came to reading her. Sometimes he got more out of observing her than talking to her.

Sabrina raised and lowered her shoulders in a vague, dismissive way, trying to tough it out for a second. Failing, she blurted out, "Are you sure I won't embarrass you?"

Since when was his mother this insecure? That last guy had really done a number on her by walking out,

Matt thought. Maybe it was lucky for him that the bastard had vanished the way he had, because if he had the man in his sights right now, he might not be responsible for his actions.

"Why?" he asked, feigning amusement. "What are you planning on doing?"

Sabrina gazed down at her freshly polished pink nails, acting unusually flustered. "Nothing," she declared breathlessly. "But, well, these are people you work with, right? People whose opinions you probably value?"

"Right. These are down-to-earth people," he emphasized. "Not born-with-a-silver-spoon-in-their-mouths, critical-of-everyone-who-breathes Southampton people." He paused for a moment, ignoring the doorbell that had just begun to ring. "You're a survivor, Mom." He gave her hand a squeeze. "You could never embarrass me."

But his mother apparently remembered it differently. "How about the time you came home early from school and walked in on me and—"

He was *not* about to go there. It had taken him a while, all those years ago, to purge from his brain the compromising sight of his mother and her then "boyfriend" in bed.

"Okay," he allowed, "maybe that one time. But I've never been embarrassed by you, the person." He gave her forehead a quick kiss. "Ready?"

Sabrina took a deep breath and smoothed down the skirt of her yellow-and-white sundress, even though it was lying perfectly flat.

Swallowing, she nodded. "Ready."

Ushering her gently over to the door, Matt opened it. Kendra was standing in his doorway, her hair pulled back in two short, sassy pigtails. She was wearing a white peasant blouse that ran out of material just shy of the top of the waistband of her frayed, faded denim cutoff shorts.

Matt certainly hadn't been prepared for this. He all but did a double take at the expanse of tempting, creamy skin.

"You look like a teenager, Good," he told her. "A *young* teenager."

She cocked her head. "I don't know if you just complimented me or put me down." Ignoring any further exchange with her partner, Kendra put her hand out to the slender, petite strawberry-blonde woman standing next to him. "Hi, I'm Kendra, Abil—Matt's partner," she introduced herself, smiling warmly.

"I'm Sabrina Abilene," the woman said, flashing Abilene's smile at her. They had the same slightly tilted curve of the lip on one side, Kendra noted. "Did my son just call you 'Good'?" the woman asked her, slightly confused.

"That he did," Kendra answered, then realized that, from a mother's point of view, that "name" might be misconstrued. "It's a long story."

Sabrina smiled brightly. "I'd love to hear it sometime."

Backed into that one, Kendra thought. "If there's a lull at the barbecue," she promised, then glanced at her watch. "In the meantime, I think we'd better get going."

Abilene waited for his mother to cross the threshold,

then following, he turned to lock the door behind him. "You didn't tell me we'd be punching a time clock."

"We don't," Kendra answered. "But if you want to park somewhere relatively close to the house, it pays to show up early. Depending on how many people are coming today, any latecomer might have to walk about half a mile or more to get to the house."

Sabrina looked from her son to his partner, waiting for some punch line.

"You're kidding, right?" she asked as she got into the passenger seat in Kendra's car.

Kendra glanced at her partner. "Have you warned your mother how big the family is?" Not waiting for a response, she continued. "And that doesn't begin to touch on any friends who might have been invited." Her focus was back on his mother as Kendra pulled her vehicle away from the curb. "I know this word tends to get overused, but the chief's parties are *legendary*. The food is fantastic, and the people—" she smiled at the woman "—well, they have a way of making you feel glad you're alive."

"Is it that way for you?" Abilene asked from the backseat.

Kendra fully expected to see a smirk or a cocky half smile on Abilene's lips, but when she spared him a glance over her shoulder, he actually seemed serious. As if he'd just asked something he wanted answered, not eventually, but now.

"Sometimes," she allowed cautiously, again addressing her words to his mother. For some reason she couldn't explain, saying that to him would have felt way too personal. "Anyway, I think you'll have a great time, Mrs. Abilene."

"Oh, call me Sabrina," the woman told her with feeling, then tagged on an emphatic "please."

Kendra didn't ordinarily feel comfortable calling someone's mother by her first name, but this woman seemed exceedingly youthful. She made a guess that Sabrina Abilene had to have been awfully young when her son was born.

"All right," she said to his mother, "if you insist."

"I do," Sabrina told her with a soft little smile. She seemed to relax a little for the first time since before her son had come to pick her up.

"Your mother's very nice," Kendra said, tossing the words over her shoulder to the man sitting directly behind her. "What happened to you?"

"The 'nice' gene made a U-turn and doubled back when it realized it was going into my body," Abilene quipped without hesitation.

"That's not true," Sabrina protested. "You're a very good son."

But Kendra nodded as if Abilene had just recited chapter and verse of what she'd already suspected.

"That would go a long way toward explaining things," she murmured under her breath, even as she smiled broadly at the passenger to her right and said, "I'm sure he is, Sabrina."

"Come in, come in!" Andrew Cavanaugh greeted them warmly less than a beat after Kendra rang the doorbell. Because they were guests, the former chief of police and acting patriarch of the family first shook

Sabrina's hand and then her son's. "Good to see you again," he told Abilene.

Turning toward Sean's daughter, Andrew embraced Kendra. Her immediate reaction was to stiffen. The next moment, she forced herself to relax. She wasn't entirely successful.

"Better," Andrew said, laughing as he released her. "We'll get you into this hugging thing yet. It's an acquired taste." There was a twinkle in his eye as he said it.

Even back during his hectic days as chief of the Aurora police department, Andrew Cavanaugh was nothing if not a devoted family man first, a servant of the people second. Nothing and no one was ever more important to him than family. He was a firm believer in "the more, the better." Kendra's slight resistance to being absorbed by the family was nothing new to him.

He was accustomed to reluctance. It had taken patience to bring around some of his late brother's children. Until a couple of years ago, he hadn't even known of the triplets' existence and they—Ethan, Kyle and Greer—had believed themselves to be the children of a dead war hero, not the illegitimate offspring of a policeman shot in the line of duty. And there'd been the four stepchildren—Zack, Taylor, Riley and Frank—that his younger brother Brian had brought into the family fold when he'd married his former partner, Lila McIntyre.

But all that paled in comparison to the eight new members they had uncovered when the hospital mixup had come to light.

They were all trying to work out the emotional logistics. But, for the most part, Andrew felt that it was coming along rather nicely, all things considered. Sean Cavanaugh had already been embraced as the long-lost brother. Even their father, Seamus, had left his idyllic life in Florida, pronouncing it "boring," and had returned to Aurora to meet the son he'd never known. The reunion had gone so well, that the once-vibrant police officer who'd fathered them all made up his mind that he would stay.

Their numbers were growing by leaps and bounds and Andrew, for one, couldn't be happier about it.

"Why don't you grab something to drink—or eat—and introduce Sabrina around?" Andrew suggested to his niece.

Kendra glanced into the living room and the family room beyond. She was still trying to get everyone's names straight herself.

"I didn't bring my player's handbook," Kendra confessed wryly.

Andrew didn't see that as a deterrent. "No shame in asking. Sometimes I forget a name, too," he confided with a wink.

"Must be your advanced old age," Seamus said to his son as he came up behind him. He clamped a hand down on Andrew's shoulder.

Andrew laughed as he half turned to look at his father. "Careful, old man, or I'll hide your teeth," he warned.

"These are all mine," Seamus assured Kendra and her partner and especially Sabrina as he pulled at a couple to show how solidly embedded they were. "You must have me confused with yourself." And then he bowed gallantly, although not as low as he once could have, before Sabrina. "Tell you what, why don't I do the honors for this pretty lady?" he suggested. Straightening, he gallantly offered Sabrina his elbow. "Let's go dazzle the natives, shall we?"

"He's some character," Abilene commented to Kendra as he watched his mother be whisked off by the oldest of the Cavanaughs.

"You'll get no argument from me on that score," Andrew agreed.

Matt hadn't thought that the chief could hear him. He didn't want the man to think he was being flippant about his father. "I'm sorry, sir, I didn't mean—"

Andrew waved the apology away. "Sure you did. And you're right. Dad *is* a character. And a handful." He watched as his father seemed to disappear into the crowd with his newfound charge. "Brian and I still haven't figured out how to handle him."

"You don't 'handle' a man like that," Sean told his newly discovered older brother as he joined the small circle, finding a place beside Kendra. He brushed a kiss against his daughter's cheek by way of a greeting, never missing a beat of the conversation. "You just get out of his way before he mows you down. It's what you do with a force of nature."

Approaching from the family room, Brian Cavanaugh laughed as he overheard Sean's assessment of their father. "You're a fast learner," he commented with approval. "But then, you *are* a Cavanaugh." He patted Sean on the back.

"No self-esteem issues in this crowd," Lila Cavanaugh laughed as she slid in beside her husband. She smiled at Matt. "Hi, you must be Kendra's partner, Matt Abilene."

"I must be," he agreed affably, shaking the woman's hand. He'd been here perhaps a couple of times before, invited by a friend of a friend of one of the Cavanaughs. Once had been for a Christmas party. The family was even warmer than he remembered. "And you're—"

"Hungry," Lila confided, looking at Andrew. "Isn't it almost about time that you fired up the grill, Chief?" she asked.

"Just waiting for someone to suggest it, Lila," Andrew told her. For Matt's benefit, he nodded his head toward the still very pretty blonde and said, "And she's Lila, who's much too good for Brian but she sticks by him anyway. She used to be his partner, you know. Back in the day. I figured she was way too good for him even then." Before Brian could utter a comeback, Andrew took charge of both his brothers. "C'mon, you two, you can help."

"I can't cook," Sean protested, falling into place beside Brian and behind Andrew.

"Okay, but you can lug, can't you?" Andrew asked as they went out.

"Lug?" Kendra asked uncertainly, looking to Lila for a possible explanation.

"He's probably referring to the propane tank for the grill," Lila guessed.

"That he is. Andrew likes to make people feel useful," Rose, the former chief's wife, told the two newcomers as she drifted by them with a tray filled with tiny smoked-cheddar cheese stuffed mushrooms. "Have a couple," she offered, holding the tray lower so that

Kendra and Matt could make their choices. "Hopefully it'll tide you over as you find your way around this maze," she told them. "There's always a lot of smoke when Andrew barbecues. I think he does it on purpose. It's almost like watching a magic act. Just follow your nose and you can't go wrong."

"Well, they certainly are a friendly bunch," Kendra commented just before she took a bite out of the stuffed mushroom she'd selected.

Matt regarded her for a long moment. She was a complicated piece of work. In his partner's place, he would have welcomed being part of this forceful family.

"You don't sound as if you know whether that's a good thing or not."

"I do know that it's pretty overwhelming," she freely confessed.

By now she should have gotten somewhat used to it, he thought.

Looking around, he could see his mother in the center of a small cluster of people. Even at this distance, he could see how wide her smile was. She was enjoying herself. He felt a sense of relief.

"My mother seems to have taken to it like a duck to water," he observed. And then he surprised Kendra by shifting gears. "Why's your guard up?"

She had a choice of denying his observation, ignoring it or telling him the truth. Caught off guard, she went with the truth.

"I find it hard to get close."

"Because they won't let you in?" Even as he asked, he knew that couldn't be it. The Cavanaughs were family-oriented to a fault—and for them, "family" included the men and women of the department as well.

"Because *I* won't let me in," she told him simply.

She'd told him this much, so Matt decided to dig a little further. "Why? You don't strike me as the naturally shy type."

Finished eating, she balled up the napkin in her hand. "No, just supercautious."

"Why?" he asked again. "Have you been burned?"

The choice of words was enough to startle her. She covered it quickly, but he'd seen the sudden wariness, the quick intake of breath, the single second of pain in her eyes to know that somehow, without meaning to, he'd managed to strike a nerve.

"Want to talk about it?" he asked quietly.

There was no way she wanted to talk about it, especially not with someone she would have to see day in, day out, at least until this case was solved. After that, maybe one of them could get a transfer.

"No."

He knew when to push, and when to back away. "Okay. I can respect that. Me, I don't get close because I've watched my mother do it for most of my life and all she ever managed to get for it was kicked in the teeth."

To him, it was a simple object lesson. You put yourself out there, as his mother did, you were asking to have your heart tossed into a shredder. He figured that relationships, if they had a prayer of working, developed slowly, over time. They didn't burst upon you like fireworks on the Fourth of July.

She felt as if she was looking at him for the first time. He'd suddenly become more than simply two-dimensional. "So you've made up your mind that it wasn't going to happen to you."

Shrugging, he looked away, pretending as if something else had caught his attention—rather than her. "Something like that."

"How's that going for you?" she asked, curious. Tom hadn't had much to tell her about Abilene. Maybe she could find out from the horse's mouth.

"For the most part, okay." He looked back at her. Nope, no doubt about it. He was attracted to her. More than just a little. And seeing her like this, with so much skin to peruse, just brought this fact home to him that much faster. "But there's this one woman who's really driving me crazy. It's like she's gotten under my skin. You know," he continued in a lower voice, "like an itch I just can't scratch."

Had it suddenly gotten warmer in here? Had to be the press of all these bodies milling around, using up the oxygen, she told herself. "What'll happen if you do scratch it?"

And hadn't he been asking himself that same question since he'd first laid eyes on her? "Most likely it'll be like nothing I've ever experienced before—and quite possibly mark the end of civilization as we know it."

"Then maybe you shouldn't scratch that itch," she told him. Because, tempting though it seemed right at this moment, they *were* partners and things could get very awkward if they did give in to the moment. "If it means saving the world, and all."

"Maybe," he conceded loftily. Then he went on to admit, "But I have been thinking about scratching an awful lot lately."

That was the exact moment that she felt her lips go dry. Which made talking more difficult. She had to all but push out the words.

"Keep me posted on that." She tried clearing her throat and even the sound seemed to get stuck.

"Don't worry," Abilene promised her quietly, "you'll be the first to know." Without thinking, he put his hand lightly against her back, meaning to guide her into the living room.

Kendra fought hard not to shiver in response to the single stroke she could have sworn she felt against the small of her back.

Served her right for not wearing enough clothing, she silently chided herself. But then, she had a feeling that she would have felt that—whatever *that* was—even if dressed in a heavy suit of armor.

The next moment, another group of Cavanaughs— this particular one composed of twenty to twenty-eight-year olds—converged and surrounded her partner and her. Within less than a heartbeat, it felt as if they were assimilated into the group's collective.

Like the classic science fiction line, resistance was futile. She'd discovered that the last couple of times she'd been invited to one of Andrew's "unofficial" parties. Not only that, she always seemed to leave the party a couple of pounds heavier and with a slightly shifted perspective on at least one if not more things.

Since this was a more structured party, she had a feeling she had even less of a chance of remaining on the outside, looking in.

And the thing of it was, she was surprised to realize, that she had less and less of a desire to *be* that outsider.

Chapter 10

Close to ten hours into the party and the crowd had only thinned out slightly.

Some of the younger Cavanaughs with very small children had said their good-nights and then gone home. But a lot of the others with sleepy children had availed themselves of portable cribs or one of the beds that had been left standing in rooms that Andrew's five adult children had long since vacated.

This way, tired grandchildren and grand-nephews-and-nieces had somewhere to lie down and, most likely, recharge their batteries. It was an exceedingly family-friendly house, Brian had told her during one of her first visits, and always had been.

Right now, she found it difficult to move around without tripping over some member of the family, or, in some cases, a member-to-be.

And everyone, apparently, seemed to be in excellent spirits. There were no arguments, no nasty flares of temper over some sensitive subject. As a general rule, everyone within the Cavanaugh domain seemed to get along.

She supposed, if she had to be part of a larger family than the one she'd been born into, this one wasn't all that bad.

And she'd never seen her father looking happier. It was as if he'd finally found that "missing piece" of himself he'd once told her about. That missing piece that made him feel so restless sometimes. Maybe somehow subconsciously, he'd felt he wasn't where he was supposed to be when he was growing up in the Cavelli household.

Not that he had cut that family off when his real identity had come to light. That wasn't her father's way and it wasn't theirs, either. She and her siblings still touched base with the aunts, uncles and cousins they'd known all their lives.

Their family had just expanded, her father had told her more than once.

But watching him tonight, Kendra knew that this was where her father felt he belonged. And that was good enough for her. She made up her mind then and there to change her name to Cavanaugh.

Permanently.

"Do you think that maybe we should get going?" Abilene suggested, coming up behind her. The barbecue had been over for quite a while now. Everyone was stuffed to the gills and while it wasn't late, it had been a very long day. He looked at her, waiting for her reaction. "What do you think?"

Kendra was surprised that he'd left the decision up to her. Maybe the man wasn't such a knuckle-dragging Neanderthal after all. And she could see that he did genuinely care about his mother. She'd already given him points for that.

"I think maybe you're right," she agreed. Then, scanning the immediate area, she asked, "Where's your mother?"

Abilene realized that he'd gotten so caught up with both Kendra and the Cavanaughs, he'd lost track of his mother.

"I don't know," he admitted, looking around. He thought for a minute. "I haven't seen her since just after we sat down to eat."

"Which time?" Kendra asked.

There had been wave after endless wave of food. If she continued attending these little impromptu feeding fests, she would either have to have all her clothes let out or her mouth sewn up.

He was still scanning the area for his mother. Her particular color of strawberry-blond hair tended to stand out. So far, though, he hadn't seen her. "The first time," he told Kendra.

"Well, don't worry, your mother has to be around here somewhere. Nobody could have possibly made off with her in a house full of cops," she assured him.

It took a little while, weaving their way through the various clusters of family members and gently extricating themselves from conversations that threatened to draw them in, but they finally found Sabrina. She was in the backyard, several yards past the patio. She was sitting on the porch swing, rocking.

And Matt immediately saw that his mother wasn't alone.

"My father seems to be bending your mother's ear," Kendra observed as they came closer to the couple.

"She doesn't look like she seems to mind," Matt noted.

Sean and Sabrina appeared completely oblivious to their approach. Despite the swirling din of noise coming from the house and other parts of the yard, the two single parents might as well have been alone.

From where they stood, Kendra thought, Abilene's mother gave the impression of hanging on her father's every word and he, in turn, looked as if he was trying very hard to entertain her.

Was this the start of something? Or just an evening's interlude? She knew which side she was rooting for. Her father had been very vocal about getting her "back on the playing field," but deliberately deflected any of her comments about the fact that he had *not* done the same after her mother died. He merely shrugged and said that once was enough for him.

Maybe that had changed, she thought, watching as Sabrina threw her head back and laughed at something her father had said.

"Think they might need a chaperone?" Matt asked her. She couldn't quite tell if he was kidding.

Kendra smiled. "This might be the best thing for both of them," she commented with growing enthusiasm. "My dad's certainly not going to make off with any of your mother's money or things, and she might just remind him that he's more than simply an active part of the police department and a father."

When Abilene looked at her quizzically, she elaborated. "When my mother died, a side of him seemed to just vanish. But obviously, it just went into hiding," she said with a satisfied smile. "It's nice to see him embrace that part of himself again—even for a little while."

She missed hearing her father whistle. He always used to whistle when her mother was alive. When she died, he just stopped, as if he didn't have anything that happy, that carefree to whistle about any more. And the light had gone out of his eyes.

"I hate to break this up, Mom," Matt said as they reached the couple, "but Good here wants to get going."

Sean looked up at his daughter. "'Good'?" he questioned, more amused than confused.

She instantly thought of the way her father might have interpreted the nickname. Horrified—this wasn't the kind of thing adult children shared with their parents even if they *were* very close—she was quick to offer up a denial.

"Oh, no, it's not what you think—"

Sean stopped her before she could get wound up, holding his hands up in front of him as if to block the onslaught of words. "I'm not thinking a thing," he told her innocently. "And don't worry, Matt, I can take your mother home." He flashed a smile at his companion on the swing who appeared contented enough to begin purring. "Most likely it's on my way."

"Actually, it's not—" Kendra began, then stopped abruptly. She didn't want to throw cold water on whatever it was that her father was planning. "—Unless you take the scenic route," she amended. She looked at her new partner. "Okay, Abilene, I guess it's just you and me in the car. Just like every other day," she added with a deliberately weary sigh.

Apparently, Abilene couldn't help himself. His eyes skimmed along her torso and Kendra could have *sworn* she felt his gaze touching her bare skin. Touching her in places that definitely increased the heat level.

"I don't know about that," Abilene commented. "I don't remember you *ever* coming into work dressed— or undressed—like that." Appreciation resonated in his voice.

"It's a barbecue," she told him. "Not a spring formal."

"Definitely nothing formal about what you're wearing," he agreed. Turning back to his mother, he grinned. "See, I told you that you'd have a good time. Next time, you'll know not to doubt me." Leaning down, he gave her a quick kiss to the cheek. "Don't stay out too late."

Sabrina shook her head. "Last time I looked, I was the parent, you were the child."

"Look harder," Matt advised, the grin on his lips widening. Turning away, he began to walk toward the house with Kendra. "Your father going to be all right?"

That was *not* the question she thought he would ask. "Your mother's not exactly a femme fatale out to bilk him of his life savings," she pointed out.

"No, but she does tend to respond to kindness rather quickly." He laughed under his breath. "She might have them going steady before the morning light."

Kendra found the old-fashioned term almost sweet. This man definitely had layers to him. "It's nice of you to be concerned, but my dad could really use a little excitement in his life that doesn't involve piecing together dead bodies or reconstructing homemade bombs. I think it's kind of nice, really," she told him.

Entering the house through the sliding-glass door, she looked around for the chief. Family or no family, she wouldn't feel right about leaving without thanking him first.

"What do you think is kind of nice?" Matt prodded when she just left the sentence hanging there.

"Flirting at their age. Or whatever the current term is for what they were doing." She shrugged, feeling a little self-conscious. "I'm a little out of practice these days."

"Right." There was no missing the sarcastic tone surrounding the single word. It all but vibrated and was a total match with the smirk on his lips.

"I am," she protested.

Finding Andrew, Kendra wove her way over to that side of the living room. The former police chief and all-around amazing chef was sitting back on an overly large sofa, his wife nestled beside him, and both were engaged in a conversation with half a dozen other members of their family.

"A hottie like you?" Abilene mocked in a low voice only she could hear.

"—who's consumed with her work," Kendra tagged on.

They both thanked their host and then withdrew, promising to be at the next gathering which, according to what Andrew called after them, would be there "before you know it."

"Only if you want to be," Abilene said, picking up the thread of their conversation the second they turned away from Andrew and the others. "Why do you want to be consumed by your work to that extent?"

The night air was cool in comparison to the way it had been earlier that day. The lack of humidity at this hour made it feel rather pleasant. It was a good night for a walk, Kendra thought. But, because they had arrived fairly early, the car was parked not too far down the street.

Kendra walked quickly, as if to distance herself from his question.

As if that was possible.

Abilene was waiting for an answer. She didn't have to look at him to know that he was.

She tried to go on the attack. "Aren't you getting a little too personal here?" she countered.

"Personal is if I asked you what you weighed or what you had under those short-shorts besides an incredible pair of legs." His eyes seemed to be gleaming as he allowed himself to envision her wearing even less. "*This* is taking an active interest in my partner's psychological profile."

She laughed shortly. "Oh, is that what it is?"

"Yes," he answered, as somber as if he was stating his case before a judge. "If somewhere down the line, something suddenly makes you snap, I need to know if I should be prepared for that burnout mode—or not."

She didn't take offense at his scenario. He was just trying to rattle her cage—and that was rarely done these days.

"You could always change partners," Kendra said.

He inclined his head, as if to acknowledge changing as a possibility—if he wanted it to be.

"Let's say I don't want to," he told her.

Releasing the locks on the car, she opened the car door on her side.

Well, that was a surprise. She'd just assumed that he wanted to be away from her as much as she told herself she wanted to be away from him. Who knew?

"You're not going to drop this, are you?" she asked him.

Abilene got in on his side and watched her for a long moment before answering. "What do you think?"

She blew out a breath. "I think I should have told you I was dating someone exclusively."

He shook his head. "I already know you're not."

About to turn the ignition, her eyes opened wide. "You asked around about me?" There were few things she hated as much as someone prying into her background. That she had tried to do the very same thing with Abilene was beside the point.

He saw the quick flash of temper and did what he could to head it off and set her straight. "No, but if you were 'dating someone exclusively,' he would have been here and the *two* of you would have been by to pick my mother and me up."

She snapped her fingers as if that was a stunning revelation. Actually, it *was* a pretty clever deduction on his part—especially considering that she'd expected not all that much from him.

"By George, you *are* a real detective, aren't you?" she cracked.

He took the comment, as he took everything else, in stride. "Told you I was." He waited a beat as she began to drive down the street, then continued with his mission to unravel his partner. "So?" he prodded.

She sat up a little straighter, bracing her shoulders as if the words she was about to say wouldn't relax her. When she spoke, it was in a slow, hoarse whisper, as if her voice would break at any moment.

"My fiancé killed himself on the day we were supposed to get married." She couldn't bring herself to refer to it as their wedding day, but it would have happened had Jason not been trapped in that awful fire.

"What?" He needed details and did his best to try to coax them out of her. "Wouldn't it have been easier just to cancel the wedding? Just as quick and a lot less messy?"

She wasn't saying anything. *Maybe his comment had been too flip.* He debated retreating and decided that this would always be out there until she told him the whole story. They had to deal with it and then sweep it away. Curiosity didn't motivate him. He wanted to help. For the first time since he'd met her, she wasn't the feisty little powerhouse, plowing over him. She was a woman who had been badly wounded.

"There's more to it," he told her simply. "What aren't you telling me?"

Her eyes were stinging badly. She didn't know how much longer she could keep the tears at bay. She didn't want to cry in front of this man, and yet, there was nowhere to go inside her.

"What I'm not saying is that Jason was a great guy. We'd dated all through high school and all he ever wanted to be was a fireman," she said, remembering the young man he had been. The one who had captured her heart so completely.

"So he became one." And with that, she thought, his fate had been sealed. "He went at his job each and every day like the hero that he was." She pressed her lips together, searching for strength to continue, to finish the story. "On what turned out to be his last day on the job, four of his buddies were trapped on the third floor of a crumbling apartment building. Jason had just come out with this old man he'd rescued. He didn't even stop to catch his breath, he just went charging back into the building."

She stopped for a moment, afraid her voice would crack. Abilene waited, instinctively knowing that his silence was all she could handle right now.

"The floor beneath them collapsed. His friends died, burned almost beyond recognition. The other firemen managed to save Jason, but he had burns over 85 percent of his body." Remembering those awful days, waiting for him to wake up, she had to take a shaky breath. Tears began to slide down her cheeks but she pushed on. "Eventually, he lost a leg. I kept trying to tell him that he was lucky to be alive, but he'd look at me with those dead eyes and tell me that he didn't feel so lucky.

"Every day he slipped away a little more. There was no way I could reach him, no matter what I said or how hard I tried." That was what hurt even more than seeing him like that. That she couldn't help the man she loved. "I just couldn't get through to him.

"He had God knows how many skin grafting operations—they had to scrape away all his burned skin and replace it. In between, the hospital tried to get him to work with a team of physical therapists. He tried in the beginning, but then he'd just tell them to leave him alone. That he was useless.

"I was there every morning, every evening. The moment I was off duty, I went to the hospital to be with him, to offer my support. But it didn't do any good." The tears were coming faster now. She wiped them away with the back of her hand. "He just lost his will to live. And then, on the day we'd set to get married, someone—and we never found out who—managed to bring him a gun despite all the security measures in place at the hospital."

Kendra was talking in short bursts now, as if she couldn't draw enough air into her lungs to speak in long sentences.

"And he put that gun to his temple—and he pulled the trigger. And then he didn't have to be that broken man in the hospital bed anymore. He found his peace—and all the rest of us—his family, his friends, me—we were left in hell."

She was crying now, almost uncontrollably, hating herself for allowing this breakdown in front of a witness.

"Pull over," Abilene ordered.

They were still a couple of miles from his apartment complex. Maybe she hadn't heard him correctly. She felt shell-shocked. "What?"

"Pull over," he repeated in a firmer voice.

When she did, pulling up the hand brake and turning off the engine, he leaned over and put his arms around her. Kendra struggled for a second, not wanting his pity, but he remained firm, holding her despite the awkward angle.

And then whatever was left of her strength broke down completely and she just cried. Cried so hard that her entire body shook.

He said nothing, letting her cry it out as he continued to hold her.

Chapter 11

Kendra cried for several minutes, cried, despite struggling hard not to, as if her heart had just broken into tiny little pointy pieces inside her chest.

And then she stopped.

Abruptly.

Finally pulling herself together, Kendra blew out a long sigh that shuddered through her body. Lifting her head from her partner's shoulder, Kendra used the heel of her palm to wipe away some of the damp streaks along the length of her cheeks—she couldn't begin to erase all of them.

She was torn between lashing out at him because he'd been a witness to this breakdown, had drawn it out by his kindness, and apologizing for letting her emotions get the better of her around him.

Pressing her lips together, Kendra looked at Matt's

shoulder again. There was almost an oblong-shaped wet mark on the light blue material.

Her tears.

"Sorry," she murmured, then cleared her throat, attempting to negate the raspiness that came out when she tried to speak. "I didn't mean to get your shirt soggy like that."

A soggy shoulder was so far down on the list of his concerns, it didn't even begin to register. He laughed shortly.

"It'll dry," Matt told her, dismissing the unnecessary apology with a shrug. "Want me to drive?" he offered, thinking that, after crying so hard, perhaps she was exhausted and didn't feel up to driving.

To her, the question had pretty much come out of the blue. Her ability to navigate a vehicle had nothing to do with the temporary breakdown of emotions she'd just suffered.

"Why would I want you to drive?" Kendra asked. "I didn't short-circuit my wiring by crying. Just give me a second."

She paused, taking in a deep breath, as if that somehow helped her to center herself. To put this break from her customary closemouthed approach behind her and forget about it.

And she's back, he couldn't help thinking after her flippant comment. *Shields up and all.*

Although Matt liked Kendra's bravado, he had to admit that the vulnerable woman he'd just glimpsed did appeal to the protector in him. He supposed that was because he had never quite gotten over his Eagle Scout training as a boy. Damsels in distress—any kind of distress—had always been a weakness of his.

"Take all the time you want," he urged. "The evening's not going anywhere."

She meant to say something flippant about his comment. Instead, what came out went back to her emotion-fueled moments where she'd bared her soul to him. She really should have held it together instead of falling apart like that, she silently chided.

What was she thinking?

"I'm sorry."

"For what?" he asked. "For being human? I kind of already suspected that you might be, except that I didn't have any proof."

She wiped away another stray tear. "And now you do." It was part question, part assumption.

Matt inclined his head magnanimously. "And now I do," he agreed.

"It shouldn't have happened. My breaking down like that," she said, trying very hard to distance herself from the event by viewing the whole thing in a clinical light. Was this going to make working together harder, now that he knew about her pain? "That's why I never talk about Jason and what happened."

"Not with anyone?" he asked, surprised. Even without the Cavanaughs, she had a pretty big family and from what he'd seen and heard, they were a tight, close-knit bunch. They had to have known what happened to her fiancé.

In answer to his question, Kendra shook her head. Taking another long, deep breath, she turned the key in the ignition, then put her hands on the steering wheel and started to drive again.

"No," she finally said.

Okay, he was no psych major, but anyone with an

ounce of common sense could see what was coming down the road in that sort of a situation.

"You know, keeping that kind of thing bottled up inside you can make a person just explode at the worst possible time," he told Kendra.

The wording struck her as funny, though she suppressed the laugh. But not the laughter in her eyes. "There's a good time to explode?"

Abilene inclined his head in agreement. Poor choice of words, he told himself. "Point taken."

He didn't strike her as the type to spread rumors. But the truth, well, he just might be willing to pass that along if he perceived it as an amusing true anecdote. She didn't want to take that chance. Would asking him to keep silent about what had just happened make him refrain from talking about it—or just encourage him to tell anyone who would listen?

Like everything else, she decided, it was a gamble.

"Look, what I just told you," Kendra began haltingly, "I'd rather you didn't talk about it with anyone."

Matt snapped his fingers, as if he'd just lost out on something big. "Well, I guess there goes my blog post for today."

He said it so matter-of-factly, for a split second Kendra actually thought he was being serious. Slanting a look at her partner, she asked cautiously, "You're kidding, right?"

"I am definitely going to have to work on my delivery," he murmured, as if to himself, then said, "Yes, I was kidding. I don't have this driving need to share every little thing I hear with the immediate world. Let the world entertain itself some other way," he told her, hoping to put her mind at ease.

Or as at-ease as someone as wired as Kendra Cavelli/ Cavanaugh could be, he amended.

They had reached his apartment complex and within another minute or so, Kendra brought her car to a stop in a guest parking space that was only a few feet away from the door of his ground-floor apartment.

Instead of saying good-night and getting out, Abilene turned toward her and said, "I appreciate your inviting my mother to the party. I think she really enjoyed herself. It was just what she needed to feel better about herself."

He meant every word. Why did he suddenly feel so awkward saying this? And why the hell did he feel like some gangly teenager who didn't know where to put his hands? What was it about this woman that kept rubbing away his guard?

And then, having absolutely no intention of extending any sort of an invitation, Matt still heard himself saying, "Would you like to come inside for a minute?" as he nodded toward the apartment door behind him. "I don't have anything fancy to drink," he warned. "But I do have a couple of beers with a foreign-sounding label slapped on the bottle."

Kendra laughed. Was that meant to impress her? Or did he think she was some sort of a snob? God, nothing could be further from the truth.

"I don't need anything 'fancy,'" she assured him. "And I drink beer, even without foreign-sounding names written on the label."

"So that's a yes?" he asked, his hand on the handle of the passenger door, waiting.

After purging her soul, she didn't want to be alone, at least, not right now. Talking about it to her partner had unearthed just too many memories, memories she didn't know if she could handle in her present frame of mind. So, accepting the lifeline he'd just tossed her, she shrugged in response to his question.

After all, she had to keep in character. Otherwise he might suspect just how very vulnerable she actually was.

"Sure, why not?"

"Can't remember when I've had a more eager acceptance," he said wryly, getting out. He came around quickly to the driver's side and opened the door for Kendra before she could do it herself.

Ignoring the hand he offered, Kendra swung her legs around and got out. "I'll just bet," she answered with a short laugh.

He looked at her for a moment. "Meaning?"

"Just that your reputation precedes you."

"I don't have a reputation," he informed her mildly. "Unless you're referring to the one about my caseload." It was her turn to look confused, so he elaborated. "I led my division in the number of cases I closed," he said.

"And in the number of short-term relationships you amassed," Kendra interjected. That was what she'd initially been referring to when she'd mentioned his reputation.

"All amicably ended," he was quick to point out. "No promises of a rose garden or happily-ever-afters. Just a good time to be had by all. And then we went our separate ways."

"Your mother's influence?" she guessed. It didn't take much to put two and two together.

"Maybe," he allowed as he unlocked his front door

and let her walk in ahead of him. "Or maybe I'm just not built for a long-term relationship."

"Maybe," she echoed. Some people weren't. She now thought that she belonged in that group as well. "If you never make a promise, you can't break it." *And then your heart doesn't get scarred.*

"Exactly," he agreed, closing the door.

They were standing inside his apartment now, with only the single low light that he always left on illuminating the immediate area and holding the darkness at bay.

Was that what made her appear particularly appealing to him? That illumination whispering of things not seen?

But then, he'd found himself attracted to her off and on—mainly on—since they'd first been paired together. The pull had only grown stronger, and right now, he was having a really hard time resisting it. A larger and larger part of him didn't even want to continue resisting. If there was fallout because of it, he'd deal with that later.

"So," he said in a low, deliberate voice, "I guess we both know where we're coming from."

"I guess we do," she agreed, never taking her eyes off his.

Suddenly, this was not just a philosophical exchange about the nature of relationships and how to avoid disappointment. There was an underlying current pulsing between them and she would bet anything that he was as aware of it as she was.

"Want that beer now?" he asked, nodding toward the darkened kitchen on his left and the refrigerator that was there.

Suddenly mesmerized, Matt couldn't seem to draw

his eyes away from her lips, watching them move as she answered, "Not particularly."

"Then what would you like?" he asked, every syllable undulating seductively along her bare throat and shoulders.

Kendra didn't answer. At least, she didn't say anything out loud.

But he could have sworn that somehow between them, the word *guess* vibrated, sending off shock waves. Tempting him to take her.

He gave up the pretense of resisting.

Like a man walking on a beach for the first time after a particularly cold, desolate winter, Matt tested the incoming waters slowly.

Taking her face in his hands, he framed it gently, then, almost in slow motion, he lowered his mouth to hers. Their lips touched lightly, then pressed.

Then kissed.

The kiss deepened and grew, taking them both to a high, sharp edge neither one of them had even been sure existed.

And then he kissed her again.

And again.

Until they lost count and lost their sensibilities as well. What began in slow motion suddenly grew and multiplied in speed and urgency.

As pulses and heart rates sped up, so did the tempo of their needs. Hands flew, caressing here, tugging there, learning, absorbing, reveling.

Bringing unbridled pleasure with every stroke, every touch.

She'd purged herself of all her tears and found that she needed to somehow fill the emptiness that had been left behind within her, the emptiness that had been haunting her these last eighteen months.

Needed, ever so desperately, to feel *alive* again.

She needed to *feel* like a woman, to be *regarded* as a woman.

And his hands, as they passed over her body worshipfully, made her want things she thought she'd never want again.

The more he kissed her, the more he touched her, the more she wanted him to. On some logical plane, Kendra knew she should be backing away, calling a halt to this before it went too far. Before she couldn't control what was happening inside her.

Abilene was her partner, a man she would be working with for at least a while and this might create some awkwardness between them.

But she didn't care.

Didn't care because what she was feeling right now was absolutely *wonderful,* like attending her own rebirth, with heat, stars, sunshine and explosions of happiness all rolled up into one, lighting her up like a Roman candle.

It had taken less than two minutes to undress her.

Kendra pulled away his shirt, tugged at his belt, desperately wanting him to be as naked as she was, as vulnerable as she was.

Now.

It took longer to undress him than it had her, but that was because her fingers seemed to be fumbling. And he had more on to begin with.

When his belt became stuck, she yanked at it in frustration and heard Matt laugh softly. Her eyes darted up to his face, but the amusement in his eyes wasn't at her expense. Instead, it seemed to give her a sense of sharing. Like they were laughing at something *together*.

"I'll do it," he told her, stilling her hands.

And then, just like that, there were no more barriers in the way. Just like that, she found herself on the sofa, expecting the next moment to bring with it fulfillment—and an ending.

She was only half-right. There was fulfillment as he pleasured her in ways that took her breath away, even as they brought a shower of stars swirling about in her mind's eye, but there was no ending.

Instead, the climax she experienced dovetailed into another wild, skyrocketing ride, leaving her to hang on for dear life.

To her unsuspecting delight, she quickly discovered that droll words were not the only things that could roll off Abilene's tongue. He could all but make it do tricks.

She felt it, and his lips, passing along her skin, drawing in closer and closer to its target and then suddenly, as he thrust into her extremely sensitive core, there was an avalanche of stars and sensations shooting all through her.

Kendra caught herself digging her fingernails into the cushions, arching up into him as she tried to absorb every nuance, every wondrous feeling that this man was capable of creating within her.

Breathing hard, she pulled his face up to hers. Drawing as much air into her lungs as she could, Kendra pressed her lips to his, determined to at least partially affect him. Trying to make him feel as helplessly exhausted and crazy as he had just made her.

With her hands, her lips and her tongue, mimicking his style, she managed to bring Matt figuratively to his knees.

A long breath shuddered through his aching body.

Matt stared at her in wonder. She was one hell of a fast learner. He didn't know how much longer he could hold himself in check, not when his entire body begged him to let go, to enjoy the wild sensation that had so swiftly built up within him, demanding to be released.

But Matt wanted to be certain that he had taken her up as far as she was capable of going, wanted to be sure that she bordered on exhaustion and had no resolve left.

He couldn't put it into words that made sense, even to himself, but he felt a kinship with this woman to whom life had been so subtly cruel. Felt a kinship and at the same time felt a need to somehow make it all up to her, even though none of it was his fault.

Who knew—maybe his early nomadic life with his mother had somehow fried his circuits so that he was incapable of thinking clearly.

He didn't know.

All he knew was that once he and Kendra had begun making love, he became determined that this was the experience she would remember no matter how many years she lived.

Because God knew he was going to remember it even with his dying breath.

That was the surprise of it. Wanting to pleasure her, he'd uncovered a world of pleasure himself. So much so that part of him wanted it to continue and stretch out as long as humanly possible.

But he knew his limitations, his boundaries. He had reached the end of his tether and it was time for the final volley.

Shifting his body over hers, Matt drew her into his arms, kissing her over and over again and then he began the final phase.

A new wave of passion washed over him as he entered her.

One was made out of two.

And then, with swift, sure movements, the upward ascent began, growing quicker and quicker in tempo. As they clung to each other, both scrambled to the highest point on the peak before them.

Eighteen months of celibacy exploded within Kendra the moment she and Matt reached that much-desired plateau together.

Euphoria embraced her as hard as Abilene did, holding her tightly in its grasp as her heart hammered wildly.

She was panting as if she'd just sprinted the last mile of a twenty-six-mile marathon.

Kendra clutched on to the moment—and the man—knowing in her heart that both would be gone from her life all too soon.

But they were here now, in the moment, and that was all that mattered to her.

Tomorrow was still an eternity away.

Chapter 12

"You know what this means, don't you?"

Abilene's question broke the silence that had been hanging between them these last few minutes as euphoria receded and the world came back into focus.

Kendra slanted a wary glance at him. Instinctively, she braced herself, although exactly for what she was unable to say.

She could feel her body tensing anyway.

"What?" she asked, her voice toneless. If he was going to say something flippant, she was determined to be blasé.

"Well, the way I see it," Matt began slowly, struggling to keep the grin out of his voice. It was a short battle and he lost. "We're going to have to change your name from *Good* to *Fantastic*." He shifted so that he was able to face her now. "Or maybe some word that's even better than that. What's better than *fantastic?*" he asked her.

"Your ability to spout absolute nonsense," she told him, shaking her head.

She was doing her best to look irritated, but there was no denying that inwardly, she was grinning fit to kill. Matt was teasing her, but also telling her that he had enjoyed their interlude just as much as she had.

"I beg to differ," he contradicted. "You were not on the receiving end of you." He grinned as he wound a long, blond strand of her hair around his finger, absently noting how soft and silky it felt. Just the way she did. "I was."

Kendra could never really handle genuine compliments of any sort for more than a second—and this was a whole new level of compliment—without blushing or feeling awkward. Or both.

"Kendra," she blurted out. "My name is Kendra. You can call me Kendra, or, on a good day—and if I let you—you can call me Kenny. Or you can call me Cavanaugh if you want to keep it strictly business."

"Only when we have our clothes on," he told her, teasingly referring to the "strictly business" comment she'd just made. And then he replayed her words in his head. "Wait. What? Back up a minute. You said I could call you *Cavanaugh?*"

She sighed. Now where was he going with this? "That's right."

Curious, Matt propped himself up on his elbow and looked down into her face. "When did you make up your mind about that?"

She supposed she owed him an explanation—and

if she withheld it, he'd poke and prod at her until she told him. Might as well get it over with now and spare them both.

"When I saw how happy my father was today. He looked as if he'd finally found his niche." Her father was very dear to her and it was nice seeing him like that. God knew he deserved all the happiness he could find after struggling to be both mother and father to all seven of them.

"And he hadn't before?" Matt asked, curious. As he spoke, he slowly drew his fingertips along the inviting curve of her hip, skin against skin. Seemingly oblivious to the effect he was having on her.

But she knew better.

"Not entirely," Kendra admitted. She was trying to appear aloof, but it was difficult to concentrate on what she was saying. Her body began to vibrate in anticipation again.

"The Cavellis are all good, decent people, but I always had the impression that Dad felt kind of out of sync around them." She tried to give him an example. "You know, like when you have a pair of shoes that don't quite fit, even though they're the right size— Will you please stop that?" she finally said, unable to pretend that she was unaffected any longer. "I can't think straight when you do that."

"And do you want to?" He shifted again, this time his body provocatively touching hers. "Think straight?" he asked innocently—but there was definite mischief in his eyes.

"Yes, of course I want to think straight— Oh, the hell with it," she cried, giving up.

And with that, she wound her arms around his neck and kissed him, surrendering any and all pretense of indifference to the magic that this man conjured up whenever he so much as touched her.

"My sentiments exactly," he echoed with a laugh. The next second, Matt lost himself within her.

The body wash she'd used that morning still managed to linger along her skin and it was filling his head, effectively adding to the heat swirling through his veins.

Although she would have never suspected it, making love the second time with Matt was even better than the first time. The stakes had become even higher, the need to pleasure, to excite, even greater.

There was nothing "business as usual" about this second trek through the fiery regions of Matthew Abilene's lovemaking.

He surprised her in a hundred different ways.

She was surprised by her own wild desire, by the ever-shifting newness of his techniques and by her own unbridled responses to what he was doing to her.

And she was equally surprised by her almost fierce desire to bring this man with the fabulous lips and tongue up just as high, making him just as mind-numbingly delirious as she was.

And the most frightening part of this second encounter with Matt was that it only made her want more. Made her want to do this heated, frenzied meeting of bodies and spirits again and again to the exclusion of absolutely everything else.

This lovemaking came before eating, sleeping, *breathing*.

Before everything.

She wanted this passion, this insatiable desire to continue forever, without end. Logic, something she'd always bowed to, dictated otherwise. But she had no use for logic—not tonight. Not here, not now.

But eventually, despite their youth and their stamina, sheer exhaustion caught up to them both. It had already made away with their ability to think or make any sort of decisions.

They fell asleep in each other's arms. Kendra had absolutely no memory of when.

The gleeful noises of raised voices followed by the sound of water being splashed penetrated Kendra's subconscious a number of times, going deeper each time.

It finally roused her and she had no choice but to reluctantly wake up and open her eyes.

Kendra's first bewildered thought was that she had no idea where she was.

But then the weight of the very masculine, very muscular arm lying across her chest caused her memory to return.

Abilene.

She'd slept with Abilene.

Over and over again.

Each thought, coming on the heels of the last, alarmed her more and more.

Oh, God, what had she done in a moment of absolute weakness and insanity? Was she completely out of her mind?

Not that it hadn't been wondrous. Even looking back, in a growing state of panic, she still had to admit to that. The man had a fabulous technique—she had to give him his due.

An extraordinary technique learned and perfected, no doubt over a period of time, on heaven only knew how many willing young women who had passed through the man's life and through his bedroom sheets. Sheets that they'd moved to at some point during the night and that were now wrapped around her.

But what was going to become of their working relationship now that they'd been this intimate? Was he going to expect to "grab a little loving" as Jason used to call it, whenever the spirit moved him?

When they were going over a crime scene and were left on their own, would he suddenly have an itch he wanted scratched?

She would have to set Abilene straight about that right up front. Otherwise, this just wasn't going to work.

Okay, that was the plan, she told herself. The minute he woke up, they were going to talk.

"So who won?"

Startled, she almost yelped. Instead, she pressed her lips together, shifted and saw that Abilene was looking at her.

Grinning.

The big dumb lug was awake. For how long? Had he been staring at her the whole time? Why hadn't she known that?

Her brain felt like a briar patch, all tangled up and thorny.

And what the hell was he talking about, anyway? "What?" she asked, confused.

"Who won?" he repeated. "You had this look on

your face like you were conducting some sort of an argument in your head. I was just wondering which side won, that's all."

When had she become this transparent, and to him of all people?

"Nobody 'won,'" she retorted.

What did he think, that she heard voices?

Well, don't you? Sometimes? Just calm down, she schooled herself.

Taking a breath, Kendra was just about to tell her partner about the ground rules she felt needed reinforcing, but she never got the chance. He interrupted her again.

"Oh, good, then you're not renouncing or denouncing anything that went on last night," Abilene concluded, pleased.

That made her stop for a moment.

"Does that happen often for you?" she asked. What kind of a woman made love with him and then turned around to revile him about it? Maybe he was so lighthearted in his relationships because he was afraid that something might set her off.

Stop defending the man. Sometimes a wolf is just a wolf, not an enchanted prince, she reminded herself sternly.

"Nope." It didn't happen at all, because the women he picked all knew the rules ahead of time. "But then, I have to admit, you're not like the rest."

Right, I'm "special." And if I believe that, you have a bridge you want to sell me—retail.

"Nice platitude," she quipped out loud. "Is that supposed to make me breathe a sigh of relief and then, out of gratitude, issue you carte blanche so you can feel free to do anything you want with me once we're outside of work?"

He knew if he laughed, she was liable to haul off and hit him. Getting annoyed at her sarcastic tone would probably get him the same reaction.

So he held the laugh in check and tried honesty.

"No, that's supposed to let you know that I think you're unique right down to your toes." He could see that she was tensing, as if she expected some kind of a confrontation on some level. "Easy, Cavanaugh, I wasn't planning on another go-round, at least, not without an invitation." Although, God knew, just looking at her had him ready and able. "Now, since this is my place, what would you like for breakfast?"

"My clothes."

Matt never missed a beat. "Boiled, scrambled, sunny-side up?" he asked as if she were talking about eggs and hadn't just requested the shorts and shirt that had heated him up so much in the first place. "By the way, you're welcome to stay just as you are for as long as you'd like."

In response, she slid off the bed, tugging the sheet around her as she went. Somehow, she managed to do it regally, looking like a displaced Greek goddess in search of a private section of heaven for herself. As far as he was concerned—at least for this morning— heaven was right here, held captive in Kendra's eyes.

She still hadn't said anything about what she wanted to eat. And she definitely wasn't taking him up on his suggestion that she remain just as she was.

"Okay, be that way," he said good-naturedly. "Since

you made no requests, I'm making a Denver omelet," he informed her.

Instead of putting on any of the clothes that had been haphazardly discarded on the rug, Matt stood up, incredibly oblivious to his naked state, and walked over to the small bureau. Opening a drawer, he took out a pair of washed-out denim shorts that were badly frayed along both cuffs and pulled them on.

Kendra chastised herself for not being able to tear her eyes away. He really was a magnificent specimen of manhood.

"Don't you want to put on underwear first?" she heard herself asking.

He shrugged dismissively. "I'm just throwing something on to make breakfast. I'll get more formal after my shower," he promised.

Breakfast. Abilene'd been serious about his offer, then. Now *that* was surprising. "You really cook?" she asked.

"Haven't killed anyone yet," he told her matter-of-factly.

Which brought her back to the amount of traffic this apartment had to have seen in the last few years. That should keep her grounded, she thought. She was just one of many.

"So it's a package deal?" Kendra asked him flippantly. "You serve up a hot night and then a hot meal in the morning?"

"You make it sound like a bed-and-breakfast pamphlet," he said, amused. "And to answer your question, no, it's not a package deal. At least, not usually," he amended because, after all, wasn't that what he was doing right now? "Let's just say that you bring out the best in me."

She didn't understand. "But you just said you've never managed to kill anyone with your cooking—if you weren't talking about women who've spent the night with you, who were you talking about?" she asked. It was obvious that she didn't believe him and was just curious to see how Abilene intended to wiggle out of this.

"My mother," he told her simply. By the way she was staring at him, he knew she hadn't been expecting that for an answer. But it was true. "When I was growing up—and there wasn't some guy she'd opened up her heart to lying in bed next to her—she'd hold down sometimes two, three part-time jobs, trying to make ends meet for the two of us. That left her pretty tired. So on Sundays, I'd get up early, sneak into the kitchen and make her breakfast with whatever I could find in the refrigerator."

For a second, Matt had left her almost speechless. But she rallied quickly enough.

"My God, you sound like some kid in one of those after-school specials that they used to love to air on the Family Channel," she told him, getting somewhat accustomed to the plaintive puppy-dog eyes he had turned her way.

"Too tame?" Matt asked, amused, as he began to walk out of the bedroom and into the small kitchen.

Kendra trailed after him, still wearing the sheet around her like a flowing toga. She moved more slowly than she liked, careful not to trip over the excess material. That would have been all she needed, to fall flat on her face in front of him. With her luck, the sheet would somehow unravel, leaving her far more exposed than she would have liked.

Kendra paused to awkwardly pick up her discarded shorts, top and the undergarments that went with them. Clutching them against her, she followed Matt the rest of the way into the kitchen.

She was having trouble reconciling what he'd just told her with the image she had of him. "That helpful little wide-eyed boy doesn't really jibe with what I know about you."

He opened up a cabinet and took out a heavy iron skillet, placing it on a burner adjacent to another, smaller pan. Watching him, she decided that maybe the man actually did know his way around a kitchen.

"You mean with what you *think* you know about me," he corrected.

Oh, now he was going to tell her that he was a closet saint? "What? What I saw in public is just your secret identity and this is the real you? You're a master chef who perfected his skills making Sunday brunch for his mother?"

"It was breakfast, not brunch," he corrected. "And I didn't claim to be a master—at least not at cooking," he said, looking at her over his shoulder. The sexy grin on his lips went straight to her gut as if it was mounted on an arrow that he'd just shot. "People are complex, Cavanaugh." Opening the refrigerator, he began to take out what he needed. Unlike when he'd been a boy, this refrigerator was well stocked and had a lot for him to choose from. "You ought to know that."

The last remark had her radar going up. Was that

a crack? About what, exactly? "What's that supposed to mean?"

Did she want to pick a fight? he wondered. Why? Because she'd enjoyed herself too much and was now waiting for him to disappoint her somehow, the way her fiancé had? Or was she just plain ornery?

He had a feeling it wasn't the latter.

"That you're not the only one with several layers," he answered simply. "Why don't you take a shower while I make breakfast?" he suggested, his voice mild, completely nonconfrontational. And then he grinned wickedly as he added, "Unless you want to wait until I'm finished out here and then we can take a shower together."

"Worried about conserving water?" she asked. California had its share of droughts off and on and they were never completely out of the woods.

But to her dismay, rather than take the bait, Matt wound up disarming her again with another sensual grin.

"Conserving energy was the very *last* thing on my mind when I suggested showering together."

Meaning she would have found out what it was like to make love in a shower stall while her body was being pelted by water.

Why did that sound hopelessly erotic to her? It was just water, for heaven's sake. What was it about this man that just a simple suggestion from him could cause her breath to literally back up in her lungs like that?

Hell, he could achieve the same result with just a look, a phrase with a double meaning.

After all, it wasn't as if she was some untried, vestal

virgin. Granted, she hadn't made love in a year and a half, but whatever pent-up energy, emotions and combustible feelings she'd been harboring all these months had all emerged, exploding out and making their presence—and exodus—known in a glorious shower of fulfillment.

So how could she be thinking about going to bed with this man all over again as if last night had never taken place?

Or was that because last night *had* taken place and she was desperate to re-create it?

She just didn't know.

But Matt did.

She had a gut feeling that Abilene knew exactly what was going on in her head. He *had* to. There was no other reason why he was looking at her so knowingly right now.

"Bathroom's right back there," he told her, pointing toward the bedroom again. "You'll find fresh towels in the linen closet on your way there. Breakfast will be ready soon. Don't take too long," he warned. "Or I'll be forced to come looking for you."

"Wouldn't want that," she quipped.

He merely smiled. "That remains to be seen," he said under his breath.

But she heard him.

Kendra hurried away, giving herself a mental count of ten minutes to shower, dress and be back in the kitchen. Eleven, tops. Otherwise, she had absolutely no doubt that Abilene would make good on his promise to come looking for her.

The trick, she thought as she stepped into the light

beige tiled shower, was not to allow herself to dawdle because that would mean that she *wanted* him to come into the shower with her.

And if that happened, she knew damn well that neither one of them would have any interest in the hot meal he'd have left waiting on the stove.

Chapter 13

Forcing herself to hurry through her shower, Kendra was just about to turn off the water when she became aware of the noise.

Knocking?

No, more like pounding. Impatient pounding. The noise sounded like a woodpecker trying to penetrate a petrified tree.

Abilene.

But why was he pounding? Was this some Jekyll/Hyde thing? What did she really know about this partner of hers, anyway?

Thinking that any second the man who had made the very earth move last night would just barge in, she grabbed a towel and wrapped it around herself.

"Hey!" she heard Abilene call through the door. "We finally got lucky!"

Lucky? Was he actually saying what she *thought*

he was saying? Denigrating the whole interlude from last night by describing it with the crass term of *getting lucky?*

She felt a hot flash of anger.

"'Lucky'?" she echoed, securing the towel around herself as best she could. "How can you say that?" she demanded.

"Well, what the hell would you call it?" he asked, mystified by her reaction. He'd thought she'd be happy. "Wong just called, said we got a hit on Burnett's ATM card."

The last part of his sentence dribbled from his lips in slow motion because she'd pulled open the door, her eyes flashing, obviously ready to confront him and give him a piece of her mind. Why, he didn't know. What she gave him instead was an eyeful.

Never mind that he'd already seen every inch of her unclothed. This was somehow even sexier. The towel was barely large enough to cover the essentials. Had she been a woman with a longer torso, she would have had to make a judgment call as to which part of her she wanted to protect more from being exposed to appreciative eyes.

Coming to, Matt held up a piece of paper with the information he'd just hastily jotted down while on the phone with the other detective.

"I've got a location, but it's Sunday. Nobody's going to be at the bank to help us." And then he grinned at Kendra. "God, you smell better than what I'm cooking."

"I'm not sure if that's a compliment or not," she retorted. Though she could have gotten sidetracked more easily than she was happy about, Kendra forced herself to focus on the paper in Abilene's hand. "We can get the name of the bank manager, have him come down to the bank and let us watch the footage on the surveillance camera," she said. He'd been staring at her with a strange expression on his face the entire time. Impatient curiosity finally got the better of her. "What?"

"Why did you get so mad when I knocked on the door just now?"

"First of all, you didn't knock, you pounded. And second, to answer your question, it was because I thought—I thought—" If she admitted to her mistake, he'd think that *she* thought there was something more to last night than just casual sex. Kendra decided that it was a subject better left untouched. "Well, never mind what I thought—"

The moment she stopped talking about it, the answer suddenly dawned on Matt. His grin was back, broader than before, if that was possible. "Oh, you thought I meant the other kind of lucky."

"We don't have time for this," she informed him primly. "This is the first lead we've had on our suspect since we found that woman's body. We need to follow it up. And I need to get dressed."

She could all but feel his eyes raking up and down along her body. If there was more time…

But there wasn't and she had to remember that. She was a police detective *and* a Cavanaugh now. That meant she had a great deal to live up to. That didn't involve grabbing a little morning delight before going after a murder suspect.

"You might get more cooperation if you don't," he told her.

Kendra frowned, waiting for him to leave before she discarded the towel and started getting dressed. "I'll chance it."

Matt nodded toward the kitchen. "I'd better go turn off the stove."

She could feel her stomach begin to growl. The prospect of a long morning loomed before them. "Wrap the breakfast up to go," she called after him. "Shame to see it go to waste."

Matt looked back at her over his shoulder, his eyes taking one final tour over her wet, barely covered body. "My sentiments exactly," he confessed with a sigh he didn't bother to suppress.

She forced herself to cross to the door and then shut it, leaving Abilene on the other side of it. Otherwise, with only a towel acting as a barrier, she wasn't sure just how long she would be able to resist her very sexy partner and his bedroom eyes. Especially when she knew exactly what the man was capable of doing to her.

C'mon, Kenny. Focus, focus, focus, she ordered herself, moving as quickly as she could.

"You come here from a picnic?" Detective Alexander Wong asked her when she first walked into the squad room just ahead of Abilene.

For a couple of minutes back there, she'd thought about making a quick run home to change into something a little less skimpy, but she didn't want to waste the time. She was too eager to see if this lead did *lead* somewhere. And, since she was fairly certain that the squad room would be mostly empty, she thought she could get away, just this once, with wearing something

that made the usual casual clothes seem formal in comparison.

"Long story," she told Wong with a dismissive wave
of her hand. She shot Abilene a warning look in case
he had any ideas about picking up the narrative for the
other detective's sake.

For now, Abilene was humoring her.

"Hey, I've got time. Fill me in," Wong all but begged.

"Some other time, Wong," she told him, "when this
case is behind us."

Along with about fifty years or so, she added silently.

She wouldn't dare admit to *anyone* that she'd spent
the night in Abilene's apartment. Not that she was
ashamed of what had happened last night—she was,
after all, an adult—but neither did she want it broadcast
on the morning news. What she did and who she did it
with after hours was her business and she intended to
keep it that way.

"Spoilsport," Wong complained, all but pouting. It
still didn't prevent him from sending long glances her
way.

"Yup, that's me," she admitted cheerfully. "Now that
we have that out of the way, where are we on getting
the bank manager to come down?"

"Still trying to track him down," Abilene told her,
chiming in. Getting the name and contact number for
the bank manager had been his assignment the second
they had set foot in the squad room. He held up the
telephone handset that he'd been on. "All the calls keep
going to his voice mail."

There could be more than a dozen reasons for that.
But right now, Kendra zeroed in on only one. The rea-

son she *didn't* like and hoped wasn't true. "Think he could be dead, too?"

"Could be," Matt allowed, hitting the Redial button on the keypad again. "But let's not get ahead of ourselves," he cautioned.

"That would have been a good rule to go by last night, too," she murmured under her breath as she sank down in her chair to check out something on her monitor.

"Guess we've got a basic difference of opinion on that," Abilene told her.

She flushed, then quickly struggled to get herself under control. She hadn't thought he'd hear her, what with the air-conditioning unit struggling to come on and making rumbling noises.

Clearing her throat, she became all business. "Do we know where Mr. Bank Manager lives?" she asked. In response, Matt held up a piece of paper with the man's home address on it. Leaning over her desk, she took possession of it. "Okay, let's go."

Abilene looked at her as she rose behind her desk. "Go?"

"Yes, 'go,'" she repeated. As lead on the case, she didn't owe him any explanations, but because he was looking at her, waiting, she said, "I'm feeling antsy and this is our only lead. Let's see if Mr. Bank Manager is home and just not answering his cell phone. He might think he deserves some time off because it's Sunday."

"Poor delusional fool," Abilene quipped, seeing the look in Kendra's eyes. He quickly rose and followed her out. The bank manager had no idea what he was in for, Abilene thought with a grin.

* * *

This time, they did make a quick stop at her apartment. If she was going to be questioning a bank manager, she needed to have on something a little less casual than a pair of frayed shorts and a blouse that only came halfway down to her midriff.

Leaving her partner in the kitchen, she dashed into her bedroom to change. She opted for a black sleeveless pullover and a pair of jeans that had taken on her shape even when she wasn't in them. The transformation took her exactly five minutes, counting entry and exit.

"Let's go," she declared as she sailed by him and out the door.

Matt took a long look at her as they hurried back to his car. "I dunno. Maybe the manager'd be more inclined to talk to you if you stayed dressed the way you were," he speculated.

Getting in the car, she secured her seat belt. "If it's all the same to you, I didn't want him thinking I was going to trade a lap dance for a confession," she told him as he got in on his side.

"You know how to give a lap dance?" he asked, intrigued. The car rumbled to life and they quickly pulled out of the development.

"Eyes on the road, Abilene—" She struggled not to let on that the gleam in his eye secretly pleased her. "And as for your question, giving a lap dance can't be all that hard."

"Well, then, you'll have to show me sometime," he told her.

She laughed shortly. "In your dreams, Abilene." Kendra couldn't help thinking that her words would have held a great deal more weight if they hadn't just spent the night together.

Matt spared her a lingering, appreciative glance. "There, too."

"The road, the road, watch the road," she ordered. If the grin on his face was any wider, she couldn't help thinking, it would have probably split his face right in half.

Kendra turned out to be right. The bank manager, a Howard Hanna, had turned his cell phone off because it was Sunday and he was trying to spend some uninterrupted quality time with his family.

Politely apologizing for separating him from that same family, Kendra explained that it was an emergency. The person they were looking for had most likely killed his girlfriend. And, as luck would have it, he'd used his ATM card to access his savings account at Hanna's location. They needed to see last night's tapes from the surveillance camera.

The bank manager seemed hesitant. "Can I see your IDs again?"

Kendra and Matt both took out their wallets and let him examine each in turn.

"Satisfied?" Kendra asked.

"Well, you know those can be faked," Hanna said, still not looking completely convinced.

"You're welcome to call the chief of detectives with our shield numbers," Kendra told him.

"He doesn't like to be disturbed on a Sunday," Abilene told him matter-of-factly. "But he'll talk to you and back up our story."

Hanna appeared torn for a moment, then shrugged. "No need to disturb him. I guess you're on the level. I'll take you to the bank," he agreed.

He accompanied them on the short run to the bank, but he was still uneasy about surrendering the surveillance tapes.

"I'm usually supposed to clear this with the corporate offices," he explained. "Technically, the video feed belongs to them, not me."

"Well, you can call them," Abilene agreed. "But remember, by the time your request goes through all the proper channels, Mr. Hanna, our suspect could very well kill another woman—or just disappear. And that would be on you," he added seriously, wielding guilt like a sharp scalpel.

"We really do need your help," Kendra told the manager, trying to appeal to his sense of decency.

They were playing good cop/bad cop, Abilene mused. And watching Kendra, he had a feeling the woman was appealing to the man's other senses as well. He'd already noted the way the manager kept looking at her—like a hungry stray mutt wanting to steal a bone from beneath another dog's nose.

Not that he blamed him, Abilene thought.

Hanna's dark eyes seemed to dart back and forth as he thought things over. It was a short battle.

"All right, wouldn't want him killing someone else because I couldn't get you a release fast enough through channels," the manager told them—mainly Kendra.

They arrived in front of the bank branch where Burnett had used his card. Hanna took out an impressive set of keys and selected a key from among them to open the outer door, then quickly fed the security code into the keypad, disarming the alarm.

The inside of the bank was eerily quiet and the dormant air was stifling. No doubt eager to have the whole thing behind him, Hanna hurried over to the small room where the ATM video feed was recorded and stored.

The room could barely accommodate the three of them, especially since the manager was more than a little overweight.

"Now, when did you say this was?" Hanna asked.

Matt glanced down at the notes he'd made right after Wong had called this morning. "Early this morning. According to the hit that came up, Burnett withdrew two hundred dollars from his savings account."

Hanna fast-forwarded through the videotape from the first half of that day. "Just two people used their ATM cards this morning," he said. He stopped the tape, rewound it and started it again so that they could see for themselves that he hadn't missed anything. "One of our senior citizens took out eighty dollars from her savings account," he narrated as he played the image for them on a small flat screen. "And a teenager wearing his cap backwards like some would-be punk was the only other customer to use the ATM." He turned from the monitor. "He took out the two hundred dollars you were talking about. Is he your killer?"

"No," Kendra cried, frustrated. She knew what Burnett looked like. There'd been a couple of framed photographs of the man with his now-dead girlfriend in the apartment. Under no lighting and under no circumstances was the man in the photographs the teenager on the tape.

"Are you sure those were the only two people at the ATM this morning?" Kendra pressed.

"I can play it again for you," Hanna offered. "But I've already gone through it twice, so unless your guy's invisible—"

Matt could feel Kendra's frustration mounting, not to mention his own. He pointed to the screen image of the teenager. "Can you get a close-up of the name on the account he's accessing?" It wasn't a request, but a politely worded order.

"Sure." Since this *was* his home turf, the manager seemed confident. He centered on the desired documentation, then enlarged it several times over, each time doubling it in size. "But you just told me that this isn't—"

"'Ryan Burnett,'" Kendra read the name out loud. "That kid has Burnett's ATM card and he's obviously got the password." She looked up at her partner and could see that Abilene was thinking the same thing. "The kid had to have somehow gotten his hands on the card."

"Maybe even killed Burnett to get it," Abilene speculated. "Hell, maybe he's the one who killed Summer in the apartment." Instead of answers, they just had more questions.

Kendra looked back at the teenager's face. She shook her head. Something in her gut was telling her no. "I don't know, Abilene. He doesn't look like a killer to me."

"That's what they said about Baby Face Nelson, too," he pointed out, mentioning a romanticized gangster from the late twenties and early thirties.

She had no idea who he was talking about, but his tone clued her in. "Just when I think there's hope for you, you turn cynical on me, Abilene," she couldn't help commenting.

While he couldn't deny the charge, he could amend it. "Only sometimes, Cavanaugh. Only sometimes."

She was surprised that she liked the sound of that. She could feel a mellowness returning, something that had been absent from her countenance for too long a time. For eighteen months.

Maybe she'd been fighting everything too hard, including the circumstances that had recently arisen. Up until now, she'd felt that if she accepted the fact that she was part of such a large law enforcement family, she was somehow being disloyal to the people she'd always believed were her extended family.

Now's not the time for philosophical ruminations, she upbraided herself. There was a case to solve and apparently more than one person to bring to justice.

Or so it seemed.

Damn, there was nothing simple about this so-called simple case.

Their first step had to be to find out who this teenager was and how he was mixed up in all this.

"Okay, how do we find this kid?" she asked Abilene, thinking out loud. Before her partner could say anything, she turned to the manager and asked the man a very obvious question. "Mr. Hanna, have you ever seen this teenager before?"

The bank manager shook his head adamantly. "No. I don't recognize him."

"Are you sure?" Matt pressed.

The man remained firm. "Positive."

Kendra sighed. "Can't ask for more than that."

Playing a long shot, Kendra and Matt went back to Ryan Burnett's apartment building and questioned all his neighbors. When they showed the photo of the teenager lifted from the surveillance tape, no one could recall ever having seen him around.

"I suppose we could get a court order to confiscate the ATM and bring it to the lab to check the outside for fingerprints," Kendra said halfheartedly an hour later as they faced each other across their desks in the squad room.

"Half the city's fingerprints might be on that keypad," Matt pointed out.

"Yeah," she said with a sigh. "So near and yet so far."

"Speaking of near, how about grabbing a bite to eat and heading back to my place?" he suggested.

They were alone in the squad room. Wong had gone home half an hour ago and he'd been the last one there with them. There was no longer a reason to keep her voice low the way there had been earlier—Wong had ears like a bat and he also loved gossip.

"Look, just because I spent one night with you doesn't mean that I'm going to hop into bed with you every time you smile," she informed Matt.

"I know that," he told her solemnly, then asked, "So, how does pizza sound?"

She hadn't been able to resist him when she'd been operating on all four cylinders. In her present condition, she knew damn well that she didn't stand a chance and was only going through the motions of holding him at arm's length for form's sake. She didn't want to appear supereasy.

The truth was that spending another night with him sounded incredibly appealing.

"Perfect," she told him with a tired sigh. Switching off her computer, she rose to her feet. "As long as you promise no anchovies."

He pretended to sigh as he followed suit. "You drive a hard bargain."

Kendra laughed shortly as she crossed the empty squad room. "Hey, I'm a Cavanaugh. We're supposed to be born tough."

"So the legend goes," he agreed, letting her walk out first. "Okay, no anchovies."

Once she crossed the threshold into the hallway, he hit the light switch. The squad room fell into darkness, except for a single light left on in the lieutenant's office. Lately, everyone had been reminded to do their part to conserve energy.

He intended to follow the letter of the request—at least at work. In his apartment, though, it was a whole different story—and he couldn't wait to get there to watch it unfold.

Chapter 14

Several days went by, shrouded in frustration. Their investigation had ground to a complete standstill. There were no more sightings of the teenager using Ryan Burnett's ATM card and no one had seen Ryan himself, not anyone in his building nor at his workplace. They had left instructions at both places to be called immediately if the man turned up.

The phone, in that respect, remained exasperatingly silent.

In the interim, Matt ran off copies of the teenager's photo that they had lifted from the initial bank surveillance tape and then had them distributed to all the other bank branches in the county as well as the surrounding counties. They were hoping that greed could prompt the teen to tap into a second ATM.

After a week had gone by, there still hadn't been any new hits.

They were swiftly running out of innovative ways to approach the problem.

"Damn!"

The softly muttered curse had Kendra looking up from the papers on her desk and at her partner. Despite everything, her expression instantly softened. Their case might not be going anywhere, but it seemed as if they were.

Not that she had the slightest idea *where* it was that they were headed, but for now, the holding pattern they were currently engaged in had her waking up with a smile each morning despite the frustration she was professionally encountering.

When it came time to leave the precinct for the day, it made no difference if they walked out together or separately and at different times—they still wound up together that evening.

In each other's arms.

And neither one of them minded.

Kendra refused to explore what was happening, refused to think beyond the moment because she knew from experience that the next moment could bring with it devastation and events that could very well blow her life apart. So she told herself she wasn't invested, that she was simply enjoying the moment and the very steamy, teeth-jarring fact that the good-looking man seated across from her in the squad room was one incredible lover.

And that, she told herself over and over again, was enough for her.

If at times she wondered how he felt about what was happening between them, she forced herself to block the questions and think of something else. *Anything* else. In this particular situation, ignorance *was* bliss—because knowing, most likely, would bring with it some sort of excruciating pain and if she could avoid it, even by simply sticking her head in the sand, she was going to do it.

Besides, she reminded herself, there was no basis to believe that anything of a permanent nature would ever be in the offing. The man had a history of loving 'em and leaving 'em. Fruit flies had longer relationships with one another than Matt Abilene had with the women who passed through his life, and she was vaguely aware that she was already pushing the time limit.

But if she pretended oblivion and said nothing, maybe he wouldn't notice and this moment they were sharing would continue a little while longer.

It was the only plan she had.

"Another dead end?" she asked, nodding at the phone.

Coming to, he replayed her question in his head and had no point of reference. "What?"

"You just said 'Damn,' so I'm asking you if that's another dead end. Our case," she prompted when he looked at her quizzically. "You remember, dead body in bachelor's apartment. ATM hits by a third party." She cocked her head, looking up at the face that had already turned up several unnerving times in her dreams. "Any of this ringing a bell for you?"

"Yeah, yeah." For now, he waved away her question and her reference. This wasn't about their case, but something far more personal. Something that caused him worry and concern on a regular basis. Why couldn't he have a normal mother who went off on tour buses with her friends and gambled twice a year in Vegas? "She's still not answering," he said in frustration.

It was Kendra's turn to be confused. *"She?"* She was only focused on one *she* right now. "The dead woman?"

"No," Matt bit off, exasperated not so much with her as with who he was trying to reach—and couldn't. "My mother." In an effort to make more sense, he back-tracked and said, "I keep leaving messages on her phone and she's not picking up or returning my calls."

That didn't sound all that unusual. After all, he and his mother had separate lives to live. "Maybe she went away for a while."

He shook his head. "Not without telling me."

She laughed softly, wondering if he knew what that sounded like. "You realize that you're making noises like a parent."

He couldn't remember a time when he wasn't the re-sponsible one, the one who watched out for his mother instead of the other way around.

"With her I always have been." He dragged his hand through his wayward dark hair and looked accusingly at the telephone handset again. "Other than one message on my voice mail in which she said all of two words, I haven't heard from her all week."

Kendra humored him and asked for more details. "And those two words were?"

"Thank you. She said, 'thank you.'" He said the words as if they held some hidden insult.

Kendra smiled and nodded knowingly. "Ah."

She had his attention immediately. "What do you mean, 'ah'? Was that some form of female-speak that I'm not getting?" he asked.

This was a side of the man she found amusing. And strangely endearing, although there was no way she would ever say that to him.

"In a way," she admitted, and then she decided to clue him in, at least in the way she interpreted it. "I think your mother was thanking you for taking her to the gathering at the chief's house last weekend."

"Okay." He continued looking at her, waiting for further enlightenment. He didn't see any reason for his mother to simply say that and nothing more. "Okay," he repeated, this time with a touch of frustration because Kendra was obviously seeing something that he didn't. "Fill in the blanks for me. What is it that I'm not getting?"

"That your mother probably hooked up with my father."

He could feel his protective side rising up. There was an edge to his voice as he asked, "*Hooked up* in the old sense or in the new sense?"

That was a subject she neither wanted to explore nor talk about at length.

"Either way, I think your mother's happy. And I caught my father humming the other day when I came down to the lab with our possible suspect's photo. My father doesn't hum," she told him, in case the significance of that escaped him. "At least, he hasn't since my mother died."

Matt was still stuck at the starting gate as the significance of what she was saying began to sink in. "Meaning your father and my mother—"

"Had a good time," Kendra said euphemistically. And then, because she wasn't really able to read her partner's expression, she continued in their individual parents' defense, "Hey, they're both consenting adults...." Not wanting to go into any sort of detail, Kendra deliberately let her voice trail off.

"My mother's been through the ringer emotionally," Matt protested. He definitely didn't want to see that happening to the woman again. Didn't want her taken advantage of again, even unintentionally.

Kendra did her best not to take offense and just focused on the fact that her partner was worried about his mother—not that Abilene was inadvertently insulting her father.

"And my dad's not the kind of guy to just have a fling without any thought to possible consequences—not like some people."

That brought the conversation to a skidding halt. Her partner's vivid green eyes narrowed as he looked at her. "Was that meant for me?"

Denial at this point would have been useless, so rather than retreat or pretend that he'd misunderstood her, she stuck by her words. "I don't see anyone else in this conversation."

And that was when the alarms went off in her head. What the hell was she doing? Since when did she behave like a "typical female," to use one of her brothers' labels, acting as if she wanted to know "where this relationship is going"? That wasn't her. At least, that wasn't her anymore, right? Because she didn't want a relationship, just something casual, nothing more, she silently insisted.

"Sorry, forget I said anything," she told Abilene with a dismissive wave of her hand. "I'm just punchy, that's all. The important thing is, don't worry about your mother. If my dad's spending time with her, then she is definitely in safe hands. He's the old-fashioned type—chivalrous to a fault," she added with emphasis, because Abilene still looked pretty unconvinced.

The phone rang on his desk just then, preventing her partner from responding to her assurances about her father and his mother.

"Abilene," he snapped impatiently into the handset.

Kendra watched him and decided that it wasn't his mother finally returning his calls. An alert expression had come into his eyes. This had to be about the case.

"We'll be right there," he promised, hanging up. Matt looked at her. "We've got a hit."

She was on her feet immediately, grabbing what she needed and shoving it into the pockets of her jacket. "He showed up at another branch of the bank? Is he still there?" she asked eagerly.

Matt shook his head. "The bank security guard saw the kid through the glass doors, apparently making a withdrawal. By the time he got outside, the kid had driven away."

Kendra blew out a breath. "Terrific," she bit off in frustration.

"Actually, yes."

"Go on," she prompted.

"The guard got a partial plate number," he explained as they hurried out of the squad room.

"You could have led with that," she told him in exasperation. "Well, every little bit helps." She tried not to allow herself to get too excited. This could lead to just another dead end—then again, maybe they had gotten a little closer to finding their perpetrator.

Instinctively, Matt knew that she'd want to take the stairs rather than wait for the elevator, so he headed in the opposite direction of the elevator banks, toward the door to the stairwell.

When he was directly behind her, Kendra smiled to herself. The man was learning.

"I'm sorry," the security guard, a retired former patrolman with the Aurora P.D., apologized for the third time in as many minutes. "I was on my break and coming in through the other entrance when I spotted the kid you're looking for. He was just finishing up and by the time I got over to that side of the building, he was driving away." The guard had already given them the paper with the partial license plate he'd managed to copy down. "It was one of those little cars, you know, looks like it belongs in a toy box."

"A smart car?" Abilene guessed. It was the smallest-looking vehicle that he knew of.

The man shook his head. "No, it's a mini-something-or-other."

"A Mini Cooper?" Kendra asked.

"Yeah, that's the one. Mini Cooper," he repeated, relieved to get that off his mind. "It was navy and white," he described.

Kendra nodded. Finally, they were getting some pieces to work with. "We're going to need to see the surveillance tape," she told him.

"Sure, I already told the assistant manager you'd be asking," he informed them, then added, "The bank

manager's out today," as he led them inside the bank
to speak to the woman.

They got luckier.

The teenager's car was parked directly behind him
as he'd made the withdrawal and the rest of his license
plate was visible after the in-house tech at the police
station worked her magic for them and removed the
glare from an adjacent window.

From there, the steps became easier.

"Hello, Scott Randall," Abilene declared as he pulled
up the Mini Cooper's registration. Armed with the teenager's name, they pulled up his driver's license.

Which was where it looked as if their streak of luck
ran dry.

The man whose name was on the registration for
the car looked like—and was, according to his date of
birth—a senior citizen.

"If that's a teenager, then I belong in nursery school,"
Kendra commented as she came around to her partner's side of the desk and looked over his shoulder at
the photo on the driver's license he'd pulled up on the
screen.

"Maybe it's the kid's father," Matt speculated.

"More like his grandfather, is my guess," she said,
shaking her head. "Either that or there are a hell of a lot
of people involved in this case." Going back to her side
of the desk, she sighed, took out her weapon and hol-
stered it. "It's all we've got. Let's go pay Mr. Randall a
visit and ask him if he knows who's been using his car."
She rolled her eyes, thinking of worst-case scenarios
as she walked out of the room. "And I swear, if he tells

us his car was stolen and he was just getting around to reporting it, I'm going to scream."

She probably would, too, Matt thought. "Just give me fair warning, that's all I ask," he said to his partner as they went toward the stairwell again.

The car in question was not parked in front of the house listed on the DMV registration.

Big surprise, Kendra thought, getting out of the Crown Victoria. She braced herself for the disclaimer she anticipated coming from the man they were about to question.

Matt pressed down hard on the doorbell. When the door opened a couple of minutes later, a rather befuddled, somewhat overweight man with flyaway white hair looked at them over the tops of his rimless glasses.

"Can I help you?" he asked, one hand still on the door. It was obvious he was prepared to swing it shut at a moment's notice.

"We certainly hope so, Mr. Randall," Kendra said in her most soothing voice. "Do you by any chance own a navy-and-white Mini Cooper, license plate number—"

The man held up his hand, stopping her before she could launch into the sequence of numbers. "Don't read the numbers to me. Waste of time," he informed her. "I can't picture them in my head. I've got to see the numbers written on a piece of paper or something."

Perfectly happy to play along, Kendra handed the man the paper and Scott Randall peered at it very carefully, blinking his eyes several times.

And then he raised his eyes to hers. "What about the car?" he asked cautiously.

"Then you *do* own it," Matt said, wanting to establish that fact first.

"And if I do?" Randall's small brown eyes went from Kendra to Matt like tennis balls moving in slow motion. "Who's asking?"

"Detectives Abilene and Cavanaugh," Kendra said, nodding toward her partner as she held up her identification for the man to see. Abilene took his out and did the same.

For form's sake, Randall studied one, then the other. And then sighed deeply. "What's he done now?"

"'He'?" Kendra echoed.

"Yeah. Scottie. My grandson." Each word sounded as if it weighed more than a ton on his tongue before he uttered it.

Kendra took out the photo she and Abilene had been showing around for the past few days.

"Is this your grandson?" she asked, mentally crossing her fingers. She held her breath, waiting for the man to answer.

He did reluctantly after a beat. "Yeah, that's Scottie."

"Does Scottie by any chance live with you?" Matt asked.

The old man laughed. "Does he live with me? Ever since he was three days old and his mother, my daughter, left him on my doorstep and took off." He shrugged haplessly. "Just as well. That girl could never take care of any living thing. All her pets always died. She kept forgetting to feed them," he confided. And then he grew very serious. "What's this all about?" Randall asked, growing somewhat distressed. "Scottie's a good boy," he assured them. "He just can't seem to get his act together."

Kendra felt sorry for the older Scott Randall, but there were rules about discussing ongoing investigations, namely: don't. So her hands were tied and she was forced to ignore his question.

"Where can we find Scottie right now?" she asked the old man.

He thought for a moment. "At Fashions for Less on Windom and Halladay. He's a stock boy there. It's not that he doesn't work hard," the man quickly added. "He just can't seem to hold on to anything. This is Scottie's fifth job since the beginning of the year," he confessed, embarrassed. And then he looked at them again. "Please, what's he done?"

Kendra threw him a crumb—it was the best she could do. "Hopefully something minor."

"Have him call me when you find him," Scottie's grandfather called after them as they walked away from the house.

Kendra raised her voice. "We'll do our best," she promised, fervently hoping she could keep her word. "Poor guy," she murmured under her breath as she and Abilene walked back to the unmarked vehicle they'd left parked at the curb.

Her partner paused and looked at her over the roof of the car. "You know, you act tough, but you're pretty softhearted," he noted.

She didn't want him extrapolating from there and going in directions she wasn't comfortable with.

"Depends on the situation," she said crisply. She got into the car on the driver's side. "I just felt sorry for the old man." In her opinion, it was hard not to. "He does a good deed, takes in his daughter's kid—a kid she thought nothing of abandoning," she added with a shake of her head. "And now his payback might be that he raised a killer." Although she still had a long way to go before she was convinced of that.

"Maybe not," Matt speculated. "Nothing about this case is cut-and-dried," he pointed out. "For all we know, this kid could be an innocent dupe in all this."

Now *that* surprised her. She spared him a glance at the next light just to be sure he hadn't morphed into someone else.

"Well, look at you, Mr. Optimist." She grinned. "Nice to know there's a streak of optimism buried in there somewhere."

He shrugged off her words and said flippantly, "I guess maybe you're contagious. I should have gotten my shots first before we got…'started,'" he finally concluded.

"Maybe you should have," she agreed.

And while they were at it, she added silently, she should have gotten hers—against him. Because God knew he was definitely getting to her. Here they were, on the cusp of possibly catching a break in the case, and all she could think of was being alone with Abilene tonight.

Something was definitely wrong with this picture. And she was really going to get hurt if she wasn't careful.

Chapter 15

"Murder? What murder? Whose murder?"

Scottie Randall croaked out the questions, his voice getting higher and reedier with each panicked syllable he uttered. His head looked as if it was on the verge of spinning around like some character in a grade B horror movie.

Kendra and Matt had found the nineteen-year-old exactly where the teen's grandfather had said he would be, working in the back room of Fashions for Less, stocking the shelves. They took Scottie back to the precinct with them for questioning and at the time, he seemed happy enough to get away from the airless stockroom and go with them.

But once the tone changed and the questions began coming, his affable smile melted into confusion and then shock.

"I didn't kill nobody," he protested again, genuinely frightened. His eyes were pleading. "You gotta believe me."

Any second now, their suspect was going to get hysterical on them, Matt thought. Time to change tactics. He spoke to the teen slowly, calmly, doing what he could to soothe him and distance Scottie from any possible breakdown. A breakdown wouldn't help them or answer any questions that needed answering.

"We'd really like to believe you, Scottie, but that account you've been taking money out of, that's not your account."

He shook his head and for just a second, it occurred to Kendra that she was looking at someone incapable of lying to save his life. "No, it's not."

"It belongs to someone who's currently missing," Kendra told him. She'd come up on his other side so that between them, she and Matt had become the teen's human bookends.

"He's not missing, he's right there," Scottie cried, his head swiveling to look from one detective to the other and then back again. "In his apartment." He ran his hand along the back of his neck. "Jeez, he said there wouldn't be any trouble."

"Hold it," Matt held up his hand. "In his *apartment*? You took the money back to his apartment? What's the address?" he asked.

Scottie rattled off the address of the building where Summer's body had been discovered. Ryan Burnett's apartment building.

The superintendent had been instructed to call them, night or day, if the man returned. So far, that call hadn't come in.

"And you didn't think it was odd that Burnett was sending you to withdraw money for him?" Kendra asked the teenager.

The thin shoulders rose and fell haplessly. "He said he was real busy and that if I got the money out for him, he'd give me a—a—he called it a service charge," Scottie remembered, brightening as he repeated the phrase.

Like a frantic puppy, eager to please his master and not quite sure who that master was, he looked from Kendra to Matt and then back again. "And he was alive when he took the money from me," he said adamantly.

"And when was that?" Matt asked.

"Today," Scottie cried. "Right after I took out more money for him." He lowered his voice, as if to share a confidence. "I said it would go faster if he just went in and took the money out himself, but he said this was just fine for him." He shrugged. "I guess he knows what he's doing."

"And this is the address you went to?" Kendra turned the paper she'd written the address on around so that Scottie could see it.

He gazed at it intently, then looked up at her. "Yeah."

"You're sure?" Matt pressed, his eyes pinning the teen down.

"Yeah." This time there was less confidence in his voice. He was growing nervous again. "Why?"

Instead of answering, Kendra took out the folded photograph of Burnett that she had in her pocket. "And this is the man you gave the money to?"

He stared at the photograph as if he was waiting for it to do something. But it didn't. Finally, he looked up. "No, that's not Ryan Burnett," he told her.

"What apartment number did you go to?" Kendra asked.

"Better yet," Matt interjected, "why don't you just take us there?"

Scottie shook his head. "I can't."

Uh-oh, here it comes, Kendra thought. Maybe he was a far better liar than she'd thought and this innocent, wide-eyed thing was just an act. "And why is that?" she asked.

"You left my car in the parking lot," Scottie whined.

Kendra exchanged looks with Matt. It was obvious her partner was thinking the same thing she was. That this particular teen was not the brightest bulb in the ceiling fixture.

"We'll drive," Kendra told him, gently placing her hand against the back of his shoulder and giving him a slight push toward the door. "You just lead us to the apartment."

The teen was agreeable to that. "Okay, but then can you take me back to work? This is my first week and I don't want them to fire me yet."

Yet.

The last word amused Matt. The teen obviously had a game plan that involved not working too hard. With that kind of attitude, Scottie was a perfect candidate for someone with a devious mind-set to use as his lackey and errand boy.

The question was, exactly *who* was pulling these strings?

"We'll have a patrolman bring you back after you take us to the apartment where you last saw Ryan Burnett," Kendra promised.

Though he continued to look a little uneasy, Scottie's panicky expression had disappeared. It was obvious that he took them at their word. Considering the kind of people she was accustomed to dealing with, Kendra decided that Scottie Randall was an exceedingly trusting soul—which, again, made her think of him as ripe for the picking for anyone who wanted to operate from behind the scenes.

Maybe they were finally on the right path to wrapping this up. God, she hoped so.

When they arrived at the apartment building where Summer Miller's body was first discovered, Scottie took them up to the third floor. Ryan Burnett's floor. But when she and Matt turned to go to the left, Scottie remained standing where he was and looked at them with curiosity.

"It's over this way," he told them, indicating an apartment down the hall on the opposite end of the hallway.

Definitely not Burnett's apartment, Matt thought. The last time they were here, canvassing the floor, this was the young, friendly actor's apartment.

Were the twists and turns in the case *ever* going to lead them to a conclusion?

Scottie rang the doorbell at the apartment in question. The noise coming from inside the apartment was rather loud and had most likely drowned out the sound of the doorbell.

"We'll take it from here," Matt told him.

Moving the teenager aside, Matt fisted his hand and pounded against the door. When there was no response, he pounded even louder.

"I can get the super," Kendra offered, raising her voice to be heard above the blaring music inside.

Who listened to that kind of stuff without going deaf? she couldn't help wondering.

"Might not be a bad idea," Matt agreed, raising his voice as well.

"Can I go back to work now?" Scottie asked them hopefully.

Kendra nodded at the patrolman who'd arrived at the scene. "Take him where he needs to go. And Scottie," she added as a footnote, as she turned to look at him, "don't leave town."

Scottie bobbed his head up and down vigorously and seemed rather excited about the standard warning she'd issued.

"Cool," he pronounced, then turned to go with the patrolman.

"Cool," she repeated under her breath. Kendra shook her head. It took all kinds.

In the interim, Matt had given pounding his fist against the door one more try. This time, he was successful and it opened.

A man somewhere in his mid-thirties or so who appeared to be feeling very little pain stood in the doorway, using the doorknob to help him maintain his vertical position. He squinted at them—predominantly at Kendra.

"You the entertainment?" he asked. It was obvious that the idea pleased him.

"Detectives Cavanaugh and Abilene," Kendra informed him, holding up her badge as Matt held up his.

The man grinned. "Yup, you're the entertainment,"

he declared, weaving just a little as he backed up and held the door all the way open for them. He leered at her in anticipation as she passed him. "Guess it's going to take you a while to get out of all those clothes, isn't it?"

"Longer than you could possibly imagine," she answered crisply.

"Hey, Tyler, who hired your strippers?" their doorman asked, tossing the remark back over his shoulder into the general throng.

"What?" Tyler Blake worked his way to the front door. Kendra noted that the genial smile on his lips faded just for a moment before he brightened and said, "Detectives, have you come to do me the honor of staying for my bachelor party? I'm getting married Saturday," he told them, repeating a fact that he had already mentioned in the last interview he'd had with them. "You're welcome to come to the ceremony, but right now, I've got to get back to the party. My best man went through a lot of trouble throwing this together at the last minute and it wouldn't be polite not to enjoy myself."

Matt placed a hand on the actor's shoulder, stopping him in his tracks as the latter began to retreat.

"We'll write him a formal apology," he promised. "Right now, my partner and I have a few more questions for you."

Tyler turned around slowly and looked at Matt. "It can't wait?"

"It can't wait," Kendra assured him firmly. "You need to come down to the station with us."

With a resigned sigh, he said, "All right." Tyler latched onto another man who appeared more intoxicated than the one who had opened the door. "Jeffrey,

I've got to go talk to these people. Don't let the party die down."

"No chance, Ty-man," his friend promised with a wide, silly grin.

As they left, Kendra could foresee the neighbors calling the police about the noise shortly—if they hadn't done so already.

"What is this about?" Tyler asked once they were at the precinct and he was seated in one of the interrogation rooms.

During the entire short ride to the station, the out-of-work actor had said nothing, as if gathering his thoughts together and deciding how he wanted to play the scene. When he finally opened his mouth, he sounded unbelievably calm in Matt's opinion.

"I think you already know the answer to that," Matt said quietly, his eyes riveted to Tyler's very blue orbs— contacts?

Matt gave the impression of looking into the other man's mind and after a few moments, it seemed to work because Tyler's carefully reserved facade abruptly began to crack.

Tyler did not appear to be able to sustain the performance he had wanted to render.

"Just for the record, why don't you tell me?" he finally said.

"Okay, 'just for the record,'" Matt obliged him. "Why do you have Ryan Burnett's ATM card and password and why are you emptying out his bank account?"

Tyler sat up straight, indignation suddenly emerging from every pore. "Who told you that?" the man demanded angrily.

"Scottie Randall," Matt said matter-of-factly. Then, for leverage, he added, "We caught him on the bank surveillance tape making the withdrawals. He said you gave him the card and he seems to think that you're Ryan Burnett."

Unprepared to have it all unravel right in front of him so quickly and without a prepared script at the ready, Tyler panicked.

"He's lying!"

Kendra shook her head. "Scottie's not clever enough to make up a lie. His brain works on a much less complicated level than yours," she told him. "Now, why don't you save us all some time and just tell us the truth? Where is Burnett?"

Stalling, Tyler looked from her to Abilene, then finally said, "Ryan's in Costa Rica. I'm supposed to wire him the money as soon as I get it. I forgot because of the party, but I'm going to do it tomorrow morning. I swear it."

"You know what I think?" Matt said, shifting so that he was directly in the man's line of vision despite Tyler's attempts to turn away from him. "I think you're lying, Tyler."

"No, I'm not," the other man insisted fiercely. "Ryan asked me to do this for him and then he just took off."

Matt leaned in closer, eyeing him. "The police department was pretty good about installing a first-class air-conditioning system at the precinct for days just like today. It would take about three hours to defrost a bag of frozen peas—but you're sweating," he pointed out. "Why is that?"

"My body rhythm's out of sync," Tyler answered, a note of mounting desperation entering his voice. "I've always been like that. Drives my fiancée crazy."

"That happens when a person's nervous," Kendra said, joining in on the psychological attack. "Especially when they're lying."

Tyler's voice rose half an octave as he insisted again, "I'm not lying."

"Aren't you?" Kendra probed, maintaining eye contact just as Matt had. "If I call all the airlines, I'm going to find out that Ryan never booked a flight to Costa Rica, aren't I?"

"Private plane," Tyler blurted out. "Ryan was on a private plane. It belongs to a friend of his. I don't know the name."

"Not necessary," Kendra told him. "But just so you know, there would be a flight plan filed with the control tower," she said mildly.

"Easy enough to find out," Matt agreed.

It was all blowing up in front of him. A drained Tyler dragged both hands through his hair, looking as if his head had suddenly become too heavy for him to hold up any longer.

His breathing grew heavier, more labored. And then he cried out, "Dammit!"

"Yes?" Kendra moved her chair in closer. "Are you asking to revise your story?"

"It wasn't supposed to get out of hand like this. It was supposed to be so simple." He looked now like a frightened man who was watching his future, his entire life slip through his fingers. "If she'd just married me a little sooner, none of this would have happened. It wouldn't have been necessary. But she said she wanted to be 'sure.' I didn't have time to wait for 'sure.' I needed to get the money *now*."

"Necessary?" Kendra repeated in disbelief as she stared at the man. Was he serious? "Since when is murder necessary?"

"Since it had to look as if Ryan killed his girlfriend and then, overwhelmed and afraid of the consequences of what he did, fled the country."

Matt closed in on the man. "Burnett didn't kill her, did he?" When Tyler didn't answer, he repeated more sternly, "Did he?"

Tyler stared down at his fingertips. "No," he said in a quiet whisper.

"But Burnett is dead, isn't he?" Matt pressed. Tyler continued to avoid looking at either one of them and just stared vacantly at the top of the table before him. "Isn't he?" Matt repeated, raising his voice harshly. He was losing patience.

Suddenly, the actor's head jerked up, a naked, desperate look in his eyes.

"I didn't *want* to kill him. You've got to believe me," he cried. "But I had to. They were going to kill me if I didn't come up with the money and Burnett was the only one I knew—besides my fiancée—who had any real money in the bank."

"Back up," Kendra interrupted. "*Who* was going to kill you and *what* money?" she asked Tyler.

The sigh came out more like a shudder. The actor's

shoulders seemed to cave in on him. He looked every bit the broken man.

"The money I owed this loan shark. He called himself a 'money facilitator,' but he's a freakin' loan shark, all right." Misery filled his eyes as they began to tear up. "I never gambled before. Suddenly, I couldn't stop. It was like this rush, this high. At first, I couldn't lose—and then, I couldn't win."

The story was so stereotypical, Kendra found it hard to listen. How could people just throw their lives away like that?

"It's all I thought about," Tyler was saying, wringing his hands now. "I didn't want to eat, I didn't want to act. I just wanted to *win*."

"But you just kept losing," Matt guessed. The gambling bug had bitten him once or twice while he and his mother had lived in Vegas, but he knew enough to steer clear and not start what he might not be able to finish.

"Yeah," Tyler said wistfully. "That winning hand, the one that was going to turn everything around for me, that was out there, just out of reach and no matter how much I tried, I just couldn't wrap my hands around it." He looked up at Matt. "I bet everything I had—and everything I didn't have—until I was in just too deep to get out."

"Why didn't you just try to borrow the money through regular channels?" Matt asked.

Tyler laughed. "If you were a bank, would you lend me money? Besides, it was too big a sum to even apply for. I owed almost half a million dollars. I couldn't ask anyone for that kind of money."

"So you killed him for it instead?" Kendra asked incredulously.

Tyler didn't answer. It was as if he just couldn't bring himself to form the words.

"Where's the body now?" Matt asked.

"At a construction site. That big mall where the physical fitness chain is going to be building their latest franchise. I buried him there." An extremely sad, ironic smile played on his lips. "He was always into physical fitness. I thought it would be a good final resting place for him. They're going to be pouring cement tomorrow morning."

"No, they're not. Their work plans just got delayed," Kendra said, picking up the telephone handset. She intended to call the chief of Ds. If anyone could get a temporary stop-work order issued, it was the chief.

"Look, I get why you might have killed Ryan. You were desperate and he looked like your only way out," Matt said, trying to get answers while the actor was still volunteering them. "But why kill his girlfriend? Was she there in the apartment at the time? Did she walk in on you when you were killing Burnett?"

He shook his head. "No, she came in later, looking for him. I had to make it look as if he had a reason to just disappear. I wanted to make it look logical. If he killed Summer, he wasn't going to hang around until someone put two and two together."

Matt shook his head. It took all kinds to make a world, but it still never ceased to amaze him how very different people could be.

"Maybe you should have followed that advice yourself," Matt suggested as he took out his handcuffs.

"Stand up." When the actor did, Matt cuffed him. "Tyler Blake, you're under arrest for the murders of Summer Miller and Ryan Burnett..." he began, reading the out-of-work and definitely out-of-luck actor his rights.

Glancing over, he saw Kendra hanging up the phone. "The chief's going to get the construction company to back off until we can locate Ryan Burnett's body." She looked at Tyler. "Any helpful hints to follow?"

The actor appeared to be slipping into a world of his own. Before he made the transition, he said, "Look for suitcases."

Terrific, Kendra thought grimly. *The body was in pieces.*

Chapter 16

"God, this is one day I just want to put behind me," Kendra said late the next day.

Not only was she struggling to get her exhaustion under control, but her sense of revulsion as well. That morning, armed with a temporary stop-work order and with the help of two cadaver dogs, Kendra, Matt and two other detectives working with them, plus several patrolmen recruited to do the initial digging, were able to go over the grounds and locate the suitcases. In all there were four—four suitcases each stuffed with some part of Ryan Burnett's decomposing body.

All four suitcases were photographed in the exact place where they were found, carefully documented, and then sent over to the medical examiner. The body of the missing accountant then became one giant jigsaw puzzle until it could be verified that they did indeed find all of him.

They had.

The horrible stench, when she and Matt had witnessed the opening of the first suitcase, was still with her, despite the fact that the last of the suitcases had been opened over five hours ago.

"I don't think I'm ever going to be rid of that smell," she told Matt wearily. It seemed to hover around her no matter which way she turned.

Matt wasn't experiencing the same reaction, but he could understand hers. "Right now, it's just all in your head," he assured her.

"It feels more like it's all in my nostrils," she complained.

Matt smiled at her across the desks. "That's because you have a vivid imagination. It'll pass," he promised her with a certainty that was meant to comfort her. "In the meantime, I'll see if I can find some vanilla candles for you when we leave here. What?" he asked, when he saw the bemused expression on her face.

Kendra shook her head. "I just can't picture you picking up scented candles, that's all." He'd struck her as way too macho to even *know* that vanilla-scented candles existed.

"Is that your way of saying you think I'm insensitive?" His voice gave nothing away. She had no idea if she'd insulted him or he was just baiting her.

Kendra winged it. "No, that's my way of saying I can't picture you doing typical 'girlie' things. Hell, I don't do typical 'girlie' things," she admitted. She'd never even lit one scented candle in her life, thinking of it more in terms of a fire hazard than something needed to create a romantic mood.

"Then maybe you need lessons," Matt teased. And then he shrugged. "It was just something I read in a magazine article while trapped in a dental office, waiting for a root canal." Stretching, Matt pushed back from his desk. "You ready to call it a night?"

Oh, so ready, she thought. Instead of answering his question directly, Kendra pretended to take him literally and announced, "Night," then rose to her feet.

"I guess you are," he murmured under his breath. Pushing his chair in against his desk, Matt was all set to walk out of the squad room when his cell phone began to ring. With a sigh, he looked down at it to check the caller ID.

Kendra saw his eyebrows rise in a silent question, as if he was surprised to be on the receiving end of a call from whoever was on the other end.

"Who is it?" she asked.

He looked at her as he opened the phone and raised it to his ear. His expression told her that he had no idea what this was about. "Your father."

"We didn't find Burnett?"

It was the first thing that occurred to her. She couldn't think of another reason why her father would call Abilene—but then, he knew she was acting as primary on the case. Why wasn't her father calling her if there was some news? It didn't make any sense.

Listening closely to the limited exchange between Matt and her father gave her no further clues.

"Yes, sir," Matt said, ending the call. He closed his phone and slipped it back onto his belt. Seeing the unanswered question in her eyes, he said, "He wants to see us."

But the case was all but wrapped up, wasn't it? Why the eleventh-hour call?

"What's wrong? Wasn't that Burnett in the suitcases?" she asked as they headed out toward the bank of elevators.

Matt shook his head. "He didn't say. Just that he wanted to see us. We'll find out soon enough."

She sighed as she pressed the Down button beside the elevator. Within less than a minute, the elevator doors were opening on their floor, ready to take them to the basement and the CSI lab.

She got on and pressed B. "I don't think I can stand one more twist in this case, at least not tonight. I don't remember when I've felt so drained." Did that sound as whiny to him as it did to her?

The half smile that curved Matt's sensual mouth told her that he could remember a time.

She knew immediately what he was thinking of. "Not a word," she warned.

She didn't trust the utterly innocent look on his face one bit.

Getting off the elevator, she marched ahead of him to the lab.

"Well, we're here," Kendra announced to her father as she pushed the door open. From the looks of it, the day shift had all left and the night shift hadn't arrived to take their place. Either that, or they were all out on a call. In any case, that didn't concern her. Her father's summons, however, did. "Okay, tell me. What's wrong?" she asked.

Her question took Sean by surprise. "Since when have you become such a pessimist?"

That was easy. Kendra could document the exact time and place for this last wave of uncharacteristic dark outlook on her part.

"Since a seemingly perfectly affable man took it upon himself to hack his trusting neighbor into four pieces in order to keep a loan shark from possibly doing the same to him."

"If you put it that way, it's understandable, I suppose. I'm just not used to your being so bleak in your outlook." Sean moved aside what he was working on and came around the steel table to join the pair he had sent for. "But this isn't about the case," he told her.

It was her turn to be caught by surprise. "Then what is it about?" Kendra asked uncertainly.

Rather than answer her, Sean Cavanaugh directed his words to her partner. "I thought that you should be the first to know—" And then he stopped. For the first time in a long time, he felt somewhat uncomfortable. Shaking his head, Kendra's father laughed to himself. "I'm really out of practice here," he confessed almost sheepishly to them.

Though Matt looked puzzled, it took Kendra less than a second to put all it together. Ordinarily, her father was quiet confidence personified. She could only think of one thing that would strip him of that confidence.

She stared at her father, stunned. "Are you trying to ask Abilene's permission to date his mother?"

"No," Sean answered honestly, then explained, "We're already doing that." Taking a deep breath, he started again. "I just wanted you to know that it's becoming serious."

"How serious?" Matt asked. There was no indication in his low, monotone voice how he felt about the matter.

Sean's eyes looked directly into Matt's. "Serious," he repeated, as if the word was enough to convey it all. And then he ratcheted it up several notches. "If it continues this way, I'm thinking of asking your mother to marry me."

Kendra's mouth dropped open. For a moment, she didn't know whether to congratulate her father or hint that he was out of his mind. Wasn't this going too fast?

"You're kidding."

"No, I'm not," he assured her solemnly.

She knew he had as much of a right to happiness as anyone. More. But he was a novice here, as far as she was concerned. "Don't you think you're rushing things a little?"

Her choice of words made her father laugh softly. "At your age, I'd be rushing it. At mine, *time* is what's rushing. I don't have as much of it left as I once did. And as you do," he told them, looking from his daughter to Sabrina's son. "I just wanted to make sure that you didn't have any major objections," he told Matt.

"And if I did?" Matt asked.

Sean gave him an honest answer. "I'd hear you out and then we'd discuss them."

At least the man wasn't trying to snow him—and he wasn't backing off, either. Apparently, his partner's father had the courage of his convictions. He liked that.

"Can't ask for anything more than that," he told Sean with an understanding smile. "I just want my mother to be happy."

Then they were on the same page, Sean thought, relieved to have this over with.

"So do I, Matt. So do I. Well, that's all I had to say," Sean told them, rounding the table again to his original side. He began locking down his station. "I didn't mean to keep you," he apologized. Sean glanced at his watch. "Hey, I've got to get going myself. I told your mother I'd meet her for dinner tonight at that little Italian restaurant she likes." Sean smiled broadly at them as he shed his lab coat and hung it up on the back of the door. "See you both at the next family gathering."

Kendra suddenly came to. "And you don't have anything new to tell us about the man subdivided in the suitcases?" she called after her father as he started to walk out.

"Only that it's the man you were looking for," he said just before the door closed in his wake.

Her father was serious about Abilene's mother. The words swirled about her head like a news headline.

She was vaguely aware that her partner was wordlessly ushering her out of the lab.

Was this relationship between their parents going to change things between them? she wondered. Matt seemed to like her father, but there was a world of difference between liking the head of the day shift CSI unit and liking the man who was dating his mother.

It occurred to her—not for the first time—that she didn't want things to change between them. Not for any reason. She didn't want this interlude they found themselves in to end, even though she'd been preparing herself for just that eventuality since the moment it had begun. Status quo had suddenly become very important to her.

The silence between them was deafening. They'd been driving in it for the past five minutes. Finally, she couldn't stand it any longer. "Are you angry?"

Matt continued watching the road. "No, why would you think that?"

Wasn't it obvious? "Well, you're not saying anything."

Her logic escaped him. "That doesn't automatically mean I'm angry."

She was willing to accept that, as long as he explained the silence. Why wasn't he talking to her? "Okay, then what are you?"

"Thinking," he answered.

About the case? About their parents? He had to give her more of a hint than that. "About?" she asked impatiently.

She was definitely not prepared for what Matt said next. "Us."

"Us?" she echoed. Was she right? Was he looking for a way to end this? Her mouth felt sandpaper-dry as she asked, "What about 'us'?"

"What your father said back there started me thinking," he began, then glanced at her. "I realized that I still don't know where 'this' is going," he confessed, referring to what was happening between them, "but I'm beginning to think I know where I want it to go."

Why did that spark such a sense of panic within her? Panic no matter how this played itself out. If Matt told her he wanted to take their relationship to the next level, she was terrified of being disappointed in the end, the way that Jason had disappointed her. But if Matt told her he wanted his space, then the disappointment she lived in fear of would be right there.

There was no winning in this.

"Oh?" Kendra did her best to sound cavalier. "Care to share?"

This time the look Matt spared her was longer. And penetrating. "Do I have to?"

She took his words at face value. "Well, it'd be nice to know what you have in mind."

Matt shook his head as he turned left at the light. She didn't understand. "No, I meant I don't think I have to say it out loud—because I think that you already know where I want this to go."

It didn't change a thing. Either way made her nervous. She didn't want to pin down what was going on between them, didn't want to give it a name—because things with names tended to disappoint you in the long run. And she'd already had her heart ripped out once.

"Let's just table this for now, okay? Please?" she asked.

He *knew* she was going to say that. It still didn't make it any easier for him to hear. He kept his disappointment to himself. "You don't have to run from this, you know."

Oh, yes, I do. Because you're only going to hurt me. Big-time. She'd never thought she'd ever fall in love again, but she had. It had snuck up on her and knocked her knees out from under her.

Because she loved him, because she didn't want either of them to be hurt, she did her best to try to make him understand. "Look, I've already been there once, had it blow up in my face once—"

She'd given him the opening he wanted and he seized it. "Right. *Once,*" he emphasized, interrupting her. "When you were engaged to Jason. But newsflash, Cavanaugh," he said, deliberately using her last name, reminding her of how things did change in life, "I'm not Jason. I don't have a hero complex with unrealistic expectations for myself. And I don't have any unrealistic expectations for you, either."

"Nice to know." There was a tinge of sarcasm surrounding her words.

Matt continued as if he hadn't heard her or picked up on her tone. What he had to tell her was too important to get sidetracked by minor details and wounded pride.

"Hell, you've already exceeded any expectations I might have had beyond my wildest dreams," he said with finality. "All I have to do is look at you and I find myself wanting you more than I even want to breathe."

"*Really* nice to know," she said, amending her original response and definitely eliminating the sarcastic tone that had come with it.

"My point was," Matt went on, "that I don't know where this is going, but I want to give it every chance to get to the right destination." They were at a red light and he looked at her intently. "I want to go the distance with you."

"I thought we already were."

She was being flippant. It was, he'd come to understand, one of her defense mechanisms.

"Not that distance," he laughed, and then he grew serious again. "The *big* distance—the kind of distance that your mother and father went. The kind," he said with feeling, "that your father is proposing to go with my mother."

Her mouth was now drier than dry. She was surprised she wasn't croaking as she asked, "Are you asking me to marry you?"

"Not yet," he told her honestly. "But there is a distinct possibility that we will be having that conversation in the not-too-distant future." Then, before she could protest, he assured her, "I know what you went through and I don't want to rush you. And I know how I felt about the thought of marriage—until I started dealing with you. Things change, and they don't always have to change for the worse." He waited for her to stay something. When she didn't, he prodded, "Well?"

"Drive faster," she said.

"What?"

"Drive faster," Kendra repeated firmly. "I want to carry on this conversation at my place, preferably without so many clothes in the way," she said, ending her statement with a wicked wink that had his stomach tightening, then flipping over.

"Kendra, I'm serious."

Yes, he was, Kendra thought. It was the first time she'd heard him say her name. "I know," she told him, her tone utterly subdued as she looked at him. Her smile was warm—and full of promise. "So am I."

Matt stepped on the gas and sped up.

Epilogue

The moment Kendra slammed shut the front door of her apartment, the blizzard of clothing began, falling on the floor, marking their path.

By the time Matt and she had gone the short distance from her door to her bed, there no longer remained anything between them except the very intense desire to share all the heated pleasures they had come to discover in each other's arms.

In the relatively short time they had been together, Kendra had learned an infinite number of ways to make love, to give, sustain and get the maximum thrill from intimate rituals and she was incredibly eager to revisit each and every method, each and every movement.

Her heart was pounding wildly as she found herself on the receiving end even as she made plans to reverse the tables on him.

The first spectacular climax occurred within less

than five minutes of her unlocking her front door. More followed, but by then she could no longer gauge time and space, only heat and exhilarating bursts of pulsating pleasure.

Exhaustion never felt so wonderful.

"No fair, no fair," she gasped in protest, "you're ahead."

"I'll let you catch up," Matt promised, murmuring the words against the sensitive skin along her throat. "I just wanted to prove to you that I'm serious."

"So am I," she breathed.

A salvo of energy infused her. In a moment she was switching positions with him and climbing on top, doing her best to at least partially drive him as crazy as he had already driven her.

And then, into this mutually acceptable madness, a jarring noise began to invade. It continued, taking on shape until she recognized it for what it was.

Ringing.

"Dammit, it's my cell phone," she cried in frustrated annoyance, not wanting to surrender a moment of what was happening. "I should have dropped it in a glass of water when we came in."

"You'd better take it," Matt recommended. His words would have had more conviction had he not been pressing his lips and other parts of his body against receptive parts of hers.

Delicious waves of heat and passion were licking at her as Kendra struggled to clear her head and reached for the phone she'd flung somewhere on the nightstand.

"Cavanaugh," she declared into the phone. It took more than a little effort and she struggled to try to keep that shred of her brain that was still functioning receptive. And then her eyes flew open. "Say again?" The next moment, she sighed. Resigned. "Damn. Okay, keep me posted if there's any more news. Thanks. I appreciate it."

Closing her phone, she let it slip from her fingers, already forgotten.

But she'd piqued Matt's curiosity. "What was that about?" he asked, even as he trailed his lips along her naked shoulder.

Another, more heartfelt sigh preceded her answer. "The actor escaped."

He raised his head to look at her. "What?"

She filled him in as best she could, given that her body was once again tingling in high anticipation of the magic she knew was to come.

"Wong just called. Somehow, Blake got his hands on a guard's uniform and walked right out of jail. Nobody knows where he is."

He asked because he knew procedure, not because he wanted to. "They want us to go after him?"

There they had lucked out. For now. "Wong and Ruiz already said they were on it, but they don't hold out much hope." She had to admit, though, if only to herself, that there was a part of her that felt they had not heard the last of Tyler Blake.

But, right now, none of that mattered. The only thing that did matter was the way that Matt made her feel: incredibly alive and hopeful.

"Then we can go back to what we were doing," he concluded, never really having stopped.

Every part of her smiled in response. "Absolutely."

"Good," he said, both to the situation and recalling the nickname he'd teasingly given her the first day they'd met.

In either case, it was the last thing either one of them said for the rest of a very long, inspired and delicious evening.

* * * * *

Lily pulled violently away. "You don't get it, do you? I trusted you and this is what happens. You accuse my father of murder."

She lurched to her feet and opened the door.

"Where are you going?"

"I want you to leave." She darted around him, then pushed him, managing to shove him back several steps.

"Lily, please. Listen to me—" She ran out the door with John close behind her.

I know you love me, he thought, just as a heavy weight slammed against the backs of John's knees. They buckled. He landed on the ground with a muffled curse, catching himself with his hands. A series of punches caught him in the face. His lip split open. With a guttural yell, he heaved off his attacker and sent him flying several feet away. His thoughts went to Lily. Were there more? Did they have her?

Dear Reader,

My second Mills & Boon® Intrigue is centered around one tragic night that changes the lives of my hero and heroine—but not forever. One family suffers a horrible loss, a young girl's budding love is shattered and a young man's hopes are dashed, yet in the end things are made right. Not because of a miracle, but because two people are willing to face their fears, seek the truth and trust in each other.

In real life, tragedy doesn't always give way to happier times. Those who hurt others aren't always caught. Those who suffer aren't always made whole again. Yet even in a world filled with fear and darkness, one truth shines bright—love is powerful. It heals but it also gives strength. It's what enables humanity to press on despite the challenges we face and, with hope in our hearts, to believe that something better waits for us.

I hope you enjoy Lily and John's story and that it empowers you to keep moving toward your own Happily Ever After, whatever that may be.

Wishing you much love and happiness,

Virna DePaul

IT STARTED
THAT NIGHT

BY
VIRNA DePAUL

First published in Great Britain 2012
by Mills & Boon, an imprint of Harlequin (UK) Limited,
Eton House, 18-24 Paradise Road, Richmond, Surrey TW9 1SR

© Virna DePaul 2012

ISBN: 978 0 263 89567 4
ebook ISBN: 978 1 408 97748 4

46-1012

Harlequin (UK) policy is to use papers that are natural, renewable and recyclable products and made from wood grown in sustainable forests. The logging and manufacturing processes conform to the legal environmental regulations of the country of origin.

Printed and bound in Spain
by Blackprint CPI, Barcelona

Virna DePaul was an English major in college and, despite a passion for Shakespeare, Broadway musicals and romance novels, somehow ended up with a law degree. For ten years, she was a criminal prosecutor for the state of California. Now she's thrilled to be writing stories about complex individuals (fully human or not) who are willing to overcome incredible odds for love.

Since I began this story it has undergone numerous changes. To everyone who helped it come to fruition, thank you!

Hugs to Holly and Matrice for all your support!
And as always, love to my boys,
who are my brightest light.

Prologue

August 28
8:45 p.m.
Sacramento, CA

John Tyler sat in front of his house as the sounds of the party inside drifted toward him. He closed his eyes, trying to find comfort in the darkness. Instead, he felt trapped, unable to forget Tina Cantrell's parting words.

"Lily's a good girl. Too good for you. If you care about her at all, send her home and stay the hell away from her."

John opened his eyes and faced the truth.

Lily's mother was right.

Sixteen to his twenty, Lily had her whole life ahead of her and their friendship had already caused a rift between her and her parents, one that had only widened once her father had left. John didn't want to be the cause of further sorrow for her. Despite how he felt about her—despite the fact he wanted more and so did she—it couldn't happen. His leaving town tomorrow would be a fresh start for both of them. He didn't even know what he was going to do for money, but he had a friend in Seattle he could crash with for—

He heard footsteps. For a moment, he wondered if Lily's mom had returned, but then *she* came into view.

Lily. Sweet Lily, his sister Carmen's best friend. Even though he'd been forewarned, the shock of seeing her here, now, almost brought him to his knees.

The house lights cast her in a dim, almost surreal glow. His eyes immediately took in her loose hair, and the simple black dress that cinched her unbelievably tiny waist and revealed her pale arms and legs. She'd rimmed her eyes in black makeup that made their faintly exotic tilt even more mysterious. Her mouth was tinted red.

Lord, she was beautiful. He'd known she had a crush on him, but neither one of them had ever acknowledged it. He'd wanted to. Sometimes he'd felt desperate to take her love and give her his in return. But thankfully he'd never done so. She was still innocent, unsullied by his choices and reputation.

He jerked his chin at her and clenched his fists. "A little late for you to be out, isn't it? Carmen's not—"

Lily ran toward him and threw her arms around his neck. Automatically, he wrapped his arms around her to steady them both.

"I'm not here for Carmen." Her body trembled and he realized she was crying. He frowned when he thought he smelled alcohol on her. Frowned harder when he saw what appeared to be red marks and scratches on her neck and a purple mark on her pale cheek. Raising his hand, he touched it gently.

"What's this?"

She lifted her chin but didn't answer. Leaning down to examine her eyes, he softly inhaled; the scent of alcohol faded, replaced by the fruity scent of her shampoo. But her pupils were dilated, indicating she was under the influence of something. Then again, she was also upset, which could explain—

"I have to tell you before you leave," she whispered. "I love you."

John dropped his hands and straightened. Panic and temptation warred within him. Knowing he needed to make her leave for both their sakes, he patted her shoulder. "I love you, too, small fry. You know that. You're family."

She frowned, clinging to him when he tried to pull away. "I don't need more family. I can't handle the one I have."

"Lily—"

Moving quickly, she placed her hand on the back of his head and pulled his lips down to hers.

Her body, so small and fragile, pressed against him.

Her lips clung to his, soft and sweet.

And for one second—just one—his lips responded.

He jerked away and staggered back. She'd already lost her father to another woman. He couldn't risk alienating her from her mother, too. "Go home, Lily."

The confusion on her face was unmistakable.

"I—I love you—"

"What's this about, Lily?" He pretended to search the darkness. "Did you and your parents plan this?"

If she'd looked confused before, now she looked stunned. "What?"

"Your father the cop. Are you trying to set me up? He didn't get me on drug charges, so why not try for statutory rape?"

She just stared at him.

He grabbed her arms. "Are you?"

She pushed futilely against his hold. "N-no," she said. "I'm alone. I just needed you to know how I feel."

"Well now I know. And you know what? It doesn't mean a damn thing."

She swallowed audibly. "I—I don't believe you," she whispered, tilting up her chin. Looking like she was getting ready to fight him until he admitted he was lying.

Damn, she was amazing.

Desperately, he said, "That's because you're a kid."

She paled. "Kid?" she whispered and backed up.

"Yeah. A kid."

Hurt spread across her features and his stomach clenched. He forced himself to continue. "Here's some advice. Lose the makeup. It makes you look trashy. And whoever taught you to kiss didn't do a very good job."

She froze and stared at him. "You can teach me—"

Shouts of laughter interrupted her. She looked over his shoulder, her eyes widening so much they practically swallowed her whole.

Whirling around, he saw his ex-girlfriend Stacy surrounded by her friends. All standing in the open doorway. All laughing at them. At Lily.

John gritted his teeth and struggled for calm, when all he wanted was to rip them apart. Instead, he walked toward Stacy with determined steps, grabbed her face, and kissed her hard. Her tongue eagerly surged against his, wet and agile, and she grasped his hair, her long fingernails cutting into his scalp in a way that had always been arousing.

He felt nothing. Nothing but desperation.

Tearing himself away, he saw the smug satisfaction in Stacy's eyes. "Now why don't you..." He turned toward Lily and stopped.

She was gone.

Chapter 1

Fifteen years later...

Lily Cantrell opened her front door and stared at the man who had his hand raised to knock again. He was tall, dark-haired and wore a yellow button-down shirt and jacket with jeans. His shoulders were broad and his eyes were still the most beautiful shade of blue she'd ever seen. Despite the years that had separated them, he'd been the only man she'd ever loved, even after he'd rejected her so ruthlessly. Even after...

"Hello, small fry," John said, his voice deeper than she remembered. "It's good to see you again."

The years had perfected his masculine frame. He'd gotten bigger. Broader. The strong angles of his cheeks and jaw provided a rugged framework for the dark slash of his eyebrows above his pale blue eyes, and the prominent thrust of his nose and the sensual line of his wide mouth proclaimed him to be a bit of a barbarian. Fine lines gathered at the corner of his eyes, telling her without a doubt the boy she'd loved had grown into a man to be reckoned with.

John pushed back his hair in a familiar gesture that twisted her insides with longing and pain.

"You going to invite me in, Lily?"

Invite him in?

Instinctively she raised a hand to her cheek. Fifteen years ago, her mother had slapped her for the first and only time. All because Lily had insisted on going to see *him,* this man, the boy her mother had warned was too old for her and would only end up hurting her. She'd been right, but Lily never had a chance to tell her so. She'd never had a chance to say she was sorry for the terrible things she'd said. And she'd never had a chance to say goodbye.

Before any of that could happen, her mother had died. Now, days before the man responsible was to be executed, John suddenly showed up?

Her first instinct was to slam the door. To hide. To run. But she couldn't.

She wouldn't.

She'd acted like an ungrateful, selfish child once and soon afterward her mother had been murdered. She wouldn't disgrace her mother's memory any more than she had. She wouldn't run from this man now.

She stepped out onto the porch, shutting the front door behind her. "What do you want, John?"

He didn't smile, but she could swear his eyes did. "Good to see you, too, Lily. Can I come in?"

She shook her head. "Answer my question."

"I'd really like to talk about it inside—"

"And I'd really like you to tell me why you're here before I call the cops."

"No need. They're already here." He pulled out a thick black leather flasher wallet and showed her a shiny badge and accompanying picture ID.

"You're a cop?" She couldn't disguise the shock in her voice.

He'd been the ultimate bad boy. Accused of doing drugs and worse.

"I'm a detective with El Dorado County Sheriff's Department."

"El Dorado County? But why—" Realization made her eyes widen. "Is this about the execution?" The execution of her mother's murderer wasn't something Lily was taking any pleasure in. In fact, with the dreams having started up again, she'd been trying not to think about the execution at all. She just prayed that afterward she and her family would find some measure of peace, peace that had been eluding them. Her work with her art-therapy patients helped a lot, but—

John's jaw tightened. "I'm not here to cause trouble. This doesn't have to be a battle between us, Lily."

He's changed. Still intense, but more controlled. Confident. He didn't need to play the bad boy anymore. He was prime alpha male, sure of himself, not caring what others thought about him.

Well, she'd grown up, too. "This *is* about the execution, isn't it?"

He blinked and cleared his throat. "Talking to the victim's family isn't unusual during the last stages of the appeal process. Chris Hardesty's claiming innocence, so—"

"I don't understand." The calm façade she'd adopted cracked slightly. "Who cares what he's saying now. You have the evidence. You have the trial transcripts. His confession. Why are you reopening my mother's case?"

"We're not reopening the case, Lily, but the Attorney General's Office wants me to follow up on some leads. There's been a series of murders in El Dorado, murders I've been investigating, and the modus operandi for all of them are similar to your mother's. At first we thought they were copycat murders, spurred on by news coverage of the approaching execution, and they probably are, but…"

When he hesitated, her heart beat in a furious rhythm,

pounding in her ears. His words left room for doubt and for a second it shivered through her.

No. No matter what I dream, the evidence shows Hardesty killed Mom. But if these murders were similar, that meant...

"Someone's been stabbed?"

He didn't say anything and a wave of dizziness hit her.

"Look, I'm not saying Hardesty's innocent. Just that it needs further investigating. Hardesty says—"

A laugh burst from her, raw and ugly. It horrified her. Made her sound like she was on the verge of hysteria. She knew exactly how convincing Hardesty was. "The police investigated. I don't know why you people are doing this."

He narrowed his eyes and shifted the bag on his shoulder, a black satchel she noticed for the very first time. "You people?"

"Yes. Hardesty and his attorneys. The D.A. Now you. All you do is cater to the criminals. In the meantime, forget about the victims—"

John shook his head. "I never forgot about you. And somehow I don't think you forgot about me, either."

The innuendo in his voice shocked her. So did the tugging in her stomach. She remembered telling him she loved him. She remembered kissing him at his party—the party to which she *hadn't* been invited. And she remembered what he'd said in response.

Here's some advice. Lose the makeup. It makes you look trashy. And whoever taught you to kiss didn't do a very good job.

The memory still hurt and she clung to that pain with all her might.

Yes, remember how he hurt you. Remember what happened that night.

"Did—did you know I get letters from them just about every week?" she asked. "Begging me to visit him in prison so he can convince me of his innocence. And the D.A., he hasn't even—"

Anger lit the flame in his eyes to a bonfire. "His attorneys had no right to ask that of you." He stepped closer. "Stay away from them, Lily."

Involuntarily, she crossed her arms and stepped back until she hit the front door. "I don't need your advice."

"I'm giving it to you anyway. I let you down before, but I swear, I'll help you through this. Trust me."

"Why? What's in this for you?"

"Nothing. I gave up what I wanted a long time ago."

Her pulse quickened. "What do you mean?"

"You have to know it wasn't easy for me to turn you away that night. In fact, it was one of the hardest things I've ever done."

Feeling sucker punched, she couldn't believe he'd actually brought that night up. Humiliation filled her as she remembered what she'd said to him. How she'd clung to him, devastated that he was leaving town, begging him to wait for her. The way his friends had laughed at her.

"I threw myself at you. You mocked me. You kissed Stacy in front of me!"

He advanced on her so fast she couldn't have run even if she'd had room. Bracing his arms on the door on either side of her, he leaned down until she could smell his spicy cologne and sun-kissed skin.

She suddenly had the feeling he was fighting to keep his hands off her. She shivered in fear and unwanted desire.

"You were sixteen! Even if I wasn't too old for you, your father thought I was a petty thug. You already hated him because he'd left your mother. I was causing nothing but problems for you. What did you want me to do?"

Love me! she almost shouted. Like I loved you. But she choked back the words, dropping her voice to a harsh whisper. "All I want is for you to leave us alone. Leave *me* alone. Assign someone else to the case. You can work the recent murders without having to interact with me or my family."

The flare of anger in his eyes dissipated. He pushed away from her and shook his head, pity flooding his eyes. "I'm not going to do that. I can help. This isn't just about your mother anymore. It's about you. Two of the three girls look—"

"I don't want to hear it." She looked at the ground and felt the fight leave her body. She'd beg him if she had to. She raised her gaze to his and forced herself not to look away. "Please John. I fought with my mother that night. And then afterward, when I found her—she was lying there—killed by a man I—I'd befriended—"

Her voice broke and she struggled to breathe.

"Your mother's death wasn't your fault, Lily. And it wasn't mine. But this isn't going to just go away. And neither am I."

Propping her hands on her hips, she thrust out her jaw, the words coming out before she could stop them. "My father's a judge now. I'm sure he can arrange to have this reassigned to someone who didn't know the victim or the witnesses."

John's eyes narrowed and his smile made her shiver. He dropped his bag with a thump and once again moved toward her. "I don't like being threatened, Lily. And I'm sure your father wouldn't do something so foolish. Let the experts do what needs to be done, small fry."

She tried to shove him away, but he grasped her wrists, easily holding her hands against his chest. Her fingers flexed, wanting to sink deeper into his taut muscles. Wanting to pull him closer.

Whimpering, she pulled away and he released her. Jaw clenched tight, he glanced down a split second before his horror-filled eyes met her own.

She looked at the bloody images. Her mother. Her beautiful mother. Nausea rushed straight into her throat.

John cursed. "I'm so sorry, Lily—"

Backing away from him and shaking her head, she whispered, "Why are you doing this?" She fumbled for the door knob behind her.

"Lily—"

Finally, she got the door open, stumbled inside, then stared at him one last time.

"I just want to help, small fry."

"Then leave me alone." With bone-shattering control, she closed the door and engaged the lock with a quiet click.

John swiped his hands over his face in frustration. Damn, that had gone even worse than he'd expected. He shoved the photos and papers that had fallen back into his satchel. Standing, hands on his hips, he stared at Lily's front door, cursed, then made his way to his car. Once inside, he simply stared some more at Lily's house.

He hated it.

The small blue-shingled A-frame with black shutters fit in well with the cozy downtown Sacramento neighborhood. Older but not outdated. Paint holding up well. Certainly nothing extravagant. But it had a generic green lawn. No flowers. No decorations. No welcome mat. It was simple and quiet.

It reminded him of Ravenswood, the rehabilitation clinic he'd been admitted to after her mother's murder, the place he'd visited her only once before her agonized screams had chased him away, resolved never to come back. And it wasn't at all what he'd imagined for her.

Even at sixteen, Lily Cantrell had been complex. Colorful. Unpredictable. Dark, soulful eyes. A crease in her left cheek that never quite developed into a dimple when she smiled. A quick laugh and quicker temper.

She'd been more complex than her staid, generic home revealed. She still was.

And she was more beautiful than ever.

Her face was a mix of her father's Anglo background and her mother's Asian roots, pale skin with freckles and slightly slanted eyes. She still had shiny dark hair and a petite frame, but she'd gained enough weight to give her luscious breasts and hips where before she'd had none.

Her mouth seemed different, too. Less innocent. More sinful. Soft and full.

Rolling his shoulders, he closed his eyes. He'd hoped the

passage of time and his current assignment would create some
kind of natural barrier against any lingering feelings they
had for one another, good or bad. He should have known it
wouldn't happen.

He'd always felt a strong connection to Lily. She'd been
the ultimate good girl and he the neighborhood bad boy, but
they'd been drawn to one another, first by the friendship between their mothers, then by the sheer pleasure of each other's
company. Eventually, he'd trusted her in a way he hadn't ever
trusted his own family. Years ago, when his girlfriend Stacy
Mitchell had accused him of dealing drugs, he'd told Lily the
reason she'd done it—to hide the fact that she'd been doing
it herself. That her father hit her and her uncle had done far
worse. Wanting to protect Stacy despite what she'd done, he'd
cautioned Lily not to tell anyone. She'd believed him and refused to give up their friendship, causing enormous strife between her and her parents.

Lily's relationship with her cop father had suffered the most,
leaving Lily particularly vulnerable when Chris Hardesty, a
homeless man who had started hanging around at a nearby
park, befriended her. Eventually, it was that friendship that
had led Hardesty to Lily's mother, Tina.

John reached for his cell phone and dialed the office number
of Deputy Attorney General Lucas Thorn.

"Hi," he said when the man answered. "This is John. I just
saw Lily Cantrell and she wasn't happy about it. Don't be surprised if you get a call from Judge Cantrell fairly soon."

"Damn. I was hoping she'd cooperate. Doesn't she get we're
trying to speed Hardesty's execution along, not stall it?"

John frowned at Thorn's choice of words. *He* wasn't trying
to speed anything along, just trying to make sure both The
Razor and Tina's murderer were brought to justice, regardless
of whether they were the same person or not. He knew Thorn
wanted the same thing—he was probably just frustrated that
the governor was taking Hardesty's claims about The Razor
seriously. "Did you tell the governor that a patch of Sand

LaMonte's hair had been shaven, too, just like the girls before her?"

Thorn sighed on the other line. "I did. He doesn't see it as a significant deviation from how Tina died. She was stabbed just like Tina. And as you already pointed out yourself, LaMonte looks even more like Tina than the victims before her."

More like Tina. And more like Lily, John thought. Which was the only reason he was here. Once again, he stared at Lily's door, as if doing so would give him another glimpse of the young girl who'd turned into a beautiful albeit mistrustful woman.

Had he been wrong to believe Lily's life was in danger? Or had he simply used his fear to justify seeing her, when he'd sworn long ago to leave her in peace?

But it was Thorn who'd asked John to look into Tina Cantrell's case. Thorn who hoped John's findings would mollify the governor and rule out any connection with The Razor. And contrary to jumping at the opportunity, John had even expressed reluctance at first.

"But I knew the Cantrell family. We were neighbors. Our mothers were friends," he'd said.

Only Thorn hadn't seen that as a problem. It was a long time ago, and he trusted John to look at the evidence objectively. Besides, Thorn reminded him, looking into Tina's murder was just a formality. It wasn't as if anyone actually believed Hardesty was innocent.

Still, John hadn't wanted to dig up old memories or the pain that came with them. Plus, looking into the case meant probably having to interview Tina's family, including Lily. Better to let a stranger handle it, right?

But then something had struck him....

Inside his car, he reached into his satchel and shuffled through the photos until he had the right one, the one of The Razor's latest victim, LaMonte.

Like the other victims, neither her purse nor the jewelry she was wearing had been disturbed. And she looked startlingly like Tina Cantrell and her daughter, Lily.

The Razor's other victims had been dark-haired and petite too, something he'd registered, of course, but it wasn't until he'd put all the photos side by side that he saw just how much each subsequent victim looked more and more the way Lily had at sixteen.

It had to be coincidence. After all, if The Razor had killed Tina, why had he waited so long to kill again? Granted, they couldn't know for sure he hadn't killed other girls in other locations, but still…

In the end, logic hadn't mattered. In that moment, he'd feared Lily was in danger. He still did.

Even after all the separation and regret, he wasn't going to walk away. Even if it meant having to face her and their past, he wasn't taking any chances. Lily had implied he was trying to hurt her and her family, but all he wanted to do was make sure they were safe, her most of all.

Fifteen years ago, she'd offered her love to him and he'd done what he'd thought was best. But in doing so, he'd hurt her. Terribly. Keeping her safe now was the least he could do.

Thorn's comment about speeding along Hardesty's execution once again echoed in his mind. It had just been a poor choice of words, John told himself. Thorn's caseload had gotten intense in the past few months, which had to have contributed to his breakup with Carmen. It still pissed John off, especially when he saw how badly Carmen was taking the breakup, but he knew Thorn was hurting, too. It was obvious any time Carmen's name came up. Plus, he'd worked with Thorn for years. He trusted him. He was a good guy.

Too bad Lily no longer trusted *him*.

Chapter 2

It was barely past dawn when John strode up to the El Dorado County Sheriff's Satellite Office. Despite the prominent flagpole with the state and national flags in front, the squat tan building looked like a strip-mall dental office. Still, he loved working here, only about an hour north from where he'd grown up. The South Lake Tahoe scenery was idyllic—lush green trees, sparkling water, and snow-capped mountains. The pace was slow. The people relatively peaceful. It was a constant challenge that so many acted immune to the dangers of larger cities.

The murder of local girl Sandy LaMonte and the others before her proved they weren't.

Going through the police reports in Tina Cantrell's case hadn't weakened his belief in Hardesty's guilt. As Thorn kept telling him, the evidence against Hardesty was solid. But John also couldn't shake the feeling that he was missing something. Something having to do with Lily's hostility yesterday—even as understandable as it was—as well as her father's subsequent refusal to talk to him.

He hesitated before entering his office and thought about Lily. It didn't take long before his erection strained against the fly of his pants. John took a shaky breath.

It had been the same reaction he'd had yesterday. It was like he was twenty years old again and he couldn't keep his body from wanting her no matter how unwise the response. Back then, he'd pushed her away when she'd come to him. And now? Now he expected her and her family to…what? Forgive him? Understand? Cooperate?

He snorted. Right. What a mess.

With a sigh, he finally went inside. He greeted the receptionist and then went into the back office that he shared with the office's three deputies.

"Hi, John." Deputy Tom Murdoch appeared in the doorway just as John sat down behind his desk.

He motioned Murdoch inside. "Hey. Anything helpful from LaMonte's parents?"

Murdock shook his head. "She had a habit of hitchhiking from their home in Incline Village. Who knows where he picked her up. Here are their statements."

John took the folder and opened it. Yesterday, sitting in his car outside Lily's house, he'd studied a close-up photo of LaMonte's face. This photo focused on her stab wounds. On film, LaMonte's injuries seemed even more severe than they had in person at the crime scene, which was the opposite of what one would expect. But without her face as a distraction, without the nerves and adrenaline and compassion that had rattled through him at the crime scene, all John had to focus on were her torn flesh and blood.

The photos themselves seemed inhumane. Cold. As cold as the man who'd done this. He set the file aside. Hopefully, the guy had left plenty of evidence behind.

"What about the jacket we found?"

"Doesn't look like it belonged to her, but it's being tested along with the evidence collected from her body. The coroner found a credit card she'd tucked into her sweater pocket."

John remembered the thin gold chain around LaMonte's neck and the small earrings in her ears. Was it ethics or simply disinterest that had kept her killer from taking them and the credit card? He hadn't taken anything from his other victims either, even though Diane Lopez had at least fifty bucks still on her and Shannon Petersen had half-carat diamonds in her ears.

"The coroner confirmed sexual assault," Murdoch said. "Took a vaginal swab and other evidence from the body."

"It'll match the others." John sighed. "So we're back to square one. We've got his DNA, but no one to connect it to."

"What about DNA evidence from the Tina Cantrell case?"

"Never done. Back then, it wasn't required and Hardesty confessed so why waste the time or money."

"Is having the evidence tested the next step?"

"For some reason, the defense hasn't asked for it. And the prosecution's position is it's not needed, so Thorn's certainly not going to." In fact, Thorn had been adamant on that point. As he'd pointed out, "It's costly, unwarranted, and could potentially just complicate things. If another person's DNA is found on her body, it doesn't prove Hardesty didn't kill her. It just gives the defense another opportunity to delay the execution while they talk about a phantom suspect."

But he'd left out one crucial fact, one he was smart enough to know. Another person's DNA could show Hardesty hadn't been working alone. He might have had an accomplice. An accomplice who was at this very moment on the loose—the man they'd dubbed The Razor. Soon, John was going to talk to Chris Hardesty about that possibility.

"Right now," John continued, "Thorn just wants me to look over the evidence we already have and explore any possible holes. To appease the governor so the execution goes forward as planned."

"And what if Hardesty's telling the truth? What if The Razor really killed Tina Cantrell?"

John stared at Murdoch but didn't say anything. He didn't have to.

If it turned out the same man killed Sandy LaMonte, the

two other girls, and Tina Cantrell, then the media would have a field day. He could see the headlines now:

Innocent Death Row Inmate Barely Escapes With His Life.

"Hopefully it won't come to that," John said. "Listen, Murdoch. I appreciate you working the extra hours on this. As soon as we eliminate the theory that the same man killed Tina Cantrell and Sandy LaMonte, Hardesty's claims of innocence are going to have zero credibility. But I trust you to keep focus on what's important. No matter what happens with the Cantrell case, we still have to find the animal who's killing these girls."

"Sure," Murdoch said, then hesitated. "How young do you think the next one's going to be?"

Grimly, John opened the file and flipped through the photos until he found one depicting LaMonte's face. He knew Murdoch was thinking of his own teenage girls. "I don't know." The Razor's first victim had been twenty-five. His second, twenty. LaMonte, eighteen. Were their decreasing ages significant? Was Tina's? She'd been forty when she'd been killed.

Murdoch paused on his way out. "Oh, the A.G. stopped by about ten minutes ago looking for you. Something about Tina's daughter slapping a guy at the murder scene fifteen years ago. He wants to talk to you about it right away."

John closed his eyes and raked his hand through his hair. "Great," he drawled.

When he opened his eyes, Murdoch stared at him. "I take it this isn't good news?"

John laughed humorously. "No. It isn't."

"Why?"

"Because I'm the guy she slapped."

August 29
12:45 a.m.
Sacramento, CA

John's little apartment was trashed. The smell of pizza and beer and other things made him dizzy, and all he wanted was for the last few stragglers to leave. Especially his ex-girlfriend, Stacy.

Tormented by the hurt look on Lily's face before she'd run away from him, John nudged Stacy toward her roommate. "But I don't wanna go, Johnny. I wanna shtay here with you."

Patting her arm, he passed her into her roommate's arms along with twenty bucks. "The cab's waiting. Here's enough for the fare and tip."

"Hey! Where's the party?"

Three men John vaguely recognized jogged up the walkway. Gritting his teeth, he blocked the doorway. "Sorry," he said, although his tone telegraphed the opposite sentiment. "Party's over."

One of the men punched another in the chest. "I told you we shouldn't have stopped."

His friend rubbed his arm. "Like you didn't want to know why there were cop cars swarming down the block!"

It was unsettling how fast John thought of Lily. He lunged and grabbed the guy's shirt. "What are you talking about?" Eyes wide, the guy jerked his thumb in the direction of Lily's street. "We—we saw some cop cars in front of a house. A murder, it sounded like. The neighbors said the Cantrells lived there."

John released him with a shove and started running. He ran as if his life was in danger. He ran faster than he'd ever run in his life.

Heart pumping, John's legs wobbled every time his feet hit concrete. He pushed himself to go faster, ignoring the terror stiffening his muscles and hitching his breath.

She's fine. He doesn't know what he's talking about. She's fine.

But when he turned the corner to her street, he knew Lily wasn't fine. Three police cars were parked haphazardly in front of the house. An ambulance. A white van imprinted with the word *Coroner* in large, block letters. Yellow tape bordered the front walk, keeping out the crowd that had gathered there.

Guilt flooded through him. If he hadn't messed with her feelings, she wouldn't have run off. Had he put her in danger? Had she been hurt because of him? John stumbled, moving forward, pushing through the crowd and shouting Lily's name.

A uniformed cop grabbed at his arm, but he jerked away and dodged around him.

Relief washed over him when he saw her. She was sitting on the front stoop, her eyes dull and vacant, her body painfully frail under an oversize long-sleeved shirt and sweats. "Lily!"

She didn't look up at his call, but the cop standing next to her did. He rushed forward and planted himself on the sidewalk, blocking John's view of Lily.

"I'm sorry," he said, not sounding sorry at all, "but you need to leave."

John craned his neck and caught sight of Lily's father standing just inside the doorway. Their eyes locked and John instinctively flinched. Fear. Grief. Anguish. There were no words to describe the other man's torment. Blood stained the foyer's white walls.

"Lily!" He tried to push past the cop standing in his way, only to be shoved back.

"Knock it off, or I'm going to have to take you in."

Mindless with worry, John tried to dodge to the left, grunting when the cop got him in a choke hold. "Lily," he gasped, needing to know. "Is she hurt?"

The cop shook John's head like a maraca. "She's not hurt. But she's in shock. Now ease up, man. You are going to back off. Do we understand each other?"

John's panic subsided just a hair. "Yeah," he breathed. "Okay."

Slowly, the cop loosened his grip. "What's your name?"

"My name is John Tyler. We're—we're friends."

Before the cop could respond, an EMT jostled by them and guided Lily to her feet. He led her down the walkway toward the ambulance, passing within two feet of John.

Lily walked slowly, almost robotically. She stared straight ahead. Didn't acknowledge him in any way.

All John could think about was her declaration of love and the way he'd thrown it back at her earlier that evening. "Lily," he murmured.

She stopped.

John held his breath, waiting for her to speak. Scream. Cry. Anything.

Tentatively, he reached out and touched her face, surprised when the cop didn't stop him.

"Lily. It's John. Are you okay?"

He saw a flare of recognition in her eyes just before she reached out and slapped him. Staggering back, John felt someone grab his arm to steady him.

Grief flashed in Lily's eyes. And then there was nothing.

The EMT walked her to the ambulance and helped her in. Her father quickly followed. John watched the ambulance drive away, then collapsed to his knees. In his peripheral vision, he once more saw blood. Then he threw up.

"John!"

John's head snapped back at the sound of Murdoch's raised voice.

"Dude, you can't just drop a bomb like that and not explain. You were there when Tina Cantrell was killed? And her daughter slapped you? Why?"

It was the last thing John wanted to talk about—hell, he'd just mentally relived it and his heart was aching—but Murdoch was working the investigation, too, and he had a right to know.

"Lily, Tina Cantrell's daughter, and my sister, Carmen, were best friends growing up. The night of the murder was my last night in town. My ex-girlfriend planned a going-away party for me so I canceled dinner plans I'd made with Lily and Carmen weeks before. It hurt Lily. A lot."

"And she slugged you."

Yes, but not because of the canceled dinner. Because she'd defied her mother to come to him and he'd pushed her away.

And because she had blamed him.

Some part of her had blamed him for her mother's death, just like she blamed herself.

"Did Thorn know—"

"He knows my family and Lily's family were neighbors. That our parents were friends. As to the fact Lily slapped me that night..." John shrugged. "It was in the police report, which Thorn has. But I never told him myself."

"Why the hell not?"

"Because it wasn't relevant." He'd thought about it a lot. It was a gray issue, but not a true conflict. Lily, after all, wasn't a suspect in the case. "Chris Hardesty has already been convicted for Tina's murder. To the extent he's challenging that conviction, it's just a last-ditch effort to stop the execution. I'm only looking into the case to eliminate the notion that someone else killed Tina and is now killing these girls."

"But what if Hardesty's exonerated? What if the investigation begins to focus on Lily's father? Or Lily herself?"

Laughing, John shook his head. "You can't be serious. The father, maybe. Even though he was a cop, he and Tina were estranged, so he's still a P.O.I. in my opinion. Lily? Ridiculous. If you saw her, you'd see what I mean. And even if some evidence turns up to implicate her, we weren't lovers. She was a kid who had a crush on me. Thorn would handle questioning her, not me."

"Sounds like you've got it all figured out." But Murdoch, his disapproval self-evident, still didn't leave.

Scowling, John growled, "You got something to say to me, Murdoch?"

"It just seems like you're working really hard to justify working on this case."

"Justify? I've been working The Razor murders for almost a year. I'm not letting him get away from me now."

"I can take over—"

"Don't piss me off, Murdoch. I have a job to do, and I'll do it. I want this guy. I want him bad. And I'm gonna get him. There's no evidence The Razor killed Tina. But if I find something indicating otherwise, I won't ignore it."

"You're a good cop. I'm not saying otherwise. But—"

"Look, I've got to call Thorn. Keep me posted, okay?" He looked down at the file, deliberately dismissing the other man. After a second, Murdoch stiffly said, "Sure," then left.

John looked at the phone and thought about calling Thorn, but he wanted to talk to Lily before he did. He also wanted to follow up with some witnesses. The cops who'd reported to the murder scene. And the man who'd been dating Lily's mother fifteen years ago, the man Lily had often referred to as "the gym rat." Park, he reminded himself.

The guy's name had been Mason Park.

He wouldn't want to mess up and call him "gym rat" to his face, even if Lily could appreciate it.

Remembering Murdoch's concerns about a conflict, John snorted. There was no chance in hell Lily had anything to do with her mother's death. Anyone who said otherwise was just plain stupid.

Chapter 3

Lily was running.

    Running from her mother, who'd slapped her.

    Running from John, who'd hurt her.

    Running but going nowhere.

    Suddenly, she stopped. She saw two figures wrestling, each trying to gain control over the other but neither succeeding. The dance continued for minutes. Hours. Days. The entire time, she watched, unable to move, unable to scream. Although she couldn't distinguish one from the other, couldn't see more than shadows, she knew who the figures were. A dark-haired woman, dressed in blue silk and heels. And a grizzled dirty man with tangled white hair and vacant blue eyes. The homeless man she'd talked with at the park.

    Her mother and Hardesty. Dancing. Yelling. Fighting.

    She saw a sharp steel blade, already stained red, sink into flesh, then make a wet, sucking sound as it retracted. Again and again the motion repeated itself, the sucking sounds be-

coming shrill screams that ended each time the knife withdrew and began once more when it hit its mark.

Then things quieted. The knife and the blood disappeared. Two figures became three. Then four. Then five.

She clearly saw her mother, huddled on the ground. A tall shadow of a man—somehow she knew it was a man—lifted her mother into his arms and carried her away. Her mother reached out to her, pleading with her. "You don't know, Lily. You don't understand. He's not the man you think he is."

Light flashed and Lily tried to run, but her feet were glued to the ground with blood. Her stomach heaved and she fought the urge to throw up.

A man grabbed her arm on each side.

The first was Hardesty.

The second was her father.

"You'll be rewarded for your kindness," Hardesty said. "You'll be rewarded."

"It's all your fault, Lily," her father moaned. "Remember. It's all your fault."

Lily jerked awake, stifling the scream climbing her throat. Sweat drenched her clothes, chilling her. She immediately raised her hand to her face. It was flushed but dry. She turned onto her side and curled back into a ball.

Even in sleep she couldn't cry. Couldn't let out the grief inside her. Like a malignant growth that had become a part of its host, excising it would bring death as surely as the disease itself. She needed to hold on to the grief to survive. To keep her from making the same mistakes.

Only why were her dreams back, worse than before? What did Hardesty's words mean? And was her father's presence alongside Hardesty a twisted form of self-punishment or a hint of something else? Some repressed memory?

But that was ridiculous.

Seeing John was playing with her head, that was all. How could it not? The guy was threatening the closure she and her family needed. The closure her mother deserved. And as powerful as her attraction had been to him in the past, she couldn't ignore the way her body had responded to his closeness. When he'd caged her in and towered over her, every nerve in her body had gone ballistic.

It was some kind of chemical reaction, and she wasn't a young girl to be carried away by hormones. Not anymore. Hardesty was guilty and she'd fight John and the D.A. and the governor himself if they tried arguing otherwise.

Forcing herself to her feet, Lily walked to the kitchen and filled a glass of water from the sink. She drank in desperate swallows, even as she caught sight of the blinking red light on her answering machine. Needing to compose herself, she'd turned the ringer off after John had left. Slowly, she walked over to it, and pushed the Play button.

Her brother-in-law's voice came on and she sighed with relief that the message wasn't from John or one of Hardesty's attorneys.

"Hey, Lily, this is Aaron. Damn. I was hoping you'd be home. Listen, Ivy and Ashley have been fighting like crazy and I'm getting frustrated."

Frowning, Lily put down her glass. Aaron sounded frantic even though Lily's sister, Ivy, had always tended to butt heads with her daughter, fourteen-year-old Ashley. Even Lily's father and stepmother, Barb, had stepped in, spending more time with the girl in an effort to give her and Ivy breathing room.

"I know you two—I mean, I know you're busy, but I thought you could come over for dinner tomorrow night? Ashley's going to a dance and I'm driving her, so you'd have time to talk alone. Ivy could really use someone right now and I know you'd want to help her. You have such a big heart, Lily."

You'll be rewarded for your kindness, Hardesty's voice whispered in her mind.

Lily instinctively covered her ears. She bit her lip but heard her panicked whimper anyway. Slowly, she lowered her hands.

"—can call me at work. The number's—"

Lily lunged and pressed the Stop button. She knew the

number and she wasn't a fool. Aaron's message had to be some kind of sign. Despite how her sister had pulled away from her after their mother's death, Ivy needed her. And Lily needed her, too.

Seeing John had shaken her to the depths of her soul, and not simply because of the investigation.

She was too afraid of the memories.

Too afraid of the panic coming out of nowhere.

Too afraid of suffocating in the darkness when she lay in bed, trying to hold off sleep but knowing eventually the dreams would claim her.

Most of all, she was afraid of how John had made her feel. He'd shattered the control she'd fought so long to achieve. Made her feel things she hadn't felt for years.

Lust. Longing. Recklessness.

Those feelings scared her most of all.

Even though it wasn't quite 7 a.m., Lily knew Aaron would already be at his law office. She picked up the phone and dialed his number.

"Aaron Bancroft."

"Hi," she said, feeling more grounded just hearing Aaron's voice. "It's Lily."

"Hey, Lily! You got my message?"

"I did."

"And?"

"And it's perfect timing. I'd love to come to dinner. Have you already asked Ivy—"

"That's awesome, Lily!"

Lily chewed her lip. "But are you sure it's going to be all right with Ivy?"

Aaron gave a strained laugh. "Come on, Lily. You're family. You know you're welcome to come over any time. Ivy'll welcome the company."

If she felt better, she might have called him on his blatant lie. "Still, I'll call her. After work—"

Once again, he interrupted her, an impatient edge to his voice. "Don't piss me off, Lily. Please."

She felt her brows lift. She'd known Aaron since before her parents split up. He'd never used that grim voice with her before. "But—" She hesitated, remembering his atypical request for help. Even if Ivy didn't welcome her with open arms, Aaron and Ashley would. "Okay. Thank you. And—well— my father and Barb, they won't be there, will they?" Despite how she'd threatened John with going to her father, she didn't think she could handle seeing her dad. Not when she was already feeling so shaky from seeing John.

"No. But he misses you, Lily. You might want to give him a call."

Hearing the slight reproach in Aaron's voice, Lily didn't bother to respond. She knew it was unfair, but she couldn't change how she felt—she'd never forgiven her father for leaving them for another woman. Or for failing to save her mother.

And she'd never forgiven herself.

Wearily, Lily sat on her couch. She smoothed her finger over the binding of one chenille pillow. She forced her voice to sound cheery. "See you tomorrow night." She pulled the phone away from her ear just as Aaron spoke again.

"Ivy feels helpless—like she's losing her daughter. You being here will help."

There was nothing Lily could say. She was the last person to give parenting advice, but she'd try almost anything to feel close to her family again.

Don't hope too much, Lily. Don't let yourself be hurt again. A pleasant dinner wasn't going to erase fifteen years of tension and distance.

Lily showered and dressed for work, but didn't bother with breakfast. She'd grab something on the way. At the door, she studied the picture hanging on the wall. It was of the four of them—her father and mother, her sister and herself. Arms around each other. Smiling. Happy. Reaching out, Lily traced the shape of her mother's face.

She remembered the gruesome dream, how sharp the knife had looked, how loud the screams had been, how she could almost feel the gush of blood escape from her mother's body and onto her clothes and the floor.

It was her greatest heartache. She couldn't think of her mother, couldn't look at her picture, without imagining her being hurt. Without feeling guilt for hurting her, as well.

The same thing happened whenever she saw or thought of John.

Resolutely, she straightened her shoulders and did what she always did when leaving the house. She kissed her fingertips, touched them to her mother's image, then said, "Be back soon," before heading outside.

Chapter 4

The large room at the Mercy Rehabilitation Clinic was meant for serious activity. The red-and-yellow checkered vinyl floor and cheery yellow walls had been sealed to withstand spilled paint, markers, clay, glue and plaster of Paris. Aside from Lily and Fiona, however, the room was deserted and quiet. Lily smiled at the little girl, who'd been dropped off for her weekly appointment by her new foster parents. Fiona looked positively radiant, even if she still hadn't said a word. No surprise since she hadn't talked since the accident.

"I'm making another exception for you, Lily. But I can't make it a habit. Please understand that."

Lily brought her attention back to the woman on the phone. "I know, Dr. Tyler. I wouldn't ask if it wasn't so important."

"Our prior agreement still stands. I can't talk to you about John or Carmen. I'm not even sure I—"

Before Dr. Tyler could change her mind about meeting her, Lily said, "Thank you, Dr. Tyler. I'll see you soon." Lily hung up the phone and stared at it.

She couldn't believe she'd actually called John's mother for a therapy appointment, but she had no one else to go to. The dreams were getting worse and she needed to talk to someone—a professional—about what they might mean. And John's mother was a licensed therapist, one who'd helped her after her mother's murder, so she already knew all the relevant facts about her history and her mother's case.

"Someone's here to see you."

Lily's body jerked and she let out a frightened scream. One of the on-duty nurses frowned at her.

"Sorry. Didn't mean to scare you. You okay?"

Lily forced a laugh and raised a hand to cover her racing heart. "I'm fine," she said. She glanced at Fiona again. "We were just concentrating, weren't we, Fiona?"

The little girl smiled but didn't answer. She went back to her drawing, her little tongue poking out of her mouth.

Lily shifted her gaze to the boy standing in the hallway. Albert Sanchez quickly looked away, feigning interest in the worn linoleum floor. Conflicting emotions momentarily held her paralyzed.

Albert had been discharged from the hospital less than three weeks ago, five months after he'd staggered into the emergency room with complaints of "intense headaches." Turned out he'd had a bullet in his skull. Although it hadn't taken his life, the bullet had damaged his speech and his coordination. Lily had worked with him for months, surprised by his unwavering enthusiasm for anything artistic. She'd developed a genuine affection for the boy and he'd seemed to get increasingly comfortable with her. But once he'd been discharged, he hadn't returned.

Until today.

He was a thief and a gang member. When he'd been brought in, he'd been accompanied by a group of older boys who wore their attitude and hostility as easily as their baggy, low-waisted jeans and gang colors.

His dark hair covered his skull again, and the number four-

teen tattooed on his temple, the one that marked him as a
Norteño, stood out starkly against his pale skin. Unlike his
friends, his face was clear of the tear-shaped tattoo that sym-
bolized a gang-related kill.

He has a good heart, she reminded herself. He isn't like
those other boys. She turned to Fiona. "That's beautiful,
Fiona," she said. "You keep working on that and I'll be right
back, okay?"

Fiona nodded. Lily pushed back her chair and walked over
to Albert with a casual stroll that belied the tension she was
feeling.

She propped her hand on her hip. Casual confidence, even
if it was playacting. She didn't wear her heart on her sleeve.
Not anymore.

"So, long time no see," she said in almost perfect Spanish.

He stuck his hands in his pockets and slouched. "You look
busy." He glanced at her paints before turning away.

"Hey," she said, switching to English. "Don't leave yet. I
need someone to help me paint some tiles. And if you're feeling good, why don't you help me?"

He didn't look at her, but he didn't walk away, either.

"I saw you looking at my paints." She grinned, feeling more
at ease. "And I know you didn't come just to see me. Or did
you?" Her voice was light, trying to reestablish a rapport with
him.

He turned his face slightly, and she saw the flush move up
his neck and face. Once again, she wondered how this boy,
who loved cheeseburgers, basketball and backgammon, had
gotten involved with gangs. "I need an eagle for a mural in the
pediatric ward," she said, rushing to cover up her faux pas.
"You think you're up for painting one?"

He looked at the table and paints again. Gave a long-
suffering sigh and shrugged. Despite being only fifteen, he
towered above her and had arms that were thick with muscle.
A boy trapped in a man's body. In a man's world. He took a
seat next to Fiona and Lily joined him.

Lily worked with Fiona and Albert for over an hour, slipping into a comfortable silence.

"Lily."

This time, Lily didn't jerk at the intrusion of another person's voice in the silence. And the frown on her face as she turned toward John's voice was more in reaction to her lack of fear than his sudden appearance. Why was it that Nancy's voice could startle her when John's didn't?

He stepped into the room and after a long look at Lily, turned his attention to Albert and Fiona. Almost instantly, Albert stood with a loud scrape of his chair and grabbed his backpack. "I've gotta go, Lily."

"But why—" Lily started, sighing in exasperation when Albert gave Fiona a quick wave and rushed out the door. Angry now, she turned back to John. To her shock, Fiona had left her own seat and sidled up next to him.

He crouched down next to her. "Hey, sweetie. What have you got there?"

"Fiona—"

After shooting her a look that made her protest falter like a fumbled football, John smiled encouragingly at Fiona. She handed him a piece of paper.

He whistled. "What a great drawing. Is this your cat?"

Smiling, Fiona held up one finger.

"One of them?" He laughed when she nodded vigorously. "Very cool."

Leaving the paper in his hand, Fiona skipped back to the table and started drawing again. Lily stared at her in shock. The little girl was rarely so friendly and she never shared her art with strangers. That she did so with John made Lily feel a strange pang in her chest.

"Who was that…boy? A patient of yours."

Lily said nothing but didn't miss the pause before he said "boy." Like he'd wanted to say something else. Like he was criticizing who she chose to consort with—again. Just like he had all those years ago with Hardesty.

Rubbing the back of his neck, John jerked his chin at Fiona. "She's a doll."

She didn't know why, but his words, more than his obvious disapproval of Albert, made her bristle. "Well, she's blond, just like Stacy. I guess you've still got the touch."

John stared at her, his fists clenched at his sides.

She mentally cursed her wayward tongue.

"So you don't trust anyone anymore, Lily? Not even friends?"

She looked away. "I don't have friends. I have my work. I have my family. That's all I need."

"Is that why you stopped writing Carmen?"

She bit her lip and closed her eyes at the mention of her best friend's name. *Former* best friend.

"It took her a long time to get over that, you know. She misses you."

"I never meant to hurt her." To move on, Lily had needed to divorce herself from him completely. Since Carmen was John's sister, that had seemed to require divorcing herself from Carmen, as well.

"You trusted her once. You trusted me."

Anger crowded out her guilt and sorrow. She hadn't just trusted him. She'd *loved* him. With everything inside her. With her entire heart and soul. He'd taken what she'd offered and crushed it. "Yes, and that was my mistake. I don't trust you now. I don't like you. I don't even want to look at you."

"Bull." He said it quietly, but emphatically.

She looked wildly at Fiona, who was oblivious to the drama unfolding around her, then said, "I'm at work! How dare you—"

After glancing toward Fiona himself, John shook his head. "You're right. I'm sorry." Lowering his voice to a whisper, he leaned toward her. "But one thing I'm certain of. You might not like me, Lily. But you're still attracted to me."

She tried to deny it, but the words stuttered to a halt in her throat. She couldn't speak past the desire rippling through her, making her skin so sensitive the weight of her clothes became unbearable.

A shameful heat warmed her body. And a shameful realization—she'd felt more alive in the past few minutes than she had in God knows how long. "You're insane."

His eyes narrowed and swept her body, stopping on her nipples, which she could feel straining against the cotton of her shirt. "I don't think so."

He moved as if to touch her, but a nurse stepped into the room. She paused when she saw them. "Sorry! I just came to bring Fiona to her next appointment. You okay, Lily?"

Lily didn't take her eyes off John. He turned, walked to the window, and propped an arm on the window frame to stare outside.

Trying to follow his lead, she looked at the nurse and smiled. "I'm fine. We're discussing a private matter."

The woman's gaze drifted to John. Understanding flared in her eyes as she assumed John was a patient or the distraught parent of one. She got Fiona's things together. Lily gave the girl a hug and promised to see her soon. The nurse closed the door as she left.

Lily took the offensive, trying something she hadn't yet: reason. "Look, all I care about is making sure Hardesty pays for what he did. You're not the only one who can ask questions. Maybe I'll do some investigating on my own—"

He jerked around to face her. "And put yourself in danger again? It took Hardesty killing your mother before you realized what a danger he was the first time."

The words hit her like a battering ram, causing her to stumble. Although she pressed her lips together, she couldn't hold back a whimper of pain.

"I'm sorry," he said quickly. "I don't want to fight. I came here to apologize. You didn't give me a chance… I didn't mean for you to see those pictures. I mean—" He threaded his fingers through his hair in frustration. "I feel like an idiot."

"Good," she said, but her words were empty. Slowly, she

sank into a chair and hung her head so her hair covered her face. Be fair for once, she told herself. This isn't John's fault. No matter how much his rejection had hurt, he'd never made any promises or declarations of love to mislead her. And he'd had no part in what happened afterward.

But here he was. A big, impossible-to-ignore reminder of her own foolishness.

She heard him move and raised her head. He was staring at one of the mosaics she'd made and hung on the wall, a cheery swirl of color creating a sunflower. He stroked his finger across the individual tiles. She shivered as if he'd touched her body. Pleasure rioted through her.

For several seconds, his gaze remained fixed on the mosaic. When he looked up, he studied her with the same intensity. "It fits—you being an art therapist."

She rolled her eyes—self-preservation. "I'm so glad you approve."

He sat beside her, undeterred when she cringed away. "I didn't ask for this, Lily. Believe it or not, I don't get off on hurting you. Now or in the past."

Swallowing hard, she stared at him. His voice was tinged with real regret. And suddenly she was tired of blaming him when she'd had her part in what happened that night. "Look, I read your signals wrong. I thought I meant more to you then I did and it made me act stupid." She shoved to her feet and hugged her arms to her chest. "In the end, it all meant nothing. For you, it never meant anything at all."

"That's not true." He stood and lightly gripped her arms. "I wasn't lying when I said it was hard turning you down. I was interested in you. More than I ever let on."

She sucked in a breath and her chest brushed against his. Pleasure shot through her and she raised her hand to push him away. What would it feel like to pull him closer, just once?

"I still am."

He stared at her lips, his eyes a fierce blue backlit by desire. The warmth coursing through her exploded into flames. She took a step back. "No," she whispered, doubt rolling through her.

"Yes," he countered.

She tried to turn her head, but he held her arm with one hand while he raised the other to cup her cheek. She gasped at how good his touch felt. Helplessly, she nuzzled closer, but he dropped both hands and stepped away.

She moaned, overcome with loss. He took another step back, his face stiff and unnaturally controlled. His fingers clenched and then relaxed. "But you're a witness in this investigation. And that's a line I can't cross. You were so young then—"

"You damn tease! If I was a temptation, I was one easily cast aside. You already proved that. You didn't need to do it again."

Grabbing her wrists with an infuriated growl, he pulled her against him. Her breath whooshed out of her as every inch of her pressed against every inch of him. Chest. Thighs. And every sensitive place in between.

His mouth covered hers. Need exploded in a painful rush of sensation, scaring her. She couldn't do this. Didn't know how to show him everything she was feeling. She whimpered and pulled back, her breath as quick and shallow as his.

His hands loosened on her arms. He visibly struggled for control. Before he could completely let go, Lily grabbed his face and pulled him close.

John groaned when Lily's lips softened under his. He feasted on them for several long minutes before pulling back to bury his face in her throat. "So long. I've wanted this for so long," he managed to gasp out.

Her answering moan of need, tremulous and whisper soft, shivered into him until he felt it settle somewhere in his chest. Desperate, he took her mouth again. She tasted amazing. Sweet and innocent, just as she had years ago. But at the same time, the sweetness was tempered with spice. A ripe sexuality bore itself out in the parry and thrust of her tongue against his.

Lowering his hands to her hips, he arched her into his groin, relishing her broken gasps of pleasure and the way her hands pulled at his hair. His mouth opened wider and he pushed her against the door, flattening his palms against it and grinding his aching shaft against her until he was practically drilling her. Instead of stopping him, she arched into him, opening her legs wider.

He pulled back, breathing in air like a locomotive. He clenched his fists, stepped completely away, and walked to her art table. He braced himself on stiffened arms. Only when he felt fully in control did he turn to face her.

She'd moved from the door and sat on the battered thrift-store couch, her head tipped back and eyes closed. She must have heard him move, because she suddenly opened her eyes and sat up. She kept her face averted.

"I'm sorry." John winced. "Again."

Her mouth twisted bitterly. "Poor John. You take responsibility for everything, don't you? But I'm a big girl." She rose, dusted off her hands as if she could rid herself of him that easily, and shrugged. "Maybe I just wanted to know if you'd learned anything new since I last saw you."

He wanted to take her up on her challenge. To crawl onto her body and press her into the soft cushions and satisfy her curiosity fully. But despite her taunting words, her eyes looked anything but confident.

"Bottom line, you know I care about you. I'm just trying to do my job."

She opened her mouth but nothing came out.

"You want this investigation closed?"

This time, she didn't hesitate. "Yes."

"Then talk to me. Get your family to cooperate. Your father's dodged every attempt I've made to talk to him. The more you and your family fight me, the longer it's going to take."

"You want me to hand my family over to you? To feed them to the wolves?"

Eyes narrowed, he asked, "Are you hiding something?"

"Wh-what are you talking about?"

"I can see it in your eyes, Lily. Who are you trying to protect? Hardesty?"

Her laugh was high and panicked sounding. "No one."

"Then who? Your father?"

"No." The word came out so quietly. "No," she said with more force. "Of course not."

"Because if you are, I guarantee you I will find out. Your father never liked me, but he's going to have to face me sometime."

"Don't bother my father just because yours is lucky enough to be dead."

Shock widened his eyes.

Lily was one of the few people who knew how devastated he'd been when his father, the former mayor of Sacramento, had hung himself amidst allegations of embezzlement. It had changed him into the rebellious bad boy who'd later had trouble with the law. He'd allowed few past that protective armor. His family. Lily. And she'd just—ruthlessly and deliberately—torn into his wounds.

He moved closer, stopping when she scrambled away. "I'd never hurt you, Lily. Obviously this was a mistake. You don't want to help me, that's fine. We'll see how it plays out on its own."

"I'm sorry. I just said that to hurt you."

He froze in the act of walking away and briefly glanced over her shoulder. "Well, it worked. Score one for you."

Chapter 5

John shifted his legs underneath the small wrought-iron patio table and wondered if he should come back another time. Mason Park, the man who'd briefly dated Tina Cantrell, was definitely distracted by the two kids racing around his newly landscaped backyard. John bit back a smile when he saw the little girl stick out her tongue at her brother.

It made him think of Lily.

He straightened and reached for the glass of water Park had given him.

Everything seemed to remind him of Lily nowadays. He took a long swallow and then put down his glass. "So what time were you supposed to meet?"

"Penny, don't pull your brother's hair!" Park frowned as he watched his son and daughter bicker some more. When one ran to the play set and the other kicked a ball across the kidney-bean-shaped lawn, he finally turned back to John. "Sorry, what did you say?"

The sliding door opened and Park's wife stepped out with

a bottle of sunscreen. She murmured to her kids as she slathered them up. Their kids were five and seven, and their older daughter Theresa was at a friend's. Park worked as a pharmaceutical rep and although he was about ten years older than John, you couldn't tell it. Park had been married over ten years to the pretty blonde who could pass for a college student. Tina, on the other hand, had been ten years older than Park when they'd dated.

Remembering how much Lily had resented this man, John sighed. "Tina Cantrell. What time were you supposed to meet her that night?"

"Eight-thirty. We were going to have a late dinner and then try to catch a movie. Something light. She liked comedies."

"And she never showed?"

He shook his head. "She called me before I left the house. Told me she had a family emergency and would call me later that night." For a moment, he stared at his kids, his gaze going blank as if his mind was somewhere else. "She sounded upset. I offered to come by but she said no." He smiled. "I always told her she was too proud for her own good."

"You knew her that well? And you'd only been dating, what? Two months?"

He shrugged. "Three. But it didn't take me long to discover her independent streak. She wasn't about to lean on another man. Let alone one almost ten years younger. Not after what her ex did to her."

"So your age was a problem?"

A wistful smile crossed Park's face. "For me, no. For her, sure. It took me a long time to convince her to go out with me. And when she did, I think she told herself it was just a fling."

Everything about the man, from his words, to his tone, to his expression, radiated regret. "What about you? What did you think?"

Again, Park looked at his kids. "I wasn't sure, but I didn't get the chance to find out."

Park's wife waved to him on her way back into the house and he smiled.

John studied him. He was good-looking. Your typical family man, who seemed incapable of brutally stabbing and sexually assaulting a woman. But of course looks didn't mean a thing. Ted Bundy was proof.

"So what time did she call?"

Park shifted his attention back to John. "I was about to leave to pick her up, so it was just before eight."

The timing sounded right. Tina had come to his place looking for Lily around 8:00 p.m. Phone records showed she'd called her ex before that. According to the wait staff at 33rd St. Bistro, Park had shown up alone around 8:30 for dinner and drinks, and had left around 10:30, saying he was going to a movie. When the cops had interviewed him the next day, he'd had the ticket stub in his pants pocket. Two hours later, they'd picked up Hardesty. And a day later, they'd found Hardesty's prints at the scene.

"She didn't tell you what the emergency was?"

"Something about having an argument with one of her girls. Lily, I'm sure."

The man's derisive tone made John stiffen. "Why do you say that? You ever meet her girls?"

Park shook his head. "No. She refused to introduce me to them. Showed me pictures though. They didn't look alike, but they were pretty. Like her."

Yeah. Definitely pretty. "So why do you say she probably had a fight with Lily?"

Park shrugged. "It was something Tina talked about a lot. How hard Lily was taking her father leaving. How she blamed Tina and Tina didn't know what to do. It would have been so easy for her to make Lily hate her father, but she didn't want that, even if it meant keeping the truth from her."

"The truth? Lily knew he'd had an affair. She had a new stepmother, for God's sake."

"She didn't know her father had cheated in the past. Many times in the past."

John pursed his lips and leaned back in his chair. "Doug Cantrell cheated more than once? And Tina stayed with him? I have to say that surprises me. I knew the family. Tina didn't seem like the type of woman who'd stay with a cheater." But if that was the case, that meant John's list of potential witnesses had just gotten a hell of a lot bigger. He couldn't discount the possibility that one of Doug's jealous lovers—hell, even his present wife had to be considered—had killed Tina.

"Sounds like you knew her pretty well." Park's eyes narrowed suspiciously. "You would have just been a kid when she died. Were you friends with one of her girls? The oldest one? Or even Lily?" He leaned back in his chair, nodding thoughtfully. "Tina mentioned a guy Lily was into. An older guy. What did you say your name was again?"

"Detective John Tyler. Now getting back to Doug Cantrell's affairs. Why'd Tina stay with him?"

For a moment, the two men stared at one another. Park looked away first. "For her girls. They were younger. They loved their father. And Doug Cantrell—"

Park looked over John's shoulder and paused.

"And what? What about the ex? Ever meet him?"

Holding up a finger, Park jerked to his feet. "Be right back." He jogged over to the little girl who'd fallen and was crying. He helped her up, brushing off her knees and giving her a kiss before watching her run inside. He walked slowly back to John.

"What did you ask?"

"I asked if you've ever met Doug Cantrell."

Park's face hardened in memory. "Oh, yeah. The guy was an arrogant one. Cheated on Tina for years. Married the next woman he'd had an affair with, but then had the balls to accuse Tina and me of screwing around."

John felt his brows shoot up. "When was this?"

"A few days before. He came by the house when I was there.

They started to argue and Tina kicked me out. Told me she needed to talk to the guy."

John lifted a skeptical brow. "And you just left?"

"Like I said, Tina was independent. I didn't want to scare her off by getting all he-man on her. Believe me, I wanted to pound the guy into the ground. I still remember the look he gave me as I left. He was so damn pleased with himself." Park shrugged. "But she was a grown woman. She knew what she was doing. And what she wanted." Park's mouth twisted. "Who she wanted."

"What do you mean?"

"I mean, I was younger, but I wasn't stupid. She still loved him. Even though she tried to hide it, it was obvious. She knew it. I knew it. And he knew it."

"And...?"

"And I don't know."

But his implication was obvious. Did he really think Doug had tried to reconcile with Tina and that he'd killed her when she refused? Doug Cantrell could make the same accusation against Park.

Testing him, John said, "Mr. Park, would you be willing to take a polygraph exam about all this?"

Park's eyes widened. "But—I thought—Jesus, do you think I—"

"You were cleared a long time ago. But Hardesty's making some allegations, and we need to build a solid case to present to the governor."

"I'm sorry, but I just want to forget about all this. I mean, I have my wife. My kids."

John nodded, not at all surprised. "Okay. Again, thanks." John turned to leave and was almost to the outer gate when Park called out to him.

"Detective Tyler?"

John turned. "Yes?"

Park hesitated, looked around and then approached him, not stopping until he was about two feet away. His voice was low but urgent. "How is Lily? And her sister? Tina loved them so much. I—I heard one of them found the body. That she claims memory loss. Is that true?"

John pressed his lips together. "I can't talk about that."

"Don't mean to pry. It's just, I'm not a religious man, but I often think—if there is such thing as a soul, Tina's would rest better knowing her girls are okay. You know?"

John studied the man. His refusal to take a polygraph exam hadn't done anything to make him more trustworthy in John's eyes, but it wasn't necessarily damning, either. In truth, he'd think twice himself before agreeing to take one. "I haven't seen her sister, but Lily's doing okay. As you can imagine, though, having to revisit all this is tough for her. I'm sure you understand why getting through this investigation quickly would be in her best interest."

Park nodded his head quickly. "Of course. I'm so sorry it's having to be brought up for her again. Honestly, I want to help, but—" He rubbed the back of his neck and glanced back at his kids. "I have a family now. And who knows what Doug Cantrell would do to protect himself—"

John frowned. "Just what are you insinuating?"

Park raised his hand in an appeasing gesture. "Nothing. It's just, I've always felt he got off easy because he was a cop."

Park had apparently forgotten that's what John was. "We're exploring everything, Mr. Park."

"Oh sure, sorry. It's just with the memory loss and all…"

"What," John prompted when the man hesitated.

"Well, there's all those cases about sexual abuse and women remembering it years later. I wonder if…"

Park trailed off as John stared at him.

"So now you're accusing Doug of molesting his daughters? I'd be careful who I said that to."

"Oh, I'm not accusing. I just thought, you know, it shouldn't be dismissed offhand. Right?"

"Goodbye, Mr. Park. Thank you for your help."

As John drove away, he tried to calm the adrenaline buzzing through his body. Park didn't know what he was talking about.

But yet, his mind countered, was it really that unbelievable? Incestuous molestations were a sad fact of life. Plus, he'd seen Doug manhandle Lily once after walking her home. Doug had spewed his accusations about John dealing drugs while ignoring the way Lily had gasped in pain when he'd grabbed her wrist. John had instantly seen red. He'd grabbed the older man's wrist, forgetting that he was a cop who could have him thrown in jail again. All he'd known was he was hurting Lily. He could've hurt Tina, too.

Then there was the fact that Lily resembled her mother, and that she'd had marks on her, faint but still there, when she'd come to his party.

He pulled over, rolled down the window, and took several deep breaths to clear his head. Now he was letting his imagination get away from him. Poor Doug Cantrell was no longer just a murder suspect in his mind, but a sexual abuser, as well.

Rein yourself in, John.

He started driving again, the picture of a happy family in his rearview mirror.

One thing for sure, he wasn't going to rest easy until he knew for certain The Razor was caught and that nothing—and no one—posed a threat to Lily or her family again.

Chapter 6

John worked like a madman all the next day, hunting down potential video surveillance or witnesses for any of The Razor's victims, pausing only when his stomach grumbled, calling his attention to the hollow feeling in his gut. He hadn't eaten anything but the banana and apple he'd grabbed on the way out this morning. He glanced at the clock, surprised that it was almost 6:00 p.m.

He took a break, wolfed down pretzels and a soda from the vending machine, and confirmed the office was virtually deserted. Returning to his desk, he stared at the paperwork covering the surface.

One picture bothered him more than others. Staring at it, he struggled with the frustration of knowing something—he just didn't know what—was wrong.

In the picture, Tina lay in bed; her arms were by her side with her hands resting near her stomach. Her legs were bent.

Suddenly, it hit him. It looked like someone had stretched

an arm under her knees and carried her to the bed. The way a groom would carry his bride over the threshold.

He already knew from the autopsy report that Tina hadn't died in her bed; that meant her body had been moved there. What if someone had moved her from the hard floor to the soft bed because he'd felt guilty? What if he'd moved her because he'd cared about her?

Under that theory, the positioning of her body actually supported Park's implication that Doug Cantrell, and not Hardesty, had killed Tina.

He rifled through some boxes until he found what he was looking for. A plastic baggie containing a tape of Doug Cantrell's 911 call. Walking to a table on the other side of the office, John inserted the tape into a tape player and pressed Play.

First static. Then Cantrell's voice.

"Help me. My wife and I...my daughter and I..." He sobbed. *"My wife...I just found her.... Oh my God, she's dead."*

John's stomach spasmed at the gut-wrenching grief in Cantrell's voice.

"Where are you, sir? Are you safe?"

"Yes, yes. My name is Douglas Cantrell. I'm an officer with Roseville P.D. I just brought my daughter home. My wife and I....I mean, we're divorced.... She's been murdered. Stabbed. Oh, God."

"Where is your daughter now? Is she with you?"

"Yes. Lily, come here."

John tensed but didn't hear Lily's voice. No crying. Nothing.

"Lily...she found the body but I can't get her to respond. She won't talk. She's in shock. Oh God, Lily."

The dispatcher confirmed the address and said officers were on their way. That had been at 12:35 a.m. John had arrived at Lily's house less than ten minutes later.

Picking up the phone, he called Thorn. "It's John."

"Hey, thanks for taking time out of your busy day. Or did Murdoch forget to tell you I stopped by yesterday?"

"No, he told me."

Silence buzzed in John's ear as Thorn waited for him to explain. He didn't say a word.

Thorn sighed. "Look, I know you're still pissed at me for breaking up with Carmen, but we have to work this case together."

"I'm not pissed about you and Carmen," John said, and it was true. Thorn wasn't a good friend, but he'd become a better one since he'd started dating his sister. Thorn had ended the relationship months ago, but Carmen refused to say why. "She's hurting but so are you. I'm not blind to that, just to your reasons. If you want to explain, fine."

When he responded, Thorn's voice was tight. "I talked to Doug Cantrell."

"Funny. He's been dodging all my calls."

"Not surprised. I am surprised, however, by the fact he thinks you're a druggie. And that you have a history of harassing his daughter."

"I didn't harass her. She slapped me when I tried to comfort her at her mother's murder scene. She was sixteen. Pissed because I'd rejected her. You have the police report from that night, Thorn. I'm listed on it. You telling me you didn't see that?"

"Look, I don't care about your history with Lily or her father. All I know is Hardesty's attorneys are putting pressure on the governor to stop the execution and now Doug Cantrell is putting pressure on the A.G. to drop this investigation—"

"Let him. He hasn't exactly been bending over backward to help us. Maybe we need to ask why."

"We don't need his help. You just need to tell the governor you've investigated things and you don't believe The Razor killed Tina Cantrell. Sign off on Hardesty's guilt and move on, and do it soon."

Thorn's words almost sounded like a command and John automatically bristled. He relaxed somewhat when Thorn spoke again.

"You do think Hardesty's guilty, don't you?"

"Based on the evidence we have, yes. But if he isn't guilty, the next suspect in line would be Doug Cantrell. And given that, I don't like him trying to stymie me. Especially not now."

"What do you mean?"

"I'm looking at the autopsy photos and there's some basis for believing that whoever killed Tina Cantrell knew her. Maybe even loved her."

"Hardesty's guilty, damn it," Thorn ordered, immediately making John's hackles rise again. Thorn seemed to be shoving that down John's throat quite a lot today. . . .

John rolled his neck and told himself to calm down. He reminded himself they were working toward the same goal. Despite Thorn's repeated references to Hardesty's guilt, he'd asked John to investigate, after all. "Look, the first two obvious suspects were Tina's ex and her new boyfriend. The boyfriend had an alibi. Doug Cantrell didn't."

"He didn't need one after Hardesty confessed."

Sitting down once more, John picked up the photo of Tina's body. "Did you know the body was staged?"

Thorn didn't miss a beat. "Actually, I did. It's in the autopsy report."

"The prosecution's theory was Hardesty surprised the vic in the kitchen and the fight started there."

"Right. She tried to run and he followed her into the bedroom, where he killed her."

"Seemed logical. Blood trails lead there. The pathologist said her body had been moved. She didn't die on the bed because her wounds weren't bleeding downward."

"I'm still not seeing why you're concerned."

"Hardesty never admitted moving the body. Even in his confession, he said the attack started in the living room. He never said where she died. The pathologist says she died between 9:00 p.m. and 1:00 a.m. She had lividity in her chest during the autopsy so he thinks she died while lying on her side, which caused her chest to face down. He estimates she was in this position for several hours before being placed on the bed."

John emphasized, "Several hours. Implying someone killed her and then hung around. If it was Hardesty, why? Why not get the hell out of there as fast as possible?"

Thorn clicked his tongue against the roof of his mouth, which he often did when deep in thought. "Maybe he got off on the sight of blood. Maybe he needed to clean up first, or think of a plan. He killed her. End of story."

"If Hardesty killed her, he either moved the body afterward or someone else did. If you take it one step further, one might argue the victim being moved after her death shows Hardesty didn't kill her. Not unless they'd had a relationship no one knew about."

"Damn. So we're back to the phantom suspect. I don't buy it. It's Hardesty. I know it was. Who's to say he wasn't seeing Tina Cantrell on the side?"

John thought about it. Thorn's theory seemed a long shot, but anything was possible. "So she was dating the boyfriend, but Hardesty, too. Playing both ends, so to speak. Maybe she was just too embarrassed to admit it." He felt himself wanting to grab hold of it, simply because it was a better alternative to suspecting Lily's father.

But somehow he couldn't let it go.

John stroked his chin thoughtfully. "I'll explore the possibility that Hardesty was intimately involved with Tina Cantrell. But you know, Doug Cantrell made the 911 call. The person who reports a crime is often the perpetrator."

As a cop, Cantrell could have manipulated the evidence. But he could have also manipulated other people. Even his own daughter.

Murdoch's warning of a conflict flickered through his mind, but he deliberately pushed it away. Stay with the father. That's where the evidence was leading him.

"Well, I'm not taking anything to the A.G. unless we have more than speculation. And I'd advise you to keep your mouth shut. This case started sensitive. What you're talking about now is a freaking open wound."

"I'm not accusing him. But if Doug Cantrell killed Tina and there's any chance he's The Razor, I can't ignore it, either." Even if Lily hates me, he thought with a hollow feeling.

With mixed emotions, Lily watched her niece and her two friends follow Aaron to the front door. Now that dinner was over, this was supposed to be her chance to stay and talk with Ivy. Only, now Lily was more certain than ever that Ivy didn't want to talk to her.

"Wait." Ivy practically knocked Lily down to catch everyone before they left. "I want another picture."

Ashley rolled her eyes and said with an unmistakable whine, "Mom, we're going to be late." Still, she gamely put an arm around her friend in the aqua-blue dress and smiled. As Ivy took the picture, Aaron stared at his daughter with pride and a hint of sadness. The look made Lily's breath catch.

She remembered the same look in her father's eyes when she'd gone to her first dance with Carmen.

She hadn't looked nearly as good or grown-up as Ashley. No wonder Aaron looked sad. With her dark hair braided into an intricate updo and her face lightly accented with makeup, she looked on the verge of womanhood.

"Ash, I wish you'd consider wearing your hair down. It's so beautiful—"

The smile on Ashley's face collapsed. She glared at Ivy. "For the tenth time, Mom, we all agreed to wear our hair up." She gestured to her friends, who shuffled their high-heeled feet, and their similar hairstyles. "Besides, Aunt Lily spent a lot of time styling it for me." Ashley turned to Lily. "And don't forget you said you'd come over tomorrow, Aunt Lily. I want to spend more time with you!"

Ivy glared at her. Yikes. She looked ready to throw Lily out on the street, but she gritted her teeth and turned to her daughter. "Of course your friends look beautiful, but you have particularly—"

Aaron's face reflected Lily's horror. Ashley's face turned red. "Jeez, Mom, now you're insulting my friends?"

"No," Ivy exclaimed. "I'm just saying, why hide what's obviously one of your best features?"

"Oh, so my hair is my best feature. Not my face. Great. Thanks, Mom." Ashley huffed out the front door and her friends dutifully trailed after her.

"Ashley, wait—" Ivy placed her hands on her hips and turned to Aaron. "I didn't mean to insult her friends. I was trying to give her a compliment."

Aaron nodded. "I—uh, I'll drop them off and pick them up at 10:30 like we planned." He shut the door behind him.

An awkward silence immediately filled the room. As Ivy stared at the door, she should have been the epitome of calm beauty—perfectly curled blonde hair, which she'd inherited from their father, pressed jeans and ivory sweater, flawless makeup. But the tension vibrating through her body belied the image.

"Ivy—" Lily began.

"I think I'll watch a movie in my bedroom."

Lily's heart fell. The implication in Ivy's words was unmistakable. She wanted Lily to leave. With a sigh of defeat, Lily turned and stared out into the backyard, with its small, sparsely planted garden and dollhouse-like detached garage.

"Ivy, why do you…?" She turned back to face her sister, shocked to see she was alone. Striding into the hallway, she saw Ivy close her bedroom door and heard the television come on.

Anger replaced Lily's sadness. She marched to her sister's door and knocked. Ivy opened the door and stared at her. Lily had to tilt her head to look up at her sister, and once more she realized they couldn't look more different. Be more different.

"Didn't Ashley look beautiful when she left?"

Surprised that Ivy had actually started the conversation, Lily cautiously said, "Yes."

"She looked so much like Mom. Like you." Her mouth twisted and she shook her head. "Did you finish that painting for that little girl? The one for Fiona?"

Ivy knew about Fiona? About Fiona's painting? That meant she'd actually been listening to what Lily said at dinner. "Y-yes," Lily managed to say. "She found a foster home and I wanted to give her something to warm up her room."

"That's nice. You—you're really talented, Lily. I wish I had a gift like yours."

This time, Lily couldn't disguise her shock.

Ivy laughed. "I know, I know. I'm the bitchy sister. Why would I compliment you?" She bit her lip. "But I mean it."

"Thank you," Lily whispered. The familiar silence threatened to overtake them, so Lily forced herself to break it. "I—I've wanted to talk to you."

"I know," Ivy said solemnly. "But I don't want to talk heavy with you, Lily. And that's what it'd be, right?"

"But why does it have to be heavy? What happened after Mom died? Why have you been so angry with me?"

Shrugging, Ivy looked away. "I wasn't. I'm not. I guess, I just—I just don't want to think about it. Not anymore. I have Ashley."

I have my own family, she meant. One that doesn't include you. Lily nodded to herself. "And you have Aaron—"

A shadow crossed Ivy's face, but she took a deep breath and flashed a weak smile. "Sure. Hey, why don't we watch that movie together—"

Reaching out, Lily placed her hand on Ivy's shoulder. "Is everything okay with you and Aaron?"

Ivy pulled away, tension once more pinching her features. "Mind your own business, Lily."

"I care about you. I want you to be happy. If there's something I can do to help—"

"You want to help? Stop interfering with my personal

relationships. God, it's bad enough that Ashley wants to spend more time with you than me—" Ivy paused when Lily flinched. "I'm sorry. I'm just tired, Lily."

Lily raised her chin. "Fine. I'll just leave you alone—"

"Lily."

Lily paused.

"I don't want to lose her," she whispered softly. So softly Lily barely heard her. "Ashley and I have been fighting constantly."

Lily stepped closer. "About—about what?"

"About boys. About her wanting to wear makeup. She wants to grow up so fast. And I want her to stay my little girl a little longer. Is that so bad?"

Lily shook her head. "No, there's nothing wrong with that. You and Aaron—"

A soft, bitter laugh shot out of Ivy's throat, freezing Lily in her tracks. "Aaron's never here. When he's not working, he's... God, I don't know." She covered her face with her hands. When she lifted them, she had tears in her eyes. "I think he's having an affair."

Automatically, Lily shook her head again. Ivy and Aaron had been together since high school. Since before their mother had died. Ivy had gotten pregnant shortly after that and Aaron had stood by Ivy through everything. She'd never doubted his love for her sister.

"He works late almost every night, Lily. Even if he comes home on time, he leaves after dinner. You've seen that."

"He's working on a big case. Trying to make partner."

Ivy just shrugged.

"Do you want me to call right now? Would that make you feel better?"

"No. No, you're right. I'm sure he's there. And he'll pick up Ashley. He's very responsible. I just...sometimes I wish we were more connected. You know?"

Lily thought of her empty bed at home. Her empty house. Reaching out, she placed a tentative hand on her sister's arm. "I know. And it's there. You, Aaron and Ashley. You're a family. You'll get through this, Ivy."

Ivy pulled back and Lily's hand slipped away. That's twice, she noted sadly.

Then Ivy reached out and hugged her. "I…I love you, Lily."

Stunned, Lily hugged her back. "I love you, too," she whispered.

"I'm going to wait for Ashley. Maybe she'll want to talk about the dance." At the door, Ivy looked back. "We'll talk later, okay?"

"Yes. Later."

When Ivy shut the door, joy rushed through Lily's blood like an overdose of oxygen, making her feel dizzy. She struggled to temper the feeling. She couldn't forget Ivy's behavior reflected her desperation.

On autopilot, Lily gathered up her stuff and walked to her car out front. She froze when she saw a man getting out of his own vehicle, parked just behind hers.

John.

O-kay, John thought.
So she couldn't look more unhappy to see you.
Can you really blame her?

Still, he tried. He waved. "Hi, small fry. Imagine running into you here."

She strode toward him, eyes narrow, looking exactly like she did when she was in "Ba-Lily mode." Lily in battle mode. He'd made up the term a long time ago to tease her about how ferocious she could get. He obviously refrained from using the nickname.

"Are you serious?" she hissed. "What are you doing here?"

"I'm doing exactly what you think I am. I wanted to talk to Ivy and Aaron. Since you're not cooperating, I figured they might." Plus, he'd remembered something critical that had been bugging him. Ivy and Aaron had attended his party on that night so long ago. And he couldn't remember seeing them after

Tina's little visit. Where had they disappeared to? He couldn't imagine they'd had anything to do with her murder, but he'd never considered Doug Cantrell a viable suspect, either.

She looked over her shoulder with a frown on her face, clearly distressed at the idea of him talking to them. "Look, Aaron's not here and Ivy just went to bed. She's—she's been having a tough time with her daughter and I—I really don't want you to disturb her. Please."

He could tell that "please" had cost her. He crossed his arms over his chest. "Tell you what. I'll postpone my interview for a day or two."

Relief instantly washed over her face, then disappeared with his next words.

"But you have to do something for me."

She shook her head. "I—I don't want to talk about that night—"

"I know. Neither do I. Not right now."

She tilted her head inquisitively. Cautiously. "Then what?"

Yeah, what? He didn't know. All he knew was that he wanted to talk to her for a little while. Not fight with her. Not scare her. Just enjoy being with her the way he had before everything had gone to hell. "Your art," he said desperately, saying the first thing that popped into his head.

"My art," she echoed.

"I saw some of your work at the hospital. But I didn't see any paintings. You still paint, don't you? Can—can I see something of yours?"

She looked at him as if he was crazy and truthfully he felt like it. But her art had been a way for her to open up to him back then. Maybe—

"It's seven at night and you want to see one of my paintings," she said slowly.

He shrugged. "I want more than that, Lily. I'm asking for what I think you can give me right now. One painting. Show me something you've painted recently, and I'll wait to talk to Ivy. I mean, I drove all this way, so..." He used a wheedling tone, clearly teasing, and to his surprise she actually smiled before rolling her eyes.

"Fine. Follow me home. I'll show you one painting and then you'll leave. Promise?"

"I promise," he said. She simply looked at him and he wondered if she doubted him. But then she turned away.

After a short ten-minute drive, she pulled into her driveway and stood next to the open garage door. He was hoping she would invite him inside, but instead she pointed to a large canvas already leaning against the wall.

"I just painted that. For Fiona, the little girl you met at the hospital. She's not just shy. She doesn't talk. But she's been placed with a new foster family and I wanted her to have something—"

She pressed her lips together as if she realized she was saying too much. He wanted her to keep talking. To keep listening to her voice. But Lily had trusted him enough to show him this. Trusted him enough to believe his promise. And he wasn't going to do anything to damage that small bit of trust.

He studied the painting for several seconds.

The painting was a hazy abstract of gold, bronze and cranberry, but he saw immediately the kitten-shapes she'd weaved into seemingly casual swirls of color. It was a soft, sweet painting for a soft, sweet girl. A gift to inspire peace and hope. Something he knew Lily hadn't felt for a long time.

"Will they get her another kitten, you think?"

Again, she smiled before she caught herself. "I don't doubt it. The family seems very loving. And you saw for yourself how she makes people melt."

Just like another girl I used to know, he thought. He didn't say it. He caught Lily's gaze, however, and he could tell she knew what he was thinking. His arms ached to reach out to her. To hold her.

But he'd made her a promise.

So he simply nodded. "Thank you for sharing this with me, small fry. She's lucky to have you. And so is your family."

With that, he left.

But he didn't leave behind the memory of Lily's smile. That he took with him, replaying the expression in his mind over and over again, and even in his dreams.

Lily tried watching a movie after John left but she was too restless to sit still.

Without consciously wanting to, she walked out to the garage to stare at Fiona's painting again. The more she looked at it, the less satisfied she was with the top right corner. It needed a little more color, she thought. But even as she took out her paint supplies, she knew she was just trying to distract herself.

John.

She kept thinking of him and the way he'd teased her. The way his eyes had glowed with appreciation as he'd looked at the painting she'd made for Fiona. For a moment, she'd actually forgotten what he was trying to do. Why he'd come back into her life. Maybe it had simply been a result of the talk she'd had with Ivy, but she'd felt almost happy while they'd been standing in her garage. Happy enough to want to apologize for the awful things she'd said to him when he'd come to her house. When he'd come to the hospital.

She kept reminding herself that the happiness was just an illusion.

John would no doubt go back to Ivy and Aaron's house tomorrow.

And Ivy...

She added a trail of red to the canvas.

Could Aaron really be cheating on her? He'd stuck by her through so much. The trial. College. Years of therapy.

Death. Betrayal. Blood.

Just like that, it happened.

A jolt of pain stabbed above Lily's left eye. Although it quickly subsided, an odd feeling kept her frozen.

Something was watching her. Not something behind her,

but in front of her. But the only thing in front of her was her canvas.

Without knowing why, she felt the sudden urge to destroy it. To slash at the canvas with heavy layers of dark acrylic paint and plaster until distinct textural shapes formed on top. To dip her hands in oil paint and smear it around and around the painting's surface until nothing was left of softness, or whimsy, or girlish innocence.

Enormous pressure exploded behind her eyes, making her moan. The canvas undulated, suddenly appearing ripped and torn. Bright streaks of red paint—or was it blood?—ran from top to bottom, dripping off the edge to pool on the hardwood floor.

Her brush and palette dropped from her nerveless fingers.

She whirled around at the clatter, heart beating fast, every cell in her body shouting for survival. Whimpering, she backed up, knocking against the canvas with her elbow. She imagined she felt hard fingers wrapping around her arms.

She whirled again.

"No," she moaned. "Please, no."

The blood was still there.

Traveling down. Melding into the paint Lily herself had applied. Blurring with the red strokes she'd intended to be the fluttering stream of a cat's toy ribbon. But it now resembled a body.

A woman's body, bleeding and dying.

Her mother.

Pain brought Lily to her knees as memories overwhelmed her.

Her own face, plucked and painted because she'd wanted to look older for when she saw John. Her mother's face as they'd argued. The clatter of her heels as she'd run away from her mother, when really what she should have done was run to her and never let go.

Chapter 7

At 11:00 p.m., John sat in the Sac PD break room, waiting for Officer Max Pendelton to come off shift. Pendelton had been one of the first officers to respond to the Tina Cantrell murder scene. He'd also been there when Lily had slapped John and John doubted that was something he'd forget, even years later. Sure enough, the first thing the man said when he walked in the room was, "I know you. You came to the scene the night of the Cantrell murder. You're the daughter's friend. The one she slapped."

The officer hadn't aged well. They were only a few years apart, but time had etched his face with deep grooves. He looked twenty years older. "That's right. You know why I'm here?"

"Yeah. About the Cantrell case. You were there, and you're investigating the case now? Not kosher."

Annoyed, John frowned. "I'm not investigating the Cantrell case, per se. As I told your supervisor, I'm working a series of murders in El Dorado County. I just need to rule out that the perp is the same person who killed Tina Cantrell. You want to call the A.G. handling the Cantrell appeal?"

Walking over to a coffeepot, Pendelton poured himself a cup, and added five spoonsful of sugar then stirred it vigorously. "I remember the case like it was yesterday. My first murder scene." Motioning to the pot, he offered some to John.

"No, thanks. I've already had one."

Pendelton blew in his cup, gingerly took a sip, then grimaced. "Even with a boatload of sugar this coffee is crap." He sat down across from John. "I take it you've seen the crime-scene photos?"

"The photos. The videotape of the scene. The witness statements. That's what I want to talk to you about."

"Shoot."

John weighed his words carefully, not wanting to put Pendelton on the defensive. "When you got there, who was the first person you spoke with?"

"The father. He was the only one lucid enough to give a statement."

"What about his daughter?"

"You saw her, man. She was in shock. Didn't say one word to me or my partner."

"Would you say the father was distraught?"

"His wife had just been stabbed to death. Yeah, I'd say he was distraught."

"Ex-wife," John corrected. "But you said he was lucid. What was his overall demeanor? To Lily in particular?"

"I didn't talk to him directly. My partner did. But he seemed concerned. Paternal. In control. Trying to be calm so she'd be calm. I concentrated on the girl." His eyes shifted away momentarily. "I...made a mistake. I should've led her away from the house. So much blood—all from that one tiny woman." Pendelton's face stiffened in memory. "It was my first murder scene, you know. Still the worst, in my experience."

"Was there anything that struck you about the crime scene? The body?"

"Not really." He shrugged. "I wondered why the girl's hair seemed wet, but the father said it always took a long time to dry."

John straightened. "What are you talking about?" He didn't remember Lily's hair being wet but he hadn't exactly been calm and objective.

"It wasn't sopping wet, but it wasn't quite dry, either." He shrugged again. "I asked the father about it at the hospital. Officer Cantrell said she'd gotten blood on her hair and freaked out. Wouldn't calm down until he rinsed it out. So that's what he did."

"Are you kidding me? Cantrell tampered with evidence and it's not in your report?"

"It was his daughter, man. What would you have done?"

John clenched a fist. When Lily had visited him that night, she'd been wearing a strapless black dress. A far cry from the T-shirt and sweats she'd had on at the crime scene. He'd assumed she'd changed when the cops got there and took her dress as evidence. "What about her clothes? Did she change clothes while you were there?"

Pendelton looked away. "I think the father said she'd changed before we came. To get the blood off her."

"More tampering with evidence." John slapped his hand on the table. "And you didn't think it worth putting in your report?"

Although his hand shook, Pendelton took another sip of coffee. "Didn't I?"

"No. You didn't."

"I guess I didn't think it mattered. She was a kid. And little. There's no way she could have done that to her mother."

That didn't mean the officer shouldn't have noted every detail—relevant or seemingly irrelevant—in his report. Now things having to do with Lily needed to be accounted for. "Your partner, where can I find him?"

"Drake Livingston was an old-timer. He, uh, retired right after the case. Moved to Florida, I think."

And had probably checked out long before then, John thought. No wonder the report had holes. It had been written by one newbie and one officer headed out the door. And Hardesty had been the obvious—the easy—answer. "Did the witnesses give statements at the house?"

"No. The EMT's took the girl to the hospital. Livingston and McDonald processed the scene and waited for the detectives. They interviewed the neighbors. The boyfriend, who had an alibi. They learned about Hardesty. Found out he'd killed his wife while under the influence and had served prison time before being released. Matched his prints to those inside and later got a confession out of him." Pendelton put his mug down with a thump. "Case closed."

As John left the station, Pendelton's words echoed in his mind. Case closed.

Except it wasn't closed. Not by a long shot.

Chapter 8

The night after Ashley's dance, Lily's niece once again roped her into playing beautician. This time, however, she also wanted Lily to play chauffeur. Lily didn't mind. She was enjoying spending time with her family again.

Lily snapped the clip that held up Ashley's shiny dark locks in a half-down, half-up style. "Voila."

Ashley smiled. "Thanks, Aunt Lily." She kissed Lily's cheek and then reached for her sweater. "Let's go. I really want you to meet Mike." Ashley blushed. "I—uh—I mean Tessa."

Lily smiled. "Mike-Tessa, huh? Interesting name."

Her niece blushed.

"Okay. Go get in the car. I'll just grab my coat and purse."

With a sigh of relief, Ashley ran out the door. Lily took a quick look around the room, lightly touching the ribbons and drawings that littered the walls and frilly white vanity. Such a mix of woman and girl, she thought, picking up a picture of Ashley as a toddler. She put it down next to several tubes of lip gloss and body glitter.

Ashley had taken extra care with her appearance, too much care for a simple sleepover. The number of times she'd mentioned Mike, Tessa's stepbrother, explained why.

Had she ever been that young? That innocent?

Yes. But the last time she'd experienced that wild anticipation and euphoria had been with John.

Closing her eyes, Lily shaded her face with the picture, as if it could offer some protection against the hot wave of longing that caressed her. John's kiss had been frighteningly intense, but equally liberating, proving to her without a doubt that she wasn't frigid like she'd believed. It made her wonder what sex would be like with him. She'd probably burst into flames the minute he touched her naked body, let alone penetrated her. Shuddering, she opened her eyes, blinking when the sight of Ashley's room cooled the heat thrumming through her body.

Moving down the hallway, she followed the trail of murmured voices and the smell of chicken piccata.

"—what about Lily? Remember John?"

Lily stopped in the hallway and tried not to breathe. Had John already tried to see them again?

"That was different.... She was vulnerable to that sort of thing."

"And what about me? Was I vulnerable, too?"

Aaron's voice sounded clipped. "I don't know, Ivy. You tell me. Is that why you went out with me?"

The tense silence emanating from the kitchen was palpable. In horror, Lily listened to Ivy and Aaron's escalating argument. Her eyes widened when Aaron mentioned sex. Widened more when Ivy confessed to not liking it.

Evidently, frigidity was something else the Cantrell girls had in common. Closing her eyes, she frowned when Aaron said, "I'm sick of taking the blame for your father's actions." What was he talking about?

The obvious sounds of kissing forced her eyes open. Slowly, she approached the kitchen, hoping to sneak past without them seeing her. But she must have made a noise, because Aaron ripped himself away from Ivy and looked at her. She froze.

Despite their heavy breathing and disheveled clothes and hair, Aaron tried to pretend he hadn't been about to make love to his wife against the kitchen counter. Clearing his throat, he sat at the table behind a cutting board piled with artichokes and picked up the knife.

"You guys going?" Ivy breathed out. Her face was flushed dark red and she wouldn't quite meet Lily's gaze. For her sake, Lily held back her questions.

"I realized I can't stay for dinner. I have—have something to take care of. Ashley will have a ride?"

"Tessa's father will drive her home. Her mom has to take Mike to a baseball game." Ivy raised her fingertips to touch her swollen lips, then dropped them when she saw Lily watching her.

"Okay. Well, bye." Lily shot a final glance at Aaron, but his gaze was riveted to the dinner preparations. Given what she'd just interrupted, she marveled at his slow, precise movements.

She watched the swivel of steel against wood. Her breathing escalated and her vision blurred as Aaron shifted the knife in his hands and jabbed at the individual pieces of artichoke in order to transfer them to the bowl.

A knife plunging into flesh. Over and over again. Until blood drenched the walls. Before she could stop the gruesome visions, a whimper escaped her. She looked up, flushing when she saw Aaron staring at her.

She licked her lips. "I'll—I'll see you later."

He nodded curtly.

Lily waved at Ivy, who now stared at Aaron. For a moment, Lily hesitated, wondering if she should leave Ivy alone.

Reading her mind, Ivy glanced up at her, smiled reassuringly and nodded her head. "It's okay," she mouthed. "Go on."

Rushing outside, Lily got into the car. She took a minute and leaned her head back against the headrest, drawing in deep calming breaths. She felt Ashley's eyes on her.

"Aunt Lily?"

Straightening, Lily shot her niece what she hoped was a reassuring smile. What the hell had just happened in there? "I'm okay, Ash. You ready to go?"

Ashley seemed to hesitate, then shrugged. "Sure."

Turning on the ignition, Lily glanced at her niece. "Put on your seat belt, sweetie."

She set the car radio to Radio Disney and tried to enjoy Ashley's animated singing. Normally, Lily would be singing with her, laughing at the way her niece was butchering the words, but the memory of Aaron and Ivy's argument covered her in a thick shroud of anxiety. And when she thought about Aaron gripping the kitchen knife—even though she tried not to think about it—she imagined horrible things. Felt fear bite into her so sharply she clenched the steering wheel until her knuckles whitened.

"Aunt Lily!"

Lily jerked when Ashley called her name.

"You missed the turn on Marigold, Aunt Lily."

She shook her head and laughed. "Daydreaming, I guess." She pulled over to the curb and checked her rearview mirror in order to execute a U-turn. Ashley placed a hand on her arm and she automatically covered it with one of her own, turning to give her niece a smile. Ashley stared at her with such solemn eyes that Lily immediately felt a pit form in her stomach.

"Can I ask you something, Aunt Lily?"

Lily squeezed her fingers. *She's going to ask me about her parents fighting,* Lily thought, then took a deep breath. *I'll just tell her everyone fights. That her father's stressed at work...*

"Mom never talks about it, you know. Not to me. But I know Grandma Tina was murdered."

Lily tried to hide her shock but she was speechless for several seconds. Finally, she managed to respond. "You do?"

Ashley nodded. "Some kids at school were talking about it. I went to the library and looked up some articles. I know—I know the man who did it got the death penalty."

"How does that make you feel?"

"Glad," Ashley said fiercely. "I'm glad he's going to die for what he did. Aren't you?"

"I don't know," Lily whispered.

"Why not?"

"Because what I really want is my mother back. And whether he dies or not, I'm not going to get that."

Ashley stared out the windshield, focusing on the tree-lined street. "I'm sorry."

Lily jerked her gaze back to Ashley's. "For what?"

"I made you sad. Bringing it up. I shouldn't have—"

Lily released her seat belt and leaned toward her niece, catching her in a tight hug. "Don't be sorry. You can ask me anything, Ashley."

"Really?"

"Yes. Really."

With one last reassuring pat, Lily pulled away from the curb and was almost to Tessa's house when Ashley asked, "What did Grandpa do afterward?"

"You mean after Grandma Tina died?"

Ashley nodded.

"He took care of your mom and me. Made sure we had people to talk to if we wanted to. If you—if you ever need someone to talk to, you'll tell us, right? Tell your mom?"

"You mean like a therapist?" Ashley asked drily, with all the wry sarcasm of a fourteen-year-old.

Lily laughed. "Yes, I mean a therapist."

"I'll let you guys know."

"Good. Why did you ask? About Grandpa I mean."

Without seeming to know it, Ashley started bouncing in her seat as they pulled up to Tessa's house. "There's Mike's car. He's here." She opened the door and grabbed her overnight bag from the back.

"Ashley, wait. Why did you ask about Grandpa Doug?"

With a quick glance at the house, Ashley ducked her head in and gave Lily a kiss. "Oh, it was just something I heard my mom and dad talking about once. Something about Grandpa Doug doing what he'd done because of you."

Lily frowned. "Because of me? Are you su—"

"Bye, Aunt Lily. Thanks!" Ashley dashed off just as the front door opened and Tessa came running out. Tessa's mom stepped outside and waved to Lily.

With an uneasy, troubled feeling, Lily waved back, then drove away.

Chapter 9

Outside the downtown Victorian with blue paint and white trim, Lily took a deep breath and tried to ignore the stifling heat of the midday sun. It had been over ten years since she'd seen Dr. Tyler, and over five since she'd actually spoken with her before she'd called her. It was no wonder John's mother had sounded surprised by her request for an appointment. Lily would have given anything to have never seen the woman again. And not because she hated her. She felt extremely grateful to the woman who'd essentially risked her career to help Lily find a measure of peace after her mother's death. And even though she hadn't remained her regular therapist for long, she'd been the one to bring Lily out of the darkest depths of her despair.

She walked up the steep set of stairs and entered the house. A few chairs and a large table with a puzzle in progress, as well as stacks of magazines, waited on the right. She went the other direction, toward the open door of Dr. Tyler's office.

Inside, Dr. Tyler smiled and rose from her chair to greet her. "Lily."

A rush of affection and sadness ran through her. Nora Tyler was almost sixty, but her skin was smooth and fairly taut, a testament to her dedication to stay out of the sun. She wore fashionably slim jeans and a scoop-necked emerald sweater that complemented her blue eyes and dark curly hair, which she wore loose. Her casual clothes surprised Lily. In the past, she'd always worn suits and kept her hair pulled back. The change made her seem more approachable. Lily felt the urge to hug her, but stifled it since John's mother had never been comfortable with PDAs.

With regret and an ache in her chest, she thought of Carmen. She knew she was some kind of doctor now, but that was all. Lily had read a brief bio of her in the *Sac Bee*, when the Juvenile Diabetes Research Foundation had spotlighted her efforts on their behalf. Lily normally went to the charity's annual fundraiser, but she'd deliberately missed that year's gala to insure she wouldn't run into Carmen.

"Come in, dear."

Lily stepped into Dr. Tyler's office. She'd redecorated, but she'd kept the wingback chair, upholstered in a different fabric, that Lily had always sat in. She sat in it now. "Thank you for seeing me. I know how you felt about keeping me as a patient before, but I was hoping with all the time that's passed, it would be okay. You—you're really the only one I trust with this kind of thing."

Smiling, Dr. Tyler nodded. "You know I'm happy to help you, Lily."

"This time, I can even pay you. No more pro bono stuff."

Dr. Tyler crouched next to her and took her hands in hers. "That was never an issue, Lily. Your mother was one of my dearest friends. I always regretted that we'd drifted apart before..." A shadow crossed over her face and she patted Lily's hands again before straightening. "So long as you know the same rules apply, I think we're fine for one session. But for the same reasons I gave you before, I can't take you on as a regular client, Lily. Your past friendship with Carmen and John complicates things and I don't want to jeopardize either one of us."

"Sure." Dr. Tyler had already jeopardized her career once by treating Lily. She'd had little choice since she'd been the only one that could get Lily to talk during the first year after the murder.

Lily cleared her throat as Dr. Tyler took the seat across from her. "Is it okay if I ask about Carmen? How is she?"

It was subtle, but Dr. Tyler's smile faltered. "She's fine, Lily. Thank you. We'd better get started since I have an appointment in an hour. How are you?"

Staring at her hands, Lily shrugged. "I'm not doing so well."

"I read the reports your other therapists faxed me. As of a few years ago, you were dealing with your trauma extremely well. No recurring nightmares. No anxiety. Despite being off medication for several years. What's changed?"

"I—I don't know. The dreams have come back. Worse than they've ever been."

Dr. Tyler nodded, a small furrow between her brows. "Tell me about the dreams."

Lily briefly described the dream she kept having. "It's after my father says it's my fault that I wake up, terrified. I always—I always have to take a few minutes to convince myself it wasn't real. That—that I wasn't really there." Taking a deep breath, Lily leaned back in her chair and waited for Dr. Tyler to tell her she was being ridiculous.

Only she didn't. "Aren't you going to tell me how silly that is?"

The chair creaked and Dr. Tyler leaned closer, once more covering one of Lily's hands with her own. "Tell me again, where were the others in this dream?"

Staring at their clasped hands, Lily fought back the rise of fear inside her.

"Lily."

Her gaze lifted to Dr. Tyler's.

"It's okay." Dr. Tyler stood. "Let's just talk this through." Removing her hand, she sat back.

"You said the dream started the way it always does. With you walking into the house and seeing Hardesty standing over your mother's body."

"Yes. She was crawling. Trying to get away." She glanced down again. Her fingers had clenched together so tightly that her knuckles whitened. "But this dream seemed different somehow. Even at the beginning."

"Different how?"

She shook her head. "I don't know. More colorful, maybe. More vibrant."

"Go on."

Her mouth felt dry, so she reached for the glass of water in front of her and took a sip. "I tried to run to her. To help."

When she didn't go on, Dr. Tyler finished for her. "But then someone stopped you?"

She nodded. "Yes. And then they were standing next to me. Hardesty on one side. Dad on the other. And we watched together. While someone else—not Hardesty, but someone else—hurt her and carried her away. And that's when my dad turns to me and tells me it's my fault."

Lily's palms shook and a fine film of sweat covered her forehead, chilling her. She struggled to breathe evenly.

"It's okay," Dr. Tyler urged. "You're going to be okay."

Lily leaped to her feet. "How can you say that? I can tell what you're thinking. That this is some kind of memory coming to the surface. That I witnessed my mother's murder and stood by while someone did that to her."

Calmly, Dr. Tyler shook her head. "I didn't say that." She rose and walked to a sideboard on the other side of the room. She took something out of a cabinet and Lily heard glass clink together and the sound of liquid being poured. When she turned back, Dr. Tyler carried two glasses, each with a small amount of liquid.

"It's not exactly business as usual, but we're not exactly business acquaintances, now are we?" She held out one glass. Lily stared at it, then slowly reached out to take it. Dr. Tyler lightly tapped her glass against hers. "*Salud*, Lily." She swallowed the contents of her glass, grimacing slightly, then smiled encouragingly at Lily.

Lily stared at the contents, then mentally shrugged. The offer itself had calmed her nerves. Closing her eyes, she threw back the drink, then choked. And coughed. And then laughed almost hysterically.

"What IS that?"

Dr. Tyler shook her head and laughed herself. "It's called Rumple Minze Peppermint Schnapps 100. 100 Proof. A college dorm mate used to sneak it in to our room. I keep it around for tense moments like this. Breaks the ice and all that."

Lily collapsed back in her chair. "You've changed," she whispered, then dropped her head into her hands.

She felt something stroke her hair. "So have you. It's called growing up."

Lily raised her head. "You were already grown up."

"Maybe too much. I—I pulled into myself after my husband's death. Normal, of course. I know—I know it was hard for Carmen. Even John. But then subsequent events—" she smiled sadly and stroked Lily's hair again "—made me realize I needed to get over myself before I lost everything."

Silence hung heavily between them and Lily knew they were thinking of the same woman who had meant so much to both of them.

"Do you know what your mother used to say? That you inherited not only the best of her looks, but the best of everything else. Because you had her strength and passion and ability to love, but not her weaknesses."

"Weaknesses? My mom wasn't weak."

"No. In many ways she wasn't. But neither were you. She just…she just wanted to protect you so much, Lily. Too much,

I think." Dr. Tyler smiled sadly. "Just like your father. And John—" She stopped abruptly, her expression troubled.

Despite the sudden acceleration of her pulse, Lily quickly changed the subject. "My mom was the toughest person I knew. She kicked my dad out as soon as she found out about his affair. Not many women can do that."

Dr. Tyler looked away.

"What is it?" Lily whispered.

Hesitating a fraction of a second before meeting Lily's gaze, Dr. Tyler said, "She wasn't my patient, and my priority is you. Let me tell you that your mother loved your father so much, Lily. So much that she didn't act that much differently from other women when it came to forgiving infidelity."

Stunned, Lily sat quietly for several minutes. Dr. Tyler let her have the time to adjust. To grapple with the fact that even now, her father's actions—his imperfection—could still stun her.

Then Dr. Tyler cleared her throat. "About your dreams, Lily. I can't dismiss that you may be remembering details through them. I've done a lot of work with hypnotherapy. We have so little understanding of what the mind retains without knowing it.

"Also, let's not forget the stress you're under because of Hardesty's upcoming execution. For that reason alone, it's completely natural that your dreams have become more disturbing. It's also possible—no, probable—your father's words in the dream are simply a manifestation of your own misplaced guilt."

Lily stifled a sob. "But I thought I'd let that go. I want to move on."

"And you are."

When Lily moaned with frustration, Dr. Tyler said, "Okay. Let's forget the dream for a moment. You said you've seen your sister recently. How'd that go?"

Taking a deep breath, Lily shrugged. "We've made some progress. But there are obviously still issues between us."

"And your father?"

"We've barely seen each other the past few months."

"Are you still doing your journaling?"

Lily guiltily averted her gaze.

"It'll help, Lily. Help identify a pattern."

"I just want to let it go," she said wearily. "I don't want to think about it anymore, let alone write about it."

"I know. But, if you journal your dreams, you may be able to view them more objectively. We may be able to focus in on what your subconscious is trying to tell you."

"We? I thought you said—"

"I know. But I don't see why we can't work together so long as we keep our personal lives separate. If you'd like to work with me, I'd like to give it a try. I'm wondering one thing though—have you ever considered going back on the meds?"

Lily's lips tightened. "No. I'd rather not take drugs if it's not necessary. I've been doing fine."

"It's up to you, of course. I'm just worried that you're going through a difficult time. And these panic attacks seem extreme."

"Yes, extreme is putting it mildly." She sighed and accepted defeat. "I'll talk to someone about a prescription."

"Good." Dr. Tyler rose.

"Dr. Tyler," Lily whispered. "What about hypnosis? You said you'd done hypnotherapy before. I—I'm hoping that we can give that a try. Because I can't stand these feelings anymore. I can't stand feeling like I'm missing something, something important, something crucial when a man's life is at stake."

"Well, we did our own hypnotherapy sessions to a certain degree. The meditative exercises I taught you? The ones you say you still practice? Those are all the foundation for hypnosis. It's all about getting yourself into a calm, peaceful place where you can relax. Where your brain can free itself without your even realizing it."

Lily stared at her. It was a similar principle to what she

taught her patients, only the way she encouraged them to deal with their feelings was through art. "I suppose that makes sense."

"Why don't I make an appointment for you next week? You can come back. We can talk about it. I wish I could talk more, but I'm meeting someone in about five minutes."

Lily rose. "Thank you for seeing me. It's been difficult for me, these past few days. And—and—" It was on the tip of her tongue to tell her about John. But she couldn't.

Nora Tyler stepped forward and squeezed Lily in her arms. Stunned, it took a moment for Lily to return the gesture.

"Thank you, again."

"Goodbye, Lily. We'll see each other soon."

Lily left her office, making a brief detour into the bathroom. When she came out, Dr. Tyler's door was closed and she could hear the soft murmur of voices behind it. She was almost out the front door when Dr. Tyler's door opened and John stepped out with his mother.

They both stared at one another in shock. Swiftly, Lily opened the front door, scurried outside, and shut the door behind her. She ran to her car. Nerves jangling, she unlocked her door and opened it. She wasn't surprised, however, when she felt the firm but gentle grip of masculine fingers around her arm.

"Hold on there, small fry. I can't let you slip out of here that easily."

Slowly, she turned to face him. She braced herself for images of blood and the sad memories that bombarded her whenever she saw him.

Only this time, something strange happened. All she saw was him. His dark hair and steady gaze. His tall, solid strength.

She blinked.

No cruel memories. No guilt.

The shock in his eyes had faded somewhat, replaced with a sweet combination of determination and heat. The look made her jittery and scared, but in a way that had nothing to do with the past and everything to do with the powerful kiss they'd shared.

"I need to leave," she gritted. "And you're bothering me."

The tips of his mouth quirked up, making her face heat. Damn her poor choice of words. "I mean, we said everything we needed to say to each other."

"Not everything." John pushed her car door closed when she tried to open it further. "You were here to see my mother?"

"I still can't—I can't talk about it."

He nodded. "Okay. But can I ask you another question?" Before she could answer, he leaned down and stared solemnly into her eyes. "Are you going to hate me forever, small fry? Because I don't think I could stand that."

Completely taken by surprise by his soulful tone, she froze. Her lower lip trembled. She struggled for words. Sighing, he leaned back against her car and pulled her unresisting into his arms.

She was transported to that moment when she was in his arms at the hospital. Kissing him. A frisson of longing swept through her, so powerful that she immediately fought it, slowly pulling out of his arms.

Clearing her throat, she asked, "So how goes the investigation? Have you uncovered anything new?"

He seemed more troubled by the fact she'd broken his embrace than by her question. "I'm just trying to sort a few things out. Some things don't make sense."

"What could possibly make sense about a woman being stabbed to death by a stranger?" Her voice broke and she closed her eyes, rubbing a twinge of pain that pierced her temple. She imagined a flash of movement. A knife piercing skin. Blood spatter.

"Was he a stranger?"

Her eyes flew open. "Wh-what are you saying?"

"I'm saying maybe Hardesty and your mother had a relationship that no one knew about."

"No! He was—" She shook her head. "She was dating someone."

"Hardesty was what?"

The sudden aggressiveness in his tone stunned her. She reminded herself that this man made a living interrogating people and getting to the truth. She couldn't forget that. "You know he was homeless. That he broke into our house looking for money."

"What I know is someone moved the body before you got home. The two most likely candidates are your father and Hardesty. Since you seem so sure it wasn't your father—"

"It wasn't," she said, but couldn't stop herself from thinking of her dream. She, her father, and Hardesty, all watching while someone else hurt her mother. But that wasn't real. She hadn't been there. Neither had her father. "So what if Hardesty moved the body? What difference does that make? He still killed her."

"The fact she was moved to her bed tells me the killer cared for her. Which is why I'm wondering if Hardesty and your mother—"

"No," she snapped. "My mother would never have been romantically involved with Hardesty. The idea is ludicrous."

"Maybe you're right," John conceded. "It's just a theory."

She stared at the ground but he nudged her chin up, refusing to let her get away with it. "So, you're seeing my mother again?"

"Again?" she whispered. "She—she told you she'd treated me before? But that's—"

John shook his head. "Believe me, my mother and I never talk about her patients. I found out almost fifteen years ago."

She could tell by the tense set to his shoulders that there was more to it than that. "What happened?"

His lips tightened. "I saw you together at Ravenswood. You screamed when you saw me. Wouldn't stop until I left."

She saw the pain on his face as if it had just happened. She reached out a tentative hand, but let it fall before she made contact. "I—I didn't know. I'm sorry."

John shrugged and glanced back at his mother's office. "She's waiting for me. I—I better get going."

"John?"

He stopped and turned back to her. "Yes?"

"I—I meant it. I'm sorry about what I said about your father."

"I know. Thank you. Did you deliver that painting to Fiona?"

She frowned, not at his question, but at the memories it brought back. At the fact she'd freaked out, imagining violence and blood while tweaking the painting he was now talking about. "Yes, I gave it to her this morning. She seemed to like it."

"Not surprised at all. I'm glad she's found a family to care for her."

And the thing was, he really did seem glad. Family had always been important to him. "You're meeting your mother for lunch, so things are going good? With her and you? And with Carmen?"

He crossed his arms over his chest. "It hasn't been easy. But in the past few years, we've managed to make ground. She realizes she pushed us away. I reminded her too much of my father. And Carmen just reminded her of herself, before she'd learned how to protect herself. How about you and your dad?"

Lily shrugged. "Still a work in progress."

"That's good. That you're working on it, I mean." His face serious, he jerked his chin in the way guys used to communicate. "I'll be in touch."

He started up the stairs to his mother's office.

"When?"

He froze. His eyes met hers and she could tell she'd surprised him. She'd surprised herself.

She tilted up her chin. "When will you be in touch? I—I

think it's time we finally sat down and talked, John. I know Hardesty killed my mother."

Moving back down the stairs, he began, "What—"

"No," she said, and he stopped his descent. "Not now. You need to talk to your mother and I—well, I need to go home and think about a few things. But I—I'll talk to you. I promise. Can you—can you come by my house tomorrow?"

"What time?"

"What time can you come over?"

A small smile tugged at his lips. "Four?"

Nodding, she smiled back. "Four sounds good. I'll see you then."

She watched John shut the office door just as the doors of a car parked at the curb in front of her opened. A plain woman with frizzy red hair and a boxy brown suit, and a large, overweight man with gray hair and a ponytail exited the car. The woman smiled and waved, as if she knew her. The man just glared at her with a grim, expressionless face, and his posture reminded her a little of the men her father had worked with when he was a cop.

Lily squinted but couldn't place her.

"Ms. Lily Cantrell?"

"Yes," Lily said.

She held out her hand and Lily automatically reached out to take it. "This is Oscar Laslow. He's an investigator and I'm Joanna Sherwood, Chris Hardesty's attorney."

"I'm sorry. I didn't mean for you two to run into each other."

John looked up at his mother and felt an almost childish urge to embrace her. Her face didn't reflect it, but he could imagine how troubled she was he'd seen Lily.

"I always seem to screw up where my own kids are concerned. Isn't that what you and Carmen told me? Putting my clients before the two of you?"

Still recovering from the shock of hearing his mother use

the word "screw," John shook his head. "I wasn't perfect, Mom. We both know I did things. Things I'm not proud of."

"I know. But you never hurt anyone. Not intentionally. I've never believed otherwise."

"It's okay, Mom. We've talked about this."

She nodded her head. Cleared her throat. "I know it was hard for you to leave Lily behind, but you did it because you had to. I'm not surprised you've found each other again."

John studied his mother with little surprise. "You've always known how I felt about her, haven't you?"

"Yes."

"And that's why you helped her. Because of how I felt about her. And how Carmen felt about her. It's why you paid for her to stay at Ravenswood Rehabilitation Clinic after her mother died."

Her eyes widened in surprise.

Smiling, John shook his head. "A good guess. There's no way her family could have afforded it."

"I loved her and her family," his mother whispered. "We drifted apart after your father—" She released her breath in a shuddering sigh. "But fifteen years later she's still suffering." She glanced at him in horror. "I'm sorry, I shouldn't have said that."

He nodded grimly. "It's okay, Mom. I know you can't say anything. But—but I need to ask you a question. A hypothetical question," he rushed out when he saw her frown.

"Okay. Go ahead."

"What effect does trauma have on memory loss?"

His mother stared at him and John struggled not to squirm. Please, he urged silently. Forget the rules. Forget you treated her. Help me.

She spoke calmly. "Memory loss is a defense mechanism. It allows the human psyche to block out the emotions associated with the memories. The mind will go to great lengths to protect itself. The psychological ego keeps one balanced with reality and helps balance emotions—we call it modulating emotions.

And when emotions are really overwhelmed, that ego function can become endangered. If you have ego disintegration, you are going to have something close to a psychotic state. The mind will block certain traumatic memories to keep itself sane."

John pressed his hands into his eyes. "What about if a young girl believed her father killed her mother? Could that cause memory loss?"

His mother sucked in her breath. "John—"

"Mom, please. Just answer the question."

"Of course." She nodded. "During a traumatic event, memory can be encoded somewhat differently. The person can experience the emotions without any understanding of what they are about. She can have flashes of memory, or they can show up in dreams. Dreams that are different than REM dreams. More vivid. More intense. Eventually, she might question what was real and what wasn't."

"And if, on some subconscious level, Lily—I mean, someone—was there and saw the murder?"

Her mother breathed out. "Shock could make that person malleable. Easily influenced. And if that person was young? If that person was Lily's age? She'd want to feel safe. She'd want to do anything she could to survive." She hesitated. "John, do you really think Doug…?" Her voice trailed away when John's cell phone rang.

With a muffled curse, he retrieved it from his pocket. "I'm sorry. Let me just get this… This is Tyler." He heard nothing. "Hello? This is Detective John Tyler."

"Mr. Tyler? This is Mason Park."

John glanced at his mother and mouthed he would just be a second. "What can I do for you?"

"I—I just—I lied to you before."

"Excuse me?" John snapped, immediately wondering if the man was calling to confess to killing Tina Cantrell. If that was the case—

"When you asked me if I thought it was a fling. I knew it wasn't. Not for me."

John closed his eyes and took a deep breath. "Mr. Park, I really don't have time—"

But Park wasn't listening. "I loved her. And I've thought about her almost every day since we talked. So, if you need me to take a polygraph—I'll do it."

"That's great. I'll have one of my deputies contact you to set one up."

"I mean, they're reliable, right? Have other witnesses taken one? Doug? Lily?"

"It's a complicated process, Mr. Park, one that will be explained to you thoroughly. Now, I really need to go, but please call me if you remember anything. You haven't, have you? Remembered anything?"

"Oh, no. No, nothing new."

John turned to stare out the window. He jerked back when he saw Lily still standing on the sidewalk talking to a man and woman.

He cursed.

A man and woman he recognized.

He shut his phone and lunged for the door.

Joanna Sherwood followed Lily back to her car despite her repeated attempt to stop the conversation. "We've tried calling. Writing letters. You've never responded."

Lily opened her car door, jerking in surprise when Mr. Laslow slammed it shut. The threat in his action when compared to John's just moments earlier was huge.

The sun beat down on her. Too bright. Too hot. As she stared at Laslow, anxiety and a hollow feeling of vulnerability shook her. She felt small and defenseless and exposed.

Ms. Sherwood frowned at the man. "Easy, Oscar. We're not here to intimidate her." Returning her gaze to Lily, she urged, "Please, he just wants to talk with you. Don't you think a dying man deserves—"

"Hey. Get away from her." John was suddenly back, stalking down the stairs and toward Lily with a menacing thrust to his jaw that made Ms. Sherwood's eyes widen.

Still, she remained focused on her goal. "Ms. Cantrell, please. I'm begging you—"

John stood by her side. His mother stood in the doorway, worry etching her normally serene features. "Laslow, what the hell are you doing?"

Oscar Laslow tipped his head at John. "Hey, John. Me and the PD here are just having a little chat with Ms. Cantrell."

"Well, I don't think Ms. Cantrell is interested in talking right now." He glanced at Lily. "Or am I wrong?"

Lily shook her head.

To Joanna Sherwood, John said, "In case you don't know, lady, that means no. So we'll be going inside now."

Gently taking Lily's arm, John guided her up the stairs and past his mother. Before they got inside, however, Lily stopped and tugged herself away from John. She walked to the top of the stairs and called out to Joanna Sherwood, who paused in the act of getting into her car.

"Ms. Sherwood, Chris Hardesty won't get any pity from me. You've harassed me for years. This is where it ends." She felt John stand by her side, and the gentle pressure of his arm against her shoulder gave her added strength. In a louder voice, she said, "I'm getting a restraining order. If you attempt to contact me again, you'll regret it."

Joanna Sherwood straightened, braced her hands on her hips and thrust out her chin. "Then I guess I'll have to get a court order for an evidentiary hearing. One way or another, someone needs to hear Chris's side of things."

"He killed two women," she whispered. "How can you defend him?"

"He's maintained his innocence the whole time. And now there's—"

"Lily, let's go."

Lily shook her head and she raised her eyes to John. "She thinks he's innocent. Do you?"

A shadow crossed his face and he raised his hand to cup her chin. "Come inside with me, small fry. We can talk inside."

Dread filling her once more, she allowed him to gently take her arm and lead her inside.

For the first time, she allowed the question to actually form in her mind. "What if?"

What if Hardesty wasn't the one?

Chapter 10

At work the next day, Lily gathered her things even as she second-guessed her impulsive offer to talk to John later this afternoon. As she turned to flip off the light, she sensed someone behind her, and whirled around. Hand to her chest, she smiled. "Hey," she said. "I was hoping you'd come by again. You left so suddenly the other day."

Albert shrugged. "I saw the doc. Just wanted to say hello."

"I'm so glad." She smiled regretfully. "I was just leaving for the day, but I made you something. Will you wait while I get it?"

Surprise flickered across Albert's face. She removed the package from the low cabinet across the room, then crossed back to him and held it out. He didn't take it. Just continued to look at her with suspicious, narrowed eyes. "It took me a few nights, but I think I got it right."

Slowly, he took the bundle and unwrapped it. She clasped her hands together, anxious to see if he liked it. When he saw the colorful mosaic, he pressed his lips together. *"Gracias,"* he said. "It is...cool."

Lily nodded. "It's an easy technique. I can show you—"

Albert's eyes flickered to something over her right shoulder. He morphed right in front of her. Thrust out his chin. Banked the joy in his eyes. Towered over her with a menacing presence that had her cringing.

Damn it, no! She whirled around. Three boys swaggered toward them, radiating hostility and aggression. They swept Lily with disdainful, mocking glances designed to make her feel intimidated and nakedly vulnerable. Albert immediately stepped toward them and rattled something off in Spanish while trying to lead them away.

The boy in the middle resisted. "What did she give you?" He held out his hand.

Lily shifted her body and stared at Albert. He briefly met her gaze.

"What? You need this bitch's permission? I think you're forgetting where your loyalty lies, punk."

"No, Ernesto. I'm not. Here." Albert handed Ernesto the mosaic.

Ernesto stared at it, rotating it one way and then the other. "What is it?"

Albert shrugged.

Ernesto imitated the gesture. "Well, then it doesn't matter if—" he dropped it "—it breaks." The mosaic landed on the floor with a thud. Part of one corner split from the whole. Albert didn't say a word.

"Lily."

Lily's head jerked up at John's voice. Relief swept over her so quickly that her knees threatened to buckle. He stood behind the group of boys, his body braced as if ready to strike. In a black T-shirt, leather jacket, jeans and boots, he emanated toughness, making Albert's friends resemble little boys trying to act tough. With slow, measured steps, he moved toward them until his body stood between her and the other males. "Get away from her."

Lily moved beside Albert and kept her eye on the boys. If they made one wrong move, she was going to scream like bloody hell.

Ernesto didn't say anything. Didn't move.

"Now," John commanded. He pulled back his jacket, showing Ernesto something inside. Ernesto smiled but backed up.

"Anything you say. Pig."

Ernesto looked at Albert. "Outside." Kicking the mosaic before he disappeared, he left. One of the other boys spit on the mosaic before they followed him out.

Albert stepped up to the mosaic and knelt down, his stricken expression telling her all she needed to know. She placed a hand on his shoulder. "It's okay," she whispered. "Just stay here."

He shook his head and brushed off her hand. "I...I can't..." He swallowed.

"Don't go with them, Albert. Please."

He closed his eyes for a second. "You don't understand. You don't know—" Turning abruptly, he practically ran to the doorway.

"Wait!"

He stopped.

She ran to the drawer with her purse and searched inside. Panicking when she couldn't find what she wanted, she dumped it out, then grabbed a small white card. She offered it to Albert. "I want you to call me if you need me."

"Lily..." John growled.

She shot him a look of warning. He stopped talking, but he didn't look happy. In fact, he looked furious.

She ignored him and turned back to Albert. "You're not like them, Albert. You've got talent. A talent that can speak to the world. Keep up with it."

Albert hesitated before taking the card. Backing away, his body rocking in an insolent swagger that she knew was solely for John's benefit, he left. "So that's the kind of patients you have? Street thugs?"

She stiffened, her relief and gratitude leaving her as fast as it had formed. "I work with all kinds of patients. Cancer, burn, HIV positive, and substance-abuse patients included. And you weren't exactly known for your model behavior when we were growing up."

John stared at her, his fists clenched at his sides. "My past isn't the issue here. That kid's trouble. Lily, what are you thinking? And what the hell did you just give him? Your phone number?"

She hugged her arms tightly to her chest. "I don't have to explain myself to you. Besides, Albert's a good kid. He'll stay out of trouble if he knows someone cares."

John's own eyes widened in disbelief. "He's a gangbanger. A Norteño."

She winced and pressed a hand to her aching head. "I know, but he says he's going to jump out." She began throwing her stuff back into her purse. "What are you doing here? We're not supposed to meet until four."

"I know that."

"Then why—?"

"I don't know. I guess four just wasn't soon enough for me."

He'd moved closer. She could feel the heat radiating from him—from his body, from his eyes, from the fingers that he lifted to gently caress her cheek. "I didn't mean to insult your friend. I just worry about you, Lily. I always have."

Her muscles remained stubbornly tight for several seconds. When his hand dropped away, she hid her regret with a shrug. "There might have been reason for you to. Back then. But I'm no longer a child, John. I can take care of myself."

John smiled and took a step back. "That you can, small fry. But can I walk you to your car, anyway?"

On the walk to her car, Lily started to relax. Less than an hour later, John sat across from Lily in her living room, faking a casualness he wasn't feeling. She wore the old tense, silent armor.

To give them both some breathing room, he forced himself to glance around her house. The inside of her home didn't look nearly as generic as the outside. Paintings, masks and mosaic tiles were everywhere. Framed certificates dotted the wall.

Of their own volition, his eyes returned to Lily, drawn by her fresh, feminine appearance despite the troubled expression in her eyes. She wore street clothes and a ponytail, which made his hands itch to unwind the silken strands. Every time he touched her, whether it was her hair, lips or skin, she always felt cool. But then she'd immediately start to warm.

Reading his thoughts, she shifted nervously then announced, "I'll get some drinks. Be right back." She raced from the room. She came back several minutes later with two glasses and a pitcher of what looked like lemonade on a tray, which she put down on the table. Then she gnawed on her thumb.

She poured him a glass and confirmed, "It's lemonade."

He took a drink, set down his glass, then picked up the framed picture beside it. It was a picture from before the divorce. She looked just like she had at sixteen. Sweet. Saucy. Happy. She had her arms wrapped around her mother, while Ivy hugged their father. When he looked up, she was also staring at the photo, her expression achingly sad.

Oh, baby. I wish I could make this all go away.

She saw him looking at her and straightened. The speed with which she wiped her expression clean spoke of years of practice.

He put the picture down. "I noticed your mom wore this same necklace the night of..." He cleared his throat. "Was it valuable?"

She shook her head and lifted her hand to her throat, pulling the pendant from behind her shirt. "It has sentimental value more than anything else. It has my mom's birthstone. Garnet. The other two stones are mine and Ivy's birthstone.

Aquamarine—we were both born in March. My dad gave it to her after I was born."

She tucked the necklace back under her shirt.

"And who's that?"

She picked up the picture of a smiling girl with dark hair.

"This is my niece, Ashley. Isn't she beautiful?"

"Yes, she is. Not surprising since she looks so much like you. But then again, she reminds me a little of Carmen. Something about her cheekbones, I guess." He stopped rambling, feeling like an idiot.

"She's got her first crush. A boy named Mike. Her best friend's stepbrother. Weird, huh?" Blushing, she put the frame down with a shaky hand and stared over his shoulder. "You asked me about Carmen before…I didn't mean to hurt her. It's just, after my mom…well, I didn't really keep in touch with anyone." Before he could respond to her, she took a deep breath, sat back, and twisted her hands in her lap. "All right. So, how does this work?"

"What?"

"This questioning thing."

He smiled. "Well, I'm not going to pull out my spotlight and rubber hose, if that's what you mean. Why don't we just talk about what you remember? Or more to the point, what you don't remember."

What he really wanted was to hold off on their official business for a while longer, but he knew that wouldn't be fair. She'd voluntarily chosen to cooperate. She deserved to get this over with as quickly as possible.

He took a file from his briefcase and flipped to the testimony she'd given during Hardesty's penalty phase hearing. It was very brief, focused on the discovery of her mother's body. "Your testimony at trial established you have memory blanks. Is that still true?"

She nodded. "Yes. I remember going to your party. I remember seeing you—" She flushed and looked down at her shoes. "I remember leaving. That's when my memory really starts to get fuzzy."

"Fuzzy how?"

"I remember walking home. Sort of. But it's like walking through molasses. I get glimpses of emotion. But it seems like a dream."

She glanced up. For a moment, she looked desperate to be anywhere but here. Talking about anything but this. "It seems like a nightmare." She took several long swallows. "Obviously, it wasn't a great night for me."

"For me, either," he said.

"So I was walking home. I knew something was wrong. I felt out of it. I was imagining creepy crawly things all around me, but I didn't know it was drugs at the time." She frowned. "I still don't know how drugs got into my system but I remember my dad picking me up. I remember us walking into the house. I remember…finding her. Then things get blank again. Until the next day, when my dad…my dad told me she was dead."

She closed her eyes and raised her hand to her mouth as if she was getting ready to throw up.

I can't do this, John thought. *Yet what choice do I have? If I don't make her talk about it, someone else will.* "I saw you at the party around 8:30. You fought with your mother around seven?"

Lowering her hand, she took a deep breath. "Seven-thirty."

"So what did you do for an hour?"

The way she stiffened put all of John's senses on red alert. For a moment she just stared at him, a small frown pinching her features. But then her expression smoothed and her shoulders relaxed. "I went to the park. Sat in that old cement tube. Thought about going back. But I wanted to see you. Wanted to wait until the party started. I think I fell asleep for a while."

"But you remember what happened at my house? Talking to me? Kissing me?"

Their eyes met and she could swear an electric current flared between them. "I already said I did," she choked out.

"What about the alcohol, Lily? When you came to see me, I smelled alcohol on you."

"I don't remember having anything. Maybe I got some at your party somehow—"

"What about the LSD?"

She glanced at him and flushed, obviously mortified he knew about her test results. "I already told you! I don't know how I got that."

"Had you used drugs before?"

"No. And I don't remember doing it that night. I didn't before. I don't know who—"

John rubbed his hands against his face. "Yeah." Had Hardesty slipped it to her?

What if Hardesty hadn't given her the LSD, but her father had? It made the most sense. He'd picked her up, but didn't take her home right away. He got her drunk. Gave her drugs. Then brought her home to be his alibi. His shield against accusations he'd killed his ex-wife.

At his continued silence, Lily glared at him. As if he enjoyed this. Enjoyed making her suffer. Frustration made him edgy. "I'm just trying to make sense of this," he explained. "It's important, damn it, more important than you realize. Life and death important."

He closed his eyes against the stunned look on her face. He hadn't meant to say that. But he could hear her mind working now.

"When you first came by, you said something about other girls. Other murders. What were you talking about?"

John shook his head. "Lily, let's not—"

"I want to know."

Looking into her eyes, he thought about keeping it from her. But then he reminded himself she was an adult. She deserved to know. "Someone's murdering young women. Their ages range from twenty-five to eighteen. The only thing they have in common is a practice of hitchhiking and the way they were killed." Deliberately, he didn't tell her that the others, and especially Sandy LaMonte, resembled her and her mother. He wanted her informed, not scared, not when there was no indication The Razor was targeting her specifically. Or that he even knew where she lived. "Joanna Sherwood is saying it's the same person who killed your mother."

"You're in charge of the murder investigations?"

"That's right. They all occurred about an hour from here, in El Dorado County. So even though the evidence against Hardesty is strong, there are holes I'm looking into. Because I can't take the chance that we're wrong."

She shook her head. "No wonder you've been so persistent about talking to me." Her expression twisted into one of self-disgust. "I'm sorry," she whispered.

He raised a hand and cupped her face. "It's okay, small fry," he whispered. His eyes dropped to her lips and he fought the urge to kiss her. Cursed when she closed her eyes and actually leaned toward him.

He dropped his hand.

He wanted her. He wanted her so badly. But he couldn't take advantage of her emotion or her newly found trust. Not if he wanted more from her. So he forced himself to do the last thing on earth he wanted to do.

He pulled away.

She stared at him and he struggled to catch his breath. To not respond to the aching need in her eyes. "Lily, we can't—"

"You're right." Her face showed disappointment, but only briefly. "I was just upset. That's all. Of course it didn't mean anything."

John frowned. "I didn't say that—"

She licked her lips and clasped her hands in front of her. "So what happens now? You'll tell Thorn what I told you? That we know why Hardesty did it?"

Refusing to let her brush him off, he took her hands in his. "What I meant was I can't kiss you yet. Not until things get cleared up. But I intend to kiss you a whole lot. I intend to do more than that." He rubbed his thumbs in circles, smoothing her soft skin until he felt her body tremble. "We just need to finish this first."

"Because it would be a conflict?"

Because I'm beginning to think you witnessed your father kill your mother, he thought. And even though he didn't say it, something in his thoughts must have shown something on his face.

Her eyes narrowed. "What is it? I'm not lying, John, I swear it."

"I believe you. But others aren't going to be so ready to believe."

She sat down. "So there's nothing we can do. Even though you believe me? You're still going to—"

"I'll talk to Thorn. But will you consider something, Lily? You and your father. I need you to both take lie-detector tests."

She reared back. "What?"

"Polygraphs aren't admissible at trial, but that's not what we need here. I know it seems extreme to you, but it could help us. And if I can ask your father about certain things that have come up—"

Hurt and doubt crept on her face, making him want to throw something. "This isn't about not believing you, Lily."

She frowned. "Then who is it about? Hardesty?"

He simply stared at her. Her eyes grew wide and he could see her mind spinning, evaluating the questions he'd asked her in a different light. "My father?" she whispered.

"Lily, listen to me—"

She raised her chin. "You're back to thinking that? Just because someone moved my mom's body? There's no reason to think he's involved in this."

John pushed back, knowing he had no choice. "Isn't there? According to what your father told police, he found you wandering back from my party after eleven. Do you know your mom called him hours earlier? He claims he drove around looking for you the whole time, but I think we both know that's pretty unlikely."

"I don't think any such—"

"He didn't come to my house. Why? Your mom had to have told him where you'd be. Your father—"

"My father what? Say it," she said.

"Your father was a cop. I think that's the reason shortcuts were taken in the case. Why we never knew he'd washed your hair or had you change clothes. Why the D.A. was so ready to convict Hardesty even without conclusive DNA results."

"Hardesty confessed—"

"After being kept in a room for twelve hours, with no food, nothing to drink."

"What are you saying?"

"Listen to me. You said yourself your father wanted her back. That he didn't want to leave. Maybe it was an accident. Maybe he just freaked out and—"

"You bastard," she sobbed. "You want to take him away from me, too? You want me to believe my father did that to her? And then took me there to find her?"

She was trembling so badly her teeth chattered.

Helplessness washed over him and he reached out for her. "Let me help you, Lily."

She swatted him away and stood. Damn, she looked like she wanted to throw him out the window. "Lily—"

In disbelief, he watched her pick up a vase from a small table. "Don't—" He barely got the word out before she let loose. He ducked. The vase flew over his head and smashed against the wall behind him.

Desire rushed straight to his groin. He narrowed his eyes as she grabbed several books. Thick hardbacks. She flung one and he dodged to the side. Enough of this. He shifted his weight and prepared to tackle her.

She dropped the second book with a thud and fell to her knees, laughing in harsh, hysterical bursts. "God, I must have done something really bad in a past life."

He absorbed her pain, almost reeling at its intensity. Rushing to her, he dropped to his knees and cradled her face. "Don't

say that, baby. I know it seems bad, but we'll get through this."
He had to believe that.

She pulled violently away. "You don't get it, do you? I
trusted you again and this is what happens. You accuse my
father of murder."

She opened the door.

"Where are you going?"

"I want you to leave."

"I'm not leaving."

"Then I will."

"Lily, please. Listen to me—" She ran out the door and John
ran after her.

I know you love me, he thought, just as a heavy weight
slammed against the backs of his knees. They buckled. He
landed on the ground with a muffled curse, catching himself
with his hands and immediately twisting around. A series of
punches caught him in the face. His lip split open. With a guttural yell, he heaved off his attacker and sent him flying several feet away. He got to his feet and crouched down low in
preparation for another attack. His thoughts went to Lily. Were
there more? Did they have her?

A man rushed him. He saw the face—not a man, but a boy.
The gangbanger, Albert. He'd known the kid was trouble the
second he'd laid eyes on him. Rage filled him as he imagined
the worst.

Albert paused and John wiggled his fingers in the universal
sign for "bring it on." They circled each other. Albert cursed
him in Spanish.

He shook his head. "No. I've never wanted to screw my
mother. Or a dog for that matter. You must be projecting."

Albert flushed and lunged at him. John stepped aside and
caught him in a head lock. He grunted when Albert jabbed
his stomach with an elbow, but he didn't release his hold.
He squeezed tighter, cutting off the boy's air supply until he
gasped. Albert continued to struggle like an overgrown snake.

"Knock it off," John said through clenched teeth. "What the hell is your problem?"

"You were…hurting her. I'll kill you. Don't…hurt her."

John loosened his hold a fraction.

Before he could explain himself, Albert pulled back his arm and punched John in the groin. Stars exploded behind his eyes and he gagged. Falling to his knees, he automatically tightened his hold so he dragged Albert down with him. He wheezed desperately for breath. "Stop…I wasn't hurting her."

Albert struggled to escape or do more damage. "Liar. She was…crying. Running."

"We argued. But…"

An erratic punch landed near John's groin again. It bounced off his thigh. "Enough!" He heaved himself up and slammed Albert on the ground, pinning his arms behind him and grinding his face into the dirt. "I'm a cop! I wasn't hurting her." He bent down to yell in Albert's ear as he continued to struggle. "I'm trying to help her. We fought, but she loves me, okay? She loves me!"

Albert froze as he finally heard what John was saying. John let go and barely noticed when Albert stood. "She loves me," he repeated.

As crazy as it sounded. As brief as their recent contact had been, it was true. Maybe it wasn't reality. Maybe it was based on a schoolgirl's crush. But it didn't matter. She'd said it then. And it was still true. She loved him.

It's why she'd kissed him. Why she'd opened up to him. Why she'd been so devastated when he'd questioned her about her father.

She loved him.

And God help him, he was beginning to think he loved her, too.

Despite the years.

Despite the many women he'd had since.

Despite the fact that they barely knew each other.

He still loved her.

Chapter 11

Lily knocked on her father's front door, stiffening when her stepmother Barb answered. "I'm looking for my father."

Probably in response to Lily's breathless, disheveled appearance, Barb raised an eyebrow. "Come in, Lily, and tell me what's this about." She reached out to grab Lily's arm, but Lily stumbled back.

"No. I want to talk to my father. Is he here?"

Barb pressed her lips together in that way she had when she thought someone was being "uncivilized." "He went to the store but he'll be back soon. Do you want to wait for him inside or out here?"

"I'll wait inside. Thank you."

Barb sighed. "Come in, then."

Lily followed Barb into their formal living room, grimacing as she settled gingerly onto the white, formal sofa set. She was always afraid to move when she sat in this room, afraid she'd rub some of the world's grime—her grime—onto her stepmother's spotless furniture.

Blood on the white walls. On the carpet. On the sheets.

Images tumbled through her mind. Her father cradling her mother, who wore a wedding dress and a radiant smile. Lily throwing a football at her mother, who caught it and then dodged past her father only to have him sweep her off her feet and twirl her in a circle. Her father cradling her mother's broken bloody body, weeping as he placed her on a bed.

Out of nowhere, fear paralyzed her.

Oh God. Oh God.

Lily couldn't control the bile rising in her throat.

Dad loved Mom. He would never hurt her.

Swift and merciless, a tiny, traitorous voice challenged her. You never would have thought your father would be unfaithful. Multiple times.

But an affair's different, she countered. It wasn't murder.

No matter what she told herself, however, terror filled her until she could feel nothing else. John had planted a seed in her mind, and it had grown to gigantic proportions, looming over her like a towering redwood.

She flinched when Barb grabbed her arms. "Lily, what's going on? What did John Tyler tell you?"

Lily jerked back. "Wh-what? How did you know I talked to him?"

She straightened. "It's the only reason you'd be this upset. Someone from the A.G.'s office called your father. Told us John Tyler was going to be asking questions. The bastard. Trying to turn you against your father. After all he's done. Why would you do such a foolish thing? Why would you talk to him?"

"Why wouldn't I?" she asked, confused. "We don't have anything to hide. He—"

"Is that the tack he used? I worked as a dispatcher for years, Lily. I know how cops get people to talk. It's what your father did for a living. John Tyler has always had nerve where you're concerned. In fact, I think there's another reason he's trying to get you on his side. The police suspected him, you know. They interviewed him that night."

"What?" Lily breathed out, shaking her head. Disbelief hit her anew. Automatically she rejected Barb's implication, but for a fraction of a second, she was hit by memories. Memories of her father warning her about John. Telling her of Stacy Mitchell's accusations. Memories of the way John had grabbed her that night. His strength. His aggression. She'd always believed in him, but what if she'd been wrong? What if he had been responsible for her mother's death?

"He even came to the house that night. Trying to talk to you. Your father told me—"

"What did you say?" she whispered.

Barb stared at her. "What?"

"You just said he came to the house to talk to me. When did he come to the house?"

Barb shrugged. "Your father said he came before they took you to the hospital. When the police were there."

She shook her head. "I don't remember. Why didn't my father ever tell me?"

"Why would I have told you?"

Barb and Lily turned toward her father, standing in the foyer still wearing his long, dark overcoat. "Would it have mattered? You slapped him. It was obvious he'd done something to you. I wasn't going to let the bastard upset you any more than he already had."

"I—I slapped him?" She moaned. "God, Dad! How could I not remember? You should have told me! You should have—"

Her father stunned her when he punched the wall. "Your mother was dead!" He turned to her with a fierce, angry expression. "Remember that? Remember how we found her body? John Tyler meant nothing to me. Nothing!"

He looked murderous.

"Douglas, stop—" Barb began, but he turned on her.

"What the hell are you doing talking to her about all this? We agreed never to talk to her about it. Never."

Barb cringed back. Lily rushed to her father, grabbing his arm, but when he turned on her, she found herself cringing back, as well. Terror. It filled her up like a balloon about to pop. So fast she trembled and heaved for breath.

She opened her mouth and tried to speak, but a voice—no, two voices—twisted through her head, overpowering her even though each was low and distorted.

What happened...? Remember what I told you, Lily.... Didn't mean to do it....We discovered her body together.... You were walking home when I found you...that's when we found the body.

You'll be rewarded—

When we found the body— Remember.

Remember.

He frowned. "My God, Lily." Her father took her arms and shook her. "Damn it, Lily, stop this. I'm your father, remember?"

She closed her eyes, trying to block out the voices. One sounded like her father's, but not like her father's. The other voice sounded like...Hardesty's.

Shame and confusion made her weak. Dear God, she'd doubted John. Just like everyone else. Despite all her talk of loving him and believing him, she'd actually wondered if he could have murdered her mother. Her own mind now challenged that theory, forcing her to face a possibility just as abhorrent. Even more so. What if the person she needed to fear most wasn't John, but her own father?

Her head snapped back as her father shook her again. She opened her eyes, and he slowly came into focus.

"Stop," she whispered.

He did.

"What happened?" he asked, his voice laced with worry. "Were you remembering something?"

"I—I don't know. I thought for a second..." She shook her head. Backed away from him. "No. No, it was nothing. I'm just tired, that's all."

Her father didn't look convinced. "You're sure?"

She hesitated, glanced at Barb, then back at her father. "Why didn't you ever tell me? About the other affairs."

"What?" But she could tell by the way her father paled that Dr. Tyler had been telling the truth about that. Pain almost buckled her knees at how foolish she'd been. All along, she'd blamed her mother for not giving her father another chance, when in truth she'd probably given him one chance too many.

"It's why Mom made you move out. It wasn't the first time you cheated. How many—how many were there? One?"

He glanced at Barb, who turned away and stiffly disappeared into the kitchen.

Anger made her step forward, her voice sharp. "Four? Ten?"

"Stop!" her father snapped. Lily froze and crossed her arms over her chest. Her father rubbed a weary hand over his face. "John Tyler has certainly told you a lot about me, hasn't he?"

"Not that." She wondered suddenly if John had known, though. Had everyone known but her? "But he told me some other things. Things about my clothes being changed. About Hardesty's confession being coerced. If he—if he'd had anything to do with the murder, he wouldn't want to reopen things. He'd be happy to keep things focused on Hardesty."

"And what? You think I had something to do with your mother's murder? Is that what you're saying, Lily?" Her father's face was grim, closed off into a tight expression of combined anger and betrayal. He looked like a stranger.

But she still couldn't believe it. Even knowing about the affairs, she couldn't believe he'd killed her.

Confusion flooded her. "No. No, I'm not saying that. I don't know what happened. It's just…Mom…we never talk about her and I've been so upset about this…."

Her voice broke and she covered her face with her hands, wanting to curl into herself and disappear.

Gentle fingers wrapped around her wrists and pulled her hands away from her face. Her father looked ready to cry himself. "Do you see now why you need to stay away from that man? Everything's been fine. We've been fine."

"I think he just wants to help. He wants us to take a polygraph exam."

"And did he tell you how unreliable they are?"

"So you won't take one?"

"Do I need to, Lily? Because yes, I've made mistakes. Big ones. But if you really think I'm capable of doing that to your mother—my God, the woman I loved and had two daughters with—then—then I—"

The pit of misery in Lily's stomach unfurled when her father started to sob. She shook her head. "I'm sorry, Daddy. No, of course I don't think that. I'm sorry."

She hugged her father tightly. They clung to one another in the silence of his home.

Her father straightened and swiped at his face. "Promise me you'll stay away from him." He grasped her chin with a heavy hand. "Promise me."

Slowly, Lily nodded. Her father closed his eyes and sighed with relief.

Chapter 12

Apartment 206. Two days after freaking out in her father's living room, Lily stared at the numbers on Carmen's apartment door. Despite her unease at Lily's request, Dr. Tyler had passed along Lily's message and Carmen hadn't responded until this morning. But at least she'd responded and had even offered to cook them dinner tonight.

The door opened and Lily almost reeled back at the sight of her friend, all grown up but looking young and vital in a KAPPA sweatshirt, boxers and droopy sweat socks. Her hair was braided in two low pigtails, adding to the picture of a college coed. Her blue eyes remained steady.

Neither one of them said a word, but Carmen opened the door wider and motioned her inside. She'd been expecting anger or hurt. She'd been hoping for forgiveness. She felt an odd combination of relief and disappointment that she received none of those things.

"Would you like to sit down while I finish the spaghetti sauce?"

"Um—can I help you? Or just watch?"

Carmen nodded and led the way to her small, galley kitchen. She picked up a glass from the counter. "Would you like juice or water? I'm afraid I don't have anything stronger."

"Water's good. Thank you."

Filling another glass with water, Carmen handed it to her, then stirred something aromatic that simmered on the stovetop. On any other day, the smell of fresh tomatoes, garlic and rosemary would have been comforting. Now it just made her nauseous. The silence was awkward and heavy.

"It's good to see you," Lily offered. And she meant it.

Carmen let go of the spoon. Her eyes glazed with tears. The next thing Lily knew, she was squeezed tight in her friend's arms. She wrapped her arms around Carmen and let out a shaky laugh. "Oh, thank God. I thought you'd be angry I came."

Carmen pulled back and they smiled at each other. Lily kept hold of her hands, refusing to lose the fragile connection she'd just found again. "So you're a doctor now?" Lily asked.

"And you're still an artist. Funny that we both work with kids, isn't it."

"Yeah, it is."

An hour later, Lily sipped coffee, luxuriating in being with her friend again. She'd been grilling her for the past hour and couldn't seem to get enough information about her. "You never married?"

Carmen's smile wilted, making Lily instantly tense. "No. I thought I'd found the one but it turned out to be wrong. Again. I'm not sure what happened. Things were good with us until one day Lucas just—" She shook her head. "Let's not talk about that." She looked at Lily closely. "You?"

"No." Lily bit her lip. "I saw your mother. Things between you are better?"

Carmen shrugged. "My mom and I still have issues, but I know she does her best. I know she loves me."

"And John."

"Yes. And John. They still have their issues, too. He got it in his head that she didn't trust him. She thought he'd had something to do with your mom—"

"That's ridiculous."

Carmen nodded. "John was devastated."

"Of course he was." Despite her initial anger that he could think her father a murderer, she'd calmed enough to know he was doing his best with what he had. A part of him must hate her family for all the trouble they'd caused him.

"I want to talk to you about John, Lily. I want you to know I never told him how you felt about him."

Lily tilted her head, confused. "I never thought you did."

"But I wish I had."

A startled laugh burst out of her. "Why? What would that have accomplished?"

"I don't know. Maybe it would have changed how things happened that night."

How many times had she wished things could be different? Every day. Every hour. Every second.

It hadn't changed a thing.

"He wanted to be with you, Lily. He didn't want to leave you."

For a second, Lily couldn't believe her ears. She stood, the legs of her chair scraping loudly against the laminate flooring. "Don't."

Slowly, Carmen stood, as well. "I'm not lying."

"He didn't care about me. He made that abundantly clear."

"He didn't have a choice. He was four years older and leaving town."

"He laughed at me, Carmen! Told me I looked—looked like a tramp. He kissed Stacy in front of me." She shook her head. "I don't know what you think you're doing here, but I don't appreciate it." She stood up, ready to gather her things, wanting to toss them against the wall and yell out her grief.

Carmen grabbed her arm. "Listen to me. After what

happened…John came to visit. I heard him arguing with your sister's boyfriend. Aaron told him to stay away from you."

Lily dropped her bag on the floor and sat down hard, almost falling when she missed her seat by several inches. "Aaron?"

"And John told him not to worry. But Aaron said he knew John was attracted to you. Reminded him what he'd said before. He'd said someday he wanted to be with you."

Nothing seemed real anymore. "Why—why didn't you tell me this before?"

Carmen's eyes filled with tears. "When was I going to tell you? You—you were trying to get better. You had both moved on. Without me." Hesitantly, Carmen reached out and took her hand. "And I've missed you so much, Lily. I've needed you."

Lily stared at the fingers covering hers. Her heart pounded so loud she could barely think. Slowly, Lily curled her fingers around Carmen's. "I've—I've needed you, too."

They enjoyed each other's company for several more minutes before Lily couldn't put it off any longer. "Carmen, can I ask you something?"

"Sure."

"You saw me afterward, in Ravenswood. Did I say anything to you? About my father maybe?"

She frowned. "Say anything? You couldn't talk for so long."

"But afterward. When I could talk? Did I say anything about how I got drunk? Who gave me the drugs?"

Carmen shook her head. "No. I'm sorry, there's nothing."

"You're sure?"

"Yes. Why?"

"I just—there's so much I don't remember. So much I need to know. I feel like I'm walking in the dark. I'm having so many doubts."

"Tell me," she said quietly.

And she did. Lily told her about her dreams. About the voices she'd been hearing. About what John had said about her father and the lie-detector test. And about the disturbing feelings she'd had while she'd been with her father and Barb.

Carmen listened quietly and then she nodded her head. "I think you should do it."

"The lie-detector test?"

"Yes. I don't know much about them, but I do know John cares about you. He wouldn't ask you to do something unless he thought it was important."

"But my father—"

"Do you think your father killed your mother?"

"No, but—"

"Then that's your gut reaction. Listen to it, Lily. You want the truth. That's why you came here asking me questions. But I can't give them to you. Maybe John can."

Carmen rushed to a small table and grabbed her phone.

"Who are you calling?" Lily asked in panic.

"John."

She shook her head. "No. He's after my father. I can't trust him."

Staring into her eyes, Carmen whispered, "He's the only one you can trust, Lily. Let him help you. Please."

Lily licked her lips. Really thought about who she trusted and didn't trust. Then held out her hand. "I'll do it."

Chapter 13

Something had changed between them. From the moment John had gotten Lily's message, he could feel it. He'd been shocked when he'd seen Carmen's phone number on caller ID and had known she was somehow responsible for Lily's dramatic turnaround. He hadn't brought it up to Lily, however. He didn't want to do anything to destroy the feeling of hope inside him.

"I trust you," she'd said. And she was certainly acting like it. Quiet but calm, she didn't protest as he led her into the Bureau of Law Enforcement, where his friend Brian worked. He rubbed his thumb against her knuckles, his touch both casual and proprietary. Despite what he'd told her about intimacy being a conflict, he didn't care who saw them.

Surprisingly, she didn't seem to mind, either.

Once inside, he led her up several floors and into a room where Brian was fiddling with a computer laptop. At the sight, John's resolve only grew stronger.

He intended to turn over the test results. He would do what

he needed to stop The Razor. He'd arrest Doug Cantrell if he had to. But he wouldn't jeopardize Lily. Not her life. Not her freedom. Until he knew the test results, he wasn't taking any chances, which is why he'd asked for Brian's help.

He'd known Brian for years. Trusted him. Trusted him enough to let him question Lily. And trusted that he wouldn't reveal the results or the fact of the test to anyone without John's permission.

Whatever mistakes he'd made in the past, Lily was his priority now. He wasn't losing her again.

"Thank you for getting this together so quickly, Brian."

"Is this her?" Brian asked, peering at Lily like she was an alien under a microscope. She twisted her hands together. "Ma'am, if you could just take this seat."

"Of course."

He had her fill out some paperwork and went over the exam procedures. Lily seemed surprised when Brian started reviewing the interview questions.

"It's not like in the movies," John explained. "No surprises or trick questions."

Lily nodded, but he could tell she was still nervous.

"You ready for the next step?" Brian asked.

She glanced at John and he winked at her.

"Yes."

Brian wrapped a blood pressure cuff around her arm and the rubber tubing around her chest and abdomen. "These are the pneumographs I told you about. They're just rubber tubes filled with air. Nothing dangerous. Try to relax."

Lily gave a nervous laugh. "So, uh, where's the spotlight?"

John grinned.

Brian frowned. "Spotlight?"

"You know. The one you're going to shine in my eyes."

Brain stared at her blankly.

Lily waved her hand. "Sorry. Bad joke."

John placed a hand on her shoulder and squeezed.

"Can I have your left hand, please?"

She lifted her hand, and Brian placed a band on her index and ring finger. "The fingertips are one of the most porous areas on the body. These are called galvanometers. They measure the sweat you release under stress."

Lily cleared her throat. "Never let them see you sweat, huh?"

When Brian gave her another blank stare, John caught Lily's eyes. She raised a brow and he shrugged.

"All set," Brian said.

Their playful connection vanished and he saw panic fill Lily's eyes. "Wait. I thought you were going to ask me the questions?"

John took her hand, the one unfettered by wires. He ignored the way Brian shifted in his seat. "I'm not certified to give the exam. Brian is. But I'll stay right here. I promise."

She didn't look particularly comforted.

Brian fiddled with some more wires before cursing and looking down at the pager hooked through his belt loop. He shot John an apologetic look. "I've gotta get this."

Brian left, closing the door behind him.

He couldn't stand the nervous way Lily looked at him. He swore if she twisted her hands together one more time he was going to have a heart attack. He didn't remember her doing it as a kid, and he knew it was something she'd developed after the murder. To keep herself protected.

Dramatically, he rubbed his hands together and took several slow steps toward her, then leaned down until his nose almost touched hers. "So, small fry. I think I've finally got you where I want you."

She snorted. "In your dreams."

John grinned at Lily's saucy reply. Sauciness was so much better than the nerves and panic she'd been trying to hide since they'd arrived.

"Besides, I thought you didn't know how to use this machine."

"Oh, I know how to use it." He slid his fingers across the top of the open screen, careful not to fiddle with any of the buttons or wires that Brian had set. "I just said I'm not an expert."

She waved her hand in challenge, sat back and crossed her arms. "Go for it," she said.

He raised his brows. "I can ask you anything?"

"Like I could stop you," she said drolly.

He grinned again. "True." Tapping his finger on his chin, he pretended to give it deep thought. "I know. How many lovers have you had?"

Her face turned red. "Excuse me?"

"I didn't say I was going to ask you anything about the case, now did I?"

She pursed her lips as if trying to hold back a smile. "I've had hundreds. Thousands."

"Huh." He felt the corner of his mouth tip up. "You couldn't tell it from the way you kissed me. You seemed…hungry."

Her mouth fell open and he barely suppressed a full-on laugh. Straight-faced, he said, "I could help you with that, you know."

Now she laughed. "Too bad I'm not interested."

Humor fled. Suddenly, all he could think about was making her eat those words. He stepped forward until she had to crane her neck to keep their gazes locked. The position exposed her creamy neck like a column of ivory. He had the overwhelming urge to mark her. To force her to admit she wanted him. He leaned down so he could feel her gasps for breath against his cheek.

Trailing his fingers across her throat, he whispered, "Now, now. I don't need a machine to tell me you're lying. It's written in your eyes."

Her pupils dilated and the irises sparkled amber. Wanting to taste her again, he leaned even closer.

Brian walked into the room.

"Sorry about the interruption." He looked at them. "Uh, anything wrong?"

John took a seat at a nearby table to hide his boner. "Nope. I'm good. How about you, Lily?"

He grinned when she flushed, which of course yanked her chain.

"Clever move," she said sweetly.

"What's that?" he asked even though he knew.

She glanced at Brian, who didn't appear to be listening to them. John knew better, but Lily bought it. "Distracting me so I wouldn't be so nervous. I knew exactly what you were doing."

"Did you now?"

"Yep."

Instantly serious, he said, "Then you'd know everything I said was the absolute truth, now wouldn't you?"

She fell silent, apparently not knowing what to say to that. Once the questioning started however, she answered calmly and succinctly in one-word answers, just like she'd been told.

"Is your first name Lily?" Brian asked.

"Yes."

"Are you thirty-one years old?"

"Yes."

"Do you know who stabbed Tina Cantrell?"

Lily glanced at John. She looked rattled but resolute. He couldn't help feeling proud of her. Despite her initial reluctance, it was clear she was determined to do the right thing. "No."

She and John watched as Brian jotted down some notes.

"Were you born in Sacramento?"

"Yes."

"Did you stab Tina Cantrell?"

Again, she looked at John, but answered without hesitation. "No."

"Between August 1 and August 31, 1997, did you stab anyone with a knife?"

She shook her head. "No."

"Do you live at 375 Moss Lane?"

"Yes."

"Do you know a man named Chris Hardesty?"

"Yes."

"Do you believe Hardesty killed your mother?"

"Yes."

"Have you lied about your memory loss?"

"No."

"Do you suspect anyone other than Chris Hardesty of murdering your mother?"

Lily hesitated. It was barely noticeable, but John caught it. She licked her lips. Then said, "No."

"Did you see Mr. Hardesty on the evening of your mother's death?"

"Y-yes."

"Did you talk to him about the fight with your mother?"

Lily paused. She raised a hand to her temple and winced. Then she shook her head. "I'm sorry, what was the question?"

Brian glanced at John, who nodded for him to continue. Brian adjusted some dials, then said, "I'll go back one. Did you see Mr. Hardesty on the evening of your mother's death?"

Again, Lily answered yes.

"Did you talk to him about the fight with your mother?"

She took a deep breath, and John fully expected her to say no. She didn't. Instead, she stared at her hands, swayed in her seat, then slowly lifted her gaze to his. "John—?"

He leaped out of his seat and rushed toward her.

Lily heard John calling her name and tried to speak. To reassure him she was okay. But she could barely think past the words bombarding her.

You'll be rewarded for your kindness.

Like a video on fast-forward, scenes sped through her mind. The images were accompanied by surround sound. She heard Hardesty ask her why she was crying. Saw him lying in the grass with his ball cap over his head. She felt the burn of liquor that he'd given her and the way he'd stiffened when she hugged him.

Gasping for air, her body shaking, she closed her eyes and let the memories flood her.

August 28
8:20 p.m.
Sacramento, CA

In the park a few blocks from her house, Lily shivered with cold and tears. Sitting in the huge concrete tube that served as a play structure for neighborhood children, she wondered if her mother had gone on her date or if she'd even bothered looking for her.

Tired, so tired, she closed her eyes. She listened to the wind's lonely howl. All her childish fears of boogeymen and monsters under the bed welled up. If she died right now, no one would know. If she screamed, no one would hear.

Why couldn't anyone hear her?

Biting her lip, she pulled her knees tighter to her chest and wrapped her arms around them, bending herself into a tight knot. She lost track of time. The world faded in and out, keeping time with her slow, shuddering breaths.

"Why you crying, Lily?"

Lily gasped and turned over, trying to scramble to the other end of the tube but painfully aware of her slow, awkward movements.

Chris Hardesty, the homeless man she'd talked to off and on for the past few weeks, stared at her, his bewhiskered face and dingy tattered clothes barely visible as he crouched inside the opening nearest the park's slide. Concern radiated from him, and she felt a simultaneous urge to hug him and push him away.

No one had been more surprised than Lily when she'd befriended Hardesty, but the truth was she'd been the one to benefit most from their talks. The homeless man listened to her.

He didn't judge. Didn't lecture. He simply helped her see things from all sides in a straightforward, honest way.

Even things about John.

"Come on out of there, Lily, so we can talk. You don't want me to come in after you, do you? I'll break my back trying to bend down that low."

Glancing at Hardesty, Lily swiped at her tears, sniffled, and smiled weakly. She crawled from the tube, wincing when the cement scraped her knees, and fell into Hardesty's arms. She flinched back from the mild odor of alcohol and sweat clinging to him, but was too cold to protest. He placed his jacket around her shoulders. They sat in the grass by his shopping cart and held out his silver flask. "Want some?"

"No, thanks," she murmured.

He took a long swallow, then wiped at his mouth with his sleeve. "So what happened? John leave early?"

"He's leaving tomorrow morning."

"Did he go off and do something stupid like marry that blond Amazon?"

"No," she whispered. She was so tired, she couldn't even call up a smidgen of disgust at the mention of Stacy.

"Well, then, how come you're upset?"

She opened her mouth, then shut it again. She remembered John's warning that she couldn't trust anyone, particularly this man. Even so, her body trembled with the need to share the load of her pain.

Hardesty sighed, raised himself up on cracking knees, and dug through his shopping cart. He handed her a tall bottle of tequila, the kind her mother used to make margaritas, before sitting again. "It's brand-new. You can check. Have a sip."

"No, I don't—"

He yawned. "It'll warm you up and you can tell me what happened." Lying back on the grass, he pulled the bill of his baseball cap down over his eyes.

Lily stared at him, then at the bottle. She unscrewed the cap, took a long gulp, then coughed as she tried to catch her breath. "Nasty," she whispered, but she took another sip because it made her feel warmer.

Hardesty smiled, but otherwise didn't move.

After several more swigs, Lily confided, "I got into a fight with my mom. About John. She slapped me and I—I said I hated her."

"Hmm."

Frowning, Lily nudged Hardesty with her toe. "Is that all you're going to say? Just last week you were going on and on about how I should respect my parents."

"Sometimes it's hard to respect someone who's hurt you. And I imagine by going out with another man, she hurt you. Just like your father hurt you." Lifting his ball cap, Hardesty momentarily sought Lily's gaze. "Kids and parents fight. It's always happened and it always will. I wish I had the chance to fight with my daughter. I'd want her to come back to me no matter what she said."

"So you think I should go back?"

He dropped his cap over his eyes again. "I know you'll go back, sweet Lily. It's just a matter of what you're going to do f-first."

Frowning because he was shivering, she stood and draped his jacket over him. "Thanks but you need this more than me."

"You going home?" he asked. "Or to see John?"

"I—I'm not sure yet." She rubbed her arms and stared off in the direction she'd come. Suddenly, all she wanted was to see John. Maybe he'd even take her home and wait with her, and they could talk to her mother together. She took several steps toward the park entrance, then stopped. She turned back to Hardesty, wanting to do something to repay his kindness.

"Do you need anything, Chris?"

He laughed and slowly got to his feet, put on his jacket, and rubbed his hands together. "I'm a little cold. A little hungry. If you have a few dollars tucked into that dress, I'd be much obliged."

More guilt. More regret. "I'm sorry, I don't. I left my purse at home. But my mom's probably gone and Ivy's out with Aaron. I can go back and get you something. Maybe some food—"

Hardesty shook his head. "That's okay, sweet Lily. You'll be rewarded for your kindness. Maybe not tonight, but someday. Right now, just hug someone you love. Whether it's John or your mom or dad, hold on to someone who matters to you and don't let go."

Hesitating briefly, she stepped forward and threw her arms around his waist. He startled and every muscle went stiff before he pulled away.

Her arms dropped to her sides like lead. Rejected by a homeless guy. Great. What the hell was wrong with her?

He shook his head. "Lily—"

Smiling stiffly, she raised her hand. "Thanks, Chris," she whispered as she backed away. "Take care."

Lily jerked when something warm cupped her face. Caressed it. She gravitated toward the gentle touch even as the pain inside her became almost unbearable.

"Lily, look at me."

Lily opened her eyes. John knelt beside her, his face creased with worry. Brian was gone.

"Where—?" she whispered.

"I asked Brian to give us some privacy. He was almost done anyway. Are you all right?"

Pain coursed through her. For the first time, she wondered whether she had the strength to survive. If she wanted to. "I—I think I remembered something."

Taking her hands, he squeezed them. "Was it something bad?"

She nodded.

"Will you tell me?"

Without humor, she laughed. "I have to, don't I? I'm still hooked up to this stupid thing."

Unblinking, John immediately began to remove the cuffs

and tubes that Brian had placed on her. Lily stiffened with confusion.

"John—?"

He kissed her. Swooped up and took her mouth with his tongue. Soft and slick. Hard and nimble. He moved his tongue in and out of her mouth, as if savoring every bit of sensation. She clutched at him, whimpering when he pulled away and leaned his forward against hers. Gripping her hair, he gently forced her head back to stare into her eyes.

"Will you trust me, Lily? Please?"

Brokenly, she said, "I think I talked to Hardesty that night."

She was watching him carefully, but John barely reacted to her statement. He stood and sat back down in his chair. "Okay. So you talked to him when? Before or after we saw each other at the party?"

"Before," she whispered.

"At the park?"

She nodded. "He was lying in the grass. With his shopping cart nearby."

"And then what?"

"I told him I'd fought with my mother. About you."

He listened to the rest. The only time his expression changed was when she told him about the tequila. Even then, only his jaw clenched.

"You said he mentioned his daughter. Had you talked about his daughter before?"

She nodded. "He said she was living with relatives."

"Then what happened?"

She opened her mouth but nothing came out. Grief and guilt flooded her. Her body trembled, and although John frowned, he didn't comfort her. Didn't reach out to her. She pushed herself to continue. "I—I asked him how he was. If he needed anything."

"You'd given him money before?"

"Yes." She gripped the edge of the table. "I told him I didn't have my purse." She looked away, knowing she wouldn't be able to continue if she had to look at him. "That all my money was at home. But—but that my mom was leaving soon and I'd go back later and get some for him."

Her breathing was coming so fast now she could barely talk. She looked at him, saw understanding on his features, and felt her shame intensify. "He smiled. And thanked me. And said I'd—I'd, oh God, be rewarded for my kindness."

Her shoulders slumped. "It's all my fault. I practically drew him a map to her. She died thinking I hated her. And it's all my fault."

Stunned, John stared at her.

She leaped to her feet and he tensed, prepared to grab her if she tried to run. Instead, she walked a few feet away and turned her back to face a bookshelf buried in paperwork and old tape recorders.

Unfortunately, her reasoning made sense. What she'd said to Hardesty solidified his motive and opportunity to break into her house. But that was his doing, not hers, damn it.

"You're sure this is a memory? Not something else? Not your guilt playing tricks on you?"

She shuddered. "Believe me, I've lived with guilt all these years. I know the difference."

Even secondhand, her pain pierced him. He rose from his seat and rushed around the table. "Listen to me. You were upset. Trying to be compassionate. You couldn't have known what would happen." He placed a hand on her shoulder. She gasped and whirled around. "It's not your fault, small fry."

"Yes, it is," she said dully. "It gave him a reason to go to my house. While my mom was alone. Defenseless."

His gaze didn't waver from hers. "Every house in the neighborhood had money in it. Valuables. If he decided to break into your house, it wasn't your fault. You didn't tell him where you lived. You didn't draw him a map."

She frowned. "I know, but—"

"There is no but, Lily. You were nice to him, that's all. Your mother would have been proud of you."

"My mother would have chewed me out for being so stupid. She was already so mad at me—"

With both hands on her shoulders, he gave her a gentle shake. "She loved you. She knew you loved her. She didn't believe you hated her. Not for one second."

She tried to pull away, but he wouldn't let her. "You can't know that," she choked out.

"Of course I can. Because she told me."

She jerked back as if he'd struck her. "What?"

He dropped his hands. "After you fought, she came to my house looking for you."

"You're lying," she whispered.

"No. I'm not. When you didn't return, she came to see me. She said she loved you. You were going through a hard time. And she asked me to stay away from you."

"You're lying!" She shoved him in the chest. He took one step back but didn't try to block the next shove. She hit him. She even tried biting him. And not once did he lift a hand to stop her. If it would make her feel better, he'd gladly turn himself into a human punching bag. Over and over again, she pounded her anger on him.

Eventually, she tired and stepped away. "Don't try to protect me," she whispered. "Please." She brushed her hand across her face and stared at her fingertips. She seemed stunned to see proof she was crying.

"That's why I kissed Stacy," he confessed. "Not because I wanted to hurt you. But because I knew, just like your mother did, we couldn't be together."

He lowered his face slowly, then kissed her forehead, just like he'd used to do when she was a kid. "It wasn't your fault. We don't know how many houses he went to before picking yours. Your mother loved you. It wasn't your fault."

She backed up until her back hit the door. He moved close

and pulled her into his arms, undeterred by the stiffness of her body.

He stroked her hair. Murmured it again and again. "It wasn't your fault." He kissed her temple. "It wasn't your fault," he crooned.

Slowly, she relaxed and leaned against him. Although she didn't make a sound, a river of silent tears streamed down her face. "It's going to be okay, small fry."

She pulled back to look at him, and his gaze shifted to her lips. His pulse sped up and he wanted to kiss her. To caress her. To make her forget her grief and think of nothing but pleasure. He lowered his head slowly, giving her time to back away. She didn't. She gripped his sides, pulling him close. Closing her eyes.

"Lily," he whispered before taking her mouth gently. More gently than he'd ever kissed a woman.

Chapter 14

Three days after Lily's polygraph, John arrived at San Quentin Prison to interview Hardesty. He'd spent the time searching for a connection between the cases, but there wasn't any physical evidence or links. Still, something nagged at him. He'd never been more desperate or fearful of finding out the truth. If Chris Hardesty had indeed killed Tina, Lily would never forgive herself for her careless words. If he hadn't killed her, then all the evidence pointed to Lily's father. And also made him their number one suspect in The Razor cases. Either one of those things would destroy Lily and jeopardize the fragile bond they'd begun to form.

John got out of his car and trudged up the cement incline to the main gate. It wasn't the first time he'd been to San Quentin. Still, as John passed the prison "gift shop," he marveled at the prison's million-dollar, ocean-view location. He took a deep breath of cool ocean air before being led inside to check in.

As the guard led him through the steel barred gate, he

thought once more of Lily. When Brian had returned and told them the inconclusive test results, she'd been disappointed, but also offended by his suggestion that she was hiding something.

"I'm not saying it's deliberate, Lily," Brian said. "We can't know how much your memory loss affects things. But before you had your flash of memory, before you stumbled on the question about Hardesty, you hesitated in answering a different question. The machine picked up on that and assumed you were keeping a secret."

"What question?" Lily had asked.

Brian had looked at John, who'd drafted the questions himself. "Number 11."

John hadn't been surprised. He'd seen her hesitation himself. As Brian left, John explained, "It was the question 'Do you suspect anyone other than Chris Hardesty of murdering your mother?'" Her eyes had immediately gone blank and she hadn't said a word. Not until he'd said he was going to see Hardesty.

Eyes wide, she'd said, "I want to come with you."

Stunned, he shook his head. "No."

"Why not? He's been wanting to talk to me for years."

"He's trying to prove he's innocent, Lily. He's playing you. Besides, you've just told me new information. Evidence that I need to turn over as part of my investigation."

She paled. "Am I going to be in trouble?"

Warming her arms with his hands, he shook his head. "No. But some people will doubt you. Given other evidence I've seen, they'll—they'll think you're trying to protect your father. And if you try to see Hardesty, it will look even worse. Like you're trying to manipulate the facts. Trying to manipulate me. Everything will become more complicated and our past will become an issue for sure. Do you understand?"

Very slowly, she nodded, but she bit her lip, obviously still distressed.

He pulled her into his arms. "Trust me, Lily. We'll get through this. Just trust me."

Despite his plea, he wasn't sure she did. She'd refused his offer to drive her home, saying she needed time alone. Although it was the last thing he'd wanted, what else could he do other than get all caveman on her?

For a second, the word *caveman* made him uneasy. Then he realized why. Mason Park. He'd catered to Tina's independence because he hadn't wanted to come off as a caveman. She'd died because of it.

The guard led him into the visitor's area. He froze when he saw the woman sitting several feet away in a plastic blue chair. Disbelief. Confusion. Concern. Anger. The emotions rattled into him one by one, building until the pressure forced the breath from his lungs. By the guilty look on Lily's face, she knew she only had a second or two before he exploded.

She jumped out of her chair and held out a hand, as if she could actually make things right. "I just want to look him in the eye. I won't say a word."

He clenched his teeth so hard he could practically feel a layer of porcelain grind off. "What the hell is she doing here?"

The guard shrugged. "She's been cleared for contact visitation. We had her all set to visit with Hardesty in East Block, but then she got nervous. Was going to leave. But then she heard you were coming and decided to wait for you. He eyed Lily. "Is there a problem?"

John glanced around him like an idiot, part of him wondering if he was in a dream. But no, aside from a rosy-cheeked toddler with red curls playing in a small alcove, everything he saw assured him that he and Lily were indeed standing in the bowels of San Quentin prison. He turned back to the guard. "I need to talk to her. Alone."

After glancing at the badge pinned to John's shirt, the guard jerked his chin. "You can use the conference room. Hardesty's attorneys aren't here yet. You've got fifteen minutes."

John let Lily walk in before him and then practically slammed the door shut. "What—" He closed his eyes when his voice came out harsher than he intended. Gentle. Don't lose it. "What the hell do you think you're doing here?"

Her eyes widened and he felt a small thrum of satisfaction. Good. Let her be scared. He'd told her what people would think if she visited Hardesty. That she'd only make things worse for everyone—not only the two of them, but her father.

She must have seen the satisfaction in his eyes because hers immediately narrowed. "Hardesty's attorneys have been trying to get me here for weeks," she hissed. "Years. Sherwood called me after—after we talked. I told her your concerns. She reassured me that—"

"So you what? Decided to trust the woman who's been badgering you for years rather than me?"

"They cleared me a long time ago. I thought maybe it was time to face my fears." She looked lost for a moment. "I could have gone in to see him without you. But I waited." She pulled her shoulders back and thrust out her chin. "Maybe that wasn't such a good idea."

He laughed. "So after all this time, you just changed your mind." He put his hands on his hips and pinned her with an intense stare. "Why? Are you trying to manipulate me?"

"No!"

"Here I was thinking you'd finally decided to trust me, and it's all been a game."

"I wouldn't do that. I trust you. But Brian said. . . I know hesitating on that question is going to cause problems for my father. If I could just talk to Hardesty, convince him to do the right thing, to drop his claims of innocence—"

"That's exactly what you shouldn't be doing!" he yelled. "It's called dissuading a witness. Compromising evidence. And what makes you think you could convince him to do anything, Lily? The guy's about to be executed. Do you think he cares anything about you or your family?"

His voice echoed in the room, unavoidable proof that he was losing it. Lily looked scared, and he was just too tired to argue with her anymore. "Go home, Lily. Now."

"No."

He pulled her up on her tiptoes and bent down until his nose was touching hers. Until he could stare into her eyes and identify every fleck of gold in their brown depths. Every individual eyelash. She smelled like Irish Spring and lavender, the fragrant combination so incongruous to their surroundings that it was almost obscene. It raised his ire even more until he felt like the back of his head was about to blow off. "This is not a negotiation. You are leaving right now even if you have to be escorted by two very burly men in bulletproof vests. In fact," he continued, opening the door and dragging her back to the guard waiting outside, "that is exactly what's going to happen."

She dug in her heels. "Wait just one minute. You can't do this."

He lowered his face to hers. "Watch me." Her eyes widened, but he turned to the guard. "I need someone to escort this woman to the parking lot."

The guard frowned.

"Her time slot is over, right? The prisoner's being brought here for an attorney conference. She is not an attorney."

Holding up his hands in a gesture of appeasement, the guard nodded. "Please come with me, ma'am." His voice brooked no argument.

Lily looked back and forth between them. "Don't I have a right to visit?"

The guard simply said, "You can come back another day." When John's grim face turned to stone, the guard backpeddled. "Uh, or maybe not. Now, please come with me."

Lily shot John another pleading look. "John, please, I didn't mean to do anything wrong." The guard took her arm and she jerked away. "I just wanted to see him. After what I told you—"

Outwardly, John remained unmoved. He forced a chill into his voice that he didn't feel. "Go home."

Her eyes cooled along with his voice. "Fine." She walked

away, waiting with rigid regality for the guard to open the door. The guard spoke into his walkie-talkie, the outer door buzzed open, and they left.

John felt a small twinge of guilt. He shouldn't have been so rough on her. But he was hurt. Hurt that she hadn't trusted him. That she'd chosen to talk to Hardesty and his attorney when John had warned her not to. What did that say for their future together?

He kept hoping their someday was going to come. But Lily herself seemed determined to prevent it. He couldn't fight her, too. Not when the whole world seemed determined to keep them apart.

Twenty minutes later, John was back in the small conference room waiting for Hardesty. He took several deep breaths, trying to tell himself that Lily's visit had been the result of bad judgment. That it didn't mean she was willing to manipulate the evidence just to protect her father. Manipulate Hardesty to give up his claims. Manipulate John by suddenly opening herself to him and revealing a "new" memory.

When Joanna Sherwood and Oscar Laslow walked into the room, he didn't even bother with the niceties. "What the hell were you trying to pull, getting Lily Cantrell to come here?"

Sherwood looked as calm as ever. "Mr. Hardesty asked her to come. She came. It's no concern of yours."

"Like hell it isn't." John voice thundered at her, but she didn't look at all cowed. "That woman," he said, pointing at the conference room door, "found her mother's body when she was sixteen years old. Do you get your rocks off making people suffer?"

Sherwood opened her mouth to respond but then the door opened. John bit back the rest of his tirade as a guard led Chris Hardesty inside. Hardesty was close to sixty. He had dark hair that feathered to a soft gray around his face and a closely trimmed gray mustache. Even his eyes were gray, a hazy wash of color standing out starkly against his darkly tanned and weathered face.

John sat but took some mental notes. Hardesty's hands? Together and shackled. No sharp object, even a pencil, within his reach. No ill intent in his eyes. Rather, he looked amiable. Like a man about to see his grandson kick a soccer ball.

But his grandson was an adult. And John knew he'd never seen him. He'd talked to Hardesty's daughter just this morning, and she'd told him to go to hell and to tell her father to do the same. No surprise since Hardesty had murdered her mother.

"Thank you for agreeing to talk with me without any fuss, Mr. Hardesty."

Hardesty smiled, his teeth fairly straight and unstained. "What's your name, son? John, isn't it?"

A small smile tipped the edges of John's mouth. Again, the guy was good. "That's right, sir."

"Please call me Chris."

"All right. Chris."

"I was disappointed Lily didn't come. You have anything to do with that?"

Professionalism evaporated. Hearing Lily's name pass through Hardesty's lips made him want to vomit. Standing, John narrowed his eyes and pointed a finger at Hardesty. "You keep the hell away from her."

"She's okay then?" Unbelievably, the guy really seemed interested.

"She's fine." John slowly sat, disoriented by the game they were playing. "Considering you murdered the most important person in her life."

Hardesty said nothing, forcing John to finally ask, "What? No denials? No claims of innocence?"

Pull back, he told himself. You're crossing the line. All that matters is getting more information.

Hardesty sighed. "I'd hoped you were smarter than the rest, that's all. I've done a lot of bad stuff in my life, Mr. Tyler—"

"I'd say murdering your wife is pretty bad."

Hardesty paled and closed his eyes. When he opened them,

they were glassy. "You say one more word about her, and this interview is over. We clear?"

John clenched his fists, the man's command grating. "Fine," he spit out.

"Good. I've done things, horrible things I wish I could take back. And I've spent more time in prison than out of it. But what I've got here? It ain't so bad. For the past fifteen years, I've had food. Shelter. Company. It's more than I had before."

"What's your point? Chris."

"My point is, even knowing it'll be over soon, I've been willing to take my chances with the appeal system. To spend the rest of my days in this hellhole. All I've wanted is to see Lily, but she's refused."

John frowned. "Why is it so important that you see her?"

"I don't want that little girl thinking I killed her mama. I didn't." He glanced away. "Maybe—maybe the same man is out there killing other girls now. The Razor—"

John stared at him, trying to keep his face impassive. Hardesty had sounded completely sincere up until he'd mentioned The Razor. "Oh, so this is all for her protection? Then why'd you confess?"

"Like I said, I was sick of being homeless." He grinned. "I guess I still had faith in the system. Innocent men are never imprisoned, now are they?"

He was lying. He hadn't confessed just to get three hot meals a day. "You knew her mother, didn't you?"

Genuine puzzlement overcame Hardesty's expression and John realized that even if Hardesty had moved Tina's body, it hadn't been because he'd loved her.

"So you don't want Lily thinking you killed her mother. Why's that? Because you're such a kindhearted, compassionate soul? Remember now, I've got your rap sheet."

Hardesty flushed. "I told you. Don't go there. What happened with Gracie was a mistake. A crime of passion. And I paid for it. Ten years in jail. Every day. Every second of my life. But that little girl, she was kind to me. When no one else was. I wanted to protect her, not hurt her."

John leaned closer, hoping they were getting somewhere. "Protect her from who? Her father?"

"From everything."

He barely refrained from rolling his eyes. "You say that, but your prints were in the house. You never denied you went inside looking for money."

"I knew where she lived. I'd followed her home before. Only to watch her. That's all. When she said she'd give me some money, I figured why not go in and get it. She wouldn't mind."

The muscles in John's jaw clenched. Oh God, Lily had been right. He had deliberately picked her house. "When did she tell you this? And how come you never told anyone about this before."

"It didn't matter. And she would have felt responsible."

John swallowed, regretting that she did. "So what happened? You saw the mom? Surprised her? Decided you didn't want to get caught for B&E, so why not kill her?"

"Mr. Tyler," Sherwood interjected, but Hardesty interrupted her.

"It was quiet. I thought everyone was gone. I went into the living room. Lily was there. Kneeling beside her mother's body."

John reeled back and wondered if he'd misheard. "What did you just say?"

"I said, Lily was there, too. Kneeling over her mother's body."

"Bull," John gritted between clenched teeth, fighting the urge to rip Hardesty apart.

"It's true."

"And you're just telling us this now? You're trying to tell me Lily killed her mother?" John stood and shoved the table back. Hardesty's attorney gasped and John clenched his fists, trying to stop himself from killing him. "You lying piece of garbage."

"I'm telling you what I saw. I swear it on my daughter's life."

John laughed like a madman. He knew how empty that oath was. "And you just happened to leave your shirt there? All covered with blood?"

"I was carrying that shirt when I walked in. Planning to use it as a makeshift bag. Lily was in shock. Wouldn't talk. I guess when I saw her mom, I freaked out. I tried to stop the bleeding. Didn't realize she was already long dead."

"Convenient story, but I don't buy it." John flipped his files shut and leaned across the table. "I think you went to that house wanting more than food and cash. I think you wanted Lily. And when you got there, her mom fought you. And you murdered her. The same as you murdered your wife." He shook his head in disgust, then nodded to the guard. "Get me the hell out of here."

He followed the guard to the door.

"You were Lily's friend, right? The one she was in love with?"

John froze.

"You rejected her, didn't you? When she came to you?"

Shock threatened to take him out. He slowly turned to face Hardesty. "What the hell are you talking about?"

"This interview is over," Sherwood piped up.

John strode forward and slammed his files on the table. He leaned forward, towering over Hardesty and leaning down until they were practically nose to nose. "How did you know that?"

Hardesty smiled the smile of a man who knew he'd just gotten the upper hand. "She told me she was going to your party. She came to me. Hysterical. I gave her some tequila. To numb the pain. But then she ran off. I thought she'd go to your party, then go home. That's why I went to her house, you idiot. Not to steal from her. To check on her. To make sure she was okay. And that's when I found her there with her mother."

John shook his head and backed up several steps. It made

sense. But he couldn't accept it. Wouldn't. "You can't keep your story straight."

"What I'm telling you is true." Hardesty's voice was quiet, but firm. "After I found them, someone came to the door. Someone wearing a cop hat. I ran." For a moment, guilt washed over his face. "I knew if I was found there, I'd be accused of a crime. And I'm so ashamed. Lily was like a daughter to me, and I left her there. She'd never hurt anyone, but—but maybe, with the drugs I gave her—"

John sat down. The room was silent. No one, not the attorneys, not the guard looked at him. No one but Hardesty.

"The person in the hat? What did this person look like?"

"I'm afraid Mr. Hardesty is not going there. Not right now."

"Listen—"

"I want to talk to Lily," Hardesty said. "That's all."

"Why? Because you're obviously trying to set her up. For killing her mother. So you're saying she's The Razor as well, aren't you?"

Hardesty opened up his mouth then shut it. He looked at Sherwood, who shook her head in warning. "On advice of counsel, I won't say much more. But I don't think Lily's The Razor."

"Chris—"

"No," Hardesty snapped, leveling a heated gaze at Sherwood. "We're not going that far. Lily might have done something horrible because of the drugs I gave her, but I refuse to accept she's behind these Razor killings." Hardesty turned to John. "The Razor is picking women, killing women, the same way. How do you know he won't go after Lily next? What if it is her father?"

John grabbed his things. "You'll be hearing from me," he snarled. He spared a final glance at Hardesty, once more amazed at his genial appearance. Part of the reason was he looked so robust. So healthy. Tan.

"You're designated as a grade A inmate here. So you're entitled to what? Six hours exercise in the yard a day?"

"That's right."

"And you take advantage of it? Shoot hoops, maybe?"

Sherwood rolled her eyes. "Why is this relevant?"

Hardesty leaned back and shook his head. "No, no. It's okay. I don't mind a little chitchat. A lot of the condemned here don't know how to toe the line and they get put in the hole for days. Me? I'm no fool. I might not have much time left on this earth, but I take advantage of what I've got. Do I play hoops? No, Mr. Tyler, I don't. I sit. I watch. And I absorb," he replied. "I go into that yard and count my blessings, because it's the one place that still looks like the outside."

Unsatisfied with his answer but not even knowing why he'd asked, John turned. The guard opened the door.

"It reminds me of the park by Lily's house, you know."

John stopped, every nerve standing at alert.

"I miss our conversations. About family. Friendship. Love. She loved you and you threw it away. I'm paying for my mistakes, Mr. Tyler. Now, so are you."

Chapter 15

Lily looked out her living room window for the hundredth time, but still didn't see any sign of John. She knew it was only a matter of time before he came to read her the riot act for trying to see Hardesty.

She deserved it. A part of her had known it was a stupid thing to do. But she couldn't sit idly by and do nothing. Ever since John had shown up, everything had gotten so jumbled up in her mind. What she had done, what her father had done, even what Hardesty had done—she'd needed to know for sure. She'd wanted to face Hardesty. To look him in the eye in a way she hadn't been able to in court. To reassure herself that he'd done what he said he had—what they all thought he had.

That's exactly what she'd planned. Exactly what she'd intended to do. Up until the moment she'd actually walked through the gates of San Quentin. Once she was inside and she'd seen all the guards, signed all the papers, doubt hit her.

A man she'd once befriended, a man who claimed he was innocent, was going to die.

When she'd seen John, she'd been hit by another realization. That he was a big part of the reason she was there.

Not just to see Hardesty. Not just to learn the supposed truth about her mother's death. But to see John. To make him forget that she was a witness. To choose her over principle for once.

She'd wanted him out of control. As out of control as the emotions swirling inside her ever since he'd returned. And that's what she'd gotten.

She shivered as she remembered the way he'd touched her in that small, windowless conference room. He'd been angry with her, so angry that she'd seen the fire in his eyes and heard it in his voice. She'd been ashamed of the arousal that had instantly shivered down her body and between her thighs. Of the thoughts that had popped into her head. John overpowering her in bed, caging her in with his warm, naked flesh. John kissing his way down her body until all she could see was his dark hair resting against her pale stomach. John closing his eyes, his face flushed and awash with pleasure as he entered her body.

She dropped the curtain and rubbed her arms as a shiver overtook her. She'd gotten what she'd wanted, but it hadn't made her happy. Not at all. Instead, she'd felt ashamed of herself. Manipulative. Pathetic.

She jumped when her phone rang. "Hello?"

"Aunt Lily, it's me."

"Hi, Ashley, sweetie, what's—"

"Aunt Lily, Mike asked me to go to a movie with him. Can you drive us this afternoon? Please?"

Lily bit her lip at the excitement in Ashley's voice. She had no idea what time John would be back and she didn't want to miss him. "I'm sorry, baby, but I can't. Have you asked your mom and dad?"

"Dad's working and Mom said she can't. She's too busy."

"What about Mike's parents? Can you ask them?"

"No, no, we already tried." Ashley's voice hitched with distress and Lily cringed. Maybe she could run them over—

"Wait. Tessa's father is coming to pick her up. Maybe we can ask him to drive us there. I'm going to call Tessa now. Bye!"

Lily smiled as she hung up her phone. Ashley had sounded so happy at the thought of going to the movies with Mike. So carefree. Lord, she missed that feeling.

When someone knocked a few minutes later, Lily frowned. Somehow she didn't think John would knock so timidly. She opened the door, froze in confusion, then gave her visitor a tentative smile.

Lily stared at Albert, frowning when she saw something dark on his face. It took her several seconds to register that it was blood. A split second later she noticed the older boys standing behind him.

"Albert?" she whispered.

John drove the two hours to Lily's house in an hour and a half. He couldn't stop thinking about how he'd seen her at his party close to 9:00 p.m. Three hours before her father had called 911. Did she really not remember that time, or was she covering for something? Or someone?

Had Lily just wanted Hardesty to tell the truth? Or had she wanted to convince him to keep it hidden?

Clenching his hands on the steering wheel, he struggled with his helplessness. He was like a blind man feeling around in the dark. Only he was as afraid of stumbling as he was of reaching his destination. The results of the lie detector test couldn't help her. By not telling the prosecutor she'd seen Hardesty in the park that night, she'd cast a shadow of suspicion over herself that her prison visit had magnified.

What the hell was he going to do?

By the time he turned onto Lily's street, his anger had returned, blocking out his worry. It came crashing back along with a fear he'd never known when he saw Lily struggling with several men.

* * *

Lily tried to wrench her arm out of Ernesto's tight grip as he dragged her onto the porch. When he wouldn't let go, she drew her arm back and knocked him on the side of the head.

He released her and she tried to run back inside. Ernesto caught her again and slapped her.

"No!" Albert yelled.

Dazed, Lily looked over to where Albert lay. He struggled against the hold of two others.

Ernesto grabbed her chin, squeezing tightly as he drew it back toward him.

"You see what you've done to him?" He spat out the words, his English thick with his Spanish accent. "He was one of us. Tough. Smart. Now he is just a pussy-loving artist. Art? I don't buy it." He released her chin and grabbed the hair at the back of her neck, wrenching it back. "I think he's whipped because of you." He grabbed her crotch, squeezing and twisting.

Lily bared her teeth, rage welling inside her. She believed in Albert, but his "homies" were another story. Fight! She kicked out, trying to knee Ernesto in the face. Her foot glanced off his cheek and he cursed.

He hit her again, this time a close-fisted punch that made her reel back and struggle to remain conscious. She felt him dragging her toward the house.

"Bring him, too. Let's show him what happens to a coward who'd betray his brothers for a woman."

Lily tried to wiggle out of his grasp, but he held her tight, yanking her hair, dragging her across the ground.

"I didn't betray you! I haven't talked to anyone about you."

Albert grunted when the boy holding him hit him. Again and again. Until he was barely conscious.

She opened her mouth to scream, but Ernesto covered her face with a meaty hand, the stench of his skin making her gag.

A loud explosion made her jerk. Suddenly John was there, his face a mask of panic and rage. She saw Albert's friends rush him. Tried to open her mouth to scream, but only a hoarse sound came out. John ducked, but the boys tackled him.

John kicked one of the boys, a ponytailed kid that was almost as wide as he was tall, in the knee, making him collapse and howl in pain. He sent the other boy flying into the bushes. John pulled out his gun just as Ernesto yelled, "Stop, pig!"

Grabbing Lily by her hair, Ernesto pulled her up on her feet and jabbed her in the throat with a knife. "I'll kill her, pig."

John kept his gun trained on Ernesto, not once glancing at Albert, who lay unmoving on the ground next to him. He shook his head. "Then you'll be dead, I promise you."

"But she'll die first." Ernesto jabbed the knife in her throat, making her gasp. She felt a rivulet of blood trail down her skin and into the collar of her shirt.

"Stop!" John yelled and looked like he was getting ready to put down his gun.

Their eyes met and Lily shook her head.

John hesitated, and Ernesto moved his hand.

Lily lunged forward and bit him, clamping down hard until he howled in pain.

Ernesto reeled back, but held tight. He punched her in the face and she gasped at the pain. Then he was off her.

She raised her head and saw John on top of him. Pummeling him. Over and over again. She struggled to her feet and staggered over to Albert. He was bleeding and barely conscious. But he was breathing.

The sound of flesh on flesh reverberated in her ear. She turned back to John. Ernesto lay unmoving underneath him. John flipped Ernesto on his stomach, dug his knee into his back, and pulled out a pair of handcuffs. "Call 911."

She didn't respond. She stared at his right shoulder where Ernesto's knife had cut through his jacket and a layer of muscle. Blood oozed from the wound.

"Lily."

Her eyes jerked to John's. His eyes were steady and gave her strength.

"Call the police. Now."

She nodded and ran inside.

Lily glanced at John as he spoke to one of the officers, then she rushed to the ambulance when she saw them loading Albert's gurney inside. "I called your mother. She's on her way to meet you at the hospital."

Albert nodded. "I'm sorry, Lily. I didn't mean..." A round of coughing interrupted him.

"I'm okay," she said for the tenth time. The boy seemed to accept her reassurances at last and closed his eyes. A minute later, the ambulance pulled away.

She walked toward John as he talked to one of the responding officers. Ernesto glared at her, and then at John, from the backseat of a departing cruiser as another patrol car carried away his friends.

She shivered. John was right, she thought. She was too soft. Took too many chances.

John saluted Ernesto in a mocking farewell. The boy narrowed his eyes before he disappeared.

She and John had made a dangerous enemy in the gang leader.

John came up next to her. "How are you holding up?"

"Fine." She was sore, had bruises, and was suffering from heightened adrenaline, but she was okay. "I guess you were right about not being too trusting. Even Albert—" Her voice broke and she turned to go inside. John stopped her with a touch on her arm.

"I talked to Albert," he said quietly. "He didn't willingly lead them here. He came to give you something. They followed him. Threatened to kill you unless he knocked on the door. They said they just wanted to talk to you." He looked around and saw a package wrapped in plain brown paper. He picked

it up and handed it to her. "This must be what he was bringing to you."

She stared at it in confusion but refused to take it. John tore
open the package and pulled out a small object. Lily gasped
when she saw it. She walked closer and put her hand on it,
acutely aware that her hand touched his. She stared down at
the crudely crafted mosaic, and traced the pattern with one
finger.

"It's a lily. He made me a lily."

John smiled and then raised a hand to her cheek. "I wasn't
right this time, Lily. That boy didn't want to hurt you."

She stopped, a sudden hope forming in her chest.

When she didn't resist, he gave a sigh of relief and pulled
her into his arms. He rocked her. And then he pulled back and
kissed her.

She sighed and melted into him.

John kissed Lily slowly. Gently. Taking his time. The world
had gone into slow motion and if he made a wrong move or
pushed too hard then she would disappear like smoke.

He raised his hands and gently caressed her neck. She
winced and he pulled back immediately, noting that her neck
was slightly bruised and obviously still tender to the touch.

Renewed anger blasted through him like wildfire. He
wanted to drive to the county jail and beat the gangbangers
who had done this to her. She must have sensed the intensity
of his anger because she rubbed her hands up and down his
arms. "I'm okay," she whispered.

He nodded and let go of her. His arms moved reluctantly as
if he didn't want to release her. He didn't. And neither did she.
She clung to him before catching his hand in hers and guiding
him toward the house.

Once inside, the languorous haze they were in seemed to
subside. She cleared her throat and ran a hand through her hair,
which was caked with mud. "I'll be right back. I'll get you a
towel."

"Okay."

John didn't move while she was gone. When she came back with a towel, she'd changed into baggy sweats and a T-shirt. He wondered if she'd just wanted to be comfortable or if she was hiding from him. Trying to make herself look as unappealing as possible. It hadn't worked. She looked soft. Vulnerable. As if she were afraid he'd discover something about her that was too close and personal.

Too damn bad, John thought. He wanted close. He wanted personal. He wanted anything he could get from her.

Suddenly, he remembered how out of place she'd looked in the prison. His relief that she was relatively unharmed was overshadowed by remembered anger that she'd placed herself in danger earlier that day. That her actions might indeed make it harder for him to do what he'd wanted to do all along—help her.

He took the towel she offered and swiped uselessly at the dirt on his jeans. She followed the movement of his hands, seeming unable to tear her gaze away from his arms, then legs, then crotch. John felt himself hardening and pushing against his pants.

She cleared her throat again and seemed to shake herself. "I'll make us some coffee," she murmured and tried to turn away. John took her arm.

"Later," John said, his touch gentle but his voice harsher than he intended. Her eyes widened and he released her. Forced himself to lower his voice. "We need to talk about this morning, Lily."

She turned away from him and walked several steps away. "It's none of your concern, John."

The stupidity of that comment suddenly had him seeing red. "You want to say that to me again?"

She turned and a mulish expression took over her face. "It's none—"

He strode toward her, not hesitating until he was almost on top of her.

"—of your—" she continued, taking several steps backward. "Shut up."

Her mouth dropped open, but only for a moment. She straightened her shoulders and stuck out her chin, five foot two inches of female bravado. "Don't you dare talk to me like that."

He laughed. Suddenly, all the restraint he normally tried to exercise in her presence was gone. All the things he told himself about her—that she was too small, too fragile, too innocent to handle the demands of a man like him—were forgotten.

She'd been his from the moment he'd seen her. Ten years old, eyes wide, blushing furiously at the sight of him coming out of his swimming pool. Oh, she hadn't been his in a sexual sense. Not even in a romantic sense. She'd been the missing part of his heart, the one capable of filling the void once his father was gone. He'd worried about her, teased her, protected her, anguished over her. Hell, he'd driven away from her, leaving her in that damn rehabilitation hospital, leaving her in the hands of his mother and her father, because he'd thought that was what was best for her.

And now she wanted to put herself in danger? To hand herself over to scum like Hardesty so they could crucify her? Well, she'd have to get through him first.

Her eyes widened. "What are you thinking?"

"You. You're what I'm thinking about. You…you—" He felt heat pound behind his eyes. Under his skin.

The mood in the room had changed rapidly. It was as if the danger she'd been in, both in theory and then in reality, had changed things. There wasn't any more time for playing games.

There wasn't a way in hell he was going to let more time go by without letting her know how he felt about her.

She was his.

Obviously sensing his mood, she breathed fast, her gaze darting nervously behind him to the door.

He narrowed his eyes and stalked her, not liking the way she moistened her lips with her tongue and backed away, like a rabbit catching scent of a predator. He didn't want her to fear him. Ever. But at the same time it comforted him to know she had some sense of self-preservation. She certainly hadn't shown it when she'd visited the prison. "Nothing to say? How about telling me what the hell you were thinking? Are you trying to make yourself look guilty? Because Hardesty sure as hell thinks you are."

Anger flared in her eyes and she placed one hand on her cocked hip. "You think I—? You're the one that's crazy."

He threw his hands up in the air, not trusting himself to touch her. "When I work an investigation, everyone is under suspicion, Lily. That includes the daughter of the victim. The same daughter who fought with the victim before she was murdered. The same daughter who discovered the body!"

He'd finally shocked her into silence. Her face was suddenly pale. Her eyes horrified. Her expression reminded him of the way she'd looked the night of the murder. As if her whole world had just come crashing down in the blink of an eye.

This time he did touch her. He placed his hands on her shoulders. Caressed them. "God. Don't you get it? This is not a game. How am I supposed to protect you when you do something so stupid?"

He forced himself to let go of her. Walking to the living room window, he planted his hands on his hips and stared blindly at the street outside.

As quickly as he acquired control, he lost it. Because he didn't want to scare her to save her. He didn't want to push her away in order to protect her.

Concentrating on the heavy sound of his own breathing, he told himself he needed to leave.

"You really think—" Her voice broke. "How can you think I killed my mother?"

John hung his head and sighed, then turned around. One hand covered her mouth and her eyes glittered with a moist combination of hurt and fear. Tenderness swamped him, banking his resignation and fanning his love for her.

All he'd ever wanted was to be the man she'd thought he was. To protect her. And hold her. And love her. And yes, make love to her. Knowing he couldn't say the words, knowing that she'd only think he was crazy, he wanted to show how much he loved her with his body. He struggled with the urge to pick her up and carry her to bed. To shut out the world and everything that would try to keep them apart.

Knowing she was scared, he made a desperate attempt to answer her question. "Of course I don't think that, Lily. But that doesn't mean someone else won't. Hardesty's saying you were there."

Her eyes widened and she shook her head.

"Yes. He says you told him about the fight with your mom. He showed up at your house afterward. He came in and you were with your mother. And she was dead."

She gagged. He couldn't stand it anymore. He walked up to her and caught her in his arms, hanging on when she fought him. Pulling her face into his chest, he tried not to cry for her. For the both of them.

"How do you think the A.G. is going to feel when he learns you withheld information? When he finds out you purposely went to the prison to see Hardesty, knowing I'd already told you not to?" He shook his head as guilt punched him in the gut. "How's he going to feel when I tell him I kissed you? I shouldn't have. But I did. And you kissed me back."

She tried to pull away but he wouldn't let her. He couldn't do it anymore. He was sick of it all. Sick of denying he wanted her. Sick of denying himself. Cupping her face, he raised it so he could stare into her eyes. "And you know what? I want to kiss you again. And again. And again."

Shaking her head, she only goaded him on. Just once, he wanted them to be honest with each other. He wanted to say the words out loud. To have her say them back. And for neither one of them to care about their age. Their circumstances. This damn investigation. Just a man and woman. Drawn to one another by chemistry. By history. And by destiny.

Destiny had brought him back to Sacramento. It was why he'd never fallen in love before—not enough to bind himself to another woman for life. And it was why he'd taken a job that had brought him back into Lily's life. Fate had conspired to give him what he'd always wanted but had been too stupid to take. Lily.

"Listen, you're just upset. Maybe I shouldn't have gone today. I just—"

Her attempt at reason came too late. The beast inside of him had been unleashed. And it didn't want to be put back inside its cage.

He leaned down and kissed her, smashing his mouth against hers in a desperate melding of lips and tongue. Wanting to immerse them both in his love, creating an impenetrable barrier between them and the world. When he pulled back, they were both panting and she hung limply in his arms.

"Do you hear what I'm telling you, Lily? I'm not playing games. I want you. All of you. But I want more than your body. I want to hear you laugh again. I want to watch you draw and talk to you about your dreams and tell you about mine. I want to show you how I've changed, and how I'm trying to be a better man because of you. I'm trying to be someone who deserves you."

Lily flushed until her cheeks and throat sizzled pink and her chest heaved. Her warmth seeped into his palm and radiated all the way down to his toes.

"Tell me. Just once, let's both be honest. Tell me you still want me, too."

She remained silent, reached out and placed her hand on the built-in bookshelf behind her. She bit her lip hard enough to draw blood.

"Oh, baby, don't," he whispered, rubbing his thumb softly against her lips until they parted on a thready moan. "Just tell me. Please."

She licked her lips and the tip of her pink tongue touched his flesh, hitting him like a thousand volts of electricity. He sucked in his breath and raised his other hand to her face, pulling her up on her toes and toward him.

All it would take was one word from her, and he'd let go. Give them both what they so desperately wanted. She remained quiet. Stiff in his embrace.

But she stared at him with eyes like polished amber, radiating desire. "I want you. I want all those things, too."

Chapter 16

John carried Lily into her bedroom and gently placed her on the bed. Then he proceeded to kiss her. Caress her. His lips and hands lingered and savored until she was shifting restlessly, impatiently pulling at his clothes and her own.

John laughed. "Slow down, baby. I'll take care of you."

She shook her head, not sure how to make him understand. Now that she'd admitted she wanted him—now that she knew he wanted her, too—the last thing she wanted was to waste more time. Although his touch gave her pleasure beyond words, she could barely enjoy it given the impatience and urgency coursing through her. She wanted more than mere pleasure. She wanted him inside her, finally taking what she'd always wanted to give him.

"Come inside me," she begged. "Now. Please. Don't make me wait a second longer."

She could tell he wanted to argue with her, but then his expression tightened. He stripped her and himself of the last vestiges of their clothes, but not before fishing a condom packet out of his wallet. Silently, he tore the pack open and was about to suit up, but she placed her hand on his. "I—I'm on the pill. It helps with cramps. So you don't have to. If—if you don't want to. I'm clean."

He stared at her for several long seconds while a muscle ticked in his jaw. Slowly, he slipped his hand from out of hers and laid the condom on the nightstand. "I'm clean, too. But you shouldn't take my word for it."

"I do," she whispered. "I trust you."

He closed his eyes briefly, as if saying a silent prayer, then cupped her hips and took his place between her thighs. She raised her knees and hugged him, then pulled him forward. She gasped when he gathered her wrists in his hands and pinned them beside her head.

Steadily, he sank into her, hard and thick and heavenly. She whimpered with relief and frustration. He'd given her exactly what she'd wanted, but his possession merely sparked her desire until her entire body burned.

He released her wrists and moved to cover her aching breasts. He skimmed his palms lightly over her nipples. They hardened into rigid peaks and she arched with need.

His chest heaved with his attempts at breath and he smoothed one hand over her face. "What do you want, Lily?" he rasped.

You. Just you. To be my partner. To share my life. But she was unable to form the words. Her need had left her mindless, unable to do more than twine her hands in his soft hair and pull his head down toward her chest.

"You want me to suck on these?" he asked as he tweaked her nipples between his fingers.

"Yes," she ground out. "Please."

He lowered his head and teasingly lapped at one of her nipples. At the same time, he withdrew from her, teasingly massaging her with himself. She tried pushing her breast deeper into his mouth, tried drawing him back inside her, but he resisted.

"Damn you," she said, struggling away from him.

He merely laughed and captured her hands again, holding them high above her head while he subdued her kicking legs with his own.

He immediately sucked on her nipple, pulling at her with a strong rhythm she felt deep down in her core. She struggled against his hands until he released hers, then she slipped one hand between them and cupped his sex. She stroked him until he broke free from her breast and ground himself into her hand. "God, that feels good."

She pushed at his chest. When he levered himself up on his hands and knees, she stroked him for several long minutes, treasuring each groan and tremor that shook him. He seemed barely aware when she started scooting her body down, leaving a trail of kisses down his chest and the flat planes of his stomach until her feet hung over the end of the bed. She paused at the soft hair just above his groin and he sucked in his breath. "Are you—?"

Her intent was to show him just how grown-up she was now. Her answer was a hot, wet suction. He groaned and she saw his arms shake with the effort of holding himself above her. She marveled at the undeniable evidence that he was overwhelmed by their closeness. This was another first, but not just between the two of them.

She'd never done this before. Had never wanted to. But now she was greedy, licking and sucking at him like a tigress, trying to put as much of his length into her mouth as she could.

She loved him. Her heart demanded she show him how much.

She took the entire length of him, following her retracting mouth with a tight, twisting grip of her hand. He groaned and tried to back off, but she grabbed his butt cheeks, refusing to let him go.

"Lily, stop. Lily, oh God. You're going to make me...I'm going to..."

"Yes," she whispered. "Come for me."

His hips pumped against her in strong, jerky movements. She looked up and saw he was watching her, following the movements of her mouth as if he couldn't tear his gaze away. A sound started in his chest, low, like a growl, and it got louder and louder, until he was grunting in time with their movements. She felt him swell inside her mouth and braced herself, swallowing the hot liquid that shot into her mouth as if it could bond them together forever.

He dropped to the side and off the bed, falling onto the floor with a soft thud. He covered his eyes with one hand. His body still shook with the force of his orgasm and she crawled down and on top of him, kissing him deeply, wondering if he would flinch back at the taste of himself. He didn't. He invaded her mouth with his tongue and smoothed his fingers between her legs, spreading her wide as he rubbed his thumb back and forth.

She pulled back, gasping at the ripples of sensation concentrated between her legs. When she tried to capture his mouth again, he jerked his head back, but compensated for his retreat by pushing one long finger inside her. Then two. "That was incredible, Lily."

She rotated her hips in frantic circles, feeling herself on the edge of madness. "I've never...it just felt right, with you."

She saw his eyes darken and narrow as he registered what she was saying. He spread his legs wider, forcing hers apart until she braced her hands against his chest. He moved his own hands to her hips. He lifted her up and over him. He stared into her eyes as he held her poised over him. "I love you so much, small fry," he said. "Whatever the future holds, we face it together. I promise."

She tried lowering herself onto him, but he tightened his fingers, refusing to allow it until she nodded. "Yes, yes. Together. We face the future together."

He closed his eyes, then slid her down onto his length at the same time he thrust himself up to meet her.

She screamed as he hurtled her straight into the arms of

pleasure. He lifted her up and down repeatedly, controlling her movements, forcing her to accept every sensation until she was wild for release. He wrapped his arms around her back and pulled her down, rubbing his open mouth over her breasts before settling onto one to suckle her hard. When he slipped one hand behind her and stroked his finger between her butt cheeks, he pushed her over the edge. The tremors started at her toes and wound their way through her body until she was clenching around him in endless waves of pleasure. She felt him come with her just before she soared into the heavens.

It was almost 8:00 p.m. when Lily stirred and pulled out of John's arms. She used the bathroom then soundlessly opened her drawer to pull out a fresh set of panties and a T-shirt. She jerked when she felt John's arms come around her from behind.

"I've missed you so much, Lily," he growled. "It was hell to turn you away back then—"

He stopped, as if he knew talking about the past wasn't a smart thing. Her heart leaped into her throat and tears filled her eyes. Her past was her torment, but it was also her pleasure. Love and death, inextricably united. How could they get past that?

Tears ran down her face. Tears of regret. And happiness. She turned in his arms, not bothering to hide them. Despite everything, they'd found each other again. But there was something she still needed to say. "Then why? Why did you push me away? I know you said my mother came, but—why couldn't you have believed in my love? I—I would've been strong. I would've taken on anyone for you."

He kissed her eyelids. Her nose. Her mouth. "I was a fool. I'm sorry, Lily." He kissed his way down her body. Her sternum. Her rib cage. The soft swell of her stomach. He loved every precious inch of her, retracing his journey time and again, taking his time, claiming her, until she'd melted into the bedsheets with a soft languorous sigh.

Cupping her face in his hands, he whispered, "I love you, small fry. I've always loved you."

She basked in his declaration for long minutes before finally pulling away. "So, what happens now?" she asked softly.

He closed his eyes and sighed. After giving her another kiss, he began putting on his clothes. When they were both dressed, she sat on the bed. He turned to her, fingers clasped behind his head in a take-a-deep-breath kind of way.

"I need to tell the A.G. everything. About you seeing Hardesty in the park. Trying to go to the prison. About. . .us."

She looked away to stare at her footboard as she nodded. "What will happen?"

John shrugged. "I don't know. I'll be off the case for sure. As far as whether I'll be disciplined, I don't know. But I don't care. All that matters is you."

The joy she felt at his words was overpowered by fear. "Disciplined? As in fired? But why? You couldn't have known this would happen."

John smiled ruefully. "I knew, Lily. Deep inside I knew. I've always cared about you. I just hid it well. It stood to reason I'd take one look at you and fall again. Which is exactly what happened."

Hope blossomed in her heart. She stood and threw herself in his arms. He laughed and hugged her tight and for a moment she thought—finally, everything was going to work out the way it should.

When she pulled back to look at him, however, his expression stiffened again. He looked worried. She felt a small hollow pinch in her heart and took a breath, trying to fill it. "What is it?"

He pushed back her hair and caressed her cheek with the pad of one thumb. "We've got such a history, you and I, Lily. If I had known you'd be back in my life—"

She covered his hand with hers, but the muscles in his jaw ticked. "But we're together now. That's all that matters, right?"

He nodded. "That's right. And I'm not going to let anything come between us again."

He leaned down to kiss her, but even as he did, Lily's phone rang. She let the machine pick up, sinking into his kiss. She pulled away when she heard Aaron's voice coming from the kitchen, practically yelling.

"Lily, where are you? Help me, please."

She and John broke apart, and they both scrambled to the phone in time to hear Aaron's voice break into sobs.

"Ivy's been hurt. Ashley's missing. Help me, Lily. Please."

John and Lily rushed to the hospital. He'd tried talking to her, but she'd been too upset. The horrible part was he couldn't tell her everything was going to be okay. Not yet. He'd already talked to the officers who'd responded to the report of Ashley's disappearance. Now he needed to talk to Ivy and Aaron.

Lily cried out the moment she saw her sister in the hospital bed. Ivy was pale. Bruised. Aaron huddled over her at one side of the bed while Lily fell into the seat on the other side and grabbed her sister's hand. "What happened?"

"Ivy and Ashley got into a fight. Something about the boy she likes, Mike. Ashley stormed out of the house and had just turned the corner when Ivy ran out of the house to go after her. Ivy was so upset she ran right in front of a car—and Ashley's still missing. She hasn't answered her phone. We've already checked with her friends and no one's seen them. She's never run off like this before. Never."

Aaron's voice broke and he buried his face in his hands.

John winced. He and Aaron had gone to school together. They'd played on the same football team. He'd been there the day Aaron had met Ivy, and Aaron had been the only person John had told about his feelings for Lily. Aaron hadn't approved, even before Lily's mother had been killed. Even so, John had never wished the man anything but the best.

"It's okay, Aaron," Lily said. "She's going to be okay,

right?" She looked at John for affirmation and despite how much he wanted to give it to her, he didn't agree.

Lily turned back to her sister. "Ivy. Ivy, can you hear me?"

Ivy's eyes flickered open. "Li-Lily?"

"Yes, I'm here. I'm here, Ivy."

"Where—?" Her throat locked and she coughed, the sound harsh and fluid. She tried to sit up. "Oh, God. Oh, Aaron. Ashley. A man. She got into a car with a man—"

"What?" Aaron exclaimed. "What are you talking about?"

"After she ran off. When I came out to get her. I saw her—" She was racked by another round of coughs.

John gave her a second before he asked, "What kind of car was it, Ivy? What did the man look like?"

Ivy shook her head and whispered, "Blue? Black? I don't know—I can't think—"

"It's okay, Ivy," Lily said, but her distressed gaze met John's.

Ivy's expression crumpled. "It's my fault. Ashley. Mom. It's all my fault, Lily."

Lily gasped. "No, Ivy. It's not your fault. You're going to be fine. Ashley is going to be fine."

But Ivy had closed her eyes, seeming too tired to fight the darkness anymore.

"Ivy, no. Ivy, wake up," Aaron shouted.

Lily placed her hand on her brother-in-law's shoulder. The touch seemed to ground him. "It's okay," she said soothingly. "She's sleeping. She just needs to rest. And we need to concentrate on finding Ashley."

Aaron bent down and kissed Ivy's cheek. He stayed in place for several long minutes before straightening and turning to John. With an unwavering gaze, he asked, "Will you help find my daughter?"

John nodded. "Of course." Turning to Lily, he said, "I need to interview the neighbor who saw the accident. The driver who hit Ivy. I know the cops will have already done that, but I need to do it myself."

Lily nodded and clutched his arm, her eyes revealing how truly scared she was. "Yes, John. Please. Please find Ashley."

He struggled with what to say. There was no reason to think Ashley was in danger. No reason to assume more than she was angry with her mother and had simply run away. But who was the man who'd picked her up? All of a sudden, John couldn't stop thinking about one thing—Ashley was younger than Sandy LaMonte and they resembled each other. Just like the murder victim before her. What if The Razor really had killed Tina Cantrell and was picking victims who looked like her. He'd been afraid for Lily, but what if The Razor had Ashley?

Unable to form the right words, John kissed Lily softly. She clung to him for several minutes before pulling away. "I—I'll stay with Aaron."

John shook his head. "He needs to get home. In case Ashley returns."

Lily looked at Aaron, who was once again bent over Ivy and weeping softly. "He's not going to want to leave her. I'll go instead. You can call me there."

John frowned. "I don't want you to be alone."

"What? Why?"

"I'd just feel better if… I'll have an officer assigned to stay with you. He'll meet you there?"

She nodded quickly. "Fine. Now go. I'll be okay."

He gave her another quick kiss, then left the room. He called Murdoch and asked him if he could meet Lily at Ivy's house. Murdoch agreed and John hung up. He was halfway to the hospital entrance when his footsteps slowed. With confusion, he saw Thorn and Douglas Cantrell striding toward him.

The Deputy A.G. had dark shadows under his eyes, and his normally starched clothes were wrinkled. His goatee was overgrown. Doug didn't look any better.

"How—how is she?" Lily's father asked, his panic obvious. He was so pale John wondered how he remained standing.

"She's stable for now."

"What about Ashley? Have they found her?"

"I'm sorry, sir. Not yet. But I'm going to interview witnesses myself." John turned to Thorn. Sweat dotted John's forehead and he clenched his fists. Tonight had been both the worst and best day of his life. It had shown him what an idiot he'd been to let Lily go. But this is where his cowardice ended. "I need to talk to you, Thorn. It's important. As soon as we find Ashley—"

"No," Doug said flatly. "I don't want you interviewing people about Ashley."

Stupefied, John stared at him. Slowly, understanding filled him with fury. "For God's sake, will you let the past go? I know you never thought I was anything but I'm a good cop. I can find your—"

"No," Doug repeated, his voice now soft and shaky. "I know you're a good cop. A good man. But I need you to do something for me first. And I need you to do it now."

"Where's Lily, John?"

In disbelief, John glanced at Thorn. "With her sister, of course. Why?"

Thorn stared back with a grim expression. "We've got DNA results from Tina Cantrell."

"But I thought the defense hadn't requested it. When—"

"I ordered the results myself. Asked them to expedite it. Hardesty's DNA wasn't on the body. But there were traces from an unidentified man and a female with common alleles to Tina. A blood relative. The male's DNA matches The Razor's."

"Common alleles?" He stared at Thorn, then Doug. "You think Lily...?" John laughed. Literally laughed. "So? Lily was her daughter. She lived there and she found her. Her DNA would have been all over the place."

"It was found under her nails and in saliva on her dress. Indications are that Lily bit her mother at some point that night."

Shaking his head, John said, "No. That's impossible."

"You're right," Lily's father urged. "It isn't true. That's why I need you to do something for me. Right now. Right after I see Ivy. I need you to arrest me for murdering Lily's mother."

* * *

"She's awake," Aaron said, rushing to Ivy's bedside. Lily followed close behind.

Ivy's eyelids fluttered then finally stayed open. She frowned. Looked at Lily. Then Aaron. Then started crying. "Ashley," she cried. "Where's my baby?"

Aaron carefully embraced her. "It's okay. The police are looking for her. John's looking for her. They're going to find her."

"You hate me, don't you? Hate me more than you already did?"

Lily saw Aaron's eyes widen.

For a moment, he stared blankly at his wife, then frowned. "What are you talking about, Ivy?"

"At John's party. You told me my mom was waiting for me. I made you leave. I made you drive me to that hotel so we could—so we could make love. I should have gone home and faced her. If I had—that's why I can't—why sex is so—"

Lily bit her lip and turned away. She hadn't known that Ivy and Aaron had been at John's party. That they'd been there when her mother had talked to John, leaving before Lily could get there. She also hadn't realized that she wasn't the only one plagued with guilt about that night. Wanting to give her sister and her husband the privacy they needed, she crept toward the door.

Aaron reached for Ivy's hands. "Ivy, no. We've talked about this in therapy. I thought you understood your mother's death had nothing to do with you."

"It was because I was so scared of losing you. I—I knew you'd get tired of me if I didn't sleep with you. There were so many other girls chasing you."

"What? You never told me."

"And then I couldn't even give you the sex. I know you're having an affair. Ashley hates me. And I have no idea where she is. What am I going to do without her? Aaron, what—"

"Stop it."

Lily froze and turned at Aaron's harsh words.

But despite his tone, his touch was gentle. He caressed Ivy's cheek with the back of his hand as he cried. Not once did he look away from her. "Listen to me. You were never in danger of losing me. I have always been head over heels for you. I would have waited years to make love to you if I had to. And I'm not having an affair."

"But—"

He pressed a finger against her lips. "No. Just listen. Yes, I've had the opportunity. There's a partner at work who's been coming on strong. But I told her no. Because I love my wife. I love my daughter. Do you understand?"

Ivy nodded weakly, but it wasn't good enough for him.

"Say it."

"Yes, yes I understand. But Ashley—"

"She's only been gone a few hours. Let's not worry."

Yet. The word hung between them. Aaron reached into his pocket. "I was going to give this to you tonight. To apologize for what an ass I've been."

Lily saw Aaron take a fragile bracelet from a black velvet pouch.

He unclasped the small silver chain studded with gems and put it around her bandaged wrist. "It's the one you'd been looking at, right? Ashley mentioned you'd wanted it when you went shopping together."

Ivy couldn't speak because she was crying so hard.

Aaron kissed her forehead again. "It's from the two of us. To say thank you for everything you do. Our daughter loves you, Ivy. She'll come home safe and sound. You'll see."

They hugged one another and Lily finally left. She'd go home and pick up some things. Call to check on Ivy. And before she headed over to their house to meet the officer John would send, she'd cry her own tears in private.

And hope that someday she'd have someone to hold her— John to hold her—the way Aaron held Ivy.

Chapter 17

At the Sacramento County Police Department just several blocks from the hospital, John spoke with the detectives working Ashley's disappearance. Luckily, they were experienced and sharp, and had already done everything they should have. Next, he called Murdoch and asked if Lily had arrived at Ivy's. She hadn't.

"I can't stay, John," Murdoch added. "Get an officer from Sac PD to meet her here. I just got a call that they found The Razor's latest victim, a girl named Candace Evans. I need to get back to El Dorado."

"There's been another Razor victim? Did he just snatch her?" John clutched the phone tightly. "I was thinking Ashley Bancroft might have been but…"

"I know you want to do what you can to find Lily's niece, so you stay—"

"Doug Cantrell just confessed to killing Tina Cantrell," John interrupted.

The line crackled with stunned silence. "No way," Murdoch exploded. "You don't think he's also The Razor, do you?"

"I don't know. I think he just confessed to protect his daughter."

"Protect her from what?"

"Long story. Anyway, how long has this latest victim been missing. What do we know?"

"She was taken a few days ago. Reported as a missing person. He had her, but he doesn't anymore. The vic's alive this time."

John almost pumped his fist. "She's okay?"

"Not quite. The doctors aren't sure she's going to make it. She hasn't regained consciousness. Her name is Candace Evans. She's seventeen. He—he messed her up bad. It's a damn miracle she's managed to hang on as long as she has."

"But we know it's the same guy?"

"Responding officers told me it's the same M.O. Victim is small. Dark hair. But this time she didn't have anything on her. No jewelry. No identification. A silver necklace was found nearby, her mom says it's not hers."

"How'd you ID her?"

"Her mother had put out a missing persons alert a couple of days ago. She's got a birthmark on her left thigh."

"Rape kit?"

"Done. Results will be back in a day or so."

John ran a weary hand through his hair. "Will you send me the report? Fax it here to the station." John gave him the number.

"Got it."

"Thanks, Murdoch."

"What about Lily?"

"I'll get someone over there and keep trying to reach her on her cell phone."

John hung up. Then, unable to put it off any longer, he walked to the interrogation room where Douglas Cantrell sat with Thorn. Neither man was talking. Doug met his eyes unflinchingly. Thorn continued to stare at the DNA report in front of him.

Thorn had lost weight in the past two weeks. A lot of it.

Fatigue. Weight loss. Irritability. Sure, it could simply be that Thorn was working too hard. Or that he was still struggling with the breakup with Carmen. But John didn't think so. He knew the signs of drug use better than most people.

Thorn was using something, but John had more important things to worry about. Like keeping the father of the woman he loved from going to prison.

Grim-faced, John slammed his hands on the table. "She didn't do it. And I don't think you did it, either." Not anymore. Despite the evidentiary holes he'd been looking into, John had never doubted Doug loved Lily. He'd seen that love reflected in the man's eyes when he'd confessed to killing Tina, and he'd seen his determination to protect his daughter, as well.

Doug Cantrell just stared at him, his face aged and haggard, but his eyes unwaveringly firm. "I did do it, John. I came home. I caught her dressed to go out with that—that bastard Park, and I killed her. It was a moment of pure insanity."

"And I'm supposed to believe this confession even though it just happens to coincide with the delivery of this DNA report with Lily's trace?"

"As you said, she lived there. Her DNA can be explained."

He couldn't believe he was using his own words against him. "Damn it, don't do this just because you want to save her. This won't save her. It'll kill her." And she'll never forgive me. She'd never get past the fact he'd arrested her father.

For a moment, Doug Cantrell looked furious. "And what am I supposed to do? Count on the D.A. seeing reason? Trust a jury of her peers to believe those numerous reasons for her DNA being there? You forget, I'm a judge. I see what can happen. No." He wiped his face blank of all emotion except resolve. "You're right, Detective. Tyler. This is not coincidence. I'm doing what I should have done long ago. I'm owning up to my actions. I'm not going to use my daughter to protect myself again."

John picked up the DNA report and read through it. "Skin underneath the mother's fingernails tests positive for male DNA matching The Razor's. You're not confessing to killing those girls, too, right? Well, all it's going to take is a DNA test to show it's not yours."

"Not necessarily. And tests are fallible. Deals can be made. The D.A. will want this to all go away."

"You're willing to take your chances? To be tried not only for your ex-wife's murder, but the vicious murder of three young women?"

"I'm willing to do what I must to protect my daughter."

"Damn it, sir, you need to listen to me."

Doug Cantrell stood, chest out, shoulders back. "No, John. You need to listen to me. I was wrong about you. I see that now. Help Lily through this. And please, don't bring her here. I—I don't want her to see me like this. That's all I ask." He turned to the guard. "I'm ready to go back, now."

Helplessly, John watched the guard lead Douglas Cantrell to protective custody. As a judge, he wouldn't last a day in general population.

For a moment, he let himself believe Doug Cantrell was telling the truth. That Hardesty and Mason Park and all the evidence he'd uncovered had correctly pointed to Doug as Tina's killer. Maybe Doug had killed Tina, only to return to find Lily. But then why would Lily remember him picking her up? Why would she remember them discovering her mother's body? Memory loss he could understand. But to plant false memories? How was that possible?

Unless Lily was lying.

John felt bile rise in his throat. Don't go there. There's an explanation. There has to be.

He turned, startled to find Thorn still sitting there. The man had been so quiet, John had forgotten he was there.

Once again, John thought he looked like crap. Correction—crap warmed over. His eyes were bloodshot.

"I don't buy it. It's too easy. But I can't stop it. He's determined to protect her."

"I'm sorry," Thorn said.

John cleared his throat. "Yeah, well I'm the one who messed up. I—I never should have taken this case. Not with her—"

"She means that much to you?" Thorn asked quietly.

"She means more than I would have thought possible."

At her house, Lily packed up her stuff, then called Ivy's room. Aaron said she was sleeping but doing fine. There'd been no word or sign of Ashley.

Just about to walk out the door, Lily paused to stare at her mother's picture. She thought of the grief in Ivy's voice as she'd talked with Aaron. Couldn't believe that her sister had been plagued by the same guilt and grief that she'd been, but that neither one of them had been able to find comfort with the other. Not until now.

Had she and her sister become friends again only so Lily could help Ivy deal with the loss of her daughter? The thought made anxiety spike almost uncontrollably within her. She pictured Ashley singing in the car. Blushing at the thought of Mike.

Lily's things fell from her fingers and she clutched her chest, struggling to breathe. Gaze straying to the door of her meditation room, she instinctively stepped toward it.

She didn't have time to change, but she'd take five minutes. Five minutes to sit in the quiet, peaceful room and center her thoughts. She sank to the floor, wincing when every muscle she had protested. For a moment, the pain brought her joy, reminding her what an incredible lover John had been.

She closed her eyes and tried to focus on those memories. Being held in his arms. The feel of his touch. The taste of his skin.

As long as they had each other, everything would be all

right. They'd find Ashley. They'd find out the truth about Hardesty.

Her thoughts shifted as if directed by a gentle breeze and took her back to the Tyler house.

She saw two little girls running in the grass. Climbing trees. Playing and laughing in the pool as their mothers sat and drank tea at a table nearby. She smiled when a man came into the picture, playfully grabbed one of the girls, and tossed her in the air. It was John. She was sitting at the table with Carmen, and the little girl in his arms was their daughter. Her dream of marrying John and having a family with him had come true.

She frowned when the image shifted again. Suddenly, John was pushing their daughter on a swing. A swing at the park where Lily had met Hardesty. She ran toward them, trying to call out, but her voice remained stubbornly silent. John raised his arm and waved to her. John couldn't see him, but Hardesty stood behind them. Lily felt her heart clamber into her throat and ran faster.

Suddenly, Hardesty became her father. Her father tapped John on the shoulder. John stopped the swing. He took their little girl by the hand. With a final smile at Lily, he followed her father in the other direction. Away from her.

I've got to catch them, Lily thought. Don't leave me. Don't leave—

Lily jerked when she heard a persistent knocking. Her eyes flew open. She shook off her panic and ran to the door.

"Lily Cantrell? I'm Sergeant George Cooper with the Sacramento Police Department."

Checking the peephole, she saw two tall men in police uniforms. When she opened the door, the older of the men scanned her and seemed surprised by what he saw.

"Lily Cantrell?"

"Yes?"

"Ma'am. I need to ask you a few questions."

"Did John Tyler send you? Because I'm on my way—"

The officer shook his head. "I don't know a John Tyler, ma'am. But I'd like you to come to the station to answer a few questions."

"What is this about?"

"A case entitled People versus Chris Hardesty. I understand the defendant was convicted of killing your mother. However, certain questions have come up. Questions involving Chris Hardesty, you and your father."

She straightened her spine, lifted her chin, and braced her arm against the door. "Do you have an arrest warrant?"

The two officers looked at each other. Then one answered a call on his radio and stepped several feet away.

The other man addressed her. "Look, we don't have a warrant, but we just want to talk to you."

"Then I suggest you leave. In the meantime, I'll be making a phone call to my attorney. Goodbye."

She started to close the door when the other officer jogged back. "They got him. A detective from El Dorado arrested him and brought him in—" They walked away. Lily thought she heard one of them say, "judge."

Lily swayed, but managed to back up and close the door. She leaned back against it. Slowly, her legs gave way and she sank to the floor. She stared out the window, not sure when the pitter-patter of rain started. She curled into a ball. Her mind focused on the rain, the thump thump in her head becoming louder and louder until it beat like a drum in a rhythm she'd heard before.

August 29
12:05 a.m.
Sacramento, CA

Lily grasped the sides of her head and sobbed even as she continued down the dark, deserted road. No matter how fast she ran, she couldn't wipe away the voices. Cold air pressed into her, rattling her teeth and distorting the images in her mind, blending them together until she didn't know what was real and what wasn't.

Colors flashed behind her eyes in a sickening, swirling kaleidoscope. Through the chaos, she pictured herself in a pretty black dress. Saw herself arguing with her mother. Remembered John kissing her...then Stacy.

Her bare feet twisted beneath her and she stumbled, staggering in a disorienting zigzag before coming to a jerky standstill. Moonlight filtered through the trees, illuminating the road. She started moving again, struggling to put one foot in front of the other. The images in her mind faded into shadows. She saw a raised arm. Heard the voices again. Pleading. Warning. Denial.

I didn't mean to do it. Run, Lily, run.

A sudden flash of light blinded her as a car appeared, heading straight for her. She wheeled around. The road undulated in a crazy slither of asphalt, threatening to topple her. Swaying, she reached out to steady herself but fell instead, catching herself on the ground with her hands.

The car stopped. Someone got out. Moved closer. The sound of footsteps thundered in her head. Her brain screamed for her to run, but her legs refused to cooperate, weighing her down like two leaden tubes of cement.

John. Get to John. John would help her.

She started to crawl, dragging herself across the ground with such desperation that she never felt the sharp rocks that ripped at her exposed arms and legs. And then he had her, his grip like an iron vise around her arm, dragging her up toward him.

She struggled and fought, but then her father's voice registered. "Lily, stop!"

She froze. "Daddy?"

He hugged her and she clung to him, feeling safe for a brief moment before the terror returned. "It's okay," he murmured. "You're going to be okay." He led her to the car and quickly tucked her inside before starting to drive.

"Daddy—" she whispered.

He glanced at her. "Listen to me. Your mom called hours ago. Worried out of her mind. You've been drinking. Your mother said you fought. Something about a party. That's where you were, right?"

Lily didn't respond. Couldn't. Her head throbbed and the world spun. She tried to understand what he was saying, but couldn't.

"Answer me, Lily. You ran away. You went to the party. You've been drinking this whole time. Haven't you?" His voice rose in frustration and he pounded the steering wheel with his fist. "God damn it, answer me!"

His anger jolted her and a small trickle of memory flowed through her. Again, she tried to speak, but the words, like a tooth reluctant to be extracted, stayed there.

Yes. We fought. I went to the party. I drank.

She closed her eyes, hoping that the darkness would help her think. Would stop the confusing swirl of colors in her head. But darkness didn't come, and the colors only seemed to glow more brightly. Something touched her arm. Her eyes flew open and she flinched.

Her father pulled back his hand, frowning as she cowered against the door. "It's going to be okay," he said softly. "I called your mother and—" He closed his eyes, seeming to steady himself. "Just do as I say. We'll be okay."

Her mother. He said she'd fought with her mother. Lily tried to remember, but her mind was a vast blackness, filled with nothing but pain and hazy faces. Her father stopped the car, and she stared at the house.

At the rosebushes her mother tended so faithfully once, but had started to droop with her recent neglect.

She whimpered. She didn't want to go inside, but the thought of staying outside frightened her even more.

Her father got out and walked around to open her door. He grasped her elbow and gently pulled her out. "We need to go inside now."

She resisted, pulling back. Her father overpowered her, inexorably dragging her to the house.

"Everything okay, Doug?" someone called, making Lily jerk. The man in the window next door looked familiar, but she struggled to remember his name. Tabman?

Her father turned to him. "Lily's been partying. Tina asked me to bring her home. Sorry if we woke you."

The man waved and closed his bedroom window. Taking a deep breath, her father unlocked the door. It opened silently and bumped softly against the wall.

"Tina," her father yelled. "I found her." He flipped on the light and stopped. "What the hell?"

Lily followed her father's gaze. Her heart beat faster, growing in size until it filled her throat, cutting off her breath. There was dirt on the carpeting. On the walls.

She whimpered "Mama?" and moved forward.

Her father grabbed at her.

She dodged his grip and rushed toward her mother's bedroom. "Mama, where are you?"

Lily ran down the carpeted hallway, her gait unwieldy, as if her soles were sticking to the carpet each time she tried to take another step. She tripped but clawed her way back up and kept moving forward.

"Lily, stop, come back here."

She made it to the bedroom door. A smudge on the wall. Blood. She could smell it, like rusty metal mixed with rotting mushrooms. She could feel it, staining her hands and feet in a thin viscous layer. Her mother. Where was she?

There. On the bed. Silent. Knees bent. She staggered closer, needing to know for sure.

"Mama?" she whimpered, reaching out her hand; it shook so hard she could feel the vibrations coursing through her. But there was no response.

"Lily! Don't. Come here, baby. Please."

She looked at her father, standing just inside the room, then back at her mother. Her eyes were closed. The parts of her face that weren't covered with blood were pale and waxy. Lily reached for her hand and flinched at how cold it felt. Stiff. Like brittle wood that would break in half with the smallest amount of pressure.

Lily's stomach heaved and she turned away, throwing up on the carpet. She whimpered and collapsed to her knees, covering her face with her hands.

Her mind tunneled into a tiny pinpoint of light.

Suddenly, all she cared about was reaching that light in the distance. She raced toward it in her mind. Fleeing reality. Fleeing betrayal. Fleeing anger and shame and blood and tears. The faster she ran, the dimmer the light became. Until it flickered out altogether, and she was running in the dark.

Lily still hadn't arrived at Ivy's house. The officers from Sacramento PD said a team had been sent over to get her, but after talking to her had left. "That doesn't make sense," John insisted. "I told them she needed protection. They were supposed to escort her to her sister's house, in case her niece showed up. Damn it, check again."

The rattled clerk checked her computer. "It's right here. It says here that Officers Cooper and Lennox went by to question her about the Hardesty case. They're on their way back, but they had no reason to bring her in. They didn't have a warrant."

Thumping his fist on the counter separating them, John cursed. "Where's the lieutenant in charge?" The clerk pointed to a man behind her and John immediately told him his concerns.

The portly man with thinning hair didn't know what to say. "Look, someone's got their wires crossed. You've got my guys trying to protect the same woman the D.A. wants to question about the murder of her mother. If there's some kind of mix-up, you need to talk to Morton Howe."

"Tell me where I can find Mr. Howe now."

"Don't worry about it." The voice came from behind John. "I'm going to see Howe myself in a few minutes."

John turned and saw Thorn. The other man looked ready to collapse. Even worse than before. So unlike himself. He hadn't been quite himself for a while now. It had started with the breakup with Carmen. Continued with surliness and an almost obsessive need to confirm Hardesty's guilt. And after repeatedly telling John why he didn't want to allow DNA testing in the Tina Cantrell case, he'd gone ahead and ordered the tests himself. Why?

"I need to talk to you, John."

"I need to talk to you, too. I want to know why you ordered the DNA testing on your own when you'd been determined to avoid that very thing from happening for so long."

Thorn shrugged. "It's ironic really. I wanted you to confirm Hardesty was the guilty party. That the execution would be righteous. I thought you'd be the perfect person to do that. But your updates. Your theories. They were leading to the opposite conclusion. I couldn't ignore them, John. I wanted to. Believe me, I wanted to go on believing that this was all going to end when he was executed."

"What are you talking about? That what was going to end?"

"I—I needed to know the truth no matter what the D.A. said—"

John narrowed his eyes. "What?"

Thorn just shook his head. Then he said softly, "Carmen's pregnant."

Shock came first. Then something close to pity. John could see the yearning in Thorn's eyes. And the defeat.

"This is all my fault, John."

Somehow, John knew Thorn wasn't just talking about the pregnancy. "What's your fault?"

"It's a double-edged sword, isn't it? By helping people, we get to feel a little bit better about ourselves. But what do we do when we lose? What are we left with when we try our best and it's still not good enough? What are we left with when we don't even try our best?"

When Thorn opened his eyes, they were so bleak John winced. "You can get help, Thorn. Check into a program. I can't say for sure, but she might stick by you."

Thorn's eyes widened.

John shrugged. "I had a suspicion you were taking drugs, but—"

Thorn laughed. "Yeah. But I just gave myself away. What a putz. Howe would laugh his ass off."

The air left John's lungs. "D.A. Morton Howe? What's he got to do with this?"

Thorn slouched down in his chair and stared at the ceiling. "Everything. He's—he's behind all this, John. He's why I asked you to look into Tina's case. Because it had to be done, but we wanted it done by someone with incentive to close the investigation fast. Someone who wouldn't want things to drag on for the Cantrell family."

"You said 'we.' We as in you and Howe? You're working together to make sure Hardesty's conviction sticks? No matter what? Why?"

"I—I was burned out at work. Started using to get me through the day. Thought I'd be able to control it, but I couldn't. It got out of hand but then I managed to stop. That was three years ago, right around the time I got Chris Hardesty's appeal. I was concerned how fast he was tried and convicted. I started asking Howe questions. Too many questions. He told me to back off. When I didn't, he said he knew I'd been doing drugs and would ruin me. So I let it go. I started dating Carmen. I was so happy. But then with each Razor murder, my doubts came back. I started using again. Broke up with Carmen because of it. I wanted it all to go away but it wouldn't. Then Howe called me. Told me to find someone who would nail Chris Hardesty to the wall once and for all."

Disbelief and hurt came first. "And you picked me. Then what?"

When Thorn simply stared at the ground, John almost went for him. It would feel good to take out his rage on someone. Thorn, however, didn't look like he'd last more than one punch. He was pale. Skinny. About to pass out from self-disgust.

"I'm sorry. I know it's not enough, but I am."

John didn't say anything. What could he say? He couldn't accept that apology. Not now. Maybe not ever. "What's Howe hiding?"

Thorn shrugged. "Nothing that horrible. I think he really believed Hardesty did it. Because of that, he played things sloppy. Ignored things he shouldn't have. Rushed to get a conviction. Nothing criminal at the time, but once he became D.A., he didn't want anything to come out that could possibly ruin his chances for reelection."

Thorn held out a thick manila envelope. "Take this. It's my signed declaration. Detailing everything with Howe. I don't know if anyone will believe me, but at least you'll have it. I also included my file on The Razor cases. No matter what happens with the Cantrell investigation, you might be able to use it."

He started to turn away, but stopped. "I—I messed things up, but I love Carmen, John. Tell her that. Tell her I would have loved the baby, too."

His words sent a shiver up John's spine. Thorn sounded defeated. Desperate. John didn't know what Thorn was planning to do, but Carmen would never forgive John if anything happened to him. "Thorn, listen to me—"

His cell phone rang. With relief, he saw it was Lily's home phone number. "Thorn, I need to get this—"

Looking up, John cursed.

Thorn was gone.

John brought the phone to his ear. "Lily?"

He heard static. Then long, shuddering gasps for breath. Words rushed him, too fast to understand. "Shh. Slow down, baby. Are you safe? Where are you?"

"Did you—have you found Ashley?" she finally managed to ask.

"Not yet. We're still working on it. But I told you, I'll find her." He walked from room to room, scanning the station for Thorn. "Are you okay? There are officers waiting at Ivy's house. Why haven't you—"

"I'm going to the hospital. My sister needs me. Is my father there?"

He paused. He had to tell her, but he couldn't do it on the phone. He needed to look in her eyes. He needed to be able to hold her. "Your father is with me." It wasn't a lie, he told himself. And if it was, she'd understand. After he explained, she'd understand.

"Okay. I'll see you later." As if she'd flipped a switch, her tone was suddenly devoid of warmth or emotion or grief.

"What's wrong?"

"Two officers came by my house. They wanted to bring me down to the station so I could answer some questions. I told them I wasn't talking to them without an arrest warrant or a lawyer."

"Good. That's good."

"John—" For a moment, a pleading tone entered her voice.

"What is it, small fry?"

"Tell me again. Tell me you love me."

"I love you," he said instantly. "Do you? Love me?"

She didn't speak for several long seconds. Then she whispered, "I've always loved you," before hanging up.

Despite her declaration of love, an uneasy feeling sat on his chest. He needed to get to her. He needed to explain. But what about Thorn? Carmen? Ashley? Lily was his priority, but so was everyone she loved, including her father.

John slapped the envelope that Thorn had given him against his thigh, then opened it up. He took out Thorn's declaration. Grimly, he read all the details, including the fact that Thorn had honestly thought Hardesty was guilty. That was why he'd felt okay about assigning John to the case. He shoved the declaration back into the envelope, cursing when it tangled with other papers inside. He yanked one out, and several photographs spilled to the floor.

They were all gruesome, but one in particular caught his eye. It was a color photograph of Sandy LaMonte's body. Thorn had circled a portion of the photograph in red—the section showing a chain around her throat.

A fragile silver chain.

Memory tinged at the back of John's mind. Something about The Razor's victims. How he hadn't messed with their purses or taken their jewelry. How their jewelry had run the gamut from earrings to bracelets to necklaces, and how each had a mix of stones. But there had also been something else. Something similar…

Murdoch had mentioned a chain, too, hadn't he? A chain found near Candace Evans's body?

John flipped through the rest of the pictures, but the gems were either too small or the photos too grainy to provide any details. He searched some more and pulled out the reports. The property logs. One of the victims had a bracelet with several blue stones. The female officer had identified them as aquamarines. Another had on earrings. Aquamarines. And Sandy LaMonte had worn an ankle bracelet he hadn't seen. Pearls and aquamarines.

John's heart pounded.

Different types of jewelry. Different stones mixed in with the aquamarines. It probably meant absolutely nothing.

He picked up the phone and called Murdoch.

"Murdoch, this is John Tyler."

"John—I was about to call you. Candace Evans is awake."

"Does she know her attacker?"

"Can't say. She's still pretty out of it. Can barely talk."

"You said you found a chain. A silver chain. Did it have gems on it?"

"Wait a sec. Let me check. The necklace you're talking

about had stones...hell, I don't know, what they are. But they were blue. Light blue."

"Aquamarines?"

Murdoch laughed nervously. "I don't know. Could be."

"There's our connection. All the jewelry found on your vics have blue aquamarine stones. Not exclusively. But it's there."

"You're kidding. Let me check." A few seconds passed and Murdoch put John on hold. But he came back almost immediately, this time sounding much more grim. "You're right."

"Did next of kin identify the jewelry?"

"Sometimes. Sometimes not. I mean, would you be able to identify every piece of jewelry your girlfriend has?"

John thought of Lily. Other than her mother's necklace, he couldn't say what kind of jewelry she wore. But her mother's necklace had... Realization hit him and he gasped.

"What?" Murdoch asked.

"The necklace. Lily's necklace. The one Tina was wearing when she was killed. It has aquamarine stones on it. Because it's Lily's birthstone."

Less than ten minutes later, John rushed into Ivy's hospital room. He immediately saw Lily, sitting on the bed and curled next to Ivy, who looked alert but strained. Aaron sat next to her, but stood when he saw John.

"Have you found—?"

John shook his head. "Not yet. But we have some leads." He shifted his gaze to Lily, who stared at him impassively. She knows, he thought. She knows and she hates me.

He shifted his gaze to Ivy, then back to her. "There's something I need to tell you all." He squatted in front of Lily and gripped her hands. "Something I've learned about—"

She ripped away and stood. "So it's true. That police officer was right."

"Lily?" Ivy stirred, clearly frightened. "What's going on?" Aaron went to her, but Lily held John's gaze. "He arrested Dad." Despite her anger, her pain was even more obvious.

John reached for her, but she backed away. "No, Lily, technically he—"

"Don't talk technicalities to me. Take me to him."

"I can't. He doesn't want to see you yet."

"Why would he say that?"

"He's ashamed. He confessed, Lily—"

"Get out."

"If you'll just listen to me," he said, his voice rising to be heard over hers.

"Why'd you really contact me, John? Was it just for old times? An easy lay, no matter the damage you leave behind. You're just as bad as Hardesty, aren't you? Just as bad as the murdering slime who killed my mother."

He willed his face to appear blank, but couldn't stop his heart from bleeding. "Is that what you really believe?"

They stared at each other, but she didn't respond.

"Well, you might be right, Lily. But here's the way it's going to work. You hate my guts, I understand that. But right now you need me. Right now, we need to find Ashley."

Chapter 18

Ashley had been missing for over twenty-four hours.

Those hours had come and gone in a blur, weighing Lily down with worry and pain and misery until she felt on the verge of collapse.

This might be the final straw, she thought vaguely. *How much more could she be expected to take?*

"I asked him to arrest me, Lily. I wanted it to be him."

Lily stared at her father through the Plexiglas separating them, trying so desperately to hold on to her faith. "I know you couldn't have done that to her."

Relief seemed to flash over his face before he wiped his expression clean. "I'm telling you, I did. We fought. I didn't mean to, but—" His face broke and he stared at his hands. "But it happened. I've tried to make up for it. To be a good father to you and Ivy. But when the DNA report showed up, and I knew they'd start questioning you, I had a choice. Use my own daughter again to save myself, or finally prove myself to be the man I've tried to be."

"No," she whispered.

"Yes," he insisted, his voice harsh. "Flawed. So flawed I murdered the woman I loved more than anything in the world. I—I know I can't apologize. But I can do what's right now. I can protect you, Lily."

"The police say it was my DNA on her, not yours."

Her father clenched his teeth. "You lived there. Your DNA probably attached before you ever left. Or it happened afterward. After I found you and took you home. You threw up beside her, just like the police report says. I just changed the timing."

"Why would you do that? Why would you take me there? To—to find her—"

"I'm sorry, Lily. It was stupid of me. I—I was selfish, only thinking of myself."

"So you killed her in her own bed? The one you and she—?"

He closed his eyes. "Yes," he whispered.

"No."

His eyes opened. "What?"

She smiled sadly, shaking her head. "She wasn't killed in her bed, Daddy. John told me that."

"He's wrong."

"No. Not about that. It was me, wasn't it? It really was my fault? I don't know how, but—" Pain surged through her and she couldn't breathe.

"Look at me. Look at me," her father said, tapping on the panel of glass separating them. One of the guards shifted nervously, and her father sat back, leaving his palm pressed up against the glass. "You didn't do this. Whatever you think you remember isn't right. It was me. Me."

But his words sounded weak.

Lily buried her face in her hands, her shoulders shaking. He slapped the glass again. Yelled for her. But she didn't respond. Not even when the guards came and took him away.

John strode down the hospital corridor toward Ivy Cantrell's room. John needed to ask her some questions. About Ashley's cell phone. Her social media accounts. Her address book.

He knew Lily wouldn't be around. She was at the jail visiting her father. And although she didn't know it, she'd be well protected when she left. Just as she had been since he'd left Ivy's room. He'd assigned an officer to stay with her, just like he'd told her he would.

Even though he was the last person she wanted to see right now, even though he wasn't ready to see her just yet, he wasn't letting anything happen to her. Her words had pierced his soul and done considerable damage, but he'd recover. He couldn't say the same thing if he lost her.

The door to Ivy's room was open. Ivy was in bed, alone. John cleared his throat.

Ivy raised her head. She was doing much better and a spark of hope lit her eyes. Gently, John shook his head and watched the spark die. He walked toward her and slowly sat on the bed next to her. "I need to ask you some questions, if it's okay."

She closed her eyes, but even though tears seeped out, she nodded. "Okay."

"Does Ashley have a social media account on the internet?"

"She's not supposed to. We told her she couldn't." Ivy shrugged. "Doesn't mean she didn't get one. My daughter's strong-willed."

"Just like her mom," he murmured.

Glancing at him, she said, "And her aunt. Her aunt, who's hurt and afraid right now. But who's always known what—who—she wants."

John gave her a tight smile. "Yeah, well, as I learned a long time ago, you can't—"

"—always get what you want," Ivy finished with him. Smiled weakly. "Rolling Stones. Ashley can't stand them." Her face crumpled and she began to sob. Helplessly, John watched as she lifted an arm to swipe at her tears.

A sparkle at her wrist caught his eye. "Nice bracelet," he said, every muscle in his body tensing. "I don't remember you having that on before. Did someone special give that to you?"

Ivy smiled, but before she could respond, a voice came from the doorway. "I gave it to her," Aaron stated.

John stood, eyes narrowed, heart beating fast. "Those blue stones are aquamarines, aren't they?"

"Yes. So—?"

A haze of fury swept over him, making him act before he even thought about it. Ivy screamed and Aaron let out a grunt as John shoved him back against a wall with one hand to his throat. Tension screamed down on them like a shot in the dark, and the raspy sound of John's breathing echoed in his ears.

"What are you—"

John squeezed tighter. "What's Lily's birthstone?"

Under his hand, Aaron's throat convulsed.

He leaned further into Aaron's face. "What is it?"

"Aquamarine," Aaron wheezed out. "Let go. Please."

John watched as Aaron gasped for breath. Then he abruptly let go. "You gave Ivy that bracelet. A bracelet with Lily's birthstone?"

Aaron glared at John, straightened his jacket and tie. "Are you crazy? Ivy was born a week before Lily's birthday. They share the same birthstone."

In a flash, John remembered Lily telling him that. Damn it. He'd forgotten.

"We think The Razor's been planting evidence on his victims," he explained. "Jewelry. All with aquamarine stones. The latest one was a pendant left near the latest victim, Candace Evans. And Tina was wearing a necklace with the birthstones when she was killed."

For a moment, Aaron looked confused. Then he paled. "And you thought I—? That's ridiculous. I haven't killed anyone. I'm just trying to stay sane until someone finds my daughter."

John stared at Aaron. He believed him, but… "You were dating Ivy back then. You could have done it."

Aaron shook his head. "So could you, do you forget that?"

"You willing to take a blood draw? Right here, right now?"

Aaron met John's gaze without flinching. "I will. How about you?"

"I'm a little busy trying to find your daughter. You're sure you don't know where she is?"

"A-Aaron."

At the frightened, female sound, both men turned to Ivy. Aaron rushed to her. "Oh Ivy, don't listen to him. I'd never hurt Ashley. You know that." He embraced her, and Ivy didn't hesitate in putting her arms around him. She glared at John over Aaron's shoulder.

John gritted his teeth, his muscles clenched so tight he was practically quivering. Grasping his hair, he turned and paced a jagged path in front of Aaron. "This is all crazy. I don't know where to turn. What to do."

John's cell phone rang, and he immediately looked at the screen. He pressed the Talk button. "What have you got, Murdoch?"

"Candace Evans woke up."

"Did she ID the perp?"

"No, but she was able to tell us he has a daughter. He mentioned her more than once."

"A daughter?" John glanced at Aaron, who stared back with a heated gaze clear of guilt or fear. "Did he mention her name? How old she is?"

"Not her age specifically, but she said she thinks she's a teenager. She saw a volleyball uniform in the back of his car, along with softball paraphernalia. She said he called her 'Tess.'"

The name failed to ring any bells. "Tess? Tess what? How are we going to track down—?"

"Tessa?" Ivy whispered. "What about Tess?"

John stared at her. "Does Ashley know someone named Tess?"

"That's one of her best friends," Aaron interjected.

"Give me her phone number and address. Fast."

* * *

Lily walked out of the main visiting area and outside the jail doors. She didn't know how, but she was going to prove her father was innocent. She squinted when the sunlight blinded her, jerking when someone called her name. Disoriented, she blinked rapidly, desperately trying to focus on the dark shape walking toward her. She gasped when she saw who stood in front of her.

"Barb."

Pacing the hospital room like a tiger, John waited for Murdoch to come back on the line. Occasionally, he bumped into Aaron and they'd glare at each other. But John didn't blame the guy. He was frantic with worry about his kid.

It had taken them less than twenty minutes to figure out that Park was The Razor, and was likely the person who'd killed Tina Cantrell. A call to Tess's mother and a couple of questions and they'd learned that she'd divorced Tess's biological father, but that Tess still regularly saw him along with her two half siblings, Penny and Miles, the same children John had seen running around in their backyard.

It had been Park the whole time.

He wasn't just Tina's killer. He was The Razor. Continuing to kill girls who looked like Tina and Lily. Girls like Ashley.

Now, he could practically hear Aaron and Ivy's prayers. Hoping against hope Park hadn't taken Ashley even as part of them hoped he had. After all, knowing something and maintaining hope was better than knowing nothing and speculating the worst. "You got anything for me yet, Murdoch?"

"Give me a minute. Just a minute. El Dorado County records show nothing for a Mason Park."

"Try derivatives of the name. Parks. Parker."

"Mason Parks. Mason Parker. No. Damn it. Nothing."

"He's got to have a place. Someplace local he's bringing the victims. We've got to talk to Candace Evans. See if she remembers something—"

"Wait! I've got it. A Michael Parker. 2583 West Bend in El Dorado County. A house in a secluded area. Looks like he's had it for years. What do you think?"

"How long will it take you to get there?"

"Ten minutes."

"Go."

"I'll call you."

Murdoch hung up and John closed his phone. He stared at Aaron and shook his head. "I'm sor—"

"Don't," Aaron gritted. "I know you were doing your job. I just want my daughter to be okay." Aaron gathered a sobbing Ivy into his arms.

John bowed his head and felt tears sting his own eyes.

Please, God, he prayed. Help her. Let Ashley be okay.

Fifteen minutes later, his phone rang.

He and Aaron stared at one another, fear and uncertainty traveling between them like an electric current. John answered the phone.

"This is Tyler."

"She's here. She's okay. She's scared and has superficial abrasions, but she's okay. I've got Ashley Bancroft right here with me."

"She's okay," John told Aaron. The man's face collapsed and he fell to his knees in relief.

"What about Mason? Did you catch him?"

"He wasn't here. But he's sick, John. More than sick. He beat Ashley. Tried to rape her. Only he couldn't. He freaked out. Said he needed to go after the real thing. The one who really mattered. And he's got pictures of Lily all over the place. You need to get to her. Fast."

Chapter 19

Lily rubbed her arms as she paced her father's living room. Barb had insisted on coming back here to talk, saying she had something crucial to tell her. Something that would help her understand her father's actions. As soon as they'd arrived, however, she'd disappeared in search of tea and cookies.

"I'll be right out," Barb called.

Lily stifled a scream. All she wanted was to find out what her stepmother had to say and get the hell back to Ivy, who might have news on Ashley.

Lily looked at her watch again and jumped when her cell phone rang. She picked it up. "Hello."

"Where are you?" John yelled. "We found her. Ashley's okay."

Knees giving way, Lily sank onto a couch. Cries of joy escaped her. "Thank God."

"Where are you?"

"I'm at my father's house. With Barb. She said she had something to tell me about my father, but I'm on my way—"

"No. Stay there. Stay with Barb."

"Why?"

"It was Mason Park. The man your mother was dating. He killed your mother, Lily. He's been leaving jewelry with your birthstone on the victims, only we never put it together. He's the one who took Ashley."

Lily could barely believe her ears. "You caught him?"

"Not yet. He's still on the loose. Which is why I want you to stay there. Lock all the doors. I've had an officer with you so he'll—"

"What? You've had someone watching me."

A tense silence was her only reply. "I'm sorry I didn't tell you. I was worried—"

She shook her head. "No. I'm not mad. Thank you. That—that means a lot to me. That you would worry."

"Lily, can we talk? After all this is through? Please, will you give me a chance to explain why I lied."

She knew why he'd lied. For the same reason he did everything. To protect her. But all she said was, "Yes." Then, "Thank you, John. Thank you for finding Ashley."

"I'll be there soon, babe."

Lily hung up, then jumped when Barb spoke from behind her. "Who was that?"

She was so happy, she ran to Barb, not thinking about the pot of tea she held. She wrapped her arms around her. "It's over. Daddy's going to be coming home soon, Barb."

Barb screamed in pain, not joy, as hot water soaked the front of her dress.

John hung up on Tom Raddison, the officer guarding Lily, and walked quickly to his car. She was fine. He'd be there in less than fifteen minutes. No need for the panic and terror coursing through his body.

Park was The Razor. He'd sat across from him and bought into the whole family-man image and because of that Ashley had been terrorized. Doug Cantrell had felt compelled to confess to murder. Candace Evans might still die.

He slammed his hands on the steering wheel and cursed. Despite his deception, Thorn had actually presented John with the opportunity to catch The Razor. Hell, so had Hardesty.

Even as he accelerated around a corner, John frowned. Since Hardesty had told the truth about everything else, he'd probably been telling the truth about the cop hat, too. It had to have been Doug Cantrell. Who else could it—

His blood turned cold. In a flash, he remembered Doug Cantrell's 911 call the night of the murder. What had he said to the police dispatcher about who he'd been with at the time? "My wife and I" then "My daughter and I." John had assumed Doug Cantrell had initially misspoken and referred to Tina as his current wife. They'd been married so long and it had seemed a natural mistake given the violent death she'd suffered. But what if he hadn't meant Tina, at least not at first. What if he'd slipped because Barb had been there, too?

Barb had been a police dispatcher. Everyone in town knew that Doug Cantrell wanted Tina back, which meant Barb had known it, too. That kind of humiliation and pain could have driven her to do something rash. Something desperate.

And now Lily was alone with her.

Cursing, John grabbed his phone and hit redial. "Come on, come on." He waited for Raddison to pick up. Waited some more. "Damn it." When he didn't answer, he dialed Lily's number. But that just rang, too.

"No, no, no," he repeated over and over again.

Please let her be all right. Please don't take her away from me.

Chapter 20

"Thank you again," Lily told the officer standing guard out front. "I appreciate it."

The young man with dimples winked at her. "No problem. I just talked to John and he should be here soon. I'll come in occasionally and check in on you. Just be careful with that hot water, ladies."

Lily laughed uncomfortably before shutting the door, then glanced at Barb. She sat on the sofa with her jaw set, obviously not finding humor in the fact that the young officer had run in just as she'd been stripping her soaked shirt off… But then Barb's mouth tilted and a small giggle burst from her chest. Soon, she was full out laughing.

Staring at her, Lily laughed, too.

Barb shook her head and quieted down. "Your father's been the only man to see me naked in almost twenty years. It felt nice showing a little skin to someone so good-looking." She smoothed her hair away from her face. "But let's keep this our little secret, okay?"

"Definitely."

Barb rose and regarded Lily with a serious expression. "Your father never loved me the way he loved your mother, you know."

Instinctively, Lily shook her head. "That's not—"

"Lily. Please. I'm not a fool. But he does love me, nevertheless. Oh, I know if he had it to do over again, he wouldn't. But we all make choices and have to live with them. I'm the choice he has to live with. And I've never been more grateful for anything in my life. Do you understand? Your father would do anything for you because he loves you. And I know he'd do the same for me. That's why I stay with him."

Seeing the sad acceptance on Barb's face, Lily reached out and touched the other woman's hand. "Yes," she whispered. "I understand."

Barb cleared her throat. "I need a shower before your father comes back. Do you mind if I go up for a while?"

"Not at all," Lily said. "I'll just stay here and wait for John."

After Barb left, Lily went to the window, pulled the curtains aside, and stared into the dark night. The street outside was quiet and absent of activity, the only movement being the slight sway of the London Plane trees lining the path leading to a nearby green belt. She squinted, trying to see farther into the distance, to make out shapes in the shadows.

The longer she stared, the more nervous she became. From her vantage point, and without the sound of wind and rustling leaves, the silent dance of greenery seemed disturbing.

Threatening.

Her palms grew damp as she remembered the disorienting walk home from John's fifteen years ago, and the way the trees and houses had come alive.

She stepped back and knocked against a table, jerking when a frame rattled to the hardwood floor. She heard a cell phone ring somewhere nearby. She moved toward the foyer. "Officer Raddison?"

Her own phone rang. She sighed with relief, knowing it would be John. She answered. "John—?"

"Lily, it's me."

She recognized Albert's voice immediately. She also recognized the fear that made it tremble. "Albert? What is it?"

"Get out, Lily. You're not alone."

She moved toward the foyer, intending to open the door to look for him. "Where are you? Outside?"

"No! Don't go that way. The back, Lily. You need to go out the—"

She froze when the man, bloody and disheveled, plowed through the doorway. Her first thought was that he'd been in some kind of accident. Her next thought was that Albert had set her up. Finally, she realized that Albert had been trying to warn her.

Fear dug its claws into her and twisted deep. "Go, Albert."

"Lily, I'm coming in—"

"No!" she gasped. *Don't stay. Don't watch.* "Get help, Albert," she said softly. She cut off the call as her eyes darted behind the man in search of Officer Raddison.

"He's sleeping," he said in a singsongy voice.

She swallowed hard and tried to remain calm. "Did you—did you hurt him?"

He smiled gently and tsked. "Of course I did, Lily. How else was I going to get to you?"

She wanted to scream, but her eyes caught the slashing movement at the man's side. He made short jerking movements with a knife, but didn't seem to be aware of it. A knife stained with blood.

Oh God. Oh no. Her mind immediately drew an image of the young cop, a proud father of a newborn baby, sliced and bleeding because he'd failed to anticipate the arrival of a madman. "What do you want?" she whispered.

For a moment, he looked to be in pain. "I want it to stop. The fire's burning me alive and I can't make it stop. Not anymore. You're the only one who can help me."

Fear morphed into terror. She glanced down at the knife again. "How can I help?"

"It won't go away. I have no choice, don't you see?" His voice was high. Pleading.

She took several steps back. Glanced at the stairway. Wondered if Barb would hear her if she cried for help.

"You really want me to hurt the old woman, Lily?"

Shaking her head, she bit her lip.

He stepped toward her, covering the distance she'd retreated. "You changed. You're like the others now. A whore." He raised his other hand and held out a white patch of fabric.

Lily stared at it blankly.

He sighed and rearranged the fabric. Underwear. Plain white cotton. Hers?

Would John make it in time? Though fear made her thoughts sluggish, she knew she had to stall. Keep him talking. Pretending, she asked, "Who are you?"

"I wanted her, but I wanted you more." He smiled wanly. "Two for the price of one."

Fear iced up her spine. "Who? Who did you want? The other girls? The ones with the jewelry..."

His eyes widened and he grinned with delight. "Smart girl. I thought it was a nice touch. A trade-off of sorts. They gave me what I needed, and I left them something in return."

She glanced once more at the underwear, knowing but not fully accepting. "The birthstone. How did you know? Who told you?"

He tsked. "Come on now, Lily. Don't you know? It's right there. Right around your neck."

Her heartbeat lurched and she raised a trembling hand to her mother's pendant.

Where was John?

She glanced back at the doorway and wondered, briefly, if she could overpower him. But he was big. The knife was so sharp.

"Don't even think of fighting. I'll hurt you. And I'll hurt

anyone who comes to help you." For emphasis, he slashed the knife at her belly, laughing when she instinctively jerked back. "It's for the best. I need to protect her. Kids are so innocent."

"Who are you talking about? The girls you've killed? They were young. Innocent."

He frowned. "They're old enough to know better. They shouldn't be hitchhiking. Besides, they weren't important. She's the important one. The one I have to protect."

"She? Who's she?"

He opened his mouth, then shut it. "Enough talk. I didn't come here for conversation."

Her limbs went numb and she knew John wasn't going to get here in time. It was up to her. She braced her body to run, but he shook his head and lunged for her, grabbing her by the arm in a vicious grip. She opened her mouth to scream, but he dragged her into the foyer. Moaning, she saw Officer Raddison lying on the floor facedown. Blood leaked out from underneath his body.

"See what I did to him, Lily? That's what I'll do to anyone who comes to help you. Young or old. Man or woman. I don't care. That's why I took your niece, Ashley."

He laughed when her body jerked and then went limp. Blackness settled like a veil over her.

—a bloody knife plunging into flesh over and over again. Her mother crawling, trying to get away. Ashley singing in the car to the radio—

Slowly, he took his hand off her mouth. She didn't fight. Didn't protest. She felt separated from her body. Unable to do anything but let him pull her strings.

"Good girl," he crooned, twisting her arm behind her back, holding the knife against her side. "We're going to get into my car. It'll be over soon. I promise."

He grasped her elbow, led her outside, and began pushing her toward his car. "My sweetie reminds me so much of you, even though the coloring is all wrong. A father shouldn't feel that way for his daughter. It's because I wanted you, because

I never had you, that I think that way about her. I thought the other girls would help, but they didn't. It kept coming back. But when John came to see me, telling me about you, I knew it was a sign. Even Ashley wasn't good enough. It was you all along. Once I have you, once I kill you, she'll be safe forever."

She rose out of her terror enough to gasp, "Doctors. They can help you."

"Been there. Done that. Bought the T-shirt." He chuckled at his joke. "Once you're gone, the danger is over."

She saw the green belt. They were just a few feet away from his car. The synapses in her brain started firing again, telling her if she got in that car she'd never see her family again. She'd never see John. Desperately, she said, "The police know about Tess. They know who you are—"

"Don't say her name!" Searing pain stunned her as he slapped her.

She gasped and fell to the ground, catching herself with her arms. Blood gushed from her nose. Preparing for another blow, she glanced up. Saw Albert peeking out from behind a car, his face still bruised from Ernesto's attack. The boy's fierce gaze was focused like a laser beam on Park. She saw his shoulder muscles tense as he prepared to leap out. Shaking her head, she tried to pick herself up to stop him but she didn't make it in time.

She saw Albert leap. Saw Park's face, a garish twist of sub-human features. Their bodies collided a second before Albert's slumped. Lily knew immediately that Park had stabbed him. "No!" she screamed.

Park pushed Albert to the ground and then kicked him. The boy curled into a fetal position, clutching his right side.

Lily frantically crawled her way over to him. "No, no, no," she chanted. "Albert—" Before she reached him, Park tangled his fingers in her hair and yanked her to her feet. "Please, he needs help—"

The words were barely out of her mouth before his hand shot out, quick as a snake, again making her slam back against the pavement. He grabbed her by her hair again, dragging her up until her toes barely touched the ground. She screamed as he brought them face-to-face. A smile had transformed his features. He looked elated. As if every scream fed something inside him. Something monstrous.

She gagged, bile rising in her throat.

"Look at me, Lily. My Lily." He shook her, wrenching her neck, when she didn't comply fast enough. "Look at me."

She did. A glint of metal dangled in front of her face. He was holding a thin, fragile chain.

"I'll make it fast." He opened his palm and she saw the aquamarine pendant. "Just like your mother."

Memories exploded like a land mine, hurling out pieces of shrapnel and making her whimper in pain.

She saw him struggling with her mother. Hitting her, again and again. Saw her mother fight him. As she watched, he picked up a knife from the massive butcher block in the kitchen and plunged it into her mother's chest. Her mother doubled over.

Run, Lily, run, her mother had screamed. Trying to save her because she loved her.

He turned toward her, his eyes awash with bloodlust. She glanced at Albert, who was still on the ground behind them.

"She met you at her gym. You had a date with her that night."

He grinned. "Like I said, smart girl."

"Why?" she choked out. "She liked you."

For a moment, he looked confused. As if the answer was obvious. "But I loved her," he said. "Just like I love you. All I wanted was something of yours. A pair of your panties. But she walked in on me. Freaked out."

He released her hair with one hand and caressed her cheek.

A memory of her mother formed, but it wasn't from that horrible night. It was the day they'd gotten a glamour make-over together. After she'd gotten straight As and her mother had wanted to show how proud she was of her.

No! It couldn't end this way. She wouldn't let him get away with it again. She struggled anew. "You sick monster!"

Anger twisted his features once more, making him look demonic. He started dragging her to the car. "It's useless fighting it. The others knew and you'll accept the same fate."

"John—"

He stopped and laughed. Sick, heckling laughter. "That's right, your lover. But he can't save you. My salvation will be with your last breath. All along I've been using substitutes when I should have been using you."

He grasped her arm even tighter. She went limp, throwing him off balance and forcing him to take her weight. When his grasp loosened, she lunged and raced away. Away from Albert and onto the green belt.

She knew her way. Flew across the grass and into a grove of trees. She dodged and leaped, feeling the blood surging through her veins. With Park's breaths and footsteps echoing loudly behind her, she threw herself behind one tree and turned quickly. Not away from him but toward him. She whirled and rushed him, curling her fingers into claws and going straight for his eyes.

John's blood froze when he saw the front door to the Cantrell residence standing open. He bolted out of his car.

Something closed around his ankle and he automatically kicked out while turning around. He registered the low moan of pain just as he saw Albert facedown on the ground, his arm stretched out toward him. A dark stain on the back of the boy's shirt.

He knelt down beside him, his hands gently pushing material aside. A long, jagged gash in the boy's side oozed blood. Fear for Albert, fear for Lily, made his first attempt to speak inaudible. He cleared this throat. "Who did this to you?"

"Don't know him." Albert's voice was wheezy. Weak. "A man."

"Where's the officer. The guard?"

Albert's eyes shut and he went limp, as if the energy had drained out of him. Still, somehow he managed the words: "Lily—he has Lily—go," and pointed across the street.

A scream rang out. John fumbled with his cell phone with sweaty palms. He punched 911. "This is Detective John Tyler with the El Dorado Sheriff's Office. I have an officer down, 245, and attempted 187 in progress." He rattled off the address, squeezed Albert's shoulder, and said, "I've got to help her."

Albert opened his eyes for a fleeting second and nodded. "Help her."

The two of them shared a look of complete understanding. "Whatever it takes."

John was on his feet and running, saying a quick prayer for Officer Raddison and Albert, then pushing them out of his mind as he focused on saving the woman he loved.

Following her screams, arms pumping, he rushed into the green belt, heedless of the tree branches slapping at him. Hurtling himself into a clearing, he saw her, writhing in combat with a taller, bulkier figure. For a moment, he froze, unable to believe his eyes.

His Lily—the petite, gentle girl with a heart immeasurable in its capacity for love—was fighting her attacker. And it looked like she was winning.

She screamed like a banshee, a wild, primitive sound that made the hair on his body stand at attention. She punctuated each guttural sound with a strike of her fist or a vicious scrape of her nails. She raked her attacker's face, drawing blood and gouging his eyes. He punched at her, but she seemed unaware of the blows. She ripped chunks of light hair from his scalp and he howled.

Mason Park.

John sprinted toward them, his own battle cry mingling with Lily's just as Mason brought up both hands, clasped them together, and struck Lily on the side of her head. She collapsed to the ground and her head knocked against a rock. John saw the light glint off something next to her and realized it was a necklace. A necklace with aquamarine gems.

John leaped at Mason, catching him around the middle and knocking him to the ground. John pulled back his arm and hit Park, not hearing the sound of bone and cartilage cracking beneath his fist. Not even remembering in that moment he was a cop. All he felt was rage. And the fierce certainty that this man who had dared to threaten his woman had to die.

Lily grasped her head and moaned at the stabbing pain. Shadows swam in front of her but she knew what was happening. John. She needed to get to John.

She crawled toward the blur of movement and the sound of flesh hitting flesh. Please God. Don't take him, too. And if you do, take me. I can't survive without him. I won't.

She whimpered and faltered, almost collapsing back onto the ground in terror. Dear God, Park had fooled them all. The police. John. How could he be that evil and still have gotten away with it?

Lily straight-armed herself off the ground and kept crawling. No more, she thought. I won't let him hurt us anymore. As the shadows loomed closer, her eyes focused. She almost cried out with relief when she saw John unhurt. He straddled Park.

"John," she gasped out.

He didn't respond. Didn't look at her. He wrenched Park's head up and began pounding it into the ground.

She forced herself to her feet and staggered toward him, determined to make him hear her.

"John, stop. John, it's Lily. I need you, John. I need you. Please."

He pummeled Park's head once. Twice. Then he let go, causing Park's head to fall back with a sickening, hollow sound. Blood stained John's face. His shirt. His hands. He stared at them for several long moments, as if he didn't know where he was or what he'd done.

"John," she whispered.

He jerked and his gaze instantly met hers. She almost flinched back at the savagery lighting his eyes. She'd felt the same mindless rage when she'd attacked Park, but this—my God, John looked like a warrior just come back from battle. Distant. Deadly. Crazed.

But his savagery didn't scare her. He'd never hurt her. He'd protect her, just like he'd always done.

"John," she said again, this time reaching out to touch his face. He blinked several times. She knew he'd recognized her when relief, like a tide of sanity fresh from the sea, slowly washed away the taint of rage and cruelty in his eyes.

Breaths heaving in and out of him, he lurched and fell against her. Each steadied the other. He wrapped his arms around her and leaned his head against her stomach. She tangled her hands in his hair. "It's over," she murmured. "It's finally over."

Chapter 21

It wasn't over, John thought as he stared down at Lily. She slept peacefully, but that was unusual. She was safe, but not healed. She'd been having nightmares again. In the last week, she'd had to deal not only with her own pain but her family's.

Officer Raddison and Candace Evans were both still in critical condition. Albert was stable. Ashley was going to need therapy but she seemed like she was going to be fine.

And although John had been wrong about Barb being a threat to Lily, he hadn't been wrong about her presence that night. She'd shown up after Douglas Cantrell had found Lily in the house with her mother's body and she'd helped him with his cover-up. While Doug had been walking Lily through her return-trip home and the "discovery" of her mother's body, Barb had returned to her house and disposed of the knife and Lily's clothes. She'd willingly tampered with evidence in order to protect not only the man she loved, but Lily. Although their actions would be investigated by the new D.A., the couple seemed relieved that the truth had finally come out and that Lily's innocence had been confirmed.

After leaving John that night, Thorn had gone after Morton Howe. He'd simply barricaded himself in with the man in his office and periodically threatened to shoot him until the man had wet his pants. Howe had still been covered in piss when the cops had come in and placed them both in custody. Thorn was out on bail now, but he had a long road in front of him, as well. And because she was standing by him, so did Carmen.

Lily had a lot to deal with, too. Repairing the bonds within her family. Dealing with Park's trial. Following up on Hardesty's formal exoneration. Testifying against Howe. Trying to help Carmen with her decision to stand by Thorn, despite the uncertainty of his future.

Hard times were still ahead for both of them.

But at least Lily wouldn't be alone this time.

And neither would he.

He smoothed a hand over her cheek, smiling when she crinkled her nose and butted against him like a cat. She yawned and stretched her arms before opening her pretty brown eyes.

His breath caught. She gazed at him with her heart in her eyes and for a moment insecurity flooded him.

She was too good, he thought. Too good for me.

The thought shattered when she sat up and the sheet fell, leaving her soft skin bare. He couldn't resist reaching out and cupping one small breast, kneading it gently before moving to the other. Then he reached up and caught her mother's pendant in his fingers. He stared at it. Reminded himself once more she was safe.

He leaned in and gave her a kiss. "I've gotta go."

She frowned and pouted. "What? I thought you were waking me for a reason."

He laughed. "I am." He kissed her soundly on the lips. "I wanted to kiss you goodbye." He moved back in and kissed her again, this time opening her mouth and pressing his tongue against hers. He groaned when she pulled him closer and unbuttoned the top button on his shirt. Heat shuddered through him, making him hard so fast his head spun. A second later, however, his chest tightened and he pulled away.

He captured her hands and laughed. Even to him, it sounded forced. Uncomfortable. "Enough of that, you. There'll be plenty of time for that later."

She stared at him with solemn eyes. "John—"

Clearing his throat, he rose. "I promise, babe. Hold that thought. Let me get through this first, okay?"

She pulled the sheet up and covered herself, holding it in place by leaning her chest against her bent knees. "You don't have to go."

He stopped and turned back to her. "Yeah. I do. I need to see Park again, just like you need to visit Hardesty. It's going to be hard, but we'll be okay. Because we have each other."

She smiled, grabbed his palm, and kissed it. "I talked to Fiona's foster parents yesterday. She has a new kitten. She wants me to see it."

He soaked in the beauty of her happiness, not surprised that his own chest felt lighter. "I'm glad."

"You'll come with me, won't you? To see it? To see her? Fiona would like it, too. She took a definite liking to you."

He kissed her palm this time, overwhelmed by her faith in him. "I can't wait."

When he got to his car, he hesitated. Thought about going back to her. Did he really need to watch Park's interrogation? If Lily could leave him to the criminal justice system, why couldn't he?

He turned on the engine, already knowing the answer.

Because something had changed in him that night. Something had reverted to a dark, ugly place that he thought he'd long ago left behind. He questioned himself now. Every time he touched Lily. Every time he thought of a future with her.

And that was not acceptable.

John watched Mason Park lean back in his chair and talk to Detective Bolin as if was chatting with a friend at a coffee shop. "She broke up with me. Told me she needed to concentrate on her family. I—I was desperate. I went to the house to talk to her, but she wasn't there."

"Is that when you decided to go into the girl's room?" Detective Bolin asked him. "Why?"

Park ignored Bolin and stared through the one-way mirror as if he knew someone else was there. As if he knew it was John.

"I'd seen her and Tina working out together. Before we started dating. She used to wear these skimpy shorts and thin T-shirt." Even as they watched, Park's earnest face transformed. Sweat popped out on his forehead and he licked his lips. He smirked. "I could see her little breasts through it. So sweet. Less than a handful, right John?"

Officer Newton shifted next to John, his rustling clothes grating like fingernails on a chalkboard. John braced his arms above the mirror paneling and gritted his teeth. The transformation was sickening. Park seemed to be Jekyll and Hyde. During half of Bolin's interview, he was the man John had interviewed at his house—the man with a steady job, a family, a conscience. But in a blink of an eye, depending on who and what Bolin asked him about, he would change, revealing the beast within.

John could see it. A jury would see it, too. Which meant he'd probably cop a plea. Guilty by reason of insanity. And unlike most defendants, he'd probably be successful.

For a moment, John wished he still had Park under him. And that he hadn't stopped hitting him until he was dead.

That thought horrified him more than even Park's dual personality.

"So it was her you really wanted?"

Park frowned at the detective's question, then looked confused. He shook his head. "No. She was a child. I knew that. But they were the same in my eyes. I loved them both. Wanted them both. When Tina broke it off, I couldn't bear the thought of not seeing either of them again." Park's voice broke into the petulant, cloying whine of a child. His gaze focused once more on the glass hiding John from view. "I knew I'd get another lover. That had never been hard. All I wanted was something to remember them by."

"So you stopped by her house. But only after what? Buying a bogus movie ticket you had no intention of using?"

Park smirked but didn't answer.

"You wanted a pair of the girl's underwear."

Caressing one of his manacled fists as if he was imagining caressing the white cotton he'd taken from Lily's room, Park nodded.

"And then what?" the detective asked him.

Park's glassy-eyed stare as he remembered the past made John shiver. "Then Tina came in. She came at me like a berserker. I tried to leave, but she followed me down the stairs. She grabbed a knife and went after me." He smiled thinly. "I was just defending myself."

The detective snorted. "Uh-huh. Against someone who was half your size. Is that why you stabbed her over twenty times? To protect yourself? And then what? Did you prey on other young girls?"

"I traveled a lot with my job. Had my pick of women. I—I picked girls who looked young and if I was tempted by others, I stayed away from them. Tina taught me that lesson."

"But then what happened? Your own daughter was growing. What, did she have less than a handful, too?"

Park's back snapped straight and his face contorted with anger. "Shut your filthy mouth about her."

"This guy's whacked," Officer Newton said to John. "They're never going to convict him."

John closed his eyes. Park never mentioned his daughter by name, but Candace Evans had told them enough of what he'd said to her for them to piece together the puzzle. Just as Park had been shamed by his sexual fixation with Lily, and had chosen to date her mother to fulfill it, he'd likewise been horrified when he'd found himself becoming sexually attracted to his own daughter. The Razor's first murder had occurred around the time when Tess would have been developing. In a sick way, Park had started killing in order to protect his daughter, thinking that if he reenacted Tina's murder, it would once more give him the strength to quash his impulses. To some extent, he viewed the murders as the lesser of two evils.

In the interrogation room, Bolin stood. "I need to make a call," he said, his voice laced with disgust. He slammed the door shut behind him.

John remained where he was, watching Park closely. Trying not to think about the faces of Park's wife and children as they played in their spacious backyard.

Park breathed heavily in the silence. Then he smiled again. "You know exactly when I focused on her again, right? After you came to my house." He turned to stare at the one-way mirror again, leaving no doubt he was addressing John directly even though he hadn't said his name again. "I was happy with the others until then. But then I knew they weren't enough. I needed her. Her mother's death had eased the heat for a while, and now it was Lily's turn. You showed me that. I thought Ashley might do, but while she was sweet, I wanted the real thing. Substitutes no more."

"I think you should leave, John."

John ignored Newton, even as he struggled with guilt. He'd already figured out he'd led Park to Lily. When they'd found the apartment in El Dorado he rented under a different name, they'd also found his shrine of photographs in one of the rooms—photographs of Lily and girls that looked like Lily. LaMonte and the other girls were there, clearly linking Park to their murders.

With no one in the room to respond to Park's taunting words, he seemed to lose it. He struggled against his restraints, rattling his chains against the metal chair and table. "She tried to save her mother, you know. She even tried to bite me, but she was so out of it she ended up biting Tina instead. I could've had her then. The blood, the power. It was such a rush. I didn't want to fight it. Not anymore. If Hardesty hadn't shown up—"

The door to the interrogation room opened, and Detective Bolin walked in. "Who are you talking to?"

Park ignored him, his eyes never leaving the two-way mirror.

"You think I'm a monster, but how different are you? Tina told me about you and your obsession with Lily. Even after fifteen years you couldn't stay away from her. You're just like me, only you can't admit it. You like the young and helpless, too."

John swallowed the bile rising in his throat, acutely aware Newton was staring at him.

"Do you hear me? Talk to me, you bastard. Come in here and face me."

John straightened, turned and walked out of the room. As soon as he was in the hallway and could no longer hear Park's words, he leaned against the wall outside, and tried to breathe. His heart thundered in his chest and nausea turned his stomach.

He knew they were nothing alike. He used his strength to protect and to pleasure, not hurt. But still, words from the past echoed in his mind.

Rapist. Pervert. Druggie. Punk.

They stayed with him, louder than they'd ever been, until John finally straightened and headed outside.

Later that night, John woke to the fragrance of Lily. It was all around him. On his skin. Inside him.

He felt the light press of her hands on his shoulders and the soft caress of her hair and lips against his face. Groaning, he arched up to meet her, capturing her lips with tender care. He raised his hands to bracket her waist, then lifted her up and then down until she settled onto him with a wet, heated grip. She started an easy rhythm. Deliberately, he forced his hands to his sides. His fingers gripped the bedsheets tightly.

Her cool hands left his shoulders, causing her body to sink more fully onto him. Frantically, he clawed at the mattress and sheets, trying to control the urge to grip her hips and pound into her.

Gentle, he thought. Be gentle.

"...gentle. I love it when you're gentle, John." Lily's hands framed his face, and she kissed him again, a long melding of mouths and tongues. "Be gentle sometimes," she said as she pulled away, "but not all the time." She raised herself up and off him.

"No," he gritted out, barely restraining himself from hauling her back. Throwing one arm over his eyes, he took several deep breaths. He felt her lie next to him. He hissed and dropped his arm, turning to look at her.

She slowly lifted her arms above her head and spread her limbs wide, spreading herself out like a feast for the taking. "Take me, John."

John swallowed, wanting her so much he hurt, but all he could think about was Park's accusation. That John was like *him.* That he liked to dominate Lily because she was small. Vulnerable. He shook his head, "Lily..."

"Don't hold back with me. Don't let him do that to us. I want you, John. All of you." When he still didn't move, she touched his chest with her hand, and implored, "Please."

With a tortured groan, he surrendered. He released the sheets, rolled and moved on top of her. He pinned her wrists down, and pushed apart her thighs. He paused, shaking, wanting to let go, wanting things to be the same between them, but not sure if they ever could.

She smiled up at him and whispered words of love. Words of sex. She told him how she'd always wanted him. How she'd always want him. And without another thought, John pushed forward.

Into Lily.

She'd loved him before any other man had touched her. And even though he hadn't been her first, he'd be her last.

Minutes later, when their skin was cooling and their shouts still rang in his ears, Lily lifted herself on one elbow and stared down at him. She brought his hand to her mouth and kissed it, then sucked and bit down gently on his thumb. His hips arched up and she reached down to grip him, smiling when she found him already hardening.

"I love what you do to me. I love that you don't treat me like glass. I won't break and neither will you. Nothing we do together, to one another, out of love could be wrong."

He felt overcome by the faith she had in him. Realized what a fool he'd been. He took her hand, brought it to his mouth with the intention of biting her thumb, just like she'd done to him. Instead, he kissed it. Over and over again.

Then he moved down the rest of her. And he didn't stop until he'd purged Mason Park from both their minds.

John walked out of the interrogation room feeling more tired than he'd ever been in his life. Thorn was still inside, finishing his statement to Michael Colbane, the Chief Deputy Attorney General who would decide when and how to bring charges up against ex-District Attorney Howe. Despite the shame that had sometimes caused his words to falter, Thorn had been clear-eyed and steady, resolute in his decision to bring his own drug problems and Howe's deception to light. The whole time, Carmen had sat by his side, touching him and sharing her strength.

"John."

Sighing with relief, John held out his arms. Lily instantly stepped into them. He hugged her desperately and she gasped, almost as if she couldn't breathe. He loosened his grip and tried to back away, but she shook her head and hung on. "It's okay," she whispered. "We're going to be okay."

They stayed in that position for several long moments before John pulled back. "Nothing's going to happen for a few days. What do you say we go home?"

She looked up at him with a smile. "Home? And where

would that be, exactly?" They'd been splitting their time between both places. Weekends at his place. The week at hers.

John shrugged and pushed back her hair. "Your home. My home. You pick. It doesn't matter to me. We'll be married soon anyway. Home is you, not which house we sleep in."

She didn't look surprised. She looked pleased. She sounded happy. "Is that right? You're going to make an honest woman out of me? Drag me to the altar, kicking and screaming?"

He reached up and gripped her chin, even though she was still staring him in the eye. "If that's what it takes." John held his breath. "You okay with that?"

She nodded. "More than okay," she whispered.

They turned together, ready to leave. The door opened behind them. Thorn and Carmen stepped out. Thorn looked drained, like he had nothing left inside him. Until Carmen placed her hand on Thorn's arm. He straightened just as John held out his hand. Thorn looked at it blankly before taking it. As they stared at each other, John knew Thorn saw the friendship, even if he was still having to work on forgiveness.

As Carmen and Thorn walked away, John turned to Lily and saw the certainty and love shining in her eyes.

"I love you," she said.

He reached out and pulled her close. "I love you, too, small fry."

She smiled, accepting it as truth. Even after everything she'd been through. All the ways he'd hurt her. Even after that horrible night fifteen years ago, when he'd pushed her away and, in hurting her, had become associated with one of the worst moments of her life—losing her mother. Even after that... Even then...

She loved him.

She knew she was loved by him.

And that was the greatest blessing of all.

* * * * *

& *A sneaky peek at next month...*

INTRIGUE...

BREATHTAKING ROMANTIC SUSPENSE

My wish list for next month's titles...

In stores from 19th October 2012:

❏ High Noon – Debra Webb

& The Cop's Missing Child – Karen Whiddon

❏ The Reunion Mission – Beth Cornelison

& Kansas City Cowboy – Julie Miller

❏ Detective Daddy – Mallory Kane

& Engaged with the Boss – Elle James

❏ Missing Mother-To-Be – Elle Kennedy

In stores from 2nd November 2012:

❏ Savour the Danger – Lori Foster

Available at WHSmith, Tesco, Asda, Eason, Amazon and Apple

Just can't wait?

Visit us Online

You can buy our books online a month before they hit the shops! **www.millsandboon.co.uk**

1012/46